THE ONE THAT GOT AWAY

Nicky James

The One That Got Away

Copyright © 2021 by Nicky James

This is a work of fiction. Names, characters, businesses, places, events, and incidents are either the products of the author's imagination or used in a fictitious manner. Any resemblance to actual persons, living or dead, or actual events is purely coincidental.

Cover Artist:

Nicky James

Editing:

Susie Selva

LesCourt Author Services

All rights reserved.

No part of this book may be reproduced or transmitted in any form or by any means without the written permission of the author.

TRIGGER WARNING

In this story, there is heavy focus on an incident that happened many years ago involving a child kidnapping/sex-trafficking operation. The details of sexual abuse are ***NOT discussed in any detail at any point during the story***, but the kidnapping incident itself is referred to often. The long-term mental health impact of such an incident is explored through one character and presents as:
Severe anxiety and panic disorder
OCD
Dissociative episodes
PTSD

One

CHARLIE

I wasn't imagining it.

All I had to do was wait, and I'd prove it.

Wedged out of sight in the corner, fingers idly flicking the locking mechanism at the bottom of the window, I took a mental note of the time and counted.

Early morning sunlight sparkled across the dewy lawn and refracted off the chrome rims of Dad's Impala in the driveway below. The weather report called for seasonably warm temperatures. No forecasted rain, which the blue sky, absent of any clouds, seemed to confirm.

The Beekmans were rounding up their herd and shoving them into their minivan across the street. Eight-year-old Dyson scooted under his dad's arm, making a getaway, squealing as he flew with airplane arms across the front lawn.

Casey shouted after him, looking frazzled as he buckled his youngest into a car seat. Alice, Casey's wife, was crouched, double-checking backpacks as she waved for Julia and Delilah, their four-year-old twins, to get into the van. Alice must have found something missing because she popped off the ground and raced back inside, tripping over the couple's two cairn terriers, who were barking in echoing fits at the front door.

The Beekmans were nothing short of entertaining.

One minute.

Maple, oak, and elm trees lined the street in both directions. They were bursting with new life, fresh greenery that brushed together in the gentle spring breeze. If I leaned against the windowpane, I could make out the edges of Francine LaPointe's flower beds with freshly churned soil and newly planted annuals in various shades of purple and pink and yellow. My elderly neighbor loved to garden and had been itching for the spring thaw for months.

With the May long weekend approaching, I knew Ms. LaPointe would be spending all her time sorting out her vegetable patch in the backyard. *"You can never plant tomatoes before the May long weekend,"* she'd told me once. *"All it would take is one frosty night and they'd be kaput."*

Two minutes.

I continued staring as far down the street as I could, counting the cars in each laneway, ensuring every one of them belonged. Nothing seemed out of order.

The faint rhythmic clicking of the latch under my fingers helped me count the passing minutes without rushing. It was metronomic. Soothing.

Necessary.

From the landing halfway down the stairs from the second floor, I had a good view of the neighborhood in both directions. I was familiar with people's routines and relied on them to help maintain balance in my less than ordinary world. If people diverged from their schedules, it ignited an inner disquiet I carried with me all day.

It was Monday. Monday meant Westly Huntington would drag his garbage to the curb any moment, beating the weekly pick-up time by the skin of his teeth. I checked the street in both directions again then stared at the older man's garage door.

Three minutes.

Like clockwork, it rose.

Westly shuffled outside wearing a bathrobe and slippers, dragging a black-lidded bin behind him at the same time the telltale clatter of the garbage truck announced its arrival in our neighborhood.

Four.

Alice and Casey had their crew buckled into the van. They drove off, leaving their dogs yapping in the big bay window. *"Another day, another dime,"* Casey often said. He was a decent guy. Friendly. Always tired, but that seemed understandable considering he and Alice had five kids under ten.

I scanned the street. Waited. Waited some more.

Five.

My skin prickled and itched.

I wasn't imagining it. I wasn't crazy. If I waited long enough…

I clicked the latch on the window, locking and unlocking it, back and forth, the sound echoing inside my head.

Little beads of sweat formed along my spine and at my temples. I wet my lips. *Click, click, click.*

When a blue Mazda whizzed by, the hairs along my arms stood on end. A red Sunbird drove in the opposite direction. In the distance, closer still, the garbage truck rumbled.

"I'm not imagining it." The hushed words carried a weight of familiar anxiety.

Am I?

Six.

Mr. Huntington's garage door lowered as the old man tottered back inside. The Beekmans' dogs gave up their frantic barking and retreated, likely for a nap since they had a long day of nothing ahead of them. The hydraulic whine of the garbage truck pierced the air. Closer again. My internal temperature rose to unreasonable levels. My heart beat like a war drum against my ribs.

More sweat.

More minutes.

Seven.

Eight.

Nine.

"I wasn't—"

There it was.

The white Pontiac Grand Prix appeared at the end of the road, turning off Grenadine Avenue and heading in my direction. Slow and steady like before, inching down the street at a speed far below what was posted. As it crept past my house, I ducked back into the corner out of sight, watching from a tiny slit beside the curtain. A second later, I poked my head out and followed its retreat as it drove off down the road.

Then it was gone.

Again, the license plate had been unreadable.

I clicked the window latch one final time, locking it in place, and raced down the stairs, muttering, "I *wasn't* imagining it. I saw it. I saw it four times. Four. That's something. It's got to be something."

As I passed the front door, I double-checked the deadbolt, unlocking it and locking it again, peering through the tiny crack where the door butted against the frame to assure myself the firm piece of steel was in place.

I moved along each window in the front room, doing the same to all the latches, clicking them open and closed, checking each in turn. The house was large—smaller than the house where I'd grown up but a significant size nonetheless—with an excess of ingress and egress points. More than I would have preferred.

There was a large sitting room, a downstairs office where dad worked on his models, a study, a media room, and several bathrooms, along with a garage and the enormous kitchen in the back.

The second floor was reserved for multiple bedrooms, a bathroom, and a decent-sized study I used for work. The unfinished basement had been sealed off for my sanity.

I'd worked out a system years ago, a ritual Dad called it, which I performed a minimum of four or five times a day with each and every window and door in the entire house. Was it healthy? My doctor said no. My father had no comment. We both pretended it was normal.

The kitchen was my final destination. There were far too many windows in the open space. Sunlight glistened off the granite island and appliances. The white cabinetry gleamed under its assault.

Dad was hunched over a newspaper in the breakfast nook, reading glasses perched on the end of his nose, thinning silver hair slicked back over a round head. Everything about Dad was rounder these days. "That's old age for you," he'd once said when I'd suggested a healthier diet. "If you make me eat any more damn greens, I'll dig my own bloody grave. Not worth it."

The old ticker was chugging along just fine, he'd assured me. The doctors disagreed and said his blood pressure was too high and his cholesterol needed to come down.

Dad didn't argue about the locks, so I'd stopped hounding him about his health.

When I entered the kitchen, I felt the heat of his attention as I moved along the outside wall, clicking the locks on every window along the back of the house. I had to shift aside long hanging branches from a few plants, but that didn't bother me.

I finished at the patio door and took a mental note, ensuring I hadn't missed anything, then I turned and faced my father. Wringing my hands, I pieced through the events of the past few days to ensure my arguments were solid.

Dad cocked a brow as though he knew I was about to make an announcement. Unfortunately, he read me like a book.

"I'm going to the police station this morning. Someone's following me."

Dad paused, studying me, likely assessing my decision and whether or not he could steer me away from it. "You spent damn near twenty minutes on the landing."

"Twelve."

"Boy, I'm not arguing with you. Twelve or twenty, you know you shouldn't be doing that."

"It's a white Pontiac. Older model Grand Prix. I'm guessing between 1996 and 2000. I couldn't get a read on the license plate, but it drove past twice, and yesterday—"

"Charlie. Stop."

I twisted my fingers together and shuffled my feet as I clamped my mouth shut and waited for Archie Falkingham to go on.

"Now listen. Are you listening?"

"Yes."

"*No one* is following you. If you take this to that poor man at the station again, he's going to lock your ass up. I swear to god, son—"

"I haven't committed a crime. There is no reason to arrest me."

"Don't be smart. You know what I mean. Do you want another stint in the ward? That's where this will land you."

"My suspicions are well founded. If you would just listen."

"Enough. There's only so much that man is going to tolerate. You hammering down his door every other week with these outrageous stories is going to get old, you hear me? I'm telling you. Let. It. Go. If you don't, I'm getting on that phone and telling Sofia she needs to adjust your meds again."

"But… I'm not imagining it."

Dad sucked his teeth, studying my face for a long time before he nodded at the coffee pot on the counter behind me. "Grab yourself a coffee, and I'll pour us some cereal. Breakfast, a bit of work, then you'll feel better."

My fingers twitched. "At the post office yesterday—"

"Charlie—"

"—while I was grabbing those forms—"

"Enough."

"And then again when I was at the cart return at Daisy's Market. It was right there. I looked up and—"

The bench scraped across the natural stone tile as Dad shoved away from the table. I snapped my mouth shut. Grunting, he used the table to help pull himself to his feet.

Before I could protest, he took me by the arm and guided me around until I faced the coffee pot, then he shuffled away to retrieve my ceramic mug from the cupboard—the navy one with beige speckled dots in various sizes painted around its circumference. I'd bought it at the art festival from a lady with wildly frizzy hair and a laugh that was like tinkling bells. It was my favorite mug and the only one in our extensive collection I could use for my eight o'clock coffee. The red one with the gold stripes was for my ten o'clock coffee. The moss green one with a painted pinecone on one side was for my midday coffee.

I didn't drink coffee after noon. If my doctor had her way, I wouldn't drink it at all. She claimed it exacerbated my anxiety.

I disagreed.

Dad placed the navy mug on the counter and nudged it toward me. From the table, he retrieved his plain mug with *World's Best Dad* printed on the front and placed it beside mine. "What are you working on today?"

I didn't like being dismissed, but Dad also knew I didn't like getting off schedule, so I relented.

When I reached for the coffee pot and Dad was sure I was following through with his request, he retreated to the other side of the kitchen where he dug a box of Raisin Bran from the pantry.

"Kristy is waiting on an outline for the next book. I'm stuck in the planning phase. Still trying to sort out the structure of the plot. I need to think more about it."

The sound of cereal falling into a bowl filled the empty air after I finished speaking.

"So, in essence, you'll be at that damn window all bloody day or sitting in your room."

I filled our mugs and replaced the pot under the machine. "My brain needs to be stimulated. You know those things help."

"Try going for a walk."

Dad found the milk in the fridge and poured it over the flakes to a precise level, knowing my predilections. After, he handed over the jug so I could splash a quarter ounce into my coffee and slightly less into Dad's.

"I might run some errands or go to the library. I told Kenny I'd pop into the bookstore this week sometime too. Sign more books."

Dad glared over the bowls of cereal as he carried them to the breakfast nook. His left hip was bothering him, giving him a slight limp that wasn't always present. Since it wasn't raining, he couldn't blame the weather like he often did. It was arthritis, whether he wanted to admit it or not.

Dad sat at the table, and I joined him.

We ate in silence for a few minutes before Dad sighed, peering up from under his bushy eyebrows. "Don't start this again, kiddo. I'm not an idiot. You say errands, and I know what that entails. Take a step back and analyze this whole thing with a clearer head in a day or two. You're anxious about this new book and the plot not coming together how you want. It's stirring everything up. Trust me."

"I'm not imagining it. I think Detective Graveman should know." I ate another spoonful of cereal. "Just in case," I added, not looking up.

Dad stopped protesting, but I didn't miss the way he shook his head in submission nor did I miss the indecipherable words he muttered under his breath.

We finished our breakfast and coffees. Dad rinsed the dishes and loaded them into the dishwasher while I reversed course, checking the locks on my way back upstairs. When I hit the landing and stopped at the window, scanning the street in both directions, Dad's booming voice traveled from all the way in the kitchen.

"Get off the bloody landing, Charlie, or so help me god."

I continued upstairs.

In the bathroom, I showered and worked through my assiduous routine of shaving, styling my wheat blond hair into a severe side part, gluing down any stray flyaways with an exorbitant amount of gel, dressing—tan slacks, tailored to fit, and a polo in a soft blue color that accented my eyes—and applying the appropriate amount of aftershave and cologne.

I brushed my teeth, flossed, groomed my eyebrows, cleaned out the sink, and wiped the droplets off the mirror with the cleansing cloths I kept handy.

Then I managed my pills, counting them out and taking them with a small mouthful of tap water.

Order. Control.

Before leaving the bathroom, I studied my reflection. Square, clean-shaven jaw. Pale lips with a gentle downward curve, not too thin but not overly plump either. When I tried to smile, it looked awkward and unfitting. My face was more suited to a neutral expression. I had freckles in abundance across my sharply pointed nose and cheekbones. I wasn't sure how I felt about them. They seemed boyish, which I didn't appreciate at age twenty-nine. My eyes were gray blue, a color that wasn't dissimilar to the horizon when a storm approached. Framing each eye were long lashes, long enough my sister, Adelaide, called them girly. I hadn't appreciated that. Dad had told me it wasn't worth the fight and I should let it go.

Adelaide didn't like much about me.

For a moment, I leaned in, peering deep into the pools of gray blue, seeking something I'd never been able to see. I knew I wasn't like other people, and I understood why—to a point—even though there was a dark hole in my brain I couldn't access.

I was an adult, but too many people didn't see me as such. They saw me as mentally deficient. Broken. They treated me like a child, and I wasn't a child.

They sometimes called me crazy.

"But I'm not crazy."

My doctor had reassured me several times, and she was the one with multiple diplomas on her walls. The doctors might have slapped many labels on me, but crazy wasn't one of them.

I flicked my gaze to the small line of prescription bottles at the back of the counter. There were four of them. Those bottles, those pills, they claimed differently. They mocked me. The fact that I had to take them at all proved I was far from sane. I would never say that out loud. Dad would pitch a fit and lecture me, even though there were days the truth showed in his hazel eyes. Sometimes Dad thought I was a bit off my rocker too.

Working my jaw, frowning at the man in the mirror, I tried to do what Dad suggested. I tried to think rationally about the white Pontiac. Take a step back. See it from a different perspective.

But no. It had been at the post office and again at the market, then it drove past the house twice this morning.

"I'm not imagining it."

It was the same vehicle, even though I hadn't been able to get a plate number. How many people were still chugging along in cars two decades old? I supposed it wouldn't be unheard of. But the same old car following me around? No, I *wasn't* imagining it.

I would go to the station, ask to see Detective Graveman, and explain what I saw. He would listen. Stanley always listened. If I made a report, at least someone would look into it. That would make me feel better.

"I'm not crazy."

I headed back to my bedroom. It was an ordinary bedroom—in theory. The space was meticulously organized. Not a spec of dust on the vanity, dresser, or wooden four-post bed frame. The linens were smoothed with military precision. The closet was arranged first by clothing type, then by color, shoes aligned underneath in a perfect row. The windows were spotless—and locked—and the carpet vacuumed.

But that was where ordinary ended.

My bedroom was also my sanctuary, and years ago, I'd transformed it into a place of my own imagining. It was my safety net. My escape. It was the land beyond my dreams and the setting for all my novels. My room was a gateway to Vrydindel.

Artwork hung on the walls; custom paintings I'd commission from a man in China. They depicted dragons, elves, and various other creatures from my mind. Floating shelves held an assortment of figurines: more dragons, more fantastical beasts. There were weapons, tapestries, hanging vines, and a large fountain that stood as high as the ceiling. Tiny fairy lights shone through the cascading waterfall.

In Vrydindel—in this room—no one could touch me. No one could harm me. I was safe.

I moved to the window and clicked the latch back and forth once, scanning the backyard beyond. The gardeners had shown up the previous week, and the flower beds were bursting with new growth around the perennials that were starting to come back to life with the warmer weather.

They'd taken the patio furniture from storage and had placed it on the large cement pad where it sat, waiting for a day Dad felt inspired enough to barbecue.

Abandoning the window, I collected my wallet and keys from my bedside table. I reached far into the back of the drawer until my fingers touched the cold ivory handle of the one item I took with me whenever I left the house. No one knew I owned it, and that was for the best. Dad would get that look in his eyes, and Sofia would plunge headfirst into one of her lectures. Then they'd probably drug me more because that was their answer to everything.

But in my stories, Calipnia, the main hero, never went anywhere without his weapons. No one could ever hurt him. Since I was Calipnia, I too shared his philosophy.

I stuck the switchblade into my pocket and headed for the stairs.

On the landing, I spent a quiet moment scanning the street, flicking the lock, then I continued down.

Dad was in his workshop.

I poked my head in, finding him at the table under a blaze of desk lamps all pointed at his current project. Dad built model airplanes and not the simple ones. These ones were complex and required painstaking accuracy and a steady hand. It was intricate work that took several weeks to complete. I was familiar with each stage of the process since Dad had encouraged me to join him on many occasions growing up so he could teach me the art. Each plastic piece required sanding and filing and special adhesive when fitting them together. The toxic smell of his model cement filled the air.

Dad's reading glasses sat precariously on the end of his nose as he peered through a desk-mounted magnifying glass at the wing he was carefully assembling. When he worked, his breathing changed to something more concentrated, more steadily labored.

"I'll be back in a bit," I said when I was sure I wouldn't startle him.

"Don't pester that man. If he tells you it's time to go, you listen."

I didn't respond and backed out of the room. Dad always seemed to think I annoyed Detective Graveman, but that wasn't the case. Stanley had always been nothing but kind to me. He understood my situation and listened to my concerns. After all, he was the man who'd rescued me all those years ago. Detective Graveman had my safety and best interest at heart.

* * *

The central station for the Hamilton Police Department was in a busier section of downtown and serviced a large portion of the city, including my neighborhood. It was a brown, brick, two-story structure with darkened windows that didn't allow outsiders any visual access. A wheelchair ramp wound along the far side of the concrete stairs leading to the main entrance—another wall of darkened windows with a security door front and center. The entrance was monitored by several cameras aimed in every direction.

I was familiar with the building, and the personnel inside were familiar with me. The officers who staffed the front desk rotated shifts, but I knew each of them by name. Officer Kelsey Briggs was behind the plexiglass today, her face stern as always as she did something on the computer. She had a scar that intersected her left eyebrow, and she never wore makeup. I thought she could have been pretty if she tried a little harder.

A door alarm alerted her to my arrival, and she glanced up. Her shoulders rose a fraction, and her emerald eyes narrowed. "Good morning, Charlie."

"Good morning, Officer Briggs. How are you today?"

"I'm fine, thank you." She sounded tired. "Let me guess. You aren't. What brings you in?"

"I was wondering if Detective Graveman was available. I have to make a report."

Kelsey Briggs was in her late thirties and didn't often allow emotions of any kind to cross her face—the same as many of the officers with whom I was acquainted—so when her features softened and she spun from the computer, it triggered something inside me I didn't like. My pulse quickened as I tried to read the situation.

"Sweetie, Detective Graveman retired last month. He isn't with us anymore. Didn't he tell you he was leaving?"

Retired?

"No." I wrung my hands, shuffling my loafers on the gritty tiles. Someone had traipsed mud into the building, and no one had cleaned it up. They should call a janitor.

"But... I have to make a report. It's important."

Briggs sighed again, her gaze darting to her desk phone before returning to me. "All right, but you understand it's going to be a random officer who takes your statement, don't you?"

My heart knocked faster. I didn't like anything random. Stanley and I had a system. He knew me. He understood me.

Beads of sweat prickled my upper lip. "But I really should tell Detective Graveman. He'll understand because..." I twisted my fingers together as my blood raced faster through my veins. "I can't talk to someone else. It has to be Stanley. Can you call him?"

"No. Retired means he isn't doing this anymore."

"I know what retired means." I paused, leveling out my voice, realizing I was too frantic and she was looking at me like *that*. "I'm not stupid. It's just..."

The door alarm sounded as more people entered the station. Instinct made me shuffle so they would be in my line of sight and not directly behind me.

A woman and a small child of maybe ten or eleven bustled through the door. The woman made eye contact with me, then Officer Briggs before looking away again, taking her son by the shoulder and telling him they needed to wait their turn.

"Charlie, I've got to work. Either you talk to another officer, or you head on home. Your choice."

"What about Sergeant Nikola?"

If I could talk to him, maybe he'd call Stanley.

Officer Briggs sighed again, a long and exhausted sound I recognized as annoyance. I tended to bring out those types of sighs in people.

She picked up the phone and keyed in the proper extension. "Sir, Charlie Falkingham is here. He wants to speak with Graveman, and— Yes, I told him, sir. No... No, he's asking to see you instead." Briggs paused, making small noises of affirmation a few times before, "I'm not sure that will... Yes, sir. Okay. No, I understand. I'll tell him."

She hung up and turned hardened emerald eyes on me. "Head on back. Sarge will see you. But Charlie?"

I waited.

"He's busy at the moment. One of the other officers will show you to an interview room. You can wait there, and he'll find you when he's done. It might be a little bit."

I didn't move. Torn between having my concerns heard and being made to wait in a locked room I couldn't escape from—one with no windows—made it hard to breathe.

Explosions of heat erupted in my chest, paralyzing me, causing sweat to swamp under my arms. My tongue felt thick when I tried to talk. "Could... What if..."

I glanced over my shoulder at the few hard plastic seats lining the front windows. The woman and her child occupied two of them. There were four more available. The small boy was playing a game on his mom's phone, his tongue poking out the side of his mouth.

"Maybe I'll wait here. I can do that. That would work better. You can tell him I'm out here, can't you?"

Another long-suffering sigh. "Sure, Charlie. I'll let him know."

"Thank you. I appreciate it. It's very important."

"It's always very important."

Two

TAKODA

Sergeant Nikola was spitting nails. In my four years in the department, I'd never seen him this angry, and I'd seen him plenty pissed off. Overall, he was a tolerant man. He'd been sitting pretty as sergeant for the central city branch of the Hamilton police for fifteen years. For a man in his midfifties, he was remarkably good-looking in a silver foxish kind of way. I'd made the mistake of telling him that once, despite the abundance of family photographs displayed on his bookshelf and desk. A wife, two kids, a dog. The man probably had a white picket fence at home too. It wouldn't shock me. My comment had gone down like a sinking ship.

Hot was hot. What could I say?

Once again, I'd landed in hot water, and the ocean floor looked to be my final destination.

Sergeant Nikola's salt-and-pepper hair was styled in a neat side part. It was regulation short and always appeared freshly cut. His normally friendly eyes held no warmth, and although it wasn't quite noon, a healthy amount of scruff covered his razor-sharp jaw, making me think he'd been awake for a lot of hours.

For a perpetually put-together man, even after a twelve-hour workday, his open jacket, wrinkled shirt, and crooked tie led me to believe he was a tad frazzled. I brought out the best in people.

The man was so angry he seemed to be unable to form words. For the past five minutes, he'd done nothing more than work his jaw, crack his knuckles as he clenched and unclenched his hands, and snarl in the back of his throat. Red crept up his neck and settled in his face.

For once, I kept my mouth shut.

This wasn't my first time in the hot seat, but based on the intensity of the inferno running through Sarge's system, I feared it might be my last.

When he huffed a sharp exhale out his nose and slammed his hands down on the desk, narrowing his eyes, I knew that was it.

"I don't know what the fuck I'm going to do with you. A smarter man would take your goddamn badge and walk you out the goddamn door. I've worked with some mighty fine assholes over the years, Dyani, but you take the cake. How about you tell me what happened and explain why this is the second partner you've had who has come to me and told me they'd rather quit than work one more goddamn day with your punk ass."

I shifted, making the hard-plastic seat creak as I adopted a more relaxed lean with my legs spread. I didn't want him to think he was getting to me. Shrugging, I met my sergeant's hard gaze. "I don't know what to tell you. I was just doing my job... sir," I added when his eye twitched.

"Your *job* was to respond to a drunk and disorderly on the corner of Finch and Wellington. Do you want to explain to me how you ended up causing an uproar at the Gardiner residence over three blocks away?"

I parsed through my answer, knowing if I wasn't careful, it could be the last thing I said as a Hamilton police officer.

"I was following up on a suspicion." Another eye twitch. "Sir."

"A suspicion?"

"Yes, sir."

Nikola waved his hand, urging me to elaborate. His annoyance was on full display.

"The kids causing the ruckus on Finch were Fiona McKay and Billy Handler. They're both barely nineteen, yet they were drunk off their asses. Solomon and I handled it. We *aksed* them a few questions, figuring out where they'd been and whatnot. Solomon said we should give them a warning and a ride home. I said we should lock them up in the drunk tank and teach them a lesson."

"Get to the part where you ended up causing a scene at the Gardiners'."

I shifted. The chair creaked again. "It came out they'd been at a party at the Gardiners'. Friends with the kids or something. It seemed proper to check it out, seeing as the Gardiners' teenagers are underage."

Gardiner was a huge name in the city. A wealthy family whose father was CEO of some major technology company. They were in the news a lot.

The sergeant's eyes narrowed. "It was a dinner party if I understand correctly. Not some secret teenage bash. That should have been obvious when you pulled up."

"Well, yeah. We figured that out when we got there." I shrugged. "Solomon wanted to leave, but I thought we should have a chat with Mr. Gardiner, ensure he knew he'd loosed drunken teens out into the night."

"A chat?"

"Yes, sir. A friendly man-to-man, you know."

Sergeant waited, glare intensifying.

I didn't blink, keeping my relaxed lean as I avoided bouncing my knee.

When Sarge saw I wasn't about to elaborate, he growled and snatched a paper off his desk—Solomon's complaint report if I had to guess. What a fucking bitch. Gone were the days when your partner had your back apparently. "So, you didn't enter the premises without permission?"

"I don't recall being *asked* to stay outdoors."

"You didn't break a lamp, tear down a picture frame, kick a chair, and rip the tablecloth off the dining room table, which was filled with a meal at the time?"

"I had a little accident."

"Right. A little accident."

"Yes, sir. You see…" I rubbed my nose with the back of my hand. "I tripped on the edge of the carpet when I went into the room and grappled at everything to try and save my fall. First, I snagged the lamp, then the edge of the tablecloth. Still ended up on my ass. When I tried to get up, I grabbed the chair, but it tipped over, and somehow I managed to get tangled in the tablecloth, which sent the food everywhere. I snagged the wall, grabbed the picture frame by mistake, then finally got to my feet. However, my leg was caught in the chair, and when I kicked it loose, the chair might have traveled a few feet. Unintentionally." I paused. "Sir. All just a big accident. Like I said. *Aks* anyone."

Nikola glared over the top of the report.

Sweat prickled along my spine, but I didn't look away and kept my chin high. What I'd learned growing up was that when you lied, you had to maintain confidence and believe in what you said. If I didn't believe it, Nikola wouldn't either.

My sergeant's jaw moved like he was grinding his teeth, and if smoke could have come out his ears, the room would have been clouded with it.

"Did you or did you not give Spencer Gardiner a bloody nose?"

I shook my head, fighting a smirk as I recalled the stunned look on the fucker's face as he'd tried to staunch the blood flow. "Definitely not on purpose. Another accident, sir. I feel terrible about that. We were leaving, and as Mr. Gardiner saw us out, I thought of something else I needed to mention. When I let myself back in, I didn't know he was so close to the door. It could have happened to anyone."

And if that pompous sonofabitch tried to say differently, I'd pay him another visit.

"*Aks* his wife, sir. Stephanie was standing right there. She saw the whole thing."

Nikola dropped the report on the desk and pinched the bridge of his nose as he leaned back in his chair.

"You must think I'm some kind of goddamn fool, Dyani. You spew so many layers of bullshit, sometimes I don't think there would be enough mouthwash in the world to save you from the bad breath."

"That's very clever, sir."

"Shut your goddamn mouth. Solomon is done with you, and for whatever reason, Spencer Gardiner isn't pressing charges."

Because he knows better. Serving alcohol to a minor is a criminal offense that could land the pretentious asshole in prison and taint his oh-so-precious reputation.

I held my tongue. The guy was lucky he'd walked away with a bloody nose and a few pieces of broken furniture. If I saw him in a dark alley, he'd be eating through a tube for the rest of his life. He didn't see the bigger picture. My brother was in jail because of asswipes like Spencer Gardiner who thought it was no big deal to serve alcohol to minors.

Nikola shuffled a few papers on his desk at random. "I still don't know what to do with you. Every goddamn time I turn around, I get complaints. From citizens. From other officers. Everyone. You're aggressive and mouthy, and your goddamn ego needs adjusting."

"You say goddamn a lot, sir. You got some issue with the big man upstairs?"

"Do not get smart with me, Dyani. You are walking a razor's edge right now. You should be on your goddamn knees, begging for your job."

If I was on my knees, I'd be doing something that would far exceed begging.

"I have half a mind to ask for your badge. At this rate, if I keep you around, you'll be writing goddamn parking tickets for the rest of your life. At least until you piss off the wrong person and take a bullet to the head. People don't like arrogant police officers. Don't get me wrong, a little confidence and pride in the job goes a long way, but you cross a line. You cross a big goddamn line. Don't think I don't see through you, Dyani. You have prejudices a mile long, and I can list them all. Spencer Gardiner is on that list too. If you don't like—"

The phone on Sergeant Nikola's desk rang. He snarled as he bit off whatever it was he was going to say and grabbed it.

"What?"

I picked dirt out from under my nails as I pretended not to listen. Relaxed. Composed.

So, I was without a partner again. Did that mean I'd be flying solo for a while? Would Nikola stick me at a desk and make me do paperwork until he came up with someone willing to work beside me? What punishment would it be this time? A couple of days unpaid vacation? Maybe he'd make me organize the records room. What a nightmare.

"Jesus Christ. Fine, make him wait in an interview room. I'll get to him when I get to him. I don't have time for this shit." Nikola slammed the receiver into its cradle and made an unsuccessful attempt at straightening his tie.

The twitch beside his eye intensified. A curl appeared in his lip as he moved more papers around. The perfectly gelled hair he prided himself on was starting to come unstuck.

When I caught myself bouncing a knee, I stilled and scanned my sergeant, waiting for the final verdict.

It didn't come immediately. The phone call had stirred him up and interrupted his reprimand. The cogs in his brain whirred and spun with enough intensity I could nearly see them from across the desk.

"You know what?" he said after a long pause. He nodded at whatever thought had solidified in his brain. "Yeah. That's what I'm going to do."

Sergeant Nikola met my eyes, his features set. An unnerving glint of humor shone from his core. I didn't like it.

"This is the last time I'm having a discussion with you about your performance, Dyani. The very last time. Are we clear?"

I tipped my chin in a tight nod. "Yes, sir. Crystal clear."

"The next time I get so much as a whisper, a hint of your insubordination, the next time you have an *accident,* I will march you out of this goddamn building myself, and I will do it with a smile on my goddamn face."

"Yes, sir."

"You're off the street for a month. I will find you another partner or somehow talk Solomon into giving you one last chance. You'll be typing up paperwork and doing whatever other menial tasks I can find for you. If someone wants a pencil sharpened, it's your job. If someone wants a fresh pot of coffee, you'll be the one brewing it."

I clenched my jaw and swallowed my contempt.

"If the printers need new ink, you'll be the one to change it. If—"

"I get it."

Nikola's eyes widened, and I ducked my chin, knowing I'd spoken out of line.

"If someone trails dog shit into the building, you will find a goddamn bucket and polish the goddamn floor on your hands and knees until it sparkles. Do you understand me?"

"Yes, sir."

"Now, apart from all that, I am also giving you one very important job. Mark my words. If you fuck this up, you're out the door. Consider this a test."

I glanced up, curiosity making my fingers twitch against my pant leg. That glimmer, that unsettling spark of humor radiated from him. Not good.

"Sir?"

Something twisted in my gut. Whatever this grand idea, I wasn't going to like it. His face transformed into a sinister smile. If I was reading him right, the very important job he was about to assign would be my undoing, and he knew it. He'd already anticipated I would fuck it up in the blink of an eye, and he was marching me out the door in his mind as we spoke.

"Detective Graveman retired last month. Were you acquainted?"

Graveman. I flipped through the Rolodex in my brain until I matched a name and face. Older guy. Creeping up on the wrong side of fifty if my estimate was correct. Big man. Craggy face. Stern motherfucker. I hadn't had any encounters with him, but I knew he'd been a well-respected detective before he retired. Graveman was one of the older crew who didn't like how the younger generation did things. Something about disrespect for the system and over-inflated egos.

It echoed what Nikola had been going on about for the past several minutes.

"I think so. What about him?"

"Sometimes in this line of work, we come across individuals who need a little extra care and handling due to circumstances that have altered their lives. They put a lot of faith and trust in us to help them feel safe and protected. These people have lost confidence in the outside world. Their safety has been compromised."

My spine stiffened. I didn't like where this was going.

"And?"

"And Graveman had a talent for handling those tricky situations. One in particular. Seventeen years ago, he and his partner at the time, Pugsley, cracked an ugly case wide open. A kidnapping and underground child sex-trafficking operation."

Nikola shook his head in disgust. "That's the kind of shit you never want to see. Unfortunately, his team arrived a little too late. The traffickers had caught wind the police were moving in. Every goddamn person involved at the time wished that situation had ended better than it did, but no one more than Graveman. He threw himself into that case pretty hard. But that's life, isn't it?"

Nikola's jaw tightened as he stared off into middle space, his mind seemingly caught in the past. Wrinkles appeared across his forehead. "One boy survived. One boy out of eighteen. He was twelve years old. Sometimes, victims get attached to their rescuers and form unhealthy bonds. Call it hero worship or whatever you want. Sometimes, law enforcement officers get attached to victims because their internalized guilt eats them alive. We can't help thinking, what if I had done things differently? We reprimand ourselves more than our senior officers ever could. In this case, Graveman's guilt and the victim's compromised mental health combined to form a loose, yet professional friendship if you will."

It was my turn to fidget, crack my knuckles, and tense.

"I'm not sure what you're getting at, sir."

"Little Charlie has been through a lot." Nikola chuckled, but it was a sad sound. "I guess he isn't so little anymore. That was a lot of years ago. He suffers from some extreme paranoia, among other things. Graveman was good at placating him, listening to his concerns, and following through with action plans that pacified poor Charlie. Maybe the right thing to do would have been to cut ties early on, but Graveman didn't have it in him. The problem is, Graveman isn't here anymore, and Charlie's mind isn't about to turn off just because his sounding board and sole source of security is no longer with the department. Do you see where I'm going with this?"

Yeah, I saw, and I didn't like it one bit. Nikola thought I needed to coddle some prissy boy's ass.

"So, let me get this straight, you want me to mollify some guy with paranoid delusions because Graveman didn't have the balls years ago to tell him to go to a fucking shrink?"

With a haughty laugh, Nikola leaned back in his chair, folding his hands behind his head. He was smug. Too smug. "Charlie is a sweet boy. His father worked in a position of power in this city for many years until his life was turned upside down and his son was taken. It destroyed his marriage and all his future prospects for mayor. I'm good friends with Archie Falkingham. We go way back. The Hamilton police work with his wife regularly. I'll let you connect those pieces on your own. But let me tell you"—Nikola leaned forward and pinned me with a hostile glare—"if I catch even a whiff of disobedience from you, Dyani, even a hint of unprofessionalism, you're finished."

Falkingham?

I suppressed a groan. The Falkinghams were a powerful name in the city. More so than the Gardiners. They were money. Old money. Elizabeth Falkingham was the city's appointed crown attorney. A woman who was not to be trifled with. This Charlie was her kid? No wonder we bent over backward to appease him.

Fuck my life. Nikola was doing this on purpose. He wanted me to fail so he could laugh in my face and show me the door. What better way than to hand off someone else's delicate and needy flower, knowing I wouldn't be able to handle it. Knowing how I felt about people like the Falkinghams.

"You have prejudices a mile long, and I can list them all."

He was right. I wouldn't deny it. Numero uno on that list was anyone who came from money or power. Anyone like the Falkinghams. Except this time, if I fucked up, there would be no burying my mistake under a mountain of bullshit lies.

I took a second to ensure my voice was level when I spoke. "So, I'm pushing paper, cleaning up dog shit, and taking care of some kid's weekly complaints?"

"And you will do it all with a smile on your goddamn face."

"For how long? A month?"

"Or until I feel you're fit to be an officer on my streets. Oh, and Dyani? Charlie isn't a kid anymore. He's got a few years on you if I'm not mistaken. Remember that. He might struggle with certain things, but he's far from stupid."

"Yes, sir."

Nikola pushed back from his desk and straightened his shirt and tie. "Shall we?" He waved to the door. "Charlie happens to be in the building right now. I'll introduce you."

"Yay. Can't wait," I said under my breath as I shoved out of the chair.

The bullpen was crowded with the usual bustle of officers, detectives, and support staff milling about. It was stuffy since no one had bothered opening a window to let in the fresh spring air.

The steady tapping of keyboards and murmuring of low conversations provided familiar background noise while an ancient fax machine squealed in the back corner of the room. A burnt-coffee odor lingered in the air, along with the cloying scent of microwave popcorn someone had recently popped in the break room down the hall.

I followed Nikola toward the far hallway that led to our two secured interview rooms. As we crossed the bullpen, I felt the weight of a few lingering gazes and heard hushed conversations from those who were speculating about my fate.

It was no surprise I wasn't popular among my colleagues. Being the only openly gay police officer in our district caused a lot of issues. The closet homophobes who knew better than to openly discriminate still found ways to punctuate their hatred when the upper echelon of power turned their heads. I'd learned long ago not to let people walk all over me. I had thick skin and an unfiltered mouth that didn't always work in my favor and had gotten me in plenty of trouble.

Maybe I had a chip on my shoulder, but I had plenty of reasons.

Nikola unlocked the steel door to interview room A, but after poking his head inside, he closed it again. We continued down the painted concrete hallway—modulated gray blue—until we reached the next door. Interview room B had a large one-way mirror where officers could monitor from the observation room. It was also equipped with recording devices and cameras.

Nikola unlocked the door, poked his head inside, then closed it again. "Goddammit."

He shoved past me and marched back toward the bullpen. At the first desk he came to, he tugged the phone closer and punched a few buttons, cradling the receiver between his shoulder and his ear. "I thought I told you to put him in an interview room," he barked. Nikola listened for a moment, then scrubbed a hand over his face. "No, no one told me... Yeah, all right... No, it's fine." He slammed the phone into the cradle and shoved it back into place.

When he marched away toward the front of the station, the whispers cut out, and people returned to their respective work. I rolled my eyes and followed Nikola, affecting a lazy, borderline cocky strut so everyone knew my stance on what was playing out. It was like a three-ring circus in this place some days, and there I was, the performing monkey, jumping through hoops just to appease my boss.

If I wanted to keep my job, I would have to learn how to be a yes-man like everyone else, no matter how much I hated it.

It took everything I had not to shoot the room the finger as we exited.

At the front of the station, Nikola pushed through the secured exit to the waiting area. I caught the door with my foot before it closed and leaned against it, arms crossed as Nikola wandered to the seats along the window.

There was a guy in tailored chinos, a starchy polo shirt, and leather loafers sitting ramrod straight in the farthest seat in the row. His hair—the color of straw—was so stiff with gel a hurricane would have been hard-pressed to throw a single hair out of line.

Nikola must have said his name, but I was too far away to hear the gentler tone he often used with the public. The man, Charlie, glanced up.

And my breath caught.

His features were fine—a sharp nose, a delicate jawline, thin but shapely lips, plenty of freckles, and wary eyes whose color I couldn't make out from my position by the door. He wasn't a big guy, but he wasn't one of those skinny little twinks I saw at the bar all the time either. Charlie had a slender swimmer's body that was only accentuated by his fitted clothing.

He reeked of privilege. Even if I didn't know who his mother was, even if I hadn't learned his father had once been in the running for mayor, I would have guessed this Charlie guy came from money.

Those people had a look about them. They also had an attitude I vehemently disliked.

Spencer Gardiner and his arrogant teenage kids all had the same look. His wife Stephanie too, but she had a taste for rebellion which had worked in my favor. I'd picked up on it the moment I'd walked in the door. A few flirty smiles and hidden winks, and she had turned to putty in my hands. Even if Spencer hadn't been trying to avoid a charge for serving minors—since his teenage sons were all three sheets to the wind—she'd have probably supported my claim of accidentally breaking her husband's nose on the front door on the off chance I might entertain her cop fantasies behind her husband's back.

Charlie shook his head and dashed a quick glance in my direction. He wrung his hands over and over. His milky white skin looked paler under the harsh fluorescent lighting.

Shave off a half dozen years and he could have been the poster boy for an ivy league university.

If the thought of who his parents were—who he was—didn't make my blood curdle, I'd have almost called him cute. I had a thing for that boyishly innocent look. The type of guys who acted like they'd never had a dirty thought in their lives. Those guys always loved it when a confident jock took the reins and showed them a wild night.

For a fraction of a second, I envisioned destroying the look of innocence on Charlie's face. Totally sex wrecked would look good on him.

Looks aside, Charlie Falkingham was someone I wanted nothing to do with. He was a thorn in my side. A rich, privileged pain in my ass.

I bit back as much animosity as I could and reminded myself to be nice. I didn't for a second think Nikola made empty threats, and my job was on the line.

Three

CHARLIE

"Good morning, Charlie."

I whipped my head up and found Sergeant Nikola standing a few feet away. His sudden arrival released a burst of adrenaline into my system, knocking my heart rate up a few too many notches. I didn't like surprises. Although I'd been anticipating his arrival, I'd been lost in my head for the past few minutes.

Nikola stood at a distance, hands shoved inside his trouser pockets, his smile a little too soft. His voice was mellow, gentler than the tone I assumed he used on most people. I wasn't fragile, but most of the officers at the station treated me like I was made of glass. It was irritating.

Detective Graveman didn't. He was respectful and kind. Never patronizing.

But Stanley understood me. Stanley had been there the day they'd found me. He'd been the one who'd carried me to the ambulance, cradled in his big arms.

That much I remembered.

The sense of security. The warmth.

"Good morning, Sergeant Nikola." I shuffled to the edge of the hard-plastic chair, rubbing my hands together, wringing them, knotting my fingers, doing all I could to calm my nerves. "I'm terribly sorry to bother you. I need to speak with Stanley. It's urgent. I understand he's retired now, which is most unfortunate, but if you could let him know I have something to share, I'm sure he'd want to hear it." I wet my lips. "It won't take long."

Nikola transferred his weight and seemed to consider his words before he spoke, his tone no less delicate. "You know I can't do that, Charlie. Stan's earned himself a break from this place. It wouldn't be fair."

I opened my mouth to argue, but Nikola held up a hand, stopping me. "Let me finish, son. Whatever you have to report is important. I understand that, and you know we take public concerns seriously. We would never disregard anything you brought to us. However, Detective Graveman is no longer an active member of the department, so things will have to change a bit from now on. Do you understand?"

I wasn't an idiot, but a trickle of fear raised the hairs on the back of my neck. This wasn't how it was supposed to go. I didn't nod or shake my head, still fighting with the unpredictability of the whole situation. Nikola must have seen resignation in my eyes because he continued.

"I'm going to introduce you to another officer today, one who's eager to step up and help you out."

I made my hands into tight fists, my pulse thrumming in my ears. It was then I noticed the man at the secured door that led into the bullpen. A six-foot-tall, olive-skinned, dark-eyed man who looked ready to tear me apart. His brows were severe. The cut of his jaw was as sharp as glass. I was both afraid and slightly flustered at the sight of him. Heat built in my core until I was sweating under my light polo.

The new officer's hair was buzzed short and as black as midnight. He didn't look friendly or eager to help me at all. In fact, he looked hostile. Aggravated. Angry.

Toned and tattooed arms were crossed over his chest as he leaned back against the open door. With his chin hitched at an arrogant angle, he glared in our direction. His jaw was tight and set, and his lips were pressed into a firm line.

If I were to write him into a story, he could easily play the villain.

My mouth dried as our eyes connected. The heat of his glare sent my thoughts scattering into the wind.

I refocused on Sergeant Nikola and cleared my throat. "No. No, I don't think so. That doesn't seem like something that will work for me at all. Maybe we could call Stanley and ask him if he'd be willing to talk? He won't mind. We have an agreement, and—"

"Charlie, how about you meet Officer Dyani first, and we'll go from there?"

I wrung my hands and snuck a quick glance at the man at the door again. He was dressed in a navy officer's uniform with a heavy utility belt around his waist and black boots. He wasn't a detective, not like Stanley. This man, whoever he was, was a regular patrol officer.

And he looked mean.

Before I could protest, Nikola waved the man over. Officer Dyani sauntered across the tiled floor, his heavy boots clipping along and highlighting his egotism. With his head high and his gaze focused on my face, I struggled to maintain eye contact. When he stood beside the sergeant, Dyani's lips formed a weak smile. It was fake, without an ounce of sincerity.

"Charlie, I'd like you to meet Officer Takoda Dyani."

"A pleasure." The man held out his hand.

I hesitated, then took his offered hand and shook. His grip was crushing, and I winced. "Nice to meet you. No disrespect, Sergeant, but I would feel much better if we could at least call Stanley to see if—"

"That isn't going to happen, Charlie. Dyani is more than happy to listen to everything you have to say, isn't that right?" Nikola pinned his officer with contempt. A warning that might as well have had a neon sign attached to it.

"Yes, sir. More than happy."

"Excellent. I'll let you two get acquainted. And Charlie? If, for whatever reason, Takoda here doesn't handle your concerns with the utmost professionalism, you let me know, all right?"

I nodded, even though the comment seemed to be aimed at Dyani.

Nikola clapped his officer on the shoulder and shook my hand. "Tell your dad I said hi."

"I will."

Sergeant Nikola left us there in the lobby as he trucked his way back to the secured door, carded through, and disappeared into the main area of the precinct.

When he was gone, I stood stiff, unsure where to put myself. This Takoda Dyani was imposing. I didn't like being around people who made me uncomfortable. In fact, I avoided those types of people like the plague. My social bubble was select and small.

However, my choices were slim. I could either run out of the station and forget this whole thing or relay my concerns to the young officer with eyes such a deep hickory brown I couldn't help noticing their color.

And those eyes were steadily dissecting me as I stood mute.

"How about we take this into an interview room, yeah? You can tell me what's bothering you, I'll *aks* you some questions, write it all down nice and neat and professional, and you can get on outta here. Hm?"

"Ask."

"What?"

"You said *aks*. That's improper English. The word is ask. A-S-K, not A-K-S."

Officer Dyani narrowed his hickory eyes and flexed his fingers once, making fists. The ink on his arms rippled with the tensing of his muscles. It was a mixture of portraits, symbols, tribal art, and random impressions of nature—trees, birds, vines, flowers. I didn't want to stare since he was clearly upset, but they intrigued me and stirred questions.

My tongue felt thick and heavy, and I thought I should apologize since Dad had informed me several times it was rude to correct people's grammar. But Dyani spoke first.

"I will *ask* you a few questions, and you can get outta here. Better?"

I nodded, even though it was not better, and glanced around. "I would feel more comfortable talking to Stanley."

"That isn't going to happen. Are you deaf? You heard the sergeant. You talk to me, or you talk to no one. Your choice, and believe me, my feelings won't be hurt if you jog on out that door, get your perky little ass into your million-dollar Mercedes, or whatever the fuck you drive, and never look back."

"It's an Impala. And a Mercedes doesn't cost a million dollars."

"Whatever." Dyani rolled his eyes and waved at the secure door. "Shall we?"

I glanced at the door then to Officer Dyani before scanning the police station's lobby, noting Briggs was typing away at her computer behind the plexiglass window, oblivious or purposefully ignoring us. The woman and child were long gone.

"Detective Graveman had a desk in the bullpen. Do you have a desk?"

"No."

"I can't go inside the interview rooms."

Dyani groaned and ran a hand over his midnight-black hair. It rasped against his palm, and I wondered if it was soft or coarse. It was certainly silky and shone in the overhead lighting.

When Officer Dyani's brows connected in the middle, I looked elsewhere. The stern edges of his face were daunting.

"Look, man, I don't have a desk. I'm not a detective like your buddy. I'm a dime-a-dozen beat cop just trying not to get his ass fired right now. I'll let you talk. I'll even do my best to nod and smile, just tell me where the fuck you want to sit so we can get this over with and I can go clean fucking toilets or whatever bullshit job Nikola has lined up for me. You get me?"

My insides jittered, and I backed up a step, angling for the door to outside. I thought of the white Pontiac. I thought of the sleepless nights that would surely follow if I didn't make this report. I thought of Dad yelling at me for standing on the landing. For a flicker of time, I poked at the dark hole in my mind, but when internal alarm bells rang, I pulled back.

I wrung my hands over and over, taking another retreating step. I didn't like confrontation or anger, and this man's attitude was triggering. I needed to go.

"Thank you for your time, Officer Dyani. I think it's in my best interest that I take my leave. Perhaps Detective Graveman is listed in the phone book, or…" I grimaced, knowing the odds were slim. "Or I'll call my mother. She can surely help me find him. Maybe. She might—"

"Wait. Fuck. Fuck me. Okay, look. Don't run off." Dyani held up his hands like I was a startled deer, and I winced. "Just don't leave, okay?" He cracked his knuckles and seemed to make every effort to tone down his aggressive edge. When he spoke again, it was a shade cooler than before. "You came here to make a report. I'm happy to listen. Help me help you, all right? How can I make this work so you aren't going to freak out on me and leave? If you run to your mother, I'm toast, man. You hear me? Please. No interview room. I got that. I legit have no desk. Only the detectives get that privilege. There's a common work area where we patrol officers write up reports. It's a room with just a bunch of tables and a few computers and whatnot. I can't guarantee it's private, but would that be better?"

I paused my retreat to consider. "It's in a room?"

Dyani shook his head. "I don't understand. Of course it's in a fucking room. It's not in the fucking park." He pinched his lips and forced another fake smile to his face, one rich in condescension. "I'm sorry. What do you mean?"

"The interview rooms are locked. Is this place in a locked room like that?"

"No. I mean, I can shut the door and lock it if you want. It's just down the hall from the bullpen. Adjacent to the break room. You've been down that way before, right?"

"No." I shuffled, toying with the seam on my pant leg. "Detective Graveman took my statements at his desk, or we'd go for a drive and talk. I think it will do so long as the door remains open."

"Fine."

"Are there windows?"

"Yes."

"Do they open?"

"I... No. I don't think so."

I considered for another minute, ensuring I'd examined all angles. When Dyani waved a hand, a silent question, asking if I was doing this or not, I nodded.

"Okay. I can try in there."

I followed Dyani through the secured door and down the long hall toward the bullpen. I was familiar with several officers, and we exchanged greetings while I battled with my rising blood pressure. We headed down the long concrete hallway that led to the interview rooms.

Near the end of the hallway, we rounded a corner and continued to another section of the precinct. The scent of curry, popcorn, burnt coffee, and something cinnamon battled for dominance. The breakroom was on my left. A few people lingered inside, chatting and laughing while making food or drinks. A microwave beeped. The door was propped open, and a large window ran the length of the back wall, letting in the sun. In the middle of the room was a long table where a few men in suits were eating.

Immediately following the breakroom was a similar room. Dyani shuffled around and waved a hand for me to enter first. I didn't.

It was an unfamiliar space, and I took a minute to scan from the threshold.

The long tables in this room were pushed against the walls. Several computers sat on top at evenly spaced intervals. Two of them were in use by uniformed officers I didn't know. They both glanced up quizzically at our arrival before returning to their work.

A particle board shelving unit ran floor-to-ceiling beside the window. It was filled with manuals and toppling stacks of paper, a three-hole punch, a scattering of pens, two sealed boxes of paperclips, tiny note pads with sticky backs, and someone's half-eaten apple that was brown from oxidization. Upon seeing the abandoned fruit, I caught a whiff of its sweet moldering odor which was almost overpowered by the warm scent of ink coming off the copier that sat in the corner.

The room was stuffy. A large window took up a portion of the far wall, but like Officer Dyani had said, it was the kind that didn't open. Recirculated air filtered into the room from the grated vents near the ceiling.

"Are we going to stand here all day?" Dyani asked.

I pressed my lips together, taking it all in, studying the propped door and locking mechanism by the handle. It used a key. I didn't have the key. That was a problem. I didn't like locked rooms. I didn't like not having control of locked doors or windows.

"We aren't closing the door, right?" I asked. Even though we'd worked that out beforehand, this guy didn't feel as honorable or trustworthy as Detective Graveman nor did he know my quirks. Every cell in my body was telling me to leave.

But the white Pontiac. I wasn't imagining it.

"Not if you don't want it closed."

"I don't."

"All right." Again, Dyani waved me inside, his irritation mounting if the snide look he shot in my direction meant anything.

We sat in a pair of chairs a short distance from the officers who were working. The clacking of keyboard keys was familiar. I spent many hours making that noise at home, so it was soothing in a way.

Dyani angled his chair so his back was to his colleagues. I purposefully positioned myself so I faced the door. The exit. The escape route.

"Okay." Dyani snapped a pad of paper and a pen from beside one of the computers. He crossed an ankle over a knee and leaned back in the cushioned desk chair, swiveling it back and forth as he put pen to paper. "Lay it on me. What *brang* you in here today?"

"Brought."

"What?"

"The correct word is *brought*, not *brang*."

Officer Dyani's fingers turned white where he gripped the pen. When he spoke, it was from between clenched teeth. "What *brought* you in here today?"

"Someone's following me, and I'm not imagining it."

"Explain."

I glanced at the door and back, wringing my hands. "Yesterday, I went to the post office to collect the forms I'm required to fill out when posting my signed books. They prefer I fill them out in advance to save time. I prefer it too since it means less lingering in places where I don't want to be."

"*Anyways.*" Dyani waved his hand. "Get to the point."

I hesitated. "The word is *anyway*, not *anyways*. You can't pluralize that word, it's—" I swallowed my explanation when Dyani's hickory eyes simmered with suppressed rage. "Never mind. When I left the post office, a white Pontiac Grand Prix was idling at the curb. I didn't think anything of it until I got into my car and pulled out to drive away. It pulled out too and followed me for three blocks until I turned into Daisy's Market."

"Daisy's Market," Dyani said out loud, enunciating each syllable as he marked chicken scratch on the pad of paper.

It took all my self-control not to inform him that the word Pontiac was supposed to be capitalized and wasn't spelled with a *k*.

"So when you pulled into the market, it drove away?"

"Yes."

Dyani peered up from the pad of paper, his expression flat. Bored. "So, maybe they were just headed in the same direction. It doesn't mean they were following you."

"I'm not imagining it. Plus, after I grabbed milk, bread, laundry soap, aluminum foil, the chicken breasts Dad likes that they had advertised in the flyer for only—"

"I don't need your fucking grocery list."

I shifted and laced my fingers together, staring at my thumbs. The room was too hot, and my discomfort grew with each passing second.

I swallowed a tight lump and continued. "While I was bringing my cart to the cart return outside, the white Pontiac drove by again. Slowly. Like it was monitoring me or something."

"You're sure it was the same one?"

"I'm not stupid, Officer."

"I didn't say you were. It's a common make and model, that's all."

I shook my head. "It was an older model. Late-nineties maybe? I'm not positive. It wasn't new. It was distinctively... aged. There was rust on the wheel wells, and..." I frowned, unsure how else to describe it. "Anyhow, I got in my car and pulled out onto the road to head home. The Pontiac was half a block down, idling at the curb. It was waiting for me. It pulled out when I drove by and followed me until I got to my neighborhood. Then it vanished again."

Dyani scribbled everything down, but I could tell he was gearing up to dismiss this whole thing.

"But that's not all," I said before he could speak. "This morning, the same car drove past my house twice in a handful of minutes. Slowly again. On purpose."

Dyani frowned and jotted that down as well. His penmanship was terrible, and his spelling was worse. He mumble-read back through everything he'd written down, following along with the tip of the pen like he might lose his place otherwise.

A rap at the door drew both our attention.

"Hey, Koda. I heard your ass is on the line again. What did you do this time?"

The two officers working at the computers glanced up but paid the newcomer no mind and ducked their heads again, clicking away at their respective keyboards. Dyani spun on his chair. I caught the humored curve of his lips before his back was to me. "Hey, asswipe.

How about you fuck off. I'm in the middle of an interview." He thumbed over his shoulder. "Do you mind? Important shit going on in here."

The officer at the door looked to be about the same age as Officer Dyani. Unlike the man conducting my interview, the new guy was pasty white with a lick of flaming red hair slicked back off his forehead. He was tall and too skinny without a lot of muscle mass. However, the gleam behind his washed-out green eyes hinted at the same trouble I saw in Dyani's.

The newcomer flicked his attention to me and back to his buddy. "We have interview rooms for that exact purpose, you know."

"Really? Gee, I didn't think of that. What would I do without your worldly wisdom? Piss off, man. I'm busy."

"Yeah, yeah. Keep your pants on." Then the redheaded officer glanced at me again. "If this guy gives you trouble, you let me know. I'll put him through a wall for ya."

Dyani threw a pen at the door, and it bounced off the frame as the other guy ducked out of sight. His laughter rang as he continued down the hall.

Dyani spun back around and scanned the tabletop until he found another pen and snagged it. Adopting the same casual posture as before, he pasted on a condescending smile. "Okay, so a white Pontiac Grand Prix followed you from the post office to the market to your neighborhood. This morning you think the same car drove by your house twice. Is that correct?"

"I don't think. I know."

"Did you get a license plate?"

I frowned. "No. I tried this morning, but the angle from the window was wrong."

"Of course it was. Did you get a look at the driver?"

I shook my head. "The glare from the sun reflected against the windows."

Dyani pursed his lips and tapped the new pen on the pad of paper several times before he asked, "What am I supposed to do with this?"

"Someone is following me. I'm not crazy. I'm not imagining it."

"So, you're saying you don't feel safe?"

"Would you feel safe if some unknown assailant was following you?"

"You don't know if this person means you harm. It could be a coincidence."

"Maybe, but you'll investigate it, right?"

"Investigate what? You've given me shit, bucko. All I've got here is an older model white Pontiac Grand Prix. That's it."

"Detective Graveman always followed up on my concerns. There must be a way to check your data bank for a car matching that description, or—"

I bit off the words when Dyani tossed the pen on the table. It rolled with enough force it pinged off the back wall, ricocheting and skidding under a far keyboard.

He sat forward, slapping the pad of paper down on the table. He had large hands. "You know what? That is exactly what I'm going to do. Then I'm gonna get in my car and drive around the whole fucking city until I find this older model white Pontiac in a sea of about a million other cars. Does that make you feel better? Maybe you want to pay me to be your bodyguard, that way you'll always be safe. A guy like you must be able to fund a whole protective detail. You certainly have us jumping through hoops."

The tips of my fingers turned cold. All the blood drained from my face at Dyani's sarcastic remarks. He thought I was a joke. The stuffy room turned suffocating. The walls pressed in from all sides. I couldn't move, but I needed to get away. Get out. Panic sliced like a razor at the tender edges of my mind.

So I pulled away like I tended to do when I was overwhelmed. I retreated.

I could hear my doctor's voice in the faraway reaches of my mind telling me to stop and face the emotional overload. Process the things I was feeling one at a time and express them out loud. But I couldn't do it. I couldn't move

When I retreated inside my head, life became far more basic and manageable. Stress melted away. One at a time, I eliminated all excessive sensory stimulants. Like a light switch, I simply turned them off. It was a trick I'd learned a long time ago. No more hearing, seeing, tasting, smelling, or feeling. All of it was turned down so low it might as well be shut off. All I had to focus on were the foundational requirements of my body.

Breathing. In and out.

A calm soupy nothingness surrounded me.

In the distance, if I allowed it, I could scarcely make out voices and snippets of conversations. They came through as though I was deep under water.

My name. Someone said my name over and over.

A woman's voice. A man's. Then a woman's again.

Arguing.

I let it all swirl around me in the faraway distance until the prickles of fear lessened.

"Process them one at a time, Charlie. Pick the least threatening sense and bring it back. You need to learn to face these stressors. Don't hide from them. Process them."

Dr. Sofia Menard had a gentle voice, even when she spoke inside my head, even when she wasn't really there, and her lessons were nothing more than figments of remembered sessions we'd had over the years.

One at a time, I tuned back in to my senses, taking it slow and measuring each step forward so I wouldn't get overwhelmed.

Officer Dyani's voice came through first. "I'm going to lose my fucking job. What the fuck do I do? Jesus. Shit. He's *coma toast*. What the hell's happening to him? Why is he like this? Charlie! Charlie!"

"Stop yelling at him. Just level your tone and keep talking," the woman said. "I'm going to close the door before you attract an audience."

A surge of panic made me tighten my fists. Someone was holding my hands. Shaking my head took effort. Finding my voice took more. The first few words came out garbled like when the doctor dosed me with high amounts of Xanax. "Don't close the door. Please. Don't close the door."

The pull to stay gone was almost too hard to resist.

"Don't touch the door," Dyani barked. "Charlie? Do you hear me? What the hell is going on, man?" His tone was softer. "Look, if you can hear me, then listen. I was being a dickhole. I'm sorry, okay. I'll run this car through every fucking system we've got and see what I can find. Does that help? Charlie? Shit, man. Can you hear me? Do you want me to drive around the whole city and look for it? I will. Just stop doing whatever you're doing. If Nikola sees, I'm dead. You can come and look with me. I'll let you ride shotgun so you can see I'm not bullshitting you. Charlie? Fuck me. Charlie?"

This more tender, albeit panicked, side of Dyani managed to help the transition back. I blinked a few times and stared at my hands as my senses came back online. Our hands. Dyani was holding mine. His olive skin tone a sharp contrast to my pale, nearly translucent complexion.

I became aware of many things at once. The scent of sweat and something earthier like sage and sweetgrass. The hum and rhythmic pulse of the copier as it printed and spat out paper. The husky, barking laugh of a male officer down the hall.

Dyani's warm hands rubbed mine between his palms as though trying to encourage heat back into my icy fingers. He was sitting close, our knees bumping as he leaned in and said my name over and over. It sounded nice coming from his lips, and a strange warmth pooled in my low belly as I listened to him talk.

It was an unfamiliar sensation, and I didn't know if it was a good feeling or not. It raised the hairs on my arms, and it felt awfully similar to fear, but it wasn't.

I blinked a few times, refocusing on the room. First, I checked that the door was still open. It was. Then I glanced at the two people hovering over me. Dyani and the female officer who'd been working at a computer earlier.

The female officer crouched beside Dyani and rested a gentle hand on my thigh. "Hey, sweetie. Are you all right?"

I nodded, tugging my hands from Dyani's and clasping my fingers together in my lap. "I'm fine, thank you. May I have a glass of water, please?"

"Sure thing." She rose and touched Dyani's shoulder. They shared a silent conversation before she stepped out of the room.

The other officer who'd been working at the computers was gone. We were alone.

"What the fuck just happened with you?"

I wanted to cry because this was why people thought I was batshit crazy.

"I'm not imagining the car. You think I'm crazy, but I'm not crazy."

Dyani heaved an exhausted sigh and leaned back in his chair. He looked two parts relieved and one part frustrated. "Look, I don't think you're crazy. What I don't have is very much information, but I swear to you, I'll look into it and do whatever I can. Does that work for you?

I don't know what Graveman did that was so special, but just give me some guidance. I don't want you to *misunderestimate* me. I'll work hard and sort this shit out."

I glanced up, taking in all the hard angles of Dyani's face. For the first time since I'd seen him, there was an edge of concern marking his features. Was it for me or his job?

"*Misunderestimate* isn't a word."

"What are you, some kind of word Nazi? Jesus Christ, stop fixing everything I say."

I clamped my mouth shut.

"And how is *misunderestimate* not a fucking word? I've heard it before. I know I have. You're making this shit up."

I shook my head and shrugged. "It's not."

Dyani narrowed his eyes, and I couldn't take the weight of his attention, so I glanced down at my hands again.

The female officer returned with a large cup of water, condensation fogging the glass and dripping down its sides. I accepted it and drank deeply.

The woman wandered to the copier but kept half an eye on us.

The cool drink coated my belly and helped put out the fire in my core.

But the minute I put the glass down and inhaled, sage and sweetgrass tickled my nose, and the fire roared back to life. It was him. The scent was coming off Officer Dyani.

"Will you call me with your report?" I asked, doing all I could to get my head back in the game and keep my voice level.

"Sure. Is that what Graveman did?"

"Yes."

"Fine. Do we have a number for you on file?"

"I believe so."

"Then I'll find it. Do you want me to come back to your place and drive around the neighborhood? Make sure that car isn't about?"

I considered and shook my head. It would only perpetuate Dyani's negative feelings toward me, and I was convinced he was already checking me into the nearest mental health facility in his mind.

"Here." He tore a corner off the pad of paper where he'd written my statement and looked around for another pen. When he found one, he jotted a number on the scrap in his almost illegible chicken scratch and handed it over. "That's my cell number. If you see the car again, no matter where you are or what you're doing, you call immediately. Don't wait. If you can, get a license plate number and a description of the driver, but not at the cost of your safety."

I took the paper where he'd etched his phone number and his name above it. Koda, not Dyani. "I will."

"All right. Off you go, Chucky boy, and stay out of trouble, ya hear me?" Dyani shoved to his feet and hooked his thumbs in his belt.

I frowned and peered up into his dark hickory eyes. "My name is Charlie. I don't like being called Chucky. Thank you."

Dyani breathed deeply, his nostrils flaring with the action as he plastered on another one of those patronizing, fake smiles. "Sure thing. Let me see you out."

Four

TAKODA

I escorted Charlie to the front lobby and watched him leave. The minute he was through the door, I let out an exhausted breath. "Jesus Christ. This is my fucking life now?"

Briggs glanced up from the computer with a knowing smirk. I sneered, and she shot me the finger before I headed back to the bullpen. Briggs and I got along okay. She was down to earth and had a good sense of humor.

Rumors of my new assignment would be all over the station before the end of the day. Takoda Dyani gets to babysit the psycho rich boy. Wonderful.

It still wasn't noon. It was going to be the longest day in history at this rate.

The bullpen was quieter than it had been earlier. Most patrol officers were out on the street. The few who remained were dropping off perps to the local jail located in the basement on the east end of the building, or they were filing reports before heading out again. We had a handful of detectives who all had fancy little desks. A few of them,

Roosevelt, Wan, and Myers, were huddled together, staring at a computer screen and chatting too low to be heard. Beat cops were below detectives, and detectives made sure we stayed aware of our position.

I aimed for the room where I'd taken Charlie's statement, poking my head into the breakroom on my way by. Corey Adina was pouring herself a coffee. "Hey, thanks for the help earlier."

Corey glanced over her shoulder, brow raised. "Kevin says you're in hot water again. You think antagonizing Elizabeth Falkingham's son is the way to get on Nikola's good side?"

"I wasn't antagonizing him. You heard him. He thinks a white Pontiac is following him and wants me to do something about it. No plates, no description of the driver. Nothing. What the fuck am I supposed to do with that?"

"You really don't get it, do you?"

Corey was in her mid-thirties. She wore her hair buzzed on both sides with a wide strip of bleach-blonde hair down the middle which she tied back in a short ponytail. It wasn't long enough to stay back without a gallon of product, and it often slipped out of the elastic, falling into her face. She had to fix it ten times a day, and I'd heard Nikola bark at her about regulations, stating if she wanted longer hair, it had to be long enough to stay tied back.

Corey was short but with a gym-toned body that gave her an air of strength and power several women in the department couldn't pull off. I'd called her butch once about a year ago, and she'd handed me my ass, much to her partner's delight. I'd learned my lesson that day to never piss her off. I liked her.

"What do you mean I don't get it?"

"Charlie Falkingham's case was the Hamilton Police Department's biggest fuckup in twenty years. Haven't you read about it?"

"No. It was forever ago. What the fuck do I care?"

"You're a fucking idiot, Dyani. Nikola passed Charlie off to you, right? Now that Graveman retired?"

"Yeah, so?"

"So, in other words, he's paved your way right out the fucking door. Adios, amigo. Sayonara."

I kicked the wedge out from under the door, and it slammed. I leaned against it, crossing my arms and taking a stance. "What the fuck does that mean?"

"You gonna go all macho on me? For real?" She grinned, shaking her head. "Bring it, Dyani. Your punk ass doesn't scare me."

"Just answer the question."

"It means Nikola doesn't think you have an ounce of sympathy in you, and he's counting the days until he can replace your ass without having to risk some discrimination lawsuit or some other bullshit."

I frowned. "Are you saying he hasn't fired my ass yet because I'm gay?"

"I'm saying, I have no fucking clue why he keeps you around, to be honest. You're an arrogant asshole who doesn't know when to shut the fuck up and stand down. You walk around with your cock swinging thinking you're untouchable. But guess what? If you don't bend over backward and kiss Charlie Falkingham's ass every single time he walks in that door, it won't be Nikola showing you out. It will be someone much higher up because that family has power like you wouldn't believe and a huge grudge against the Hamilton Police Department for not breaking that case faster. So I'm going to suggest you swallow this hard-done-by, pissy fucking attitude you bring to work with you each day and do your job before you don't have one. Talking to Charlie like you did? That's signing your death warrant."

I didn't have a response and ground my teeth, holding Corey's gaze until she glanced down at her coffee and took a sip. She was entirely too smug, and if she wasn't partners with one of my best friends, I might have had something more to say.

"It's bullshit," I mumbled. "What am I supposed to do? You were in the room. You heard it. I have no information, and chances are this is all in his fucking head."

"It *is* in his head. Charlie suffers from severe paranoia, among *many* other things. He just needs reassurance we are looking out for him. That's all. It's not rocket science."

"How?"

Corey shrugged. "I don't know, Dyani. Graveman was the one who took Charlie under his wing, but that man knew how to handle him. Get creative. Try not to be an asshole even though I know it's your default setting."

I growled under my breath and kicked at the garbage can that sat beside the door. It clanged and rocked, almost spilling over before landing square on its base again. I jerked the door open, muttering, "Prissy little rich boy gets whatever the fuck he wants. That's the way of the world. Waste of taxpayer money."

"Keep it up, Dyani. You're just digging your grave," Corey called after me. "I already know what I'm going to wear to your funeral."

I ignored her.

In the officers' workroom, Kevin Trampoline, Adina's partner and my best friend, leaned against the copier, scrolling on his phone as the machine whined and whirred.

"Your partner's a bitch."

Trampoline glanced up, his red hair catching the light and shining with all the damn product he put in it. It was disgusting. I needed to slap a flammable label on both him and Corey.

Trampoline grinned wide. "I like her. She's feisty. Are you all done with your interview?"

I snapped the notepad off the desk and scanned the bullshit I'd written down. "Yeah. Now I've just got to figure out what to do about it."

Trampoline chuckled. "If I'd known you were going to be wiping Charlie Falkingham's ass from now on, I'd have added more toilet paper to the supply list."

"Fuck you." I dropped onto a chair at one of the computers and logged in using my ID. I pulled up the vehicle registration site we used and stared at the empty boxes where I was supposed to input information. I didn't have any information.

"Hey, man. Question. Is *misunderestimate* a word?"

I glanced over my shoulder, but Trampoline never lifted his gaze from his phone. "I don't know," he muttered. "Sounds like a word to me."

"That's what I said. Little shit."

The copy machine stopped, and Trampoline pocketed his phone and snatched the papers from the holding tray. "Wanna grab beers tonight? We can head over to Sharky's. I need to get out."

"How about Cage? I need to get laid."

Trampoline squirmed. "Come on, man. Not Cage."

"Yes, fucking Cage. I'm having a bad day. Be my wingman."

Trampoline groaned and glanced once at the door before lowering his voice. "Fine, but Sharky's first. You know I can't go to Cage until I'm good and hammered."

I couldn't fight the grin that threatened to take over my face. "Because all the pretty boys can't keep their hands off you."

"Shut up."

Although he wouldn't admit it, I got the feeling Kevin Trampoline was a little bi-curious. As far as I knew, he hadn't acted on it, but it never took a whole lot of convincing to drag him to Cage. He didn't hate the boys' hands all over him as much as he let on. However, he couldn't do it sober. Once he was a little tipsy, he was eager to join me at my favorite gay nightclub—even when all he did was prowl with his eyes and pretend to get annoyed with all the attention he garnered playing hard to get at the bar.

Corey poked her head into the room, ending the conversation. "Hey, what's taking you so long? We've got to get out of here."

"I'm coming. Later, man," Trampoline said, smacking me with whatever forms he'd been printing." Be good."

"Yeah right. Tonight."

"Text me."

Alone, I swiveled back to face the computer and the empty little boxes asking to be filled. The blinking cursor taunted me. Make, model, plate number, color, year of manufacturing, location of registration, and VIN. The idea was to fill in as much information as possible. I typed in *white,* and *pontiak*, and *grand prix*, knowing it wasn't enough information, narrowed it to the Hamilton area, and hit enter.

It came back with an error message, telling me *pontiak* wasn't a valid entry, and did I mean *Pontiac* instead?

"Everyone's a fucking English teacher now. Yeah, I meant Pontiac, you piece of shit computer."

I stabbed at the keyboard with two fingers, fixing the word and trying again. When the sheer volume of hits soared past a hundred and kept on going, I stopped the search and added a year bracket covering 1995 to 2000. The list of hits still rose beyond a reasonable amount.

I smashed a fist on the table and shut down the site, gritting my teeth as I considered what to do about Charlie's imaginary white Pontiac.

"Hey," said a voice at the door.

I cast daggers in that direction and found Churchill, one of the precinct's detectives leaning against the frame. He was an older guy with a bad comb-over and a meaty midsection. There was a button missing on his shirt, and it pulled apart, revealing his undershirt. He wore a shit-eating grin on his weathered face as he waved a large stack of files in the air between us.

"What?"

"I hear you're doing grunt work." He tossed the stack of files on the table beside me, and they slid, some of the papers falling out from inside. "I need all of this logged by tonight. Have fun."

He spun on his heels, his fancy-ass loafers clicking on the tiled floor as he walked away. A waft of cheap cologne gusted past my nose, and I blew out a breath, waving a hand in front of my face. When a burst of laughter erupted from the bullpen, instinct wanted me to jump up and chase Churchill down, tell him his sloppy fat ass reeked of a frat house, and he could do his own damn paperwork.

But I stilled my feet, making fists until the skin over my knuckles threatened to split.

One meeting with Nikola was enough for one day, and I really didn't want to lose my job.

* * *

The shots of tequila sat in two neat rows, three deep. Kevin had met up with me at Sharky's, an old cop bar on Intrepid Park Road four blocks from the station. He'd dressed in designer jeans and a fitted T-shirt that was about two sizes too small and showed off every inch of his lean frame.

The boys at Cage would eat him alive, but I got the feeling he'd dressed that way on purpose. I, on the other hand, didn't own designer jeans and stuck with my favorite pair of worn Levi's and an old band T-shirt that was soft from years of washing. It fit a little snug, and the hem was frayed, but I liked it. It hugged my muscles and complimented my tanned skin tone and tattoos.

The atmosphere at Sharky's was tamer than Cage, but it was after eleven, and the crowd had limbered up with drinks and late-night snacks, so it was buzzing about as much as it could for a Friday night.

Some honky-tonk country music played over the speakers while the crash of pool balls smashing against one another echoed from the table in the back corner. A few guys and gals I recognized from work were having a friendly competition. A riot of laughter filled the air from a booth off to my left, and some woman squealed as she stumbled through the front door with a few girlfriends tailing behind her.

The air was rich with a mixture of cheap cologne, perfume, and beer.

"Come on. Bottoms up."

I took the offered shot glass from Kevin, and we clinked them together before upending them. Fuck lemons and salt. This was how real men drank tequila, and I savored the burn.

Kevin whistled and choked, laughing as he shuddered. "That stuff has bite."

"It'll put hair on your chest."

"I don't have that problem, asshole." Kevin yanked down the collar of his T-shirt, proving it. "Can you say the same thing? I don't think so."

"This body is as smooth as a baby's ass. I don't need a bunch of sweaty chest hair to make me a man. I've got this weapon of mass destruction instead." I grabbed myself, and Kevin laughed, shaking his head.

"Keep it in your pants, Dyani. No one here wants to see that."

I drew the next round of shots forward, nodding at them. "Come on. We're just warming up."

We pounded back the next round, then chased them down with the final pair. Kevin snapped his fingers at the bartender, calling out for more.

I took my time, scanning the bar as the alcohol absorbed into my bloodstream. The faster I could get Kevin drunk, the sooner we could get to Cage, so I didn't object when he asked the bartender for another six shots. After the day I'd had, I needed to unwind, and that was not going to happen at a stingy cop bar where most people barely tolerated me as an openly gay cop to begin with.

I heard the whispers and saw the evasive stares every day when I went to work.

After the bartender delivered another lineup, we slowed down, leaning back against the bar and taking in the atmosphere.

Sharky's had adopted a nautical theme which was borderline cheesy, in my opinion. The dark-paneled walls were decorated with fishing gear—rods, oars, and any number of mounted fish on plaques. There was even a singing big mouth bass behind the bar that Willy, the owner, still got a kick out of, even though the thing had been hanging there since the dawn of time.

Also behind the bar was a huge four-foot-long black canvas, sporting a string art sailboat. It used to hang in the main area, but people wouldn't stop strumming it like a guitar, so Willy had it moved.

A huge fishing net hung from the ceiling. Caught in its tangled mess of ropes were lures and more sea creatures. There was a ridiculous, pink blow-up octopus at the far corner, its tentacles dangling low enough patrons had to duck or get smacked in the head. One of the tentacles had long ago deflated or been popped, and it hung like a limp dick.

"So what's the deal with you getting the Charlie Falkingham drama?" Kevin asked, drawing me from my head.

I sighed and reached behind me for another shot. "Sarge is hoping it's my ticket out the door. I'm basically guaranteed to fuck this up because he knows I have no patience or tolerance for his sort."

"So don't fuck it up."

"Brilliant advice, dumbass." I slammed the shot, noting how the sting of the alcohol didn't affect me anymore. My limbs were loosening, and a pleasant warmth filled my veins. "I don't know how Graveman did it, ya know? This guy, Charlie, I guess he comes in all the time, angling for help with one bullshit story after another. The guy's fucked in the head."

"You would be too if you suffered what he did."

I paused with another shot glass halfway to my lips, considering Nikola's words from earlier. A kidnapping and underground child sex-trafficking operation. Sole survivor. Jesus. I hadn't thought about it much, but talk about fucked up.

Then I thought about Charlie and the way he'd been during the interview. The way he'd completely blanked out on me for a few minutes for what seemed like no reason at all. What had that been about?

I remembered taking his hands—his incredibly soft hands—in mine and marveling at how delicate they seemed. The fine bones under the surface of his skin seemed more fragile than they should have, like bird's bones, like the faintest pressure would shatter them.

"Why don't you give Graveman a call and get some advice?"

I blinked away from the memory. "Are you serious?" I downed the shot I was holding. At this rate, I'd be falling on my ass and paying for it tomorrow. "I don't need some retired detective telling me how to do my job."

"Uh, yeah, you do, actually. I know groveling and asking for help is beneath you, but if you don't consider it as an option, you're fucked, my man. F-U-C-K-E-D, fucked, and not the good kind."

"Whatever. I'll figure it out."

Talk to Graveman. Yeah right. It sounded like a downright awful idea. I didn't know the man well. We'd seen each other in passing, but I couldn't remember a single time we'd shared words. So I was supposed to what? Go grovel to the big old experienced detective and ask him how to handle a wispy bird of a man like Charlie Falkingham? I didn't think so.

"Think about it this way," Kevin went on, "that guy dealt with Charlie's complaints for years. Fucking years. He knows exactly how to handle him. A few tips, and you'll be golden. Nikola won't know why the fuck you haven't failed, and it will drive him crazy."

I smiled for the first time all night. If I considered it that way, the idea held merit. "Now that I like."

Kevin smacked my arm and handed me the final shot. "Last one, and now I'm drunk enough we can skip this old-man joint and go to Cage as long as you protect my straight ass from getting grabbed."

"No promises."

We clinked glasses and drained the tequila.

* * *

I pulled my beat-up Escort to the curb out front of an old craftsman-style house on the east end of town. The engine choked and sputtered. The brakes squealed, reminding me the ancient pads were finished and needed to be replaced. When I came to a stop and threw the car into park, the steady vibrations that ran through the twenty-year-old hunk of metal made my teeth rattle. It always felt like it was ten seconds from crapping out. One of these days, the poor car would take its last breath, and there would be no reviving it.

Turning the key, I let the engine die, and in my head, the whole vehicle sighed with relief. It was like an old man, begging for the grave.

I double-checked the address I'd gotten from the cranky woman working in the human resources department. It matched. It would figure the retired detective would live someplace like this. He must be collecting a nice pension.

My phone rang from where I'd tossed it on the passenger seat.

"Jesus fucking Christ. I swear to god, if that's you again…" I snagged my phone and glared at the same unknown number that had called six times over the past two days. Charlie. I was regretting giving him my personal contact information.

I'd answered his first call the day after he'd been to the station, and I had patiently explained that I hadn't found anything about the white Pontiac yet, but the guy hadn't let up. Another call had come through later that day, then another, and another after that.

I'd quit answering.

He'd left a message for me that morning, claiming he thought someone was skulking around his backyard, but when I'd called him back, worried, Charlie hadn't been able to confirm he'd seen anyone and had told me instead he'd experienced what he called a "strong feeling" that someone was there. *"The bushes definitely moved,"* he'd said.

I'd hung up on him.

Then my conscience had gotten the better of me.

I'd been given a workspace close to Sergeant Nikola's office since I'd been demoted to paperwork for the foreseeable future, and my palms had grown slick every time his phone had rung. My overactive imagination had been convinced Charlie or his mother were calling to report that I'd disregarded Charlie's concerns and was being an ass.

For lack of a better idea, I'd taken Kevin's advice.

It hadn't taken much to find retired Detective Graveman's home address. If anyone was going to tell me how to get Charlie Falkingham off my back, it would be the guy who'd dealt with him for the past decade and a half or however long it had been.

I dismissed Charlie's call, but my phone immediately rang again. Growling, I scrubbed a hand down my face and answered. "I'm working, Chucky boy. You want me to sort this shit out for you, ya gotta let me work."

Silence.

I glanced at the screen and put it back against my ear. "Hello? You there?"

"My name is Charlie, Officer Dyani. Not Chucky. You're being very rude."

I bit back a retort. "Why are you calling now? I'm actively trying to sort out your shit, but you're interrupting. Is it important?"

"Of course it is. I wouldn't call if it wasn't important."

"Of course you wouldn't." The sarcasm was rich in my tone, and I reminded myself for the hundredth time it wouldn't do me any favors.

When Charlie didn't go on, I gripped the steering wheel until the plastic creaked under my palms. "What is it? Tell me now, or I'm hanging up."

"The car. I saw it again."

I paused, forcing myself to take a steadying breath before asking, "Really? Where?"

"On Juniper. I was getting gas at the petrol station on the corner. It drove by going south toward Glendale Avenue. I think it turned."

"Did you get a plate?"

Charlie paused, his voice meek when he said, "No. There was too much traffic. But the driver was male. I looked."

"Can you do better than that?"

Another pause. "He was white?"

"Are you *aksing* me or telling me?"

"I'm not sure. He could have been white. The interior was in shadow. I suppose it could have been a woman wearing a hat."

"The person wore a hat?"

"I think so."

I bit back a frustrated sigh and worked the next words from my mouth carefully so they didn't sound too harsh. "That doesn't help me, Chucky. It could be a man. It could be a woman. He or she might be white, or black, or fucking green with yellow polka dots. Oh, and they possibly wore a fucking hat, but maybe not."

"It's Charlie. Look, if you don't want to help me—"

"I didn't say that."

I bit back another string of curses and counted to ten.

A woman came out of a house three doors down from where I sat. She had a car seat looped around one arm with a tiny baby bundled inside. The child was squawking at the top of its lungs. Over her other arm, she carried an overstuffed diaper bag, a small folded stroller, a teddy bear, and a plastic grocery bag. She fumbled to lock her front door. The strap from the diaper bag slipped, and she adjusted it, trying to find a new balance. The folding mechanism on the stroller caught the plastic grocery bag and tore a hole in the side. The contents—little jars of baby food—spilled onto the concrete stoop.

The baby continued to wail.

I pinched the bridge of my nose. "Fine. I'll look into it. I'll take your exceptional observation skills and see what I can find."

The woman down the road dropped her keys. She tilted her face to the heavens, and even though I couldn't hear her, I imagined she was praying for strength or swearing a blue streak. I sympathized with her frustrations.

"Thank you. And, Officer—"

I hung up before Charlie could say anymore. Cracking my neck, I got out of the car and pocketed my phone. The woman down the street was at her car, stowing her load in the trunk while the child continued to cry blue murder.

I spun, taking in the street.

The neighborhood had a whole upper-middle-class feel to it, with neat rows of craftsman-style homes built back in the sixties. Despite their age, they were all well maintained, with low-pitched rooflines, deeply overhanging eaves, double-hung windows, and large, covered front porches. Every lawn was manicured. Every garden was perfectly groomed.

It might not have been a neighborhood for the upper echelon of Hamilton's wealth, but it grated against something deep inside me regardless.

Stanley Graveman's house was made of tan-colored brick with white framing around the windows. A newer model midsize sedan sat in the driveway. As far as I understood, Graveman was a single man, twice divorced with no kids.

I followed a paver-stone walkway to the partially paned front door. Frosted glass windows ran the length on either side. I tried to peek beyond the glass, but I couldn't make out the interior.

I rang the bell and continued to scan the street. The spring sun was low on the horizon, turning the sky into a wash of deep purples and crimson as dusk approached. A light breeze kicked up and fluttered the new growth on a cherry tree next door. An abandoned pop can rolled down the street.

A click sounded as someone disengaged the lock. Stanley Graveman tugged the heavy door open and flinched, scanning me up and down once with a harsh and inquisitive stare.

I'd come right from work, so I was still in uniform.

"Can I help you?" he asked, his voice deep and throaty. Washed-out hazel eyes warily took me in.

"Detective Graveman?"

"Not anymore. It's just Stanley now. What can I do for you?"

For a guy in retirement, he still seemed sharp and agile. He stood like a man ready to fling shit right back in someone's face if they tried to cause a problem. He wore a pair of loose-fitting jeans and a plain T-shirt under an unbuttoned red flannel. The man sported a thick, graying beard that must have been new since my vague memories of seeing him around the station had never included facial hair. For a guy in his late fifties or early sixties, he was fit.

"My name's Takoda Dyani. I was wondering if you had a minute to chat."

"I know who you are. I think everyone on the Hamilton Police Department knows who you are. You're the kid with a chip on his shoulder who doesn't think rules apply to him."

My spine stiffened, and I glared. "What the fuck does that mean?"

"It means your reputation precedes you, Officer Dyani. How's your brother? Is he still in prison?"

"You know what? Fuck you. I don't need your help." I spat on the porch and flicked my chin in a universal fuck you as I backed away.

As I made my way down the paver stones to the sidewalk, my phone rang. Growling, I yanked it from my pocket. When the unknown number flashed across the screen, I almost launched the phone into the street. Instead, I punched the button to accept the call and yelled, "I swear to fucking god, Charlie, if you call me one more goddamn time, I'm gonna drive to your house and hang you up by your fucking balls. There is no one fucking following you. There is no one in your bushes. It's all in your fucking head. You're crazy, do you hear me? You're a fucking quack. Maybe no one has—"

A heavy weight slammed into me from behind, sending me crashing into the side of my car and knocking the wind out of me. The person tore the phone from my hand while using some impossibly quick maneuvers to contort my arms behind me at an angle that made me scream. Cold metal slapped around my wrists—handcuffs. Then a large hand pressed my face into the side of the car, the cold metal under my cheek bruising.

Stanley Graveman lowered his mouth to my ear, his beard scratching my skin as he hissed. "You stand here, and you don't move until I say so. You got it?" He applied more pressure. "Nod if you understand me."

I nodded because I was sure if I didn't, this fucker was going to snap my arm in half or break my face.

"Good. Now don't move."

He gave a final shove to the back of my head and stormed off toward the back end of my car, marching away down the street as he put my phone to his ear. "Hey, Charlie... Yeah, it's Stan. How are you?"

His voice drifted into nothingness as he walked far enough away he could chat in private. When he'd gone as far as he wanted to go, Graveman turned and glared at me the whole time he spoke with Charlie.

Their conversation didn't last long, but I remained unmoving, imagining all the things I wanted to do to this detective when I got my hands on him.

The call ended, and Graveman studied me from his position down the road. I'd seen that face on plenty of other people, and I didn't appreciate the analysis. He strutted back toward me as if he had all the time in the world, his expression giving nothing away.

"Take these fucking cuffs off me," I spat. "You had no right to—"

"Shut up. Tell me why Charlie Falkingham is calling you."

"I ain't telling you shit. Get these things off me, or I'll file a report and—"

"Wrong answer. Why is Charlie calling you?"

"Because Nikola made me his fucking caregiver since your old ass retired. Now uncuff me, asshole."

Graveman considered my answer before shaking his head. "You are the last thing Charlie needs."

"Believe me, I agree with you, but he didn't give me a choice. At this rate, I won't be that nut's problem for much longer because they're gonna fire my ass. That was Nikola's end goal. I'm not an idiot."

"Maybe they *should* fire your ass. It would be about time. Why are you here?"

"Really?" I tugged at the restraints and growled. "Are you seriously that fucking dumb?"

"Enlighten me, kid."

"Fuck you."

"I can do this all night. Retirement doesn't offer much in the line of entertainment. This is the most fun I've had since I hung up my badge. So, tell me, why are you here? Maybe if you stop being a little punk-ass shit, I'll consider taking the cuffs off."

I seethed, nostrils flaring. It wasn't the first time I'd been cuffed and slammed against a car. It wasn't even the first time it had been done without cause. This was the kind of shit that infuriated me and set my blood to boil. Growing up in the slums on the south end of town, I'd gotten used to being blamed for everything. Cops used to prowl those streets and tossed anyone in cuffs if they so much as breathed the wrong way.

"I came to get fucking advice, okay. I don't know what the hell to do to make him stop calling me. His complaints are bullshit. He's imagining things and blowing them way out of proportion. What the hell am I supposed to do?"

"So you came to me?"

"Yeah, man. Jesus. Get these things off me. They hurt."

"Don't be a whiny bitch. They only hurt because you're tugging." He held up a finger. "And the more times you tell me to fuck off, the longer I'm keeping you there."

I bit the inside of my cheek.

A car drove by, slowing as it passed us, the driver gawking. It must have been some sight. A cop cuffed by a civilian. Humiliation burned under my skin. I swore years ago that I'd never let myself be in a position of submission again.

"Now, let me get this straight. Nikola assigned you as Charlie's personal consultant. If you mess up, your ass is on the line. You came here because you got your first taste of what that means, and you can't handle it. Am I close?" Again, he held up a finger before I could speak. "Consider your words carefully."

"Yeah. All that. Now take them off, man." After an exhausting inner battle, I added, "Please."

"All right. I'll take them off, but then you're going to march your ass inside, and we're going to have a long chat. You're going to listen to every word I say to you, and if I *ever* hear you talk to Charlie like that again, getting fired will be the least of your problems. I didn't work thirty years as a detective and not learn a thing or two about evading arrest. You take my meaning?"

"Christ, yeah. Loud and fucking clear."

Five

TAKODA

I rubbed my wrists as I took in Graveman's front room. The couch where I'd been directed to sit was brown leather and went with all the other various shades of brown in the spacious sitting room. The range of rich earth tones gave the place a dim and melancholic feel. The setting sun cut long strips of golden light across the floor.

A fire burned in the fireplace, making the room overly warm, causing sweat to bead at my temples and under my arms. Surrounding the fireplace were built-in shelving units filled with books, framed photographs—mostly of a spunky and young golden retriever—and a stupid amount of awards Graveman had earned while serving. The ceiling had exposed wooden beams and hidden panel lighting. There were thick baseboards and dark hardwood floors.

A golden retriever, who was no longer the vibrant puppy from the photographs, slept on a battered rug in front of the fireplace. The old thing had barely lifted its head when I'd been shown in.

Graveman returned from the kitchen carrying two pilsners, caps removed, and handed me one.

It wouldn't have been my first choice of beer, but I took it, studying the label.

"You know, I could have your ass arrested for assaulting an officer of the law," I said, unable to keep the contempt from my voice.

"Shut up, Takoda. Drink the beer, and chill out for once. Why does everything have to be a battle with you? If you want my help, try not acting like a piece of shit for five seconds. *Please* and *thank you* go a long way."

Scowling, I downed a generous mouthful of beer. It was wet and cold, so it wasn't all bad. I picked the label and tried to gather myself so I wouldn't be so reactive.

"I'll be honest with you," Graveman said, settling in a recliner closer to the fireplace. He patted his knee, and the dog opened its eyes, whimpered once, readjusted its body—which looked like it took effort—and closed its eyes again with a single paw stretched out, resting on Graveman's foot. "I'm not any more pleased with Nikola's decision to make you Charlie's consultant than you are. It was a bad call."

"I couldn't agree more. What's your dog's name?"

Graveman studied me for a second, then glanced down at the sleeping animal. He moved his sock-covered foot, rubbing tenderly at the dog's paw with his toe. "Her name's Angel. She's coming to the end of her days. Turned fifteen last week, which is old for a retriever. Was diagnosed with cancer for her birthday. Just making the old girl as comfortable as I can now."

"I'm sorry."

Again, Graveman's attention was riveted on me.

"I like animals," I added. "I have two cats. Clover and Dandelion. They... they keep me sane most days. So, you know, I get it."

"You like animals, just not people?"

I shrugged. "I like some people."

"Hmm." Graveman shifted his weight, gaze fixed. "You're not a fan of authority, which clashes with your choice of profession. Why a police officer if you hate most people? The job is primarily dealing with the public. Makes no sense to me."

I shifted, drank more beer, and scanned the room. "How about we talk about Charlie?"

"How about you tell me a few things about yourself before I decide if you're worthy of handling Charlie? And don't think for a second that I can't halt this whole thing right here and now. Then what will you do?"

Pursing my lips, I ignored his request for information and drained my beer.

"Fine, you don't want to talk, I'll tell you what I've learned about you. You grew up in the south end in a single-parent home. Your dad took off when you were little, leaving your mom with four kids to raise and no money. She had to work three jobs to put food on the table and clothes on your backs. You grew up in a soddy two-bedroom apartment on Cecilia Court. You went to John Webber Elementary and then to Hubber Collegiate High School. Your brother has a juvie record longer than my arm, and you had your fair share of run-ins with the cops too, am I right?"

My blood boiled, and I cracked my knuckles. "How do you know all this shit?"

"Your baby sister was busted for drugs and prostitution at fifteen. She had a bad run-in with a trick a few months later and ended up in the hospital. How old were you then? If Odina was fifteen, that made you, what? Nineteen? That's a lot on your shoulders, especially since your mom was always trying to work enough hours to keep a roof over your heads."

I launched from the couch, slamming the beer bottle on the side table by his chair. "Fuck this, and fuck you. I'm leaving. I don't know how you know all that shit, but it's none of your business."

"Sit down, Takoda."

I stormed to the front door, the roar in my ears and the vibrations under my skin making me want to hit something.

Before I got my boots on, Graveman was in the front hallway. He placed a staying hand on my arm, his grip like iron. "I'm a detective, kid, and I was good at my job. When there is a hint of bad blood in our ranks, we investigate it. Immediately. So yeah, I know everything there is to know about you because the day you walked in the door, you rattled everyone's cages. People were wary. No one trusted you. I think you take advantage of the power that badge gives you because—"

I threw Graveman off and yanked the door open, but the old detective slapped a hand on the surface and shoved it closed again. "I'm not finished."

"Well, I am."

"I don't think you're a dirty cop, Dyani. That's not what I'm saying. I think you abuse your power a little more than most, but you aren't the first to take advantage of the badge. I think you've dealt with authority in your face all your life, and it's never gone over well. You have a lot of anger in here." He tapped my chest, and I smacked his hand away. "You're gay, and I bet that makes things—"

"Don't talk to me like you know me. You don't know anything."

Graveman's tone changed. It softened along with the intense look in his eyes. I didn't like it. "But I think the worst part of all, the part you carry with you everywhere you go, is the fact that your father walked out of your life without looking back and started a new life elsewhere."

I stalled, glaring into the far too calm, far too knowing eyes of a man I wasn't sure I liked. A rotting, festering, familiar rage burned in my core.

"The cops came down especially hard on you and your brothers and sisters, didn't they? Daddy took his money and left you all with nothing. Poverty and crime in the south end go hand in hand. I think those two things combined gave you profound hate for authority and for anyone who grew up more privileged than you. So answer my question. Why a cop if you hate them so much? Was it for the power? Are you doing it to stick it to the people who hurt you and your family growing up? You didn't feel like you got justice, so you're taking it now?"

I ground my teeth, the blood pounding in my ears keeping me on edge. "I don't want to talk about this."

Graveman wasn't about to let up. "Your father is Piero Sottosanti, am I right?"

My skin felt like a thousand fire ants were crawling over its surface. I couldn't answer. I couldn't go there. Not now. Not ever. I hated my father. Even hearing his name was enough to send me into a blind rage.

Graveman seemed to sense my breaking point. He nodded like he'd just uncovered his answer and waved me back into the front room. "How about another beer? We can talk about Charlie."

It took a long minute for the tension to leach from my muscles. I kicked off my boots and followed Graveman back into the bowels of the house.

Instead of sitting on the couch, I sat cross-legged on the ground beside his old, sick dog and let her sniff my hand before stroking her between the ears. She emitted a soft moan and wiggled an inch closer until her heavy body rested against my leg. Animals calmed me. They always had. More than anything else.

Graveman returned from the kitchen and handed me one of the bottles without mentioning my relocation to the floor. He sat in the recliner and watched me pet his dog for a long time.

"So you have two cats, huh?" he asked after a time.

"With all due respect, I don't want to talk about myself. I want to know how I'm supposed to help this Charlie guy so he doesn't drive me up the wall. I really don't want to lose my job."

Graveman readjusted in his seat, the leather of the recliner crinkling under his weight. "Well, your first mistake was giving him your personal phone number."

"What was I supposed to do? I'm not a fancy detective like you. I don't have a personal extension."

"No, I guess not. Then you'll need to start with some hard boundaries. Some rules. He'll listen."

I glanced at the detective. He was watching his dog, a faraway look in his eyes.

"Charlie goes through phases. For a few weeks, he'll get himself into a knot about everything, then it will cool off for a time, maybe a couple of months, then it all starts back up again. I've learned the best way to handle his concerns and get him to take a step back is to make him believe you're doing all you can for him. Make him think you're going out on a limb."

"So you lie to him, is that it? I don't have to exert energy on this imaginary stalker because he doesn't exist?"

The dog whined when my hand stilled, so I kept scratching her between the ears.

Graveman drank a generous mouthful of beer and rested the bottle on his knee. "I used to chase Charlie's ghosts all over town. I used to stay at the station long after I should have gone home for the night, my eyes burning at the computer as I sorted through endless lists of cars or people or whatever goose chase he sent me on. A red Toyota, a black Camry, a silver Firebird." Graveman shook his head. "He can't help it, Takoda. I always thought it would get better. I thought it would go away, and someday he'd stop calling."

"It never stops, does it?"

"No. It's sad, really. The man is ridiculously smart, but he's tormented. Locked inside his head most of the time with monsters from his past. He can't escape them. Charlie lives in a constant state of fear. The degrees might vary, but it's always there. If I thought for one second it would pass, if I thought there was even a remote chance I could cure Charlie's broken mind so he didn't have to worry anymore, I'd bend over backward to make it happen. I wouldn't give up. I'd do anything. I care about that kid, but I'm tired, Takoda. Seventeen years is a long time."

"So now it's my problem."

"No. Now it's your responsibility. Do you know what happened to Charlie?"

"Sort of. Not the whole story, but Nikola mentioned it."

"I have no desire to relive it, but I think you should take five minutes out of your day sometime and go dig that old case out of the record room. It's ugly, and you might not sleep at night after you read it, but maybe when you know, you'll be able to find an ounce of sympathy, and helping Charlie won't seem like such a pain in your ass. He might be a successful grown man now, but he's fragile." Graveman clucked his tongue. "Maybe it's not fair to call him that, but it's the truth."

I stared at the sleeping dog, stroking my fingers through her golden fur, remembering the way Charlie's hands had felt when I'd held them. Fragile was exactly how I would have described them. His skin had been soft and luminescent under the fluorescent lighting in the room. Underneath that fair skin, his fragile, bird-like bones had rolled with my touch. They had seemed so delicate. How easily they could crumble. It was a strange thing to notice, but the brief moment was imprinted on my mind, and I kept finding myself back there, looking at his hands. Those long fingers. Feeling them tremble.

I frowned. "Successful? What do you mean by that?"

A quirk appeared in the corner of Graveman's lips. A hint of a smile transformed the old man's face. It erased his stern edge and made him look more like someone's father or grandfather.

"Are you familiar with the name Kingston Fireborn?"

The name rang a bell, but I couldn't put a finger on it. "No."

"Bestselling young-adult fantasy novelist. Wrote the series Beyond the Mirrored Vale."

I glanced up. "That's him?"

"It is. He's made quite a name for himself. He got his first book published when he was sixteen years old. It broke the charts. Instant success. Almost unheard of for a kid that age. But that incident when he was twelve, it did something to him. Charlie kind of went away for a while. That's the only way I know how to describe it. He got lost in this made-up fantasy world inside his head. It was concerning. He lost touch with reality for a lot of years. When his doctor suggested he write it down, create the world so she could experience it too and understand, he did. It blew up from there.

"Ever since, he's written a dozen or more novels all set in this fantasy world called Vrydindel. Every one of his books has been well received. Slowly, Charlie returned to reality, but he's never been the same. The pen name was his dad's idea. For his safety. After that incident in his youth, the media got a little crazy, and Archie had to protect his boy from the hype. Last month, for the first time ever, Charlie agreed to appear on *The Morning Show* to talk about his books. Unveil himself as Kingston Fireborn for the first time. You have no idea how huge a step that was.

"This is the same boy who didn't speak a word for over three years after being rescued. The same boy who couldn't go to school any longer without throwing hysterical fits and having panic attacks so bad they landed him in the mental health ward at the hospital. That incident inevitably tore his family apart. His mother couldn't handle him and took his sister and walked away. His father homeschooled him and brought in doctors from all across the country to try to help his son. Charlie's much better, but he will *never* be the same.

"He doesn't do well in the spotlight. He has quirks a mile long. He suffers from a lot of mental health issues. Socially, he struggles. I'm fairly certain his father ensured he had legal representation in place before that interview so they wouldn't discuss his past. I was very proud of Charlie for being able to do that."

I focused on the dog again, brow furrowed. Her paw twitched as she dreamed. She yipped once, chuffed, then groaned in her sleep before calming. I placed my hand on her side, feeling her even breaths under my palm. Her ribs protruded, and I got the same sense of frailty touching her that I'd had when I held Charlie's hands.

I didn't know how to process everything Graveman was saying. It seemed so surreal.

"So what do I do?"

Graveman sighed. "You tell him what he wants to hear."

"So I lie to him, is that it?"

There was pain behind the older man's hazel eyes when I looked up. He cut his attention to the half-empty beer in his hand and rolled it between his palms. "You can't solve a problem when there isn't one to solve, Takoda. Sometimes it's about giving someone peace of mind. If Charlie thinks you've driven all over town hunting down a blue Kia or a yellow Bug or a white Pontiac." He waved a hand at me, chuckling without humor. "Then you tell him you did it. If it means telling Charlie you gave the poor kid working at the Esso a warning because Charlie thinks he did something suspicious, then you do that too. Maybe it sounds unethical, maybe that makes me a bad person, but it gives Charlie peace of mind, and that's what matters in the end."

I wasn't sure how I felt about that. In the same breath, I didn't know how I felt about dodging a half dozen calls every day either or chasing ghosts, as Graveman had put it.

"Okay. Fine. I can do that, I guess."

"Delivering news in person goes over better than a phone call."

"Right. In person." I gave the dog one last pat and put my empty beer on the side table by the recliner before getting to my feet. "I'll go over there now, bullshit my way through some story, and hopefully he'll take a breather for a bit, right? Is that all?"

"I don't suggest going tonight. Don't let him think you work around the clock, or he'll expect you to be at his beck and call at all hours. Go during the day tomorrow. Also, set some rules about your phone number, or that could end up being a problem too."

"Already is."

"He's not stupid, Takoda. As long as he thinks you're helping him, he'll listen. He'll understand."

Graveman got up and followed me to the front hallway. Before leaving the room, I glanced back at his dog, still asleep on the rug by the fire.

"She's had a good life," Graveman said, studying me without pretense. "And she's a good judge of character. You're not a bad person, but you're hard to like. Take down some of your walls, and maybe you'll see the whole world isn't against you like you think."

I met the older man's eyes. For whatever reason, this retired detective had managed to smooth the jagged edges off my anger—an anger he had drawn to the surface when I'd arrived.

"Thanks for your help."

He held a card between his pointer and middle fingers, thrusting it in my direction. "Call me if you run into a problem. My cell hasn't changed, but you won't get me at the office anymore." A hint of a smile touched his mouth. "I know Charlie can be a handful. Before you resort to throwing punches, or yelling, or doing anything that might damage Charlie any more than he's already been hurt, reach out."

I took the card, studying it. It was his old business card with an extension at the precinct he'd crossed out and a personal cell number. "Thanks." I tucked it into my wallet and tugged on my boots.

On the threshold, I glanced out at the darkened street. Night had descended while I'd been inside. The sodium lamps highlighted a golden path along the road. Most houses had porch lights or garden lights. Again, I was struck with that low burning hatred in my belly.

Hatred that stemmed from a life of poverty and growing up surrounded by kids who'd lived far more privileged lives. A life my brother and sisters and I had only dreamed about. A life that could have been possible had my father not abandoned us for a new family.

I left Graveman's house and neighborhood with a mixture of emotions chopping my brain to mulch. I wasn't sure where I stood when it came to Charlie Falkingham, but hearing Graveman speak, knowing there was a dark history behind the man who'd shown up at the police station the other day, made me reconsider how I felt.

By the sound of it, Charlie had lived a hard life. Even if it was completely different, I knew what that was all about.

At home, the old Escort gave a dying chug as I pulled into the gravel driveway and killed the engine. The hunk of metal shivered and sagged as it ticked and cooled. I sat for a while in the dark, absorbing the night. Every now and then, a waft of stale cigarettes and moldering upholstery tickled my nose. It was a smell that had come with the car when I'd bought it five years ago. It never went away, no matter how much I cleaned it. Most of the time, I didn't notice. Tonight, it was pungent.

My worn-down, one-and-a-half-story bungalow was set back off the road, shadowed behind an ancient Weeping Beech that took up a huge portion of the front lawn. The roof sagged, and many shingles were peeled back or missing, letting in the rain and rotting the inner skeleton of the house. The siding was weathered and in similar disrepair, a faded, sun-bleached yellow that should have been replaced a decade ago.

The paver stones leading to the front door were cracked and overgrown with weeds, making their way deeper into the earth each year. Someday, they would be swallowed up for good under the lawn.

If I squinted at the front window, dark with the heavy curtains I'd hung and rarely opened, I could make out two pairs of glowing eyes sitting on the inside ledge. Clover and Dandelion never failed to greet me. The two gray tabbies had shown up on the doorstep one day a few years ago and had never left.

I got out of the car and went around back, letting myself through the rusty chain-link gate into the backyard. The hinges gave a spine-stiffening squeak of protest, reminding me I needed to find the can of WD-40.

A fetid smell of sunbaked garbage hit my nose a fraction of a second before I registered the plastic garbage can lying on its side, the lid knocked off. The trash bag I'd tossed the other day was torn open, its guts spilling across the cement pad.

"Fucking raccoons."

I kicked the chicken carcass, wadded up paper towels, torn food packages, and empty tin cans back into the plastic bin and stood it up, replacing the lid. I scanned the backyard as though I might catch the mangy creatures who were responsible lingering around, but all was quiet.

My neighbor's house was dark except for the flickering blue glow of a TV in the living room. Their kitchen window was open, and the laugh track from some sitcom drifted through the night.

I found my keys and let myself inside. The back entrance landed me on a small platform. One set of stairs went down to an unfinished basement, and another set went up to the kitchen. I heel-toed out of my boots and kicked them into the dark pit of the basement before climbing sock-footed to the main floor.

The minute I was through the archway, Clover took flight, launching from the kitchen counter onto my shoulder. I was ready for her and brought my hand up to snag her back so she wouldn't gouge me with her claws as she gained traction. It had happened on more than one occasion when I hadn't been prepared, and I was in no mood to be shredded.

"Hey, boo." I nuzzled into her fur as she purred and wrapped herself around my neck, draping her long body over mine, grooming my ear, one of her disgusting habits. "You make a hell of an entrance, you know. One of these days, you're going to miss and shred my face to bits. I know it. Then I'm going to be pissed. Would you stop that? It tickles." Chuckling, I pushed her face away from my ear.

Dandelion meowed and twisted around my legs in greeting. He wasn't a fan of being held, but he'd made it his goal in life to trip me when I walked. He was the worst when I got up at night to use the bathroom. The cat was notoriously underfoot.

"I've had a shitty day, guys. How about some catnip for you and another beer for me? Sound good? I'll heat the leftovers, and we can watch *Animal Planet* together. Do you want the deep-water sea life episode with the fish and such?"

Dandelion yowled like he understood. It was their favorite program. They sat in front of the screen, oblivious to the fact they were blocking my view, and spent a solid half hour or more tracking the beasts or reptiles or fish, swatting at the TV like they could catch them.

That was fine. It would give me time to think about everything Graveman had told me about Charlie. A small part of me wanted to do some research into Charlie's past and the incident that had taken place seventeen years ago. Another part of me wasn't sure I wanted to know the details.

With an ocean episode keeping the cats entertained, I heated leftover succotash, grabbed a beer, and rested on the old couch in the living room with a laptop open in front of me. The middle of the couch sagged where the supports had broken long ago during a wild night with a guy I'd picked up at Cage. I didn't care. The memory was good, and the couch was still comfortable.

It had been my first purchase when I'd moved out on my own after graduating from the academy. It had been cheap. A floor model from a big-box furniture store. The brown suede was worn and threadbare. Numerous food and drink stains had piled up over the years, and I could identify a couple of places where other entertaining activities had left their mark too.

Unlike Graveman's home, mine was minimalistic in design. I hadn't grown up with extravagances nor did I need them, so I didn't throw excess money into home décor. I wasn't a penny-pincher, but I'd lived hard my whole life and had better things to spend my money on than pretty furniture. Every dime of my paycheck was spoken for. Food, beer, clothes, guys, and the occasional night out.

Extra cash didn't go into a savings account. It didn't pay for a new car or a better house or some retirement savings plan. Every extra penny I earned was divided into two separate slush funds. One to help my baby sister, Odina, through college, and the other to pay for a better lawyer to get my brother, Calian, out of prison.

Mom was doing better now that she didn't have four kids at home. She only worked one job and could finally give herself a break. Istas, my oldest sister, younger than me by two years, had fucked off somewhere up north, and no one in the family had heard from her in years. There wasn't much I could do for her. Last I checked, using my sources at the station, she'd married some guy in Sudbury and was spitting out kids left and right. Good for her. I hoped she was happy.

I poked at my food and sipped my beer as Dandelion swatted and mewled at the stingray taking up the whole screen. His tail swished and jerked side to side. Clover had decided this episode was uninteresting and had fallen asleep in a ball on my feet.

With a search engine pulled up, I hesitated, my fingers poised over the keys. Instead of looking into Charlie's kidnapping, I typed in Kingston Fireborn and read all about the bestselling fantasy author who'd written over a dozen books in some series called Beyond the Mirrored Vale. The latest release, *Morthanian's Quest*, had come out the previous month. I found Charlie's interview on *The Morning Show* and watched it.

Twice. And then again.

The whole thing seemed at odds with the man I'd met at the precinct, yet there was Charlie, regaling the audience with the story behind his fantasy series. His fine-boned features, his milky white skin, the splash of freckles across his sharp nose, and his pale, winter-sky eyes peered back at the camera as he spoke. I hated how vulnerably cute he was and the pull I felt more than once to pause the video when his face filled the screen.

It was during my second time through the video that I saw the truth. Looking back at me wasn't exhilaration as Charlie's tone suggested. His gaze was guarded. Troubled. Wary. Every so often, he wrung his hands together just like he'd done at the station. Twisting his fingers until I feared he'd snap one of those fine bones in half. I cringed.

As I watched the interview for the third time, I saw everything I'd missed when I'd spoken to Charlie in person at the station. He was a man who lived a nightmare every day of his life, and it was right there behind his shadowy blue eyes. He was a man who saw ghosts and monsters around every corner, in every car that drove down the street, and in the face of every stranger. I'd seen a similar look on my sister in the years after a bad trick had left her in the hospital, but this was different. Deeper somehow.

I closed the laptop and shifted it aside, unsure why I cared or was expending so much energy on someone who didn't matter.

He was just some privileged rich kid.

A vulnerable, privileged rich kid with a rough past.

So what if he was stupid cute with his freckles and stormy eyes that oozed innocence.

I hated him. I hated Nikola for placing him in my path.

Six

CHARLIE

Vrydindel surrounded me. Rolling hills. Lush green trees that stood a thousand feet tall with trunks as big around as houses and leaves that outgrew any of the ones found on earth. I was Calipnia, the demi-elf who'd recently escaped the dark shadow realm beyond the mirrored vale.

Magic crawled through my veins and tingled my blood to life. If I closed my eyes and concentrated, I could focus and control it, shield myself, or make myself invisible. Over the years, I'd grown stronger and more powerful than anyone in the realm thought possible. With Rotkiv—a powerful blood dragon—on my side, I was invincible. The next step of our journey lay ahead, but I couldn't determine what direction to travel. Did I venture south along the—

A knock at the office door brought me back to the present, and I blinked away the misty air and crisp morning light that had shimmered on the spiky grass beneath my traveling boots. The hints of neptosing roses and pluminion blossoms no longer invaded my nose. I smelled coffee and the rich musk of Dad's soap instead.

"It's ten o'clock. I brought you your coffee since I didn't think you were coming down for it."

The shadowy depths of my bedroom surrounded me. The paintings on the walls were no longer alive with action and danger. The figurines crowding the floating shelves were mere plastic. The swords with their intricate carvings, the ones that formed a crisscross pattern on the wall behind my bed, were dull and ornamental. They couldn't slice a brick of cheese, let alone a cave dweller or an evil dragon.

Ten o'clock.

"Thank you. You can leave it on my desk. I'll be in there in a minute."

"Who do you think you're fooling? You haven't been in that office all day. In fact, you've been standing in that exact spot for nearly two hours."

"I'm developing the plot for the next novel. It requires... submersion. You know that. I'm working."

"I know. I'm well aware of your *process*. God knows it's been going on for years. I'm just pointing out that you've been *submersed* long enough. You know the rules, Charlie."

"Yes. I'm aware." I wrung my hands. "I'm allowed to slip away, but I mustn't stay longer than an hour or so, or you'll call Sofia." *Then she'll load me up with more drugs until I can't think at all.* I kept that comment to myself. "Short visits only."

"That's right. Go write it down. Whatever you've discovered. Whatever plan you've come up with so far, even if it's not perfect. It can always be changed. It's time to shift gears."

I continued twisting my fingers together as I moved to the window. Dragging the heavy curtain aside a fraction, I peeked out. The sun hurt my eyes after having been in the dark for so many hours, and I squinted. My fingers automatically found the lock on the bottom of the frame, and I clicked it back and forth. Open and closed. Open and closed.

"Charlie?"

I scanned the backyard, examining every bush and tree, peering along the garden path at places where I'd witnessed odd sensations in the past. There were so many places a person could hide. Countless. I didn't like it. Anyone could be out there. Waiting. Watching. My skin crawled at the thought.

A breeze ruffled the leaves on the trees. A flock of Canada geese flew across the pale blue sky in vee formation. If they were honking, I couldn't hear them. This morning, no one was lurking in the shadows. The backyard was empty.

"Did you take your medication this morning?"

With a final click of the lock, I let the curtain fall back into place. Irritation tensed my muscles. "You know I'm diligent about those things. I have a strict routine. Taking my medication is part of it."

"It was just a question. Sometimes I need to be sure."

I met my father's eyes as I crossed to the bedside table, retrieving my phone. No calls. No texts. I frowned. It was taking too long.

As I moved my fingers toward the call button, Dad spoke. "What did Stanley tell you?"

I ground my teeth and pocketed the phone. "To wait."

Dad's gaze was steady. He held up my mug—the red one with the gold painted stripes because it was ten o'clock—and said, "Come have it while it's hot. Lord knows you hate lukewarm coffee. Might throw your whole day out of whack."

"I can't understand why Stanley won't help me anymore. He was happy to talk with me on the phone. In fact, he sounded delighted."

"Because the man isn't on the job anymore. You understand that just fine, Charlie. Don't play dumb with me. This new guy... What did you say his name was?"

"Dyani. Takoda Dyani."

"He'll sort you out."

I furrowed my brow. "I'm not so sure. He isn't a detective, and I sense he isn't fond of me."

"He doesn't have to be a detective nor does he have to be fond of you to do his job. Stanley said he would have a chat with this young man and make sure he knew all the ins and outs of your... case. He said to give him a day or so, and someone would call you. Isn't that right?"

"I saw the car again yesterday. At the gas station while I was filling up. It was brief, but I know it was the same one. The rust on the wheel wells was the same. An older model. I know it was."

"And you told the police. Now let them do their job. Patience is a virtue."

I nodded, unable to shake my frustration.

"Come on. Out of here."

I followed Dad down the hall to my office. It was a toned-down version of my bedroom. Sure, the bookcases were lined with stacks of my books and a few figurines representing characters and creatures from my stories, but the atmosphere didn't drag me into Vrydindel. Not like my bedroom.

I'd created Vrydindel when I was twelve, not long after I'd come home from... the incident. I didn't have a lot of memories about the day it was born. One day, it was just there in my head, alive and as real as everything else in the world. Only better. Safer. It was an escape. Somewhere that wasn't my house. Somewhere where I could be more powerful than all the dangers and threats of the world. It was hard to let it go, especially when it had given me refuge for so many years. It didn't matter that I was twenty-nine. Vrydindel remained at the tip of my fingers. Just in case. I'd shifted it into a career, but in the back of my mind, it would always be more.

At first, my therapist had called it a coping mechanism. Seventeen years later, I could tell my inability to let it go concerned her.

But my office wasn't the same.

A large calendar on the wall was marked with deadlines and project notes, all color-coded, a system of my own design. The desk was arranged with two notebooks, opened to blank pages, pens at the ready, in case I had to jot something down at a moment's notice. Ideas sometimes formed without warning, and it was best to be prepared before they skittered off again and were forgotten.

Post-it notes lined a whiteboard leaning against the wall beside the closet, each color representing a different element of my plot. They could be moved and rearranged as the story unfolded. Beside my keyboard were a sketch pad and a 5B pencil—I preferred the softer graphite—where I doodled ideas for new creatures that I might come across in the world of Vrydindel. I loved drawing dragons and had been doing it for years.

The large window overlooking the street was covered, as always, with heavy drapes. An ordinary floor lamp emitted artificial light into the room, giving everything a soft glow. The floor lamp in my bedroom was in the shape of a tree. Its metal frame included a twisting snake and six branches that stretched out wide. Big leaves cupped the light bulbs.

I dug my toes into the plush area rug underfoot as Dad set my coffee on the desk, careful not to disturb anything.

Habit made me veer toward the window before I sat down. I peeked out the corner of the curtain at the street below. The lock moved easily under my fingers. *Click, click, click.*

Down the road a block, parked along the opposite side of the road, was a vehicle. It could have been white, but the sun reflecting off the back window was blinding and made it hard to tell. My skin prickled with heat as I pressed my face to the glass, squinting into the distance. It was a light color, boxy. Maybe it was tan, or silver, but it could have been white. What if it was white? What if it was a Pontiac Grand Prix? If I could just see a little bit—

"Charlie, get away from the window."

"But I think—"

"Enough already." Dad's tone brooked no argument. "Sit down. Drink your coffee. Write some plotting notes or whatever it is you do during this phase. If you don't stop this nonsense, I'm calling Sofia. You were doing good, kiddo. Don't take this path again."

"It's not a path. I'm not imagining things."

But I engaged the lock and forced myself to step away from the window. It did me no good to obsess, or Dad would follow through with his threats. For all I liked my therapist, I knew she would identify my behavior as problematic, and she might consider adjusting my medication again. I hated when she did that. It made it hard to work. It made it hard to think. Worse, it made it nearly impossible to escape into the other world I'd created all those years ago. And if I couldn't go to Vrydindel, I might truly lose my mind.

I sat at my desk and opened a blank Word document. All the while, I was aware of Dad in the doorway looking on. He wouldn't leave unless he was sure I was keeping my head about me, which meant not standing at the window or going back into the shadows of my bedroom and Vrydindel.

I placed my fingers on the keyboard and typed. *Calipnia and Rotkiv take a journey across the frosted lake to the land of broken shards.* Maybe it was time to meet the ice dragons. Rotkiv would like that. He'd kept me safe enough thus far. Why not up the stakes?

When the sound of Dad's shuffling gait retreated down the hall, I stopped and listened. His heavy footfalls descended the stairs, an uneven thumping since he was still favoring his right hip.

He moved along the hallway downstairs.

Water ran in the kitchen.

I abandoned my keyboard and relocated to the window, peeling the curtains back and shielding my eyes against the sun's glare. The car was gone. Had I imagined it? No. It had been there.

Automatically, I reached for the lock and worked it back and forth. I scanned the street in both directions. Everything was as it should be. Calm. Normal. No more signs of disruption. No more white Pontiacs.

The Beekmans' van was not in the driveway because Alice and Casey were at work. The kids were in school or at daycare. They'd be home shortly after six. The dogs would lose their minds, and the kids would run screaming into the house.

Francine LaPointe's Cadillac was parked where it always was—on the left-hand side of her driveway. The right-hand side used to belong to her husband, but his Nissan had been sold after he died last year.

Westly Huntington's garage door sat open. The older man was sitting on an overturned milk carton, spit-polishing his shiny new red moped. The man was so proud of his purchase he'd spent the first two weeks driving up and down the street, waving at everyone he passed by.

Nothing was out of the ordinary.

The car was gone.

Or was it just hiding out of sight?

I pressed my face to the glass, doing all I could to see farther down the road.

Nothing.

I cocked an ear, listening for Dad. When I didn't hear anything, and a faint whiff of model cement drifted to the second floor, I knew he'd gone to work on his models.

I tugged my phone from my pocket. There was still no message from Stanley or Officer Dyani. The longer I had to wait, the more apprehensive I was going to get. Just as I decided it wouldn't hurt to call Dyani one more time, the sound of a car door closing caught my ear.

I peered back out the window and saw a police cruiser parked at the side of the road in front of the house. As Officer Dyani got out of the vehicle, I stuffed my phone back into my pocket, my heart beating a little faster.

He stepped onto the sidewalk and paused, hands perched on his hips as he studied the street in both directions. The swirling ink of his tattoos stood out more in the sunlight than they had at the police station the other day. They wrapped around both arms, swirls and curls of black ink that weaved an intricate pattern around several other pieces of art. I wanted to study them. He had nice arms. Toned biceps strained the short sleeves of his uniform, not excessive muscles like the bodybuilders in the magazines I saw at the market, but enough to show definition.

His skin was golden and smooth. His silky black hair shimmered in the daylight, short and smart. He pulled off a pair of mirrored sunglasses and perched them on his head. His intense eyes studied the houses along the street with a harsh glare. They were deep brown. Hickory, my memory supplied. With that memory came another. Sage and sweetgrass. Big strong hands cupping and holding my own.

"Takoda." I listened to how his name rolled off my tongue. I said it again, testing each syllable. I liked it.

I wondered if he would let me call him by his first name. Stanley had never minded, and I rather liked how it sounded and wouldn't mind trying it out.

Takoda had turned his attention to the house and the Impala in the driveway. He processed every angle with a dip in his dark brow and a firm set to his lips. His intense hickory eyes didn't miss anything.

When he followed the path to the front door, I latched the lock in place and let the curtain fall over the window. Abandoning my workstation, I raced out of the office as the doorbell sounded.

Takoda was there to help me. Stanley had said he would talk to Takoda, that he was new to the job and needed some direction. He'd said the reason Takoda had been so angry on the phone was because no one had given him guidance. Stanley assured me he'd take care of it.

And now Takoda was here. He would take care of the white Pontiac, and I wouldn't have to worry anymore that it was always around the next bend. Because it was, and I wasn't imagining it.

I took the stairs quicker than usual, stopping briefly on the landing to touch the lock on the window. I didn't unlatch it, but I had to ensure it was in place, then I continued on, intent on beating Dad to the door. I was too late. He was already in the front hallway when I got there.

Dad took one look at me and sighed, shaking his head. "You were at the damn window watching the street again. Good grief, child. You're going to be the death of me."

"I'm not a child, and I'll do as I please," I mumbled under my breath, but Dad didn't hear me.

He disengaged the deadbolt and tugged the door open as I perched on the bottom step, my blood pumping, my teeth digging grooves into my bottom lip. It took everything in me not to wring my hands. Dad said it was a telling sign of my rising anxiety, and I didn't want him to say I was too anxious for this meeting and send Takoda on his way.

A flutter in my belly dampened my fear, and for reasons I wasn't ready to process, I thought maybe I was a little excited to see Takoda again, even though he wasn't a detective, even though he wasn't Stanley.

Even though he'd been rude and dismissive.

Dad stood in the doorway, blocking my view. "Good morning." He used the firm, influential tone he'd told me once made people listen and respect him.

"Good morning. Mr. Falkingham, is that correct?"

"That's me. Name's Archie."

"Archie, sir, my name is Takoda Dyani. I'm an officer with the Hamilton Central Division Police Department, and I met with Charlie the other day at the station. I was wondering if he was available to chat. I've been working through some of his concerns, and I wanted to touch base."

"I'm here," I blurted, stepping off the last step. "Dad, I can handle this."

Dad didn't retreat or move from the door. I placed a hand on his shoulder, but he threw me off, not unkindly but emphasizing he wasn't going anywhere just yet. Not a word passed through his lips, but I got the sense Takoda was the recipient of one of Dad's warning glares. The kind that said a whole lot without saying anything at all.

After a minute, when Dad must have felt certain his message had been received, he stepped aside. "Come on in, Officer."

I caught the faint snarl in Takoda's nose as his gaze slipped beyond the threshold and into the house. "With all due respect, this won't take long. Perhaps you'd like to meet with me out here on the porch, Charlie?"

"With all due respect, son," Dad mimicked—and not nicely, "you can come inside and have a proper conversation with Charlie about his concerns."

His hickory eyes blazed with contempt. Takoda's lips twitched. Before he could say anything more to my father, I jumped in. "Please come in. We can go to my office. It's more private if that helps." Dad made to object, but I touched his arm. "It's fine, Dad. I'm fine meeting Officer Dyani up there. It's my concern. I can handle it."

Dad studied me a moment before heaving a heavy sigh. "As you wish." Turning to Dyani, he said, "If I hear raised voices like I did on the phone yesterday… If you think for one minute you will disrespect my son like that again, we're going to have a problem you and me. Do you hear? I don't give a rat's ass if you wear a uniform or carry a badge. If you walk into *my* house, you abide by *my* rules. You aren't throwing your position around in here, you got that?"

Takoda worked his jaw, but he gave Dad a clipped nod. "Yes, sir."

Dad waved him in.

Takoda crossed into the front hall with his chin high and body rigid. He walked like a police officer, and Dad wasn't going to like that. Stanley had been over a few times, but he acted like an uncle or a family friend.

"This way." I climbed the stairs, marginally aware of Dad staring after us.

On the landing, I fought the urge to check the lock and failed. One click. Back and forth. The heat of Takoda's stare made the hairs on my nape prickle to life. I continued on, wringing my hands because I couldn't help it.

The upper level veered in two directions. One way led to my bedroom, the other to the office, bathroom, and Dad's bedroom.

I directed Takoda to the office and waved him in first. When he breezed past me, he moved the air, and it carried the scent of sage and sweetgrass to my nose. My skin grew tight, but not in a bad way. It was… I didn't know how to describe it, but it was nice.

There wasn't an extra chair, so I asked Takoda to wait while I collected the one we kept in the bathroom. Dad used it for balance when he dressed after a shower or put on his socks and slippers. It was wooden and painted a soft cream color.

In the office again, I set it down for Takoda.

"This really won't take long," he said, flipping the chair around and straddling it backward. I couldn't help staring at his arms and ink when he crossed them over the back of the chair. He really did have nice arms.

And I was hot again. Why was I always sweltering when this man was around?

I settled into my own seat and spun to face him.

"I apologize for my father. He's overprotective and forgets I'm an adult sometimes. He means well."

Takoda waved it off. "It's fine." He glanced around, his gaze lingering on the figurines on the shelves among the books before drifting to the whiteboard and calendar, then to the desk. He was chewing gum, something green and minty. Every now and then, it poked between his teeth, then his tongue snuck out and drew it back in.

"So, you're an author, is that right?"

I tore my gaze from his mouth. "Um. Yes. Young adult high fantasy."

Takoda nodded. "I don't read much. At all, actually. *Irregardless*, that's pretty damn cool."

I pinched my lips together and must have made a noise, because warm hickory eyes darted in my direction.

"What?" Takoda asked. The gum-chewing stopped.

"Nothing." But my lips twitched as I tried to smother a grin.

"No, you squeaked. I heard it. What?"

"It's just… that's not a word."

"What's not a word?"

"*Irregardless*."

"Yes, it is. People say it all the time. I hear them say it."

"It doesn't make it a word. I have a profound understanding of the English language. I'm just pointing out, it's not a word."

"Whatever. I have a profound understanding of the English language too, and I say it is." He pressed fingers into his eyes. "Shit. Here we go again." Blowing out a breath, sending a minty gust of air in my direction, he drummed his fingers on the back of the chair as he cut his eyes to the shelves. "So, about the white Pontiac."

I sat straighter. "Did you find it? I thought it was here earlier. Down the road. Although, I couldn't be sure this time. The sun was bright, and when I looked again, it was gone."

"Yeah, so, here's the thing." Takoda hesitated, his tongue drawing a line along his upper teeth. I watched it. Back and forth. Then he rolled his gum around, and it poked out again then popped back in. "The guy who owns it lives and works in the neighborhood. He, um, drives to all those spots where you saw him, you know? It's nothing to concern yourself over. He's just... new around here."

"Oh." I thought about that. "Oh. Okay. So he just moved in somewhere?"

Takoda gripped the back of the chair so tightly the color washed out of his skin. "Yeah. New to the neighborhood."

"Where does he live? Is it nearby? It must be. Is it on the next block over because—"

"I can't divulge that information."

"Right. Privacy. I understand. But he's not—"

"He's not a threat. I promise. He's just an ordinary guy doing ordinary stuff."

I wrung my hands on my lap, processing. "You spoke with him personally?"

Again, Takoda squeezed the chair, the wood creaking under his palms. "Yes." The word came out tight. "We had a long conversation. All's good."

I nodded. "Okay. That's good. A relief."

A weight lifted off my chest. I rolled that new information around in my head. It made sense. How come I hadn't considered that? But what was most important was that I hadn't imagined the whole thing. It had been real. Takoda confirmed the car existed. I was not crazy.

"What about the person I saw? In the backyard."

Takoda bounced a knee, his nose wrinkling as he breathed heavily. "You told me it was just a sensation. A feeling. You didn't really see anyone, right?"

"No. No, I guess not. I mean... No." But it had been enough to twist my gut the wrong way.

"Is it possible you were worried about the car and it made you a little... paranoid?"

I sat straighter, prepared to defend myself. Sofia used that word a lot. So did Dad. They always made it sound like I was inventing stories when I wasn't.

"I'm not paranoid."

Takoda held up his hands. "Okay. Look. Maybe that's the wrong word. It made you overly suspicious. Is that better?" He didn't let me answer. "If you see someone in the backyard again—truly see them with your own two eyes and not just a feeling—then call the station and leave me a message."

His hickory eyes were trained on me. Deep, dark, and warm. Intense in a way that ramped up that funny fluttering sensation in my belly.

Takoda was for real. He wasn't throwing my concerns away. He was taking them seriously.

"Not your cell phone?" I asked after a minute.

Takoda sighed. "I made a mistake giving you that number. It's been brought to my attention that we have to maintain professional boundaries. I'm happy to take your calls when I'm working."

"Your sergeant? He said that? Was he upset? I shouldn't have called. That's my fault. I'm sorry. No wonder you were angry."

Takoda's knee bounced faster. The chair gave another whining creak under his hands. "Yeah. It's cool, man. I told my sergeant it wouldn't happen again." He swallowed, and his throat clicked. His jaw worked his gum more viciously. "He, um, he just wanted me to remind you that you can't call me on my cell."

"No problem. I never meant to get you in trouble."

"It's fine. So, are we good? You feel better about the whole white Pontiac thing?"

"Of course. So much better. It's a relief. I was worried. Thank you for looking into it."

Takoda nodded, but there was something in his face I couldn't read. Looping his leg over the chair, he stood and spent a minute fixing his clothes.

I did not stare at his arms no matter how much I wanted to study his ink.

We were close enough that the scent of sage and sweetgrass surrounded me once again, mixed with the soft hint of mint from his gum. I didn't know why I like that earthy scent so much, but it made me want to inhale deeply and fill my lungs.

Instead of leaving, Takoda wandered to the bookshelf and thumbed the spines of my series, mouthing the titles.

When he reached the end of the row, he picked up a dragon figurine, the one Ironstone was modeled after. He was a variety of earth dragon with gray-green scales and a forked tail. His wingspan was over thirty feet wide—in my stories, anyhow. Rotkiv and I had had a great time taking him on during Ironstone's tale. The figurine's wings were folded against its body. He looked far more subdued than he was during our adventure.

"His name is Ironstone."

Takoda glanced over his shoulder with a quirked brow. "He has a name?"

"Of course he does. He also has a book." I plucked the fifth book from my series off the shelf and showed him.

Takoda took a step closer, his scent tickling my nose, his arm brushing mine, and he took the book from my hand. "*The Roots of Ironstone*," he read.

"He's one of the oldest dragons in existence. He was born in the emerald forest east of Vrydindel. Calipnia and Rotkiv had to tame him so they could work together to… Well, I shouldn't spoil it."

"Rotkiv?"

"A blood dragon. He's Calipnia's protector. They used to be enemies, but now they quest together."

Takoda huffed, and a smile curled the corner of his mouth as he shook his head. It felt like mockery, and I snatched the book back, replacing it with the others on the shelf. Heat filled my cheeks, and my stomach soured.

"Never mind. They're for teenagers," I explained.

"Right. I'm sure kids love them. Anyhow, I gotta go. Like I said, you got a problem again, call the station and *aks* for me."

"Ask."

Takoda glared, his lips thinning. I didn't feel bad about correcting him that time and let a smile crest my face as I held his gaze.

"You know that's fucking irritating as hell, right?" But he was smiling too, and there was little to no heat behind the words.

"Dad's mentioned it once or twice."

"Maybe don't do it."

"I think I like ruffling your feathers, Officer Dyani. Plus, you mocked my dragons, so I think you deserved it."

Takoda studied me for a long time before shaking his head, his smile still present. "I didn't mock them. Goodbye, Charlie." He scanned the room one last time. "Enjoy your adventures."

His heavy boots clunked down the stairs. I didn't follow. The warm sensation in the pit of my stomach was back, and it was making it hard to think.

Retreating to the window, I pushed the curtains aside and watched as Takoda emerged from the house and walked along the front path to the sidewalk. At his cruiser, he stood by the driver's door, slid his sunglasses back in place, and scanned the street. After a long minute, he tugged open the door of the cruiser and got in.

Then he sat there without starting the engine. And I kept on watching, his scent still lingering in the room all around me.

"How'd it go?" Dad asked from the doorway, startling me. "He seems like an arrogant piece of shit if you ask me."

"It was fine."

A long pause. Silence swelled between us, and I knew Dad was waiting for a report.

Reluctantly, I turned away from the window and faced him. "Everything is fine. I told you I wasn't imagining things. The white Pontiac belongs to a new neighbor a few blocks away. Officer Dyani looked into it. I think he's quite capable."

Dad's face creased with concern as his mouth turned down. His old tired eyes studied me. "And that made you feel better, kiddo?"

"Yes, of course. I don't have to worry anymore. It's nothing. I overreacted."

"Good. As long as you're happy. That's what matters."

I spent the rest of the day immersed in plotting. The weight of worry had lifted, and I was better able to focus. I sketched the base form of a new creature I wanted to introduce in the ice world and mapped out a new path for Calipnia and Rotkiv with new trials and worldly lessons.

The doorbell rang at half past six while I was engaged in making dinner. Dad was in the lounge, napping with the TV on. The droning voices of sportscasters on ESPN had been keeping me company while I chopped vegetables.

"I'll get it," I called as I made my way to the front door. I didn't think Dad had heard the bell, seeing as he was still snoring.

It wasn't often we had visitors. In fact, it was rare. If Mom came by, she always called first. My sister, Adelaide, never bothered anymore. Perhaps it was the Beekmans, returning the casserole dish they'd borrowed last week when they'd needed an extra pan for their church potluck. Or maybe it was Ms. LaPointe, wondering if I could help her reach something on a top shelf again. She was a short woman and didn't like standing on chairs lest she lose her balance and break a hip. I'd heard all about it in painstaking detail.

A curl of warmth rolled through my low belly when I considered it might be Officer Dyani, returning with information he'd forgotten to share earlier.

At the door, I ran my thumb over the deadbolt and peered through the peephole before deciding if I wanted to unlock it.

No one was there.

Frowning, I squinted and waited, figuring whoever had rung the bell had stepped out of sight and would move back into my field of vision if I waited long enough.

They didn't.

I stepped back and peeled the sheer cover from the window that ran along the side of the door. The glass was frosted, but I could tell no one was on the front stoop.

Dad continued to snore.

In the distance, I could hear the pot of water boiling on the stove.

I disengaged the lock and opened the heavy wooden door. The setting sun cast long shadows across the front lawn and driveway. The temperature was much cooler than earlier. To the west, the sky was a fiery auburn, smearing to deep blues and indigo as it arched overhead. I glanced down the street in both directions, but everything was in order. Everything was quiet.

Who had rung the bell?

The oven timer dinged, and Dad's snoring sputtered and stopped. It must have woken him. I stepped outside, wrapping my arms around my middle, protecting myself against the chill in the air.

An uncomfortable prickling sensation climbed my spine, and my heart picked up its pace. Someone had rung the bell, hadn't they? I'd heard it. I wasn't imagining it.

Nothing on the street was amiss. I stood for another minute, scanning to be sure while doubt settled in.

That was odd. Maybe it had been the TV and I'd mistaken it for the doorbell.

As I backed up, intent on shutting the door again, something on the stoop caught my eye. On the edge of the cement step was a flattened chocolate bar wrapper with a small stone pinning it down. It was orange. A bright and familiar orange.

A jolt of anxiety electrified my blood. It was one of those moments when fear crashed in from all sides out of nowhere, overwhelming me in the blink of an eye. It had no rhyme or reason. It just was. It happened less often as I got older, but there on the stoop with the chocolate bar wrapper at my feet, it hit me like a truck. Something about this felt very, very wrong.

I toed the rock off the wrapper then flipped it over so I could see the other side even though I knew exactly what I'd find.

Reese's Peanut Butter Cups.

Reese's Peanut Butter Cups.

"Because they're your favorite," a voice from the abyss said.

Without warning, darkness blanketed my vision, my ears rang, and I couldn't breathe.

Seven

TAKODA

The call came on Friday.

I'd spent too many mind-numbing hours that week transcribing reports, filing paperwork, photocopying, faxing, replenishing supplies, and doing whatever mundane jobs Nikola found for me to do.

It was humiliating, but I'd done it without argument and with a fake smile plastered on my face.

Sergeant Nikola called me into his office around three o'clock Friday afternoon and told me to shut the door and have a seat. My muscles all contracted at once as I went through every interaction I'd had with coworkers over the past week, wondering where I'd fucked up or who I'd pissed off. My mouth had gotten away from me once or twice, but overall, I'd tried hard to behave.

Nikola settled in his seat, his hands folded under his chin as he examined me with analytical eyes that somehow saw through all my bullshit. His tie had silver and blue stripes today. His hair was neat. His jaw was freshly shaved.

"Is there a problem, sir?"

If I'd gone out of my way to keep my ass in line and I was still in trouble, I wasn't sure it was worth it. I hadn't taken his threats of walking me out the door lightly. I might have a hot temper and an issue with many things, but I didn't want to lose my job.

"I got a phone call from Archie Falkingham this afternoon."

I frowned. Charlie's father. It had been four days since I'd visited their house and chatted with Charlie about his imaginary problems, taking Graveman's advice and lying through my teeth to make the man happy. I hadn't anticipated how hard it would be. Especially when a look of unfiltered relief had crossed Charlie's face. It had felt almost cruel.

Had the lie not been good enough? Had Charlie complained to his father? Was he skeptical? Had he seen through my bullshit the same way Nikola always did? Had he thought I was insulting his dragons?

"Is there a problem, sir?" I asked again.

"Possibly. Archie's worried about Charlie. Something set him off on Monday that—"

"Sir, I was very careful with how I approached him. I did everything exactly how—"

Nikola held up a hand. "It had nothing to do with your visit. Something happened that evening. It upset Charlie something fierce. Caused an… episode, Archie called it. Archie ended up having to call Charlie's doctor. They've been monitoring him all week, and he's been… Well, I guess he's been pretty bad."

"Okay." I didn't know what pretty bad meant with Charlie. All I knew were the few things Graveman had shared. And what did this have to do with me?

"Archie normally tries to discourage Charlie from racing into the station with every problem that comes up. He knows it can be exhausting for us, but he's at a loss and is grappling for a solution right now. He was hoping you'd agree to come by the house and chat with Charlie for a few minutes. If you could reassure him, then maybe Charlie would come around. Archie's hoping you can set his mind at ease."

I frowned. Set his mind at ease? About what? That seemed to be code for go lie to the poor sucker. Graveman had done it for years, and now I was supposed to follow in his footsteps. This was such bullshit. If the guy was this unstable, he needed medical intervention.

"I'm not a doctor, sir. What the hell does he want me to do? This lying shit isn't an answer. It's a Band-Aid. Why doesn't anyone see that?"

Nikola scowled and pointed a finger at me. "Do not take that tone, Dyani. If Archie is asking for our help, it's because he's out of options. Your job isn't to ask questions, is it?"

It took an extra second before I could manage to spit out the "No, sir," without snarling. The self-restraint I'd used all week went out the window. "But this whole thing is bullshit, you know that, right? The guy is fucked in the head, and now we jump through hoops because seventeen years ago, we fucked up? That makes no sense. This isn't our problem. We aren't doing him any favors. Why am I the only one who sees that?"

"You better shut your goddamn mouth and get out of my office right now, Dyani. Go do your goddamn job before you don't have one. You have your orders. Were they unclear?"

"No, sir. I'm going." I shoved out of the chair and was halfway to the door when I added, "But you know what? If Charlie hadn't come from some big-name family with power and money, if he'd grown up in the south end, and if his mom had worked at a shitty, hole-in-the-wall diner, and his dad had fucked off with another woman, this wouldn't be a thing. We'd have rescued the kid all those years ago and sent him on his merry fucking way. Broken or not, he wouldn't have been our problem anymore. The only reason anyone gives two shits—"

Nikola shoved back from his desk, his chair flying backward and crashing into the wall. With his hands braced against his desk, a flush racing up his neck and flooding his cheeks, and an angry pulse making the vein by his temple throb, he worked his jaw. "Dyani—"

I ducked out of the room as fast as I could, slamming the door behind me before he erupted. That was ten kinds of stupid. I needed to learn to keep my fucking mouth shut.

Pausing outside his office, I held my breath and waited for the explosion. I waited for him to shout a blue streak and tell me to pack my things because I was fired.

Nothing.

Silence.

I wasn't sure if that was better or worse.

I let out a breath and cursed. I'd once again lodged my size-twelve boot in my mouth without thinking. But everything I'd said was true. Was I the only one who saw it?

I immediately left the building, grabbing keys for one of the available cruisers. If I waited any longer, Nikola might decide to print off my termination papers. The only thing that might save my ass was coddling Charlie and getting on Archie's good side so he could sing my praises to my sergeant.

I huffed a laugh as I exited into the parking lot. In all my life, when had anyone sung my praises, let alone some rich fuck with a mentally unstable son?

Charlie's neighborhood was quiet. The first time I'd visited, I'd been shocked to discover he didn't live in some ten-bedroom mansion on the north end of town where the wealthy congregated. Not that Charlie's house was small or unimpressive. In fact, the neighborhood was a newer development area that catered to the upper-middle-class population without being overly flashy. Large brick houses were set back off the road. The properties were huge with manicured front lawns, pruned hedges, flower boxes, and ornamental trees you didn't see in my neck of the woods. They backed onto a wooded area owned by a golf course and country club. Expensive vehicles sat in driveways, and there was an air of privilege I couldn't ignore.

Packing away my irritation, I got out of the cruiser and trudged to the front door, hooking my thumbs in my belt as I went, noting how my muscles refused to loosen even with a stern pep talk.

It was true. Everything I'd said to Nikola. If Charlie had been anyone else, they wouldn't have bothered with him for all these years. It was his name and his parents' position in the community that sent us jumping through hoops. It was such utter bullshit. A prime example of all the things I hated about the world. Money gave people rights the lower class never had. Kids like Odina, or me, or Calian suffered. Kids like Charlie? They got a fucking marching band on their side.

I rang the bell and waited.

Archie answered after a minute. The man looked haggard, like he'd aged a decade in less than a week. The lines on his face were deep crevices. His skin sagged, and deep purple shadows lived under each eye. The man who'd taken a threatening stance with me a few short days ago was gone.

I tipped my chin. "Afternoon, Mr. Falkingham. Sergeant Nikola said you were looking for some help, and I should come right over."

Archie leaned heavily against the door like he might collapse otherwise. He studied me like I was an insect he'd never seen before and couldn't tell if I was a threat or not. "I need your word that you're not going to cause problems if you come in here. We are walking a fine line right now, son, and I will not have you pushing Charlie over the edge."

I worked my jaw once before forcing my muscles to relax. Remembering Nikola's threats, remembering the vulnerability I'd seen in Charlie's winter-blue eyes and how it had reminded me a bit of the way Odina had looked for months after her attack, I nodded. "We're good. I'm just here to see if I can help."

"I hope so. Please come in. Can I get you a drink, Officer?"

"No, thank you. Call me Takoda."

Archie took me through the house to a large kitchen. I tried not to notice the décor surrounding me as we went. The crisp, clean lines of custom-made cabinetry, the stonework tiling, the granite countertops, the eat-in nook, and the large, picture windows along the far wall were impossible to ignore. It was deserving of an article in some modern home magazine. For a brief moment, I wondered if my dad's house was any different. He lived in a place like this with his new wife and new family—at least he had last time I'd looked him up.

I shoved those thoughts away as fast as they entered my mind. They served no purpose and would only make me angrier.

Charlie wasn't in the kitchen, but a younger Black woman in her early thirties sat in the nook with her hands wrapped around a steaming mug. Vibrant teal polish decorated each fingernail. She wore a flowy, one-piece outfit with a splash of bright patterned colors all over it, ranging from orange to red to blue and yellow. I wasn't sure how many women could pull off something so lively, but this one could have walked a runway. She was model gorgeous. Her hair was dyed amber and hung in tight, springy coils over her shoulders. She wore a delicate amount of makeup, but I got the sense she would have been just as beautiful without it.

"Takoda, this is Dr. Sofia Menard, Charlie's therapist. Sofia, Officer Takoda Dyani, the young man I was telling you about who stepped in after Stan retired."

I tipped my chin. "Nice to meet you, ma'am. Is Charlie not here? I thought I was coming to see him."

Archie nodded, pinching the bridge of his nose as he sighed. "He's upstairs. I thought we could have a quick chat first about what happened on Monday."

"Sure."

"Would you like to have a seat? There's coffee on. Are you sure I can't get you a drink or something?"

"I'm not much of a coffee drinker. Water's fine."

Archie filled a glass from a jug in the fridge, and we all sat around the table in the nook area. I traced the condensation on the glass, doing all I could not to squirm. I felt out of place in this house and with these people.

Charlie's doctor made house calls? I couldn't wrap my head around that as I remembered endless hours sitting in an emergency room as a kid because Istas had gotten strep throat again, and our family doctor couldn't get her an appointment for over a week.

I sipped my water. "So, um, what happened on Monday?"

Archie explained how Charlie claimed to have heard the doorbell, and how he'd gone outside to see who was there, and how he'd found an empty candy wrapper on the stoop which had sent him spiraling out of control.

"A candy wrapper?"

"I know it sounds ridiculous. I agree one hundred percent, but I can't discount Charlie's reaction. I know my son. I haven't seen him have a panic attack of that magnitude since…" Archie's throat bobbed. "Well, since he was a lot younger. Since he first came back to us. I thought we'd moved past those rougher days. There was a period of time when he had a lot of nightmares and woke up in a state. They continued into his teenage years until we were finally able to manage them. He's taking some strong narcotics at night now. They knock him out pretty good, and it hasn't been a problem in years. But this… episode was similar in nature."

I frowned and passed my gaze from Archie to Sofia and back. "Did you ask him why he got so upset?"

"Of course I did. He can't explain it. He's… he's not really saying much. Hardly anything at all, to be honest. He's shut down. He goes away inside his head, and it's hard to reach him. We've danced around it all week, pushing for answers but trying not to set him off. I had to take the damn wrapper away from him because he was working himself into another episode every time I turned around. I don't like drugging my son, you understand me? I hate it. Especially these higher doses of Xanax. It's a catch twenty-two. At the moment, he's retreated so far inside his head, he's almost untouchable. But it's because of whatever happened. So, I can dose him up and make a zombie out of him so he's calmer, or I can wait and hope he comes back on his own. I already spent over three years with a nearly catatonic son, Officer. Over three years when that boy didn't say a single word. I don't want to go back there. I don't know what else to do. Right now, I feel like I'm damned if I do or I'm damned if I don't."

Sofia took Archie's hand and squeezed when the older man's voice hitched. "We decided to give him the Xanax. Yesterday, we cut back his dose, hoping he'd be ready to come around and talk," Sofia explained. "He still hasn't said much. A few words, but we were hoping with some intervention from you, we could get him back on even ground again."

"You mean you want me to go up there and lie to him. You want me to tell him I'm working some bullshit case when I'm not?"

Archie's eyes watered, and I felt like a pile of shit.

"I'm sorry."

"No, no. I get it," Archie said. "This isn't your job. It—"

"No, it *is* my job, and I'm going to do what I can. So, he found a candy wrapper outside, and something about it affected him?"

Archie sighed and nodded. "Yes. I have no doubt it's nothing more than someone else's garbage floating around on the breeze that somehow landed on our front stoop. Charlie is convinced someone left it there for him. He's convinced the doorbell rang and that someone is sending him a message. I didn't hear the doorbell, and I was right there in the front room. Charlie feels threatened. Like he's in danger. That's about all I can get out of him."

"But he hasn't explained why?"

"I'm not sure he could," Sofia said, still holding Archie's hand. The old man looked like he needed the support.

"Son," Archie said, "Charlie doesn't remember most of what happened to him when he was taken. He's built a mental block around that time period, which most days I thank God for."

"Severe trauma can do that," Sofia explained further. "It's our mind's way of protecting us. Charlie suffered extreme abuse while at the hands of his captors. He doesn't remember the abuse specifically, but he can tap into the emotions and fear involved. Smells, sounds, a touch, anything that might correlate to the incident he's tucked away could easily trigger him. What Charlie is describing when it comes to the candy wrapper makes me believe there is a correlation to his kidnapping. It might be nothing more than he saw a similar wrapper while in captivity. It could be the children were given this type of chocolate as a reward for behaving. We don't know. Only Charlie knows, except he doesn't. Whatever the reason, that wrapper is calling on a memory he's buried, and it's terrifying to him. He's convinced someone left it for him as a warning or a threat. There is no telling him otherwise."

"What if he's right?" I asked. "What if all he's told you is the truth and someone came to the door, rang the bell, and left it for him to find?"

Sofia's smile was patient and a shade condescending, which I didn't appreciate. "Charlie suffers from extreme paranoia. This is typical behavior that has been ongoing for several years."

"But still. It could have happened."

"It's unlikely."

I nodded, shifting my gaze between these two people, absorbing all they were saying. "So, you think if Charlie believes the police are handling it, he'll calm down?"

"We can only hope. It's worked in the past," Sofia said.

"Please help my son." Archie's words were wet and full of barely restrained emotion. "I know this isn't ideal. I know this isn't part of your job, but I'm asking, man to man, please."

I emptied the glass of water as I considered the whole situation. What choice did I have? Nikola was probably sitting in his office, waiting for a call from Archie Falkingham, telling him I'd been an ass.

"Where's the wrapper?"

Archie rose from the table and retrieved it from a drawer. He placed it in front of me. It was nothing more than the packaging for a chocolate bar. Garbage that had likely blown in off the street, just like Archie had said.

"Do you have a large Ziplock baggie or something?"

Archie paused, studying me, then went and found one.

I fit the wrapper inside and sealed the closure tight. "Evidence bag. If you want me to lie to your son, we have to make it believable."

Archie clapped me on the shoulder and squeezed. "Thank you."

I wanted to knock his hand away. I wanted to tell him he should be ashamed of himself, but I bit my tongue. Charlie's doctor was right there, and if she condoned this behavior, who was I to judge?

"Where's Charlie?"

"In his bedroom. Don't turn on the light. He has it set how he wants it. Any changes might upset him. Keep your voice calm. He hasn't spoken more than a handful of words all week, so go easy. He might not talk to you at all."

Archie and Sofia followed me up the stairs like shadows, and I got the feeling they didn't trust me not to make the whole thing worse. Hell, I didn't trust myself.

Archie indicated a doorway at the end of the hall, in the opposite direction I'd gone before.

The door was open, and I remembered Charlie's adamance about closed doors at the station. Was it the same in his own home?

The room was in shadow, but enough light spilled in from the hallway and from around the curtains that hung over a huge window on the east side it was easy to navigate. There was also an enormous trickling fountain in the corner that was backlit. The light reflected off the falling water that cascaded down into a small basin made to look like a rock garden or pond. It was also enough illumination to highlight the major aspects of Charlie's room.

My feet stalled as I looked around. If I'd thought Charlie's office was hinging on radical, it was nothing compared to this. Large paintings filled every available piece of wall space. They depicted vicious dragons in fighting poses with teeth and tails and shimmering scales. There were elves and other unusual creatures I didn't have a name for. There were an abundance of figurines and sculptures, swords and other unique weaponry that might only be found in a fantasy world. Fake ivy ran along the ceiling and hung in places giving the effect of a forest or jungle. The high posts on the bed were draped with more leafy, vine-like growth that couldn't possibly be real, but it looked like it grew right out of the ground and was swallowing the furniture. It was like walking into another world.

And there was Charlie, sitting on the floor in the middle of it all. Not a child, but a twenty-nine-year-old man.

"The fuck," I breathed as I spun, taking it all in despite the ambient lighting.

I hadn't spoken loud, but Archie glared daggers from his position in the doorway. Knowing I was on thin ice, I clamped my jaw shut, swallowed my opinions, and wandered into the room.

Charlie was facing the fountain, the stillness in his body absolute.

I didn't know what to say, but I remembered my first visit to see Odina in the hospital and how on edge she'd been, so I approached cautiously.

"Hey, Charlie," I said as I walked toward him, ensuring my voice was soft and nonthreatening. "It's Officer Dyani. Takoda. Do you mind if I sit with you?"

He didn't respond.

I moved in front of him and lowered myself until I was cross-legged and we were face-to-face. I set the baggie with the wrapper behind me, out of his line of sight.

Charlie's eyes were open, but they were unfocused, staring somewhere into middle space. The light from the fountain danced across his features, giving him an ethereal look. The slope of his nose, the cut angle of his cheekbones and jaw, the delicate curve of his mouth. I hated how this man called out to me. I hated that he stirred something in my core whenever I was in his presence.

Charlie blinked a few times, and his vision cleared—mostly. His eyes were glassy, and he looked stoned. When his gaze landed on me, I tried to smile, but a knot in my chest made it difficult. This whole thing was pulling at me far harder than I anticipated, and I couldn't help feeling inordinately protective of the man in front of me.

"Hey, you. I hear you've run into a bit of a problem. I thought I should stop by to see if I could help you out."

Charlie didn't seem to be processing on the same level as the other times we'd talked. Based on the furrow in his brow, I thought my words weren't quite absorbing. He wet his lips as his gaze roamed my face like I was a stranger.

The guy was so fucking drugged he didn't know who I was. My anger boiled to life again, but I reined it in before it got the better of me. What the fuck were these people doing to him?

In what universe was this okay?

Without thinking, I reached out and took Charlie's hands. They were cooler than mine, softer. When the frail bones under his skin moved, my chest tightened.

"Charlie? Do you know who I am?"

His breathing changed. Deep inhales, stretching out longer than before. He blinked a few times and wet his lips again. "Officer Dyani," he said, the words slurred. "You smell good."

A sharp intake from the door made me glance over. Archie had a hand over his mouth, his eyes glistening. Sofia rubbed his arm.

I refocused on Charlie. "That's right. How about you call me Takoda today? Does that sound all right to you? We're friends, aren't we? Friends use first names."

Another deep inhale. Charlie's eyes fluttered closed for a second before he dragged them open again. "Takoda."

"That's right. And you're Charlie."

I caressed the back of his hands with my thumbs. His gaze fell to our connection and remained there. Watching. I wasn't sure if what I was doing was okay, but he hadn't pulled away, so I kept going. His fingers twitched once, then stilled.

For a long time, we sat like that. Charlie followed the path of my thumbs while I watched him, noting every single unique detail of his face, tracing the freckles across his nose, and wondering why my heart was racing.

Charlie's lips were parted ever so slightly, and I caught myself staring at them, noting how delicate and thin they were. Charlie might have been older than me, but in so many ways, he seemed decades younger.

The presence at the door reminded me I had a job to do. I had to get Charlie talking if I could, but I didn't want to freak him out either.

"This is quite the bedroom you have. It's like walking into another world."

"V-vrydindel." The word stretched out as though he struggled to form each syllable.

"What's Vrydindel?"

"My world. Calipnia's world." He wet his lips and spoke again, but it was like his tongue was too heavy. "My books."

"I'm going to have to try one, aren't I?"

"You don't read."

I chuckled. "You remember that. Can't hurt to try, I suppose." I glanced at the framed art on the walls. "Are all these dragons and creatures part of your stories?"

"Yes." He followed my gaze, eyes glassy. "That dragon is Rotkiv. He's Calipnia's protector. A guy in…" Charlie smacked his lips and made a sour face. "A guy in China. I commissioned them from a guy in China. He's an incredible artist. Better than me. Cost a fucking fortune, but it was worth every penny. They're exactly what I see in my head."

My brows hit my hairline as I studied Charlie's face. "Charlie Falkingham, did you just say *fuck*? Why do I get the feeling that's not a common word in your vocabulary? Are you going all badass on me?"

Charlie's doped-up gaze flickered to my face, and a smile touched his lips. "Dad doesn't like it when I swear," he slurred. "But I'm twenty-nine. I'm not a child. I can do what I want."

I glanced over Charlie's shoulder where Archie and Sofia continued to spy on our conversation. "He's at the door, you know?"

Charlie's eyes blew wide. "Oh no." He bit his lower lip, and it was quite possibly the most endearing thing I'd ever seen. I couldn't contain my laugh, and a second later, Charlie was laughing too. It was soft and light, but it was there.

I flicked my gaze to the door again and noted Archie wiping furiously at his eyes.

Charlie's smile slowly faded, and he sighed, glancing down at our joined hands again.

"You have nice hands. And arms. And you smell good."

I swallowed a tight lump and forced a chuckle. "Careful. You sound all flirty, and when those drugs wear off, you might kick yourself."

Charlie frowned and toyed with his lip some more, but he didn't respond.

I had to get down to business, but I hoped Charlie didn't retreat now that I had him talking.

"I hear you had a scare earlier this week. Do you want to tell me about it?"

His gaze never left our hands. His fingers twitched. When he spoke, his words were still heavy with the residual drugs in his system. They came out as more of a whisper. "He's watching me."

"Who? Your dad?"

Charlie shook his head. "No. He's going to come back for me. He's going to take me away."

"Who is, Charlie?"

He clung tighter to my hands. "They took me."

A vise clamped around my heart at those words, and I had to breathe a few times before speaking. "But that's over now, right? You know that. Detective Graveman took care of that a long time ago."

Had I read the file like Graveman had suggested, I might know better what had happened to the men involved. Were they in prison? Dead? I had no idea.

Charlie's face crumpled. He peered up and met my eyes. Only then did I notice how long his lashes were. They were damp and glued together. Pools of tears balanced precariously on the bottom edge of his lower lids. When he blinked, one escaped and traveled down his cheek. His pain hit me square in the chest.

"He's going to take me away again. He's going to hurt me."

"No, he won't." I had to resist the urge to wipe his cheek. "I won't let him. Do you hear me? Do you understand? I will *never* let that happen."

Another tear slipped free. It rolled down his cheek and clung to his jaw before falling and hitting our joined hands.

Fuck it. I pulled one hand free and brushed gently at Charlie's cheek with the back of my fingers, drying his face and catching another tear as it fell. I'd felt helpless a handful of times in my life, with Odina, with Calian, but this was the worst yet, and it knotted me up.

"No one will ever hurt you again," I whispered. And I meant it.

"You'll protect me?"

"That's my job, isn't it?"

"You won't let him hurt me?"

"I promise, Charlie. Do you believe me?"

Charlie seemed to process my words, but he nodded.

"Good. I want to *aks* you some questions now. Is that all right?"

"Ask."

I huffed a laugh and shook my head. "You did not just do that."

Charlie ducked his chin and pinched his lips together.

I gave his hand a gentle tug. "No way. You know what? I think you're bullshitting me right now, aren't you, Charlie? Here I think you've got all this head shit going on, and you're still correcting my damn words."

A hint of a smile touched Charlie's mouth, and I felt it right in my chest. It was like the sun had come out after decades of darkness.

"I'm sorry."

"No, you're not. You like fucking with me. You told me so on Monday. Say it again."

"Is my dad still at the door?"

"Yes, he is, but you're a twenty-nine-year-old badass, remember? You don't give a shit."

Charlie lifted his gaze and watched me from under his long, wet lashes. "I like fucking with you," he whispered.

"Again."

Louder, he said. "I like fucking with you, Takoda."

For the second time, we both laughed.

"All right, smartass. Enough of that. Can I *ask* you some questions?"

He nodded, but I caught a flicker of apprehension as it crossed his eyes.

"The wrapper." I brought the baggie forward, presenting it on my lap. "What can you tell me about it? How do you know this didn't just blow off the street and land at the door?"

Charlie's whole body coiled with tension at the sight of the wrapper, and I second-guessed my decision to bring it up at all.

Charlie clung to my hand with a death grip. With his free one, he reached out and touched the baggie. Even in the poor light, I could tell he'd lost a few shades of color. His eyes were haunted.

"Someone rang the doorbell. It was on the stoop. A rock held it down."

"So you think it was left deliberately?"

He nodded.

"Are you sure you heard the bell? Your dad said he didn't hear anything."

"He was asleep." With another lick to his lips, Charlie made a noise of frustration. "I can't talk well. My head's really fuzzy."

"You're doing great."

"I don't like these meds."

I ground my teeth and said as evenly as I could, "Neither do I."

Our eyes locked. It was brief, but something I couldn't name passed between us. Charlie looked down again and continued. "I was cooking dinner. Dad was napping. I heard it. The bell. I know I did. I'm not imagining it. I'm not crazy."

"I believe you. There was a rock on top?"

"Yes. Nobody was there."

"Why is this wrapper significant, Charlie? What can you tell me about it? If someone left it for you, why this particular candy bar? What does it mean?"

His forehead creased, and he shook his head. "I... I can't explain it. It's... a feeling. A bad feeling. I have these... flashes. I don't know what to call them. They're"—he paused and made a face—"memories, but they aren't solid. If I try to capture them, it's like trying to hold water in my hand. Sometimes it's easier to touch them from far away."

I glanced at the doorway. Archie and Sofia were still there. Archie was gnawing his thumbnail. Sofia seemed to be analyzing every aspect of our encounter.

I wasn't sure what Charlie meant, but I let it go because he was talking, which seemed more important than anything.

"I'm going to run this for fingerprints." The lie tasted bitter on my tongue. "Then I'll make this all go away somehow. No one's going to hurt you. Not again. I'll, um, find whoever did this and deal with them. I think it's just a prank. An ugly, terrible prank, but I want you to know I'm making it my number one priority. Does that help?"

Charlie pressed his lips together, his face pinched as he scowled at the wrapper.

"Charlie?"

He lifted his chin and met my eyes. His fear wasn't fake. He truly believed a threat existed. Had he heard the doorbell? Had there been a rock sitting on top of the wrapper? If so, was Charlie really imagining this, or was there real danger out there? How could I dismiss it?

"You believe me?"

"Yeah."

"For real? You aren't just saying that to make me feel better?"

I paused, the voices of Detective Graveman, my sergeant, and Charlie's father rolling around in my head. What made me hesitate was the fact that I did believe him.

"For real, but you need to trust I will handle it. Can you do that?"

"Yes."

"Good."

It was time to go, but the act of releasing Charlie's hand was more difficult than I anticipated. He seemed to be leaching strength from our connection. When I'd entered the room, he'd been far away. I couldn't help thinking that if I let go, he'd slip back into the darkness of his mind, that maybe I was the one thing anchoring him in place.

I gave his hand a gentle squeeze and peeled mine away. When I stood, Charlie remained sitting. His gaze drifted to the fountain, and the light played across his face.

"I'll call you real soon, Charlie. I promise."

He didn't respond until I was halfway to the door.

His voice drifted through the room on a cloud of drugs. "Thank you, Takoda."

In the hallway, Archie couldn't stop staring at me with wonder like I'd performed some miracle.

"What?" I asked, keeping my voice down.

"How?"

I glanced at Sofia then back to Charlie's dad. "How what?"

"He's barely spoken three words in a week. You just had a full twenty-minute conversation with him."

I peered back into the shadowy depths of Charlie's room and shrugged. I didn't have an answer for him, but I did know I was going to do what I could to put Charlie's mind at ease. None of this was fair. I didn't want to play this game anymore. Maybe Charlie was a privileged rich kid, but he hadn't exactly had a perfect rich-kid life. He'd been through hell. He had demons darker than any I'd ever seen. And I seemed to be the only person willing to acknowledge his issues and not bury them under Xanax.

I studied Archie for another minute before piercing Sofia with a hard glare. "Stop fucking drugging him. He doesn't like it."

Then I marched down the stairs and left.

Eight

CHARLIE

The second gift arrived the following Monday.

My head was cloudy. My teeth hurt from the constant pressure of trying to stay focused, and I couldn't write. Sofia had cut back the Xanax, but I was still encouraged to take a low dose each morning and again later in the day. It was easier to go along with her request than fight with Dad over how it made me feel. He worried, and I didn't like it when he worried.

So every minute of my day was like trudging through calf-deep mud.

I'd stared at my computer for hours without writing a single thing. I'd sketched some new creatures—because that was easier and didn't require the same brainpower—and I'd thought about Takoda.

I'd thought *a lot* about Takoda.

He'd called me three times since his visit Friday. *"Just checking in,"* he'd say. It was nice of him, and I couldn't deny how his phone calls made me feel. When I'd inquired about his progress, he'd explained how fingerprint analysis took time and that he didn't have answers yet.

In the long hours of drifting—which was how I liked to think of the times I could do nothing more than stare into space—I thought of him. His warm, strong hands holding mine, keeping me grounded so I didn't fly away into the abyss. His smile. His hickory eyes that seemed to see beyond the messed-up person everyone else saw. Sage and sweetgrass.

And his laugh.

Every time I ventured back to those few minutes we'd sat together in my bedroom, that fluttering warmth low in my belly returned. It made me short of breath but not in a bad way. All those sensations were new and... pleasant.

I wasn't stupid. I understood I felt a strong attraction to the younger officer. I just didn't know how to process it all. After what had happened to me when I was a kid, I rarely experienced those types of feelings. I noticed good-looking men on TV. I understood that likely meant I was gay since I didn't have the same reaction to women, but I'd never had a relationship. My teenage years weren't the same as other teenagers'. Fear kept a noose around my neck most days. The idea of having a relationship or exploring sexual activities had always been too unfathomable. There had never been an inclination. The barrier inside my mind seemed to completely block out those desires. Or they had, until now, which was why I was fumbling to understand what happened every time Takoda was near.

All I knew was I liked it when he was around. When he touched me. He made me feel safe.

And he made me curious.

The alarm on my phone sounded, reminding me to take my next handful of pills. I didn't usually require an alarm, but with my head so foggy, it helped. I abandoned my computer and headed to the bathroom.

With my next dose lined up in my palm, I turned on the tap, then stalled. Instead of taking the half-pill of Xanax, I plucked it from the pile and dropped it down the drain. A shot of adrenaline zipped through my system. I'd never done anything like that before, and if Dad ever suspected I was ditching pills, he'd insist I relinquish control and hand-feed them to me.

I stared at the drain. Maybe I shouldn't have done that.

I considered fishing another from the bottle, but the cloud in my brain was so annoying. Those damn pills were doing more harm than good. At the current rate, I'd never meet my deadlines. Dad would tell my publisher, and they would understand and push the date, but I didn't want special privileges. I just wanted to feel better.

I took the remaining pills—my usual ones—and headed downstairs, making a circuit of checking locks. My work schedule was off, and I couldn't sit in that stuffy room anymore while the walls pressed in and the air grew thicker.

I found my way to Dad's workroom and stood in the open doorway, watching as he filed a long, thin, gray piece of plastic I could only assume was part of an airplane wing. He was hunched over the table under a bright spotlight made from the two desk lamps. An old radio sat on top of a display case in the corner, playing the Bee Gees. Dad hummed along as he worked.

"I'm going to run to the supermarket and find something for dinner," I said when Dad sat back, examining his work.

"Huh?" He shifted on his stool, peering over his reading glasses. "No, you aren't. You can't drive when you're taking Xanax. You know that."

I wrung my hands and shuffled. "I'm fine."

"You're not. You aren't driving, kiddo. If we need groceries, I'll go in a bit. Let me just finish this wing."

"It's fine. Never mind. I'll find something here to cook."

Dad sighed, studied me a minute more, then swung around to face his project again. "You doing all right?"

"I'd be doing better if I didn't have to take the Xanax anymore. I can't work. I can't think. I'm not... I'm okay now. Takoda, I mean, Officer Dyani is working on it. Everything is back to normal. I'm not anxious." I sounded anxious.

Dad glanced back again, a small lift in his brow. "You've been chatting with that boy a lot this week, haven't you?"

"A few times. He can't tell me anything yet, but he's working on it."

"Mmhmm."

"What?"

Dad stared for another minute before shaking his head and shifting around again. "Nothing. I'm glad you feel comfortable with him. I know you were upset about Stanley not handling things anymore."

"Officer Dyani is a competent police officer. I'm not upset any longer."

"Is there a reason for your quick change of heart?"

I paused, my heartrate speeding up. "What do you mean?"

Dad set down his file and picked up a small square of sandpaper. It was the kind that worked with water, and he dunked it in a bowl. "I mean, he seems friendly."

"He is friendly."

"Are you being coy, or should I spell out what I mean?"

I stayed quiet, gnawing my lip.

Dad shifted his attention to me, and my cheeks warmed. I guessed by the way he glanced at them that they'd turned a deep red. He shifted back to his airplane. "Mmhmm. That's what I thought."

"I'll find something here for dinner," I said, not wanting to examine that line of questioning further.

I left Dad to his models and headed back to the stairs, detouring through the kitchen and every other room on the main floor, performing a ritual I couldn't seem to break. At the front door, I clicked the lock, but before I headed upstairs, I clicked it again, unlocking it. It was after three. The mailman should have come by, and I didn't think Dad had taken a break in a few hours to check the mailbox.

Before opening the door, I checked the peephole—another habit. No one was there, so I went outside. The spring day was crisp and cool. The air pebbled goose bumps along my arms when I stepped out on the stoop. My short-sleeved cotton polo wasn't warm enough, and the breeze cut through it.

Ms. LaPointe was sitting on the edge of her garden, picking weeds and grooming her new flowers. She glanced up and waved. "Hi, Charlie."

"Hi, Ms. LaPointe. How are you today?"

"I'm just dandy. Beautiful out, isn't it? I think we're finally going to get to keep this nice weather."

"Looks like."

She returned to her work, so I focused on my task.

The mailbox was attached to the wall beside the garage. Dad had said a hundred times he wanted to move it because it was a pain in the ass to get at when it snowed, but it was all words. I stepped off the stoop and made my way to the box.

It was mounted high enough on the wall that when I lifted the black lid, I had to stand on my toes to glance inside. There were no envelopes, no packages, no flyers or coupons, but at the bottom was a small yellow box.

Frowning, I dipped my fingers inside, snagged its edge, and drew it out. Crayola, it read. But it wasn't crayons. It was a small box of colorful pieces of chalk.

My reaction was instant and driven by an unconscious fear I couldn't name or understand.

I dropped the little yellow box, and the mailbox lid slammed closed on my fingers as I stumbled back a step. Tremors racked my entire body, and my lungs shriveled, stealing my ability to take a full breath.

It was the wrapper all over again.

In a flash, the cool air that had once pebbled my skin burned. My insides erupted in flames, and my palms turned slick.

I had just enough conscious thought to understand I was diving fast into a state of full-blown panic. Again. My tremulous control was slipping, and if I didn't calm down, I'd end up right back where I was a week ago. Days and days of cottonmouth and disconnected thoughts. Maybe Sofia would have me admitted and monitored.

No!

I had to fight back. I couldn't let this happen again. Pinching my eyes closed, I worked through all the breathing exercises I'd been taught. Counting. Breathing. Counting again. The world spun and tilted, but a small, insignificant part of my brain reminded me to just keep breathing, and it would pass.

My feet threatened to go out from under me, so I reached for the garage door. But I was unstable, and I tripped, clattering against it and making an awful racket.

"Charlie? Charlie, hun, are you okay?"

Ms. LaPointe.

With all my effort, I blinked the world back into focus as I found my feet. My knees knocked, but I managed to stand without leaning on the garage. Chest heaving. Beads of perspiration popping up all over.

"I'm okay," I said before she rushed over or called for my dad. "Just a little dizzy. I'm fine."

I watched her out of the corner of my eye until she returned to her garden. Panic had its claws in me, and I was barely holding on. The urge to escape, disconnect, or hide was powerful.

But the pills. I didn't want the pills again.

Or the ward.

I could do this. I could remain present.

With another stabilizing breath, I lifted the mailbox lid and trawled around inside until my fingers touched the box. I pulled it out. My hands shook.

Distorted memories slashed across my brain. But that was all they were. Distorted. I couldn't pin them down or find any clarity. They were nothing more than flashes, unclear sensations, and an overload of emotions.

Front and center was fear.

I darted my gaze along the street in both directions, knowing there was a threat out there, feeling it alive in my bones.

The street was calm. The day was bright. Nothing was out of the ordinary.

I pulled myself together the best I could and approached my neighbor while holding a death grip on the box of Crayola chalk. "Ms. LaPointe?"

My elderly neighbor lifted her head, a hand moving to keep her overly large sunhat in place as she looked out from under its wide brim. "Yes, dear?"

"Did you…" Dark spots blurred my vision, but I blinked them away. "Did you see someone put something in the mailbox?"

She glanced behind me to the box in question, but she was already shaking her head. "The mailman hasn't been by yet, love. Morty is on holiday this week. We have that stand-in again. Last time she did his route, she was always much later. Remember?"

"Oh. Okay."

"Is something the matter? You look awfully pale."

"No, no. Not at all. I'm fine."

I clung tight to the little box, my fingers slick.

"Charlie, dear, where's your father? You don't look well."

"I'm fine. Really." I forced a shaky smile and moved toward the house. "Have a nice day, Ms. LaPointe. Your flowers look lovely."

"Oh, thank you, dear," she called as I went inside.

I paced toward Dad's workroom, backtracked to the front door, changed course again, then stopped to catch my breath as I decided what to do.

If I told Dad, he would call Sofia. If Sofia came, and if they thought I was slipping, they'd want me to take more Xanax. Would they believe me if I told them someone had left this for me on purpose? It was like the wrapper. The exact same uncomfortable feelings were uprooting my panic.

They wouldn't believe me. They would pretend to, but the truth would show in their eyes.

Instead of going to Dad, I found the car keys and slipped on a pair of loafers. At the front door, I stalled. The door. I'd forgotten to lock it. My insides twisted and churned.

I threw it open and locked it behind me. In the driver's seat, I glanced back at the house. Dad would kill me, but I knew the only person who would truly listen was Takoda.

I started the car, threw it in reverse, and backed out of the driveway. My head was mush, my insides felt like they'd gone through a blender, but somehow I made it to the police station in one piece. The entire drive, I clutched the box of chalk in my fist until my fingers cramped.

Somewhere on the distant planes of sanity, I thought I should be watching for someone following me, but I was down to simple, basic commands and couldn't process beyond, *Drive the car. Tell Takoda.*

At the station, I registered my frantic tone when I demanded the guy at the front desk get Officer Dyani.

"I have to talk to him. Now. I have to talk to him right now. It can't wait. It's important."

"Charlie, why don't you—"

"No! Call him. Get him here. I'm not crazy," I shouted. But I sounded crazy even to me.

The younger officer on the other side of the plexiglass window kept an eye on me as he picked up the phone. I'd seen that look on other people's faces before.

My heart jackhammered as I clutched the box to my chest, trying to calm down, trying not to wear the wild eyes my dad said were telling. I hated when people categorized me as a freak. *Charlie Falkingham is a little insane*. I'd heard the rumors.

"Have a seat, Charlie," the man said, his tone snappy. "Officer Dyani is on his way."

I couldn't sit. I felt like I was ten seconds from passing out or having a heart attack. Instead, I paced.

The door to the back of the precinct buzzed a few minutes later, and I jolted as the sound rippled through my body. Takoda came through, looking stunning in his uniform, tattoos on display. I'd never thought of anyone as stunning before, and had I not been on the cusp of losing my mind, I might have taken a second longer to analyze that.

Takoda's hickory eyes landed on me. He must have seen something in my face—maybe I had the wild eyes despite my efforts not to—because he raced to my side, concern digging grooves in his forehead.

"Charlie? Whoa. Whoa. Hey. You don't look so good. Let's get you sitting down, okay."

He took my hand, and instantly I could breathe easier. Guiding me to the chairs along the window, Takoda encouraged me to take a seat. He sat beside me, our bodies positioned so we faced one another, our knees connecting. It was then I realized how badly I was shaking. Sweating. Panting.

Hearing Takoda's voice, feeling his warm hand around mine, smelling the essence of sage and sweetgrass, my heart found a calmer rhythm. The sharp claws of panic retracted. I was safe with Takoda. He'd promised to protect me. He'd told me no one would hurt me again, and I believed him.

I was safe. I was safe.

Exhausted from the fight to maintain control, my body wanted to shut down and take a break. Retreat and turn off altogether. I drifted. I couldn't help it. I didn't go far inside my head, but far enough I could reset.

I was safe. I was safe.

Takoda's voice cut into the darkness. "Hey. Charlie. Stay with me. Stay here." Warm fingers brushed my cheek, calling me back. "That's it. There you are. Look at me. Can you look at me?"

I could, and I did. His hickory eyes were full of warmth and understanding, but they were also brimming with concern.

"Hi," he said when my vision cleared.

"Hi."

"What's going on? Did something happen?"

The icy fingers of panic scratched down my spine, and I shivered. Takoda's hand tightened around mine.

I held out my other hand, presenting the object inside.

Takoda glanced down. It took effort to open my fingers. They ached from the death grip I'd held on the box since pulling it from the mailbox.

Takoda helped, peeling my fingers up one at a time and taking the Crayola box.

He turned it in his hand, a deep furrow in his brow. When he looked up and studied my face, he must have recognized all I wasn't saying. "Another gift." Not a question but a realization.

I nodded, unable to find my voice.

"Where did you find it?"

"My mailbox."

Takoda studied the box of chalk, wetting his lips before asking, "What can you tell me about it?"

I opened and closed my mouth, unable to explain something abstract and unclear.

Takoda glanced up when I didn't speak. "Is it like the wrapper?"

"Yes. I just… I don't know how to explain."

"It's a feeling?"

"Yes."

"This means something to you, right? And it's not good."

I nodded. "It's bad."

"Okay." He paused for a long time. "I'm going to… Can I hang on to it? I think maybe I need to talk to a detective and get some advice."

"Okay."

Takoda seemed to be thinking hard. His jaw was tight, and his lips were pressed into a firm line as he stared in the vicinity of the box without looking at it.

After a long few minutes, he met my eyes. "Are you okay?"

I considered. The panic had lessened, but it wasn't gone. "Not really. I didn't tell my dad I left. I came right here. If he thinks I'm panicking again, he'll call Sofia."

A flash of anger crossed Takoda's face. "Are they still drugging you?"

I shrugged. "A little. Just a small dose."

"If you don't want to take those drugs, you don't take them. Do you hear me? That's your choice, Charlie. Not theirs."

"It gets bad sometimes. They're just trying to help."

Takoda sighed. He didn't seem to agree. "Did you drive here like this?"

I nodded. "I shouldn't have. My head is still foggy."

"All right. I'm going to take you home, make sure you get there safely, and I'll check out the house while I'm there. Then I'm going to talk to some people about this." He held up the box of chalk. "It would really help if you could tell me more."

I glanced at the object in his hand, but there was no breaking through the barrier in my mind. All I knew was it was important. "I can't. I'm sorry."

He squeezed my hand. "It's okay. I'll figure it out."

Nine

TAKODA

I left Charlie in the lobby and headed back to my temporary desk. I'd put the candy bar wrapper in a locked drawer on Friday, unsure what else to do with it. I'd told Charlie I was running it for prints, but I was sure I'd get laughed out of the station if I brought it to Nikola.

Now I had two items, and I didn't for a second think Charlie was bullshitting me about their significance.

After finding an evidence bag, I slipped the box of chalk inside, knowing it had already been overhandled. I locked it inside the drawer with the wrapper. Once I dropped Charlie off, I planned to have a conversation with the sergeant. If he didn't take me seriously, maybe I'd consult with one of our detectives to see what they thought. If worse came to worse, I'd go back to Graveman. He'd listen.

Evidence suggested something was happening, and I couldn't shove it aside anymore without risking Charlie's safety.

When I returned up front, Charlie was fiddling with his phone. He glanced up, his winter-sky eyes the picture of worry. "Dad called," he said. "He's angry."

"About?"

"Take your pick. I drove when I shouldn't have. I'm harassing you about imaginary problems. I didn't tell him I was leaving the house." Charlie shrugged.

"I'll talk to him."

"You don't need to do that. I can handle my father. I'm not incapable." He glanced down at his phone again. "You must think I'm a piece of work."

"Cut that shit out. If I thought you were a piece of work, I'd tell you to your face. I don't exactly sugarcoat things. See that guy at the desk? That's Henley. *He's* a piece of work. Ain't that right, Henley?"

I grinned as my colleague shot me the finger.

"See? Asshole. You know who else is a piece of work? My boss. He's a real fucking dick. Ask Henley. He agrees with me."

"Fuck off, Dyani. Don't drag me into your problems. I have enough of my own." Henley sneered from behind the computer.

When I caught a hint of a smile on Charlie's face, I knew he'd be all right.

"So trust me when I say you aren't a piece of work. Come on. Let's get you home so I can take care of this."

Charlie peered up from under long lashes. There was something about the way he looked at me that made me shuffle my feet. There was depth to those haunted, gray-blue eyes, and they pulled at me.

He followed me out the back door of the precinct and into the parking lot. In the passenger seat of a cruiser, he twisted his fingers together and stared out the window. I didn't know what he was thinking, but I had to fight the urge to rest a hand on his thigh to keep him calm.

"I'm worried," he said as we turned onto the main road.

"I know. Honestly, I think someone is trying to pull a prank. It's probably nothing."

"How would they know the significance of those items? Even I can't explain it."

I stayed quiet. He was right, and I was stupid to think I could play it off so easily.

"I'm going to take care of this."

He kept his chin down the rest of the ride.

When I turned onto Charlie's street, a car, parked a short way down the road from his house, caught my attention. A white Pontiac

Grand Prix. It was facing the opposite direction, idling. Charlie didn't notice since he was staring at his hands, but I saw it plain as day. Alarm bells rang inside my head.

The minute I drew closer, the car pulled away, unrushed, and continued down the road, turning onto a street a few blocks down and vanishing from sight.

Instinct told me to step on the gas and find out who the fuck it was and why they were hanging out in this neighborhood, but I knew it would freak Charlie out, especially since I'd told him the car was nothing to worry about.

I reached for the radio, then pulled my hand back, calculating what I was going to do. A fucking white Pontiac, just like Charlie had said. Jesus Christ. All this shit was starting to make *me* paranoid.

"Takoda?"

I cleared my throat and refocused, pulling the cruiser to the curb in front of Charlie's house. My brain was spinning at a million miles a minute. In essence, it all seemed ridiculous when I considered Charlie's mental health problems and everyone's warnings that this was how Charlie acted on the regular. What did I have? A chocolate bar wrapper. A box of chalk. A random car.

"Is everything okay?" Charlie's voice was soft and tentative.

"Just thinking."

Archie Falkingham came out onto the front stoop and stood with his arms crossed, glaring in our direction.

"How about I get you inside? Do you mind if I have a look around? I want to make sure all your locks are working properly."

Charlie bit back a smile, and his pale cheeks took on color as he glanced down at his hands again, working his delicate fingers so aggressively I feared he'd snap one of the fragile bones in half.

Without thinking too much about it, I laid a hand over his, stopping the anxious fidgeting. "Stop. You're going to hurt yourself."

Charlie glanced up from under his long lashes. There was a lull where neither of us spoke.

Charlie cleared his throat. "I assure you, the locks on all the windows and doors function perfectly. It's, um... it's part of my paranoia or OCD or whatever. I check them at least four or five times a day. All of them." More color rose to his cheeks. "I know it's obsessive, and it drives my dad batty, but..." He shrugged and dropped his chin again. "I can't help it."

I could tell he was embarrassed, and I wanted to reassure him somehow. When he wouldn't look up, I did something that surprised me again. I tucked a finger under his chin and encouraged him to lift his head.

His skin was warm.

"Hey, if that makes you feel safer, then there's nothing wrong with it."

For a long minute, we stared at one another, neither of us moving to get out of the car. I couldn't explain what it was about Charlie that calmed me down when everyone else in the world seemed to rile me up. It didn't make sense, especially when I considered he lived under the same umbrella of privilege that made me hate most people.

Maybe it was his vulnerability. Maybe it was how he'd placed all his trust in me without knowing me at all.

Maybe it was that I'd failed Odina and Calian, and I didn't want to fail Charlie too.

Whatever it was, I couldn't explain it.

"Come on. I'm going to talk to your dad. You go check all those locks for me, okay?"

"Okay."

The look Archie pinned on me could have melted iron. I didn't think for a second he'd missed the way I'd touched Charlie in the car. It was nothing, just a touch, but my actions had awoken the fierce and protective fatherly lion.

When Charlie met his dad on the front stoop, Archie dragged his gaze from me and glared at his son. "I started making dinner. Would you go check it for me? I need to have a word with Officer Dyani."

"Yes, father. After I check the locks."

"For crying out loud, you don't—"

"I asked him to."

Archie turned his attention to me. I held my ground. Guys like Archie Falkingham didn't scare me. He thought he was special. He thought he was better. Maybe Graveman had been right. I wore the uniform because it gave me authority over people. It put me a step above them instead of ten steps below where I'd been my whole life.

"Inside, Charlie," the older man said.

Charlie met my eyes, and I gave him a reassuring smile. "I'll be in touch as soon as I know something. I promise."

"Thank you, Takoda."

As he passed his father, Charlie squeezed the man's arm.

Then Charlie was gone.

Archie and I didn't speak right away. Archie glared while I glared back. We were two alpha men, standing our ground, each of us trying to out dominate the other.

"Why did my son run off to the station without telling me first?"

"Do you want me to sugarcoat the answer for you, or do you want the truth?"

When he didn't respond, I shrugged.

"The truth is, Charlie felt threatened again, and he feared if he went to you, you'd call his doctor and have him drugged to the gills. I told you. He doesn't like that shit. Stop fucking drugging him."

"You shouldn't voice an opinion about things you don't understand."

"Oh, I understand plenty. Charlie is a grown-ass man, and he's able to express himself just fine. Now, are we going to talk about the real problem?"

Archie checked over his shoulder before his posture lost some of its rigid edges. "Tell me what happened."

"He received another gift." When Archie looked like he was about to interrupt, I held up a hand. "I know we didn't think the wrapper was anything important, but I think we were wrong. The way Charlie describes it, it was left intentionally, and we both know the reaction it caused.

"Today, he found a box of Crayola chalk in the mailbox. That was no accident. Charlie experienced the same visceral reaction. That isn't a coincidence. Both times, it called on something he couldn't explain because it was rooted in his past. Whoever left those items is making a statement."

Archie's brow furrowed as he listened. I saw the moment he'd gone from skeptical to concerned.

"Third. The white Pontiac."

Archie shook his head. "There is no way it's related. Charlie has always—"

"It was here when I pulled up, idling a few houses down. When it saw the cruiser, it took off. Charlie didn't notice, and had I gone after it like I wanted to, it would have freaked him out." I glanced down the road where the car had vanished earlier. "It's probably long gone now, but I saw it too. He's not imagining it."

"What are you telling me?"

"I'm telling you that I can't ignore this and lie and brush it under the rug anymore. I'm going to talk to my sergeant when I get back to the station to see what he thinks."

Archie nodded, his head bobbing.

"In the meantime, it would be best if Charlie didn't go off on his own." I shifted my weight. "Also, the clearer his mind, the better he's able to notice if things aren't right."

"I hear you loud and clear, Dyani. Don't drug him." Archie sighed. "I can't promise anything. You don't know what it's like when Charlie spirals."

"Call me. Before you resort to stuffing him full of drugs, call me."

"Because you have the miracle cure now?"

I thought of Charlie's hands in mine and the way he'd looked at me. I thought of the heavy slur in his voice when he'd tried to talk to me a few days ago. "You could let me try."

Archie scratched his jaw, his nails rasping the silver scruff. Then he studied me for a long minute. "Can I say something without you getting wildly offended?"

My spine stiffened, but I waited.

"I see the way Charlie looks at you. The way he talks about you. And I'm worried."

My skin grew hot, and part of me wanted to tell Archie to shut up because I'd changed my mind, and I didn't want to hear this.

"I've known Charlie was gay since he was five years old. I'm not a close-minded bigot. I love him no matter how God made him. Everything changed after he was taken. They did things to my boy that were enough to destroy a father's heart. I've never felt so helpless in my life. Charlie has never been the same. When most teenagers started dating and learning how relationships worked, I was still trying to get my boy to talk to me and stay present for more than ten minutes at a time. He came back in bits and pieces. But when he did, he wasn't a typical teenager. Then he wasn't a typical adult. I figured those people had irreparably ruined that part of him. He's showed no interest in relationships or cute boys on the TV or sex. He's been stunted in a way. I always thought he would be forever a child in that regard since I've never seen any indication otherwise." He paused. "Until now."

I couldn't stop fidgeting. The whole conversation made me uncomfortable, and I didn't think Charlie would appreciate his father telling me all this.

"What I'm trying to say is, until you came along, there had been no sign of sexual interest from him whatsoever."

"Sir, I'm not sure—"

"Listen to me, son. I know you've got eyes on my boy, and I see the way he looks at you too. I've watched you both together a few times now. I'm telling you this so you understand what you're getting yourself into."

"There is nothing there, sir."

Archie huffed a laugh. "You can lie to me all you want, Dyani, but I'm not a stupid man. Understand that if this goes anywhere, Charlie is extremely inexperienced. If you push too hard, it could be triggering. I don't know for sure because we haven't had to deal with it yet. I'm not telling you to back off, Takoda. I'm telling you to be mindful of how you approach this. That's all."

Part of me wanted to deny everything because there was no way I'd developed those kinds of feelings. I wasn't that type of guy. Charlie was cute, and there was a pull between us, but... Archie was wrong.

However, instead of correcting him, when I opened my mouth, all I said was, "Yes, sir."

Archie didn't say anything more, and all I wanted to do was run back to the cruiser and take off. It was a lot to process, especially since I hadn't properly acknowledged my interest in Charlie even to myself. It was there, in the back of my mind, but I'd dismissed it.

"Please tell Charlie to be careful for the time being. I'm going to see what my sergeant says. Let him know I'll call him soon."

"I will."

* * *

Nikola rubbed a finger up and down the middle of his forehead as he stared at the two evidence bags I'd placed on his desk. I'd told him the whole story. When I'd requested submitting them to our forensic department for analysis, he'd laughed and shaken his head.

I'd held my tongue at the last minute before I told him to go fuck a donkey. Now, I was waiting for instructions since I was technically an "out of commission" officer who wasn't supposed to be doing anything more than other people's paperwork.

"I'm going to be honest with you, Dyani. You've got nothing."

I clenched my jaw.

"I explained how it works with Charlie. Acting on this is doing nothing more than feeding his delusions."

"You're wrong. Archie sees it too."

"Because you've given him a reason to be skeptical. He worries about his son. Look at this." He picked up the Ziplock bag with the chocolate bar wrapper. "You have a piece of garbage that blew in off the street." He nudged the second bag with a finger. "And some kids' box of crayons."

"It's chalk. Sir."

"Did you consider this probably belongs to a neighbor's kid, and maybe someone found it and returned it to the wrong house?"

I balled my hands into fists. "No, sir. But it doesn't explain the way Charlie reacted."

Nikola sighed. "Charlie is sick. He's mentally unstable. He sees danger in the wind when it ruffles the leaves on the trees. We've been doing this with him for over a decade. I'm telling you, you can't take his word on these things."

"Agree to disagree, sir. I also have reason to believe the car he claims was following him is indeed following him. If you'd give me permission to work on this further, maybe I could find answers."

Nikola shoved the bags aside. "I'm not wasting taxpayer dollars on this nonsense. I appreciate that you've taken this liaison work seriously. For once, I'm seeing a decent human being behind that badge, and it's refreshing, but I can't justify this."

"Sir, I have reason to believe someone is stalking Charlie. Maybe I'm wrong, but what if I'm right? How would Elizabeth Falkingham feel about you dismissing a potential threat to her son?"

Nikola's face turned dangerously hostile. "Elizabeth would tell you this was nothing. Elizabeth is the one who suggested this course of action years ago, so don't think you can threaten me into action. You have nothing here. As far as I'm concerned, you need to placate Charlie like we always have and move on."

"Yeah. Fine." I snatched the evidence bags off the desk and left my sergeant's office, slamming the door behind me.

I paced, ignoring the subtle glances from other officers and the handful of detectives working at their desks. Everyone was so convinced this was nothing.

Before talking to Nikola, I'd run my suspicions by Wan, one of the younger detectives and a guy I got along with better than most. He'd listened, but after hearing my concerns, he'd told me he couldn't do anything without Nikola's permission. He'd also delicately suggested I let it go since it was a well-known fact that Charlie was paranoid, and didn't I know this was typical behavior?

In the end, I locked the wrapper and chalk back inside the bottom drawer of the desk and headed to the basement and our records room. Maybe no one wanted to help me out, but it didn't mean I was ready to shove it aside. My first order of business was to learn what I could about Charlie's past and the incident from when he was a kid. I wanted to know what had happened to the guys responsible because, for whatever reason, all these items seemed to tie back to that time in Charlie's life. Someone from his past was making an appearance again.

The administration desk outside the records room was occupied by Celia Bright, an elderly woman with frizzy gray hair that always resembled a bird's nest and glasses on a silver chain around her neck. She reeked of old lady perfume.

When she smiled, her yellowing teeth were smudged with crimson lipstick. Celia was in charge of screening civilians when they requested access to certain public records. It was my guess that she spent most of her days filing her nails and doing crossword puzzles. It wasn't like there was a lot of traffic coming through this section of the station.

I scooted around the desk with a tight smile and a greeting before swiping my card, unlocking the secured room where decades worth of files lived. We'd only switched to electronic filing six years ago. None of the older records had been uploaded, so I knew Charlie's case would be somewhere among the chaos inside.

Rows and rows of steel shelves lined the room. They were filled with thousands of brown folders, all with colorful plastic tags sticking out. Being a basement room with four concrete walls, a concrete floor, and no windows, it was dark and musty. Damp and cool. The fluorescent light overhead flickered nauseatingly. Dust and the strong scent of mildew tickled my nose.

I walked among the tightly packed aisles, checking tags and searching for the appropriate section for the year Charlie was taken. When I found it, I sighed.

I didn't know a month or a specific date, so I was going to be stuck plucking each and every file off the shelf to peek inside.

"Fuck me." I smoothed a hand over my hair and considered my approach.

Before I began, I poked my head out the door and found Celia shelling peanuts as she read the latest edition of some tabloid magazine.

"Hey," I called, grabbing her attention. "You've been here since the dawn of time, right?"

She blinked away from her article, her crimson lips puckering. "Twenty-seven years. Why?"

"You remember the Charlie Falkingham case?"

She peeled her glasses off her nose, showcasing her watery blue eyes, clouded with cataracts. "Of course I do. A horrible, horrible thing that was."

"I'm trying to find it, but I don't know the specific date. Any chance you remember?"

"I'll do you one better, young man."

She left her magazine on the desk and pulled herself upright. She was hunched and shuffled when she walked. I didn't know how old Celia Bright was, but if I had to guess, I'd have said she left her sixties behind years ago.

Her overbearing perfume choked me as she shoved me aside and shuffled into the room. She did a quick scan then took off to the section where I'd stopped looking.

Holding her glasses in place, she muttered and traced her finger along each tab, then she plucked a folder off the shelf. "Ah, here we go."

It was thick, and the edges were soft and frayed like it had seen a great deal of attention at one time.

Celia stared at the file with a look of remorse. "Poor boys," she said. "Of all the horrors in the world, there is nothing worse than a crime against children." She *tsk*ed and passed me the folder. "If you're taking that out of here, you need to sign a form."

"I know the rules."

I went through the process of checking out the old file and headed back upstairs to my temporary desk to go over it. I stopped at the vending machine on my way by and grabbed a Mountain Dew. I got the feeling I'd need something much stronger by the time I was finished reviewing the case.

I wasn't wrong.

Three hours later, my eyes burned, and my muscles ached from held tension. I had a notepad filled with names, and my mind was turning over so many thoughts I was having trouble keeping track of them.

The man responsible for kidnapping the children and organizing the sex-trafficking ring was Mateo Fabian. He'd been arrested during the takedown, along with several other men, and had later died in prison. A lot of inmates drew the line when it came to fucking with children. And this Mateo asshole had taken his operation to the *n*th degree.

The children, other than Charlie, had all been killed when Fabian and his crew had set off explosives in an attempt to cover evidence and cause a diversion so they could get away.

According to the report, fourteen other arrests were made in conjunction with the ring. Fourteen men who'd been involved to some degree or another. After some research, I'd discovered six of those men had also suffered *accidental* deaths while in prison, three were still doing time for one reason or another, and the last five were out in the world again.

The free men were all registered sex offenders, and a quick search online showed me where each and every one of them resided.

None of them lived in town. Most had set down roots in the greater Toronto area.

When I'd found out Odina had been selling her fifteen-year-old body on the street to creepy old men because she'd needed money, I'd lost my fucking mind. I'd hunted down one of the assholes and beat him to a pulp. He'd ended up in the hospital. He was lucky he was still breathing. I'd hoped in the end that his wife had found out what he'd done. He was just one of any number of privileged suits with more money than brains who'd taken advantage of a desperate teenager down on her luck. If I'd been able to find more of those fuckers, if I'd been able to catch up with the guy who'd left her broken on the street, they'd have all suffered a similar fate.

That was probably the angriest I'd been in my entire life.

Until now.

My blood boiled as I cracked my knuckles and processed all I'd read. Charlie wasn't my baby sister. He wasn't anything to me, but I couldn't shake the intense rage burning in my core when I thought of what had been done to him and the permanent damage it had caused.

A slap on my back made me jump, and I nearly swung around and popped the person in the mouth before I realized where I was and what I was doing.

Kevin must have sensed my agitation. He held up his hands, his eyes widening. "Whoa, man. What's up? I was just passing through and thought I'd say hey. You looked stressed."

My blood pressure came down a notch, but the inner rage burning in my core never left. "I am stressed. I almost broke your fucking face, asshole. Don't sneak up on me like that."

Kevin planted his ass on the corner of the desk, arms crossed over his chest. He scanned the notepad and glimpsed the file I'd been working through.

"What are you doing?"

"Looking into some stuff." I wasn't ready to get into it since everyone seemed to think I'd lost my mind. "What are you doing here?" I glanced around, looking for Corey, only then noticing how quiet it was in the bullpen.

"Clocking out, man. It's after six. Thought you'd be long gone."

"Shit. I lost track of time. Yeah, I should be."

"What are you up to tonight? Wanna grab a beer or something? Maybe head to Cage later?"

I cocked a brow, a smile growing on my face. "You're suggesting Cage? Something I should know?"

Kevin smacked my shoulder with a laugh. "No. For you, bro. You look like you need to wind down." He waggled his eyebrows.

I scanned the bullpen, thinking about the relief a few beers and a warm body might bring.

Then I thought about Charlie and his father's warnings from earlier. I couldn't help thinking that the one thing Archie hadn't vocalized was how I was the last thing Charlie needed.

He was right.

When I considered my empty house and all the heavy information I'd been reading, I knew I was never going to sleep.

"Yeah. Cage sounds good, but… I think I'm going to pass. I've got a date with two cats and *Animal Planet*. Not feeling it tonight."

"Your loss."

I wondered if Kevin would venture there without me.

Ten

CHARLIE

"I thought you said we were going to Stanley's."

The old Escort chugged and rattled as Takoda steered around another corner, weaving slowly down another backstreet in my neighborhood. It was the third loop we'd made since Takoda had pulled out of the driveway.

"We are. I'm just checking the neighborhood before we go."

"How come?"

Takoda's grip on the steering wheel changed. He worked his jaw a few times, but he didn't answer me. He was acting strange. Nervous.

"Takoda?"

He flicked his indicator and turned another corner, crawling down the road in the same fashion. "I'm making sure there is no suspicious activity. No strange vehicles. If someone is leaving things at your front door, you can't be too safe."

"Oh."

I thought of the white Pontiac. I'd seen it again several times, but I'd kept it to myself since Takoda had assured me it was nothing more than a new neighbor.

It had been almost a week since I'd received the box of chalk. Takoda didn't work this weekend, but he'd called me Friday afternoon, asking if I'd go see Stanley with him on Sunday morning. I'd agreed, but when I'd asked how come, Takoda had changed the subject.

At his request, I hadn't left the house all week. Dad had run the errands, and I'd stayed tucked away inside. My obsession with the locks had gotten worse, but Dad hadn't called Sofia. In fact, Dad had been more understanding than usual.

I wasn't taking any Xanax either, and I was managing better, despite the looming threat.

Takoda had called every day this week to check in. When I'd asked for an update, he'd been reserved about what he shared. More than once, he'd dodged my questions and found a way to get off the phone before I realized they'd gone unanswered.

"Are you okay?" I asked when Takoda left my neighborhood and got on one of the major roads that led toward downtown.

Traffic was light, but he drove slower than the speed limit, checking his mirrors to the point of excess.

"Yeah, I'm good. Just being cautious. You haven't been out of the house all week, and I want to make sure no one is following us."

He spared a glance in my direction, a soft smile touching his lips. "Are *you* doing okay?"

I wrung my hands then stopped, trying not to fidget. "I'm fine." After a pause, I added, "Tomorrow's Monday."

Another quick glance. "Yeah? What's that mean?"

"He waited a week before delivering the second gift. Tomorrow is a week again."

Takoda's knuckles whitened before he released a hand and touched my knee. It was nothing more than a graze of his fingertips, but it electrified my skin and burned long after he removed his hand.

"We're on top of this. I don't want you to worry."

"Then why are we going to see Stan? He's retired."

Takoda sighed and seemed to come to a decision. "Because no one is listening to me, and I need his advice." Takoda pinned me with hard hickory eyes. "This doesn't mean I'm not doing all I can. I'm just… having trouble getting help from other people."

I frowned. "People are usually more than willing to help me. I don't understand."

Takoda huffed a humorless laugh. "Yeah. You wouldn't."

"What's that supposed to mean?"

Takoda turned into a new neighborhood. I'd always known where Stanley lived, but my father had warned me a hundred different ways that I was never to go to the man's home, no matter how upset I was.

Takoda gripped the steering wheel tighter, and a low rumble rose from his chest. He didn't answer until he pulled to the curb in front of Stanley's house. Once the car's engine had rattled and died, he turned to me.

It was harder and harder to look Takoda in the eye. Every time I did, my skin buzzed, and my stomach fluttered. His gaze was always so intense. I stared instead at the tattoos along his arms, tracing their swirling designs upward where they vanished beneath his sleeves.

He waited, not saying a thing. I knew he wanted eye contact.

I wet my lips and flashed my attention to his face, our eyes catching. My cheeks warmed.

"I don't want to hurt you," he said after a time, his voice soft and low.

I wasn't sure what he meant, and I squirmed, wondering if he saw through me to all the new sensations rolling through my body every time he was around.

"I don't understand."

He reached out, touching my knee with the tips of his fingers again before withdrawing them. "Look at me, Charlie. This is important."

I swallowed a tight lump and lifted my chin.

"I lied to you."

I frowned.

"It was what I was told to do. The thing is, everyone's lied to you. Your dad, your doctor"—he waved a hand at the house beyond the lawn—"Detective Graveman. Everyone."

Any good feelings I'd had were washed away by a cold tide of fear. "What do you mean?"

"I'm probably going to lose my fucking job for saying this, but someone has to." He clenched his hands into fists. Another long sigh followed. "For years, everyone's been dancing a fucking jig around you, ensuring you're okay. All those times you reported problems, they told you what you wanted to hear just to shut you up. The thing is, they feel responsible for what happened to you as a kid, and your family holds a lot of power in the community, especially with who your mother is. It's been one big fucking rodeo where everyone lies just so you don't go off the rails."

I took a second to process what Takoda was saying. It didn't make sense, yet, somewhere in the back of my mind, it made a world of sense. My stomach clenched.

When I glimpsed my whole adult life from a different angle, it wasn't hard to see the truth.

Was I a joke to everyone? A freak who saw things that weren't there? What did they all see when they looked at me?

Shame like nothing I'd felt before covered me head to toe. Everyone jumped through hoops for poor crazy Charlie. Everyone.

Including Takoda.

"Hey." He reached for my hand, but I pulled away, turning to look out the window. My core was on fire, and my cheeks burned.

"Can you take me home, please?"

"No. I'm not done talking."

"Maybe I'm done hearing it. I don't need to be swaddled and treated like I'm made of glass. If what you're telling me is true, then I probably need to... I don't know... call my doctor or something because I must be more messed up in the head than I realized. She always said my paranoia was... excessive. I guess she was right."

Takoda reached for my hand again, but I dodged him.

"Will you stop that. Shut up and listen to me. I'm telling you this for a reason. I don't think you're crazy, Charlie. They pulled me into this shit and told me what to do, but they can go fuck a cactus for all I care. If I lose my job because I opened my mouth, good riddance. Fuck them. I told you that white Pontiac was nothing. I told you it belonged to some new neighbor because that's what I was coached to say. I didn't want to lie to you then, and I don't want to lie to you now. Will you please look at me?"

It took a long time until I was ready to turn around, but Takoda waited me out. I stared at Stanley's house, a stabbing betrayal pinching my heart. For years, he'd been like a hero to me. Finding out it had all been lies cut deep. I didn't know why Takoda had brought me here, but I wanted to go home. Too many times over the years, I'd wondered if a crazy person knew they were crazy. To me, I was perfectly sane.

So I guess I had my answer.

Eventually, I shifted around and focused on Takoda's tattoos for a minute before dragging my attention to his dark eyes. He was scowling, but there was a hefty amount of concern there too.

"Have you seen the car again?" he asked.

"Yes. Several times. But you said—"

"I know. I think someone's stalking you. I've brought it to my sergeant, but he won't listen to me."

"Because everyone's convinced I'm unstable."

"Maybe. Everyone but me. I think your dad is on our side too. Although he's more reserved about it. Unsure. *Anyways*, I've been looking into things on my own."

"No *s*."

"What?"

"No *s*. The word is *anyway*."

Takoda blinked for several seconds while I fought a smile, then his nose wrinkled with a mock sneer. "*Anyway*. I've been working on it by myself. I've been scouting your neighborhood before and after work, keeping an eye on things. My buddy and his partner drive the few blocks around your neighborhood several times a day too. Sarge doesn't know, and Kevin's doing it as a favor to me. But I think that white Pontiac is something to be wary of."

"Okay. Why are we here?"

"Because, despite his shitty fucking suggestions, Detective Dumbass here cares about you. I think he'll honestly listen if we tell him everything. I need some… Charlie, I don't know what to do next. I'm a stupid fucking beat cop who can barely write a parking ticket without pissing someone off. I have one foot out the door. Short of camping out in front of your house twenty-four seven, I feel like I'm waiting for something more to happen so I can tell my boss 'I told you so.'" Takoda wet his lips, and his gaze shifted away. "But I don't want anything to happen to you, okay."

I took it all in. It was more processing than I could deal with sitting in a car out front of Stanley's house, but Takoda's honesty and concern felt like the first real thing that had happened to me in a long time.

Since my rescue, every moment of my life had been experienced through varying degrees of separation. Layers of protective cushioning my brain had implanted to keep me safe. I knew I acted differently than most. I knew people didn't talk to me like they spoke to their friends or neighbors. Even my dad. I was the fragile baby bird with the broken wing, constantly needing to be rescued or reassured.

Pathetic.

Mentally unsound.

I didn't know how to change.

When Takoda reached for my hand again, I let him take it. His warm fingers wrapped around mine, his thumb brushing my skin in soothing circles.

It was calming, and it stirred those feelings to life in my belly.

"Will you come talk to Stanley with me?"

I nodded. "Yes."

"If at any point you want to leave, you let me know."

"Okay."

Stanley didn't know we were coming, so when he opened the door and found us together, his eyes blew wide. They shifted between us once before settling on Takoda.

"What's going on?" The deep rumble of his voice was familiar, but there was an edge to it I hadn't heard before.

"We need to talk."

"All right." His gaze shifted, and he took a minute to scan me before saying, "How are you doing, Charlie?"

"I'm well. Considering."

Stanley's brows met in the middle. He'd grown a beard since I'd last seen him. It looked good. Distinguished. He waved us in.

Takoda touched my arm, guiding me to the front room like he knew where he was going, and I wondered if he'd been here before. He encouraged me to sit on a cushy brown couch while Stanley lowered himself into a recliner.

Takoda moved toward a dog who was sleeping on a throw rug in front of a crackling fireplace. The golden retriever had slept through our arrival. Detective Graveman had talked about Angel a few times in the past. This was the first time I'd seen her.

Takoda squatted down and brushed his fingers through her fur, scratching her ear and talking in a voice low enough I couldn't make out the words. He continued for several minutes. I glanced at Stanley, who was also watching Takoda. There was a soft look on Stanley's face, an appreciation.

Takoda kissed his fingers and pressed them to the dog's head, then he stood and joined me on the couch, leaving only a small distance between us.

I was aware of every inch.

Takoda leaned forward, bracing his elbows on his knees as he stared at Stanley. "I told Charlie the truth."

Stanley pressed his lips together until they were white as he glared daggers at Takoda. Otherwise, he didn't move a muscle. "Meaning?"

"You know what I mean." Takoda was unaffected by the hostile stare.

For the moment, it was like I wasn't in the room.

"What are you trying to prove, smartass?" Stanley asked.

Not what are you talking about? That stung. It only proved that what Takoda had said in the car was true.

"I think someone is stalking Charlie. If everyone has their way, it'll be swept under the rug like everything else. I can't let that happen."

Stanley seemed to carefully consider Takoda's words. His eyes narrowed, but he didn't flinch or look away.

"I think you should explain yourself before I get on the phone to Sergeant Nikola and tell him what a stupid fucking shit you are."

All the muscles along Takoda's spine stiffened. Before he could snap, I placed a hand on his lower back.

"You will do nothing of the sort, Stanley." My voice came out stronger than I expected. "I know I'm ill. I know I don't perceive things the same way other people do. I know I see danger where there probably isn't. I know I've sought your help a hundred times over the years. And I also know you and everyone else have lied to me. Over and over again. Maybe you thought I'd be too stupid to figure it out. Well, I guess I was because it took Takoda pointing it out before I saw the truth."

"Charlie—" I held up my hand, stopping Stanley's interruption.

"Please listen to what Takoda has to say. I think you owe me that much."

Shame flooded Stanley's eyes. He glanced at his dog for a long time before facing me again and nodding. "You're right. Go ahead."

Takoda inhaled deeply. I gave the small of his back a gentle rub before withdrawing my hand. He glanced at me from over his shoulder, and a tiny smile appeared on his face for a minute before he wiped it clean and turned back to Stanley.

Takoda told him about the two gifts and how I'd received them. He told him about my reactions to each, which made me want to sink into the couch and disappear. Then he told him about the white Pontiac. When Takoda explained about how he'd pulled my old case file from storage and read it, a knot tightened in my belly, and shame heated my face. Although the time I'd spent in captivity was a dark blot in my memory, I knew what had happened. I knew what had been done to me.

Takoda knowing was mortifying.

Almost as mortifying as the talk Dad had had with Takoda almost a week ago. I'd been too curious when Dad had sent me inside so they could chat, so I'd gone upstairs, opened a window, and listened to every horrifying word.

My thoughts spiraled from there. While Takoda and Stanley talked about the men who'd been arrested and locked away, I evaluated every sad detail of my life, expressly focusing on the undeniable attraction I felt for Takoda and what it meant. Dad had been right about a lot of it, even though I was reluctant to admit it. But it wasn't that those sexual parts no longer existed. It was more that I'd turned them down really low so I wouldn't have to deal with them. Even today, I wasn't sure if it was fear or shame that kept me from exploring that part of myself.

But for the first time in my adult life, I couldn't seem to shut it off or pack it away like it didn't exist.

I liked the butterfly wings tickling my belly.

I liked the heat that ran through my veins.

And when Takoda touched me, I couldn't help holding my breath and wondering how much bigger those sensations could grow if I let them.

But how would I handle it? How would I react?

Was I asking for a problem?

"Charlie?" A warm hand on my thigh brought me back, and I gasped, unsure how long I'd been holding my breath while tiptoeing into territory where I had never trusted myself to venture.

Takoda's face was a picture of worry. The furrow in his brow was deep, and I wanted to reach up and smooth it away.

I didn't.

I cleared my throat and tried to smile as I glanced from Takoda to Stanley. "I'm sorry. I was… lost in my head." Words that I knew didn't help my case when I wanted everyone to think of me as rational and sane. "What's going on?"

A flicker of anger came and went in Takoda's eyes. "Detective Graveman wants to call Nikola so they can talk this over."

I met Stanley's eyes as I heard everything Takoda wasn't saying. "You don't believe me."

"I never said that. I'm sorry, Charlie, but the evidence at hand is flimsy at best. I would like to confer with Sergeant Nikola."

"Sergeant Nikola already told Takoda he won't support any of this."

"What do you want me to do? I'm retired. I don't hold power anymore."

"Bullshit."

Detective Graveman's eyes widened. It was probably the first time he'd heard me swear.

"Charlie, believe me, if I thought you were in danger—"

"I *am* in danger. I'm not imagining these things. The threat is real. Someone is stalking me. He's out there, and the only person who seems to care is Takoda."

Stanley let out an exhausted sigh and pinched the bridge of his nose.

"You know what? Fuck this. Let's go, Charlie. I shouldn't have brought you here." Takoda shocked me by taking my hand and weaving his fingers through mine as he tugged me off the couch and dragged me to the entryway. He only released me long enough for us to get our shoes on before snatching my hand again. I wasn't sure if he feared I wouldn't follow or if it was a protective gesture on his part, but I wasn't complaining—except that it was making all my synapses fire at once, which meant it was hard to think straight.

Graveman was on our heels. "You're making a mistake, Dyani," he was saying. "You're aggravating an issue that's been going on for years. Charlie is extremely—"

"Shut your fucking mouth," Takoda roared, spinning on Stanley. "Just stop. Charlie isn't fucking stupid. You're the one who told me that, and he's standing right here. Maybe if everyone would listen and stop treating him like a fucking invalid who can't make his own decisions, things would be different."

I wanted to disappear into the wall or melt into a puddle. I was both flattered and embarrassed by Takoda's bravado, but if he didn't calm down, he was going to end up losing his job because of me. Stanley might be retired, but he had power. Sway. And he was good friends with Sergeant Nikola.

"It's fine." I squeezed Takoda's hand. "Let's just go."

It was then Graveman noticed our joined hands. He cocked his head and zeroed in on Takoda again. His voice when he spoke was laced with danger. "What are you doing, kid? Do you have any idea—"

I shoved Takoda out the door, shouting, "Goodbye, Stanley." Then I slammed it behind us.

Takoda didn't say a word as we drove away, veering toward city central and weaving around the lazy Sunday traffic as we crossed through downtown. He didn't seem concerned about a tail anymore and was driving well over the speed limit.

I could sense Takoda's anger, and I didn't know how to fix it. It was all because of me and my problems. He was fighting a lone battle, taking my side and going head to head with all the people who I'd once thought had my best interest at heart.

"What if they're right and we're wrong?" I twisted my fingers in my lap as I considered. "It makes sense. I mean, I don't even know why those items affected me like they did. The wrapper. The box of chalk. I can't explain any of it because I have no memories of… that time. Maybe I'm as fucked in the head as they say. Stupid Charlie Falkingham, who lives in a fantasy world because he's too afraid to insert himself into society like a normal adult. Poor Charlie, who has been slapped with so many labels and fed so many drugs over the years, he can't possibly think rationally. He's got a thread loose. Lock him in the ward. That's where he belongs. With the nutcases. Maybe I'm sending you on this goose chase for nothing. You'll end up losing your job for some broken, mentally unstable—"

"Shut up, Charlie. I swear to fucking god, if you say one more negative thing about yourself, I'm going to pull this car over and beat your fucking ass until it shines. Got it?"

I shut up, but I didn't feel any better. The majority couldn't be wrong, could they? No one believed Takoda, and he was supposed to be the sane one of the two of us.

I feared what tomorrow might bring. I feared being without Takoda at my side. I feared the long nights ahead of me and the nagging sense that I was vulnerable and that someone was out there, waiting, watching.

I feared the dark hole in my mind where those missing weeks belonged. I couldn't go back there. I would never survive. Not twice.

Most of all, I feared the man beside me, but it had nothing to do with the lingering threat and everything to do with how he made me feel.

When we got back to my place, Dad was gone. The driveway was empty, so Takoda pulled his car into the available slot, the brakes squealing as he parked.

I figured he was dropping me off, so when he killed the engine, I stopped reaching for the door handle and rested my hands in my lap instead. The car ticked and made some ungodly noises that couldn't be healthy as it settled.

Takoda stared at the garage door, his gaze far away on a distant thought. "Can you remember anyone who might have approached you in the last month, who you didn't know or who seemed especially interested in you?"

I analyzed the past few weeks, running through each part of my day. I never left the house excessively. When I did, it was more or less for routine purposes: groceries, mailing packages, occasional visits to the library or the bookstore in the strip mall by our house. The owner of the bookstore liked me to come by and sign a few books for him to sell. Plus, I loved to explore their huge fantasy section in the back. Sometimes it gave me new ideas for my stories. If I got stuck on a plot point, a short visit often helped nudge me through to the next section.

"Not that I can think of. Nothing out of the ordinary."

"Have you received any strange phone calls? Hang-ups? People trying to sell something?"

I shook my head, feeling more and more useless. "No. Apart from my agent, no one calls me."

Takoda sighed in frustration.

I wished I knew something. I wished I could unearth a clue or recover a small memory that might help.

"The man who took you before, the one who ran the whole operation, he's dead, Charlie. You know that, right?"

I wrung my hands. I couldn't stop. "I know." But he still haunted my dreams.

Takoda shifted to face me. "I don't want to freak you out, but it's the other men I'm worried about. He wasn't working alone. You knew that?"

The lump in my throat prevented words. I nodded. "There were a lot of them."

"Some of them are still alive and have been released from prison. I'm not saying this to upset you, but it's a fact. When I looked into it, they've been out on the street for four or five years each."

"You think it's one of them doing this?"

"Maybe. They would have firsthand knowledge of what happened, right? But my question is, why now?"

The tips of my fingers were cold. I stopped fidgeting and tucked them under my thighs for warmth.

"I don't know."

Takoda smoothed a hand over his hair and cracked his knuckles once before saying, "Would you be able to look at pictures? If I printed off recent photos of the men who are out there, could you look at them? I want to know if there is a familiar face there. Maybe you've seen him while out and about and don't realize it."

My teeth chattered, so I clamped my jaw tighter, but even then, my muscles spasmed and cramped. "I... I don't know. Maybe. I should, right?"

"Think about it and let me know tomorrow. I know it might not be easy. It might mess up your head a bit."

I frowned.

"That's not what I meant." Takoda held up his hands. "What I meant was, it could be triggering. Like the candy wrapper."

"I'll look at them."

"Are you sure?"

"Yes."

"Okay. Tomorrow. I'll print them out."

"What should I do in the interim?"

Takoda dropped his head onto the steering wheel. "Fuck. I don't know. Stay inside. Don't go anywhere alone. Buy a gun." He laughed and shook his head. "I'm kidding. Sort of. Do you know any self-defense?"

I couldn't help but laugh as well. It exploded from me unchecked. The minute the laugh came out, I pinched my lips together, trying to stop it.

Takoda was grinning. "What the fuck was that? Was that a laugh?"

My cheeks were on fire. "Do I look like the kind of guy who knows self-defense?"

"I don't know. My sister is five foot three and maybe a hundred pounds soaking wet, but she could take down a man three times her size without breaking a sweat. People *misunderestimate* her all the time. Don't believe me, I'll take you to her classes." He sat back, still smiling. I didn't have it in me to remind him *misunderestimate* wasn't a word. "She's in college, but she had a rough go as a teen. She started taking self-defense in high school after an incident. Now she teaches it three nights a week. She's badass. I wouldn't fuck with her."

"Wow. Yeah, that's not me. I carry this." I dug my switchblade from my pocket and held it between us.

Takoda removed it from my hand and ejected the blade, examining it before closing it again and handing it back.

"Do you know how to use it?"

I smiled again. "It's self-explanatory, no? Stick them with the pointy end."

Takoda laughed again. "In theory. A knife is actually not a very good self-defense weapon unless you know how to use it. Could you stab a man if you were in trouble?"

I stared at the closed knife in my hand, turning it end over end. When I summoned the fear that had been born when I was twelve, I knew I could. "I think so. Yes."

"I believe you, Charlie." I glanced at Takoda, who was watching the blade. "But desire does not mean skill. Wanting to and being able to effectively is two different things."

"I know. I'd probably be pretty useless, to be honest."

"Would you be opposed to a lesson or two?"

I caught Takoda's eyes. He was serious. "You'd help me?"

"You sound shocked."

"No, I... That would be... I'd like that."

"Do you gotta write about dragons today, or would you like some company?"

Those fluttering butterflies were back. "Fuck dragons. I'd love some company."

Eleven

TAKODA

 I didn't know what was happening. I didn't know where the words had come from or why I'd jumped so hard at the chance to give Charlie a few self-defense lessons. Part of me was worried about him and the situation, sure, but it was more than that.
 Every time I was in Charlie's presence, my fiercely protective side ignited. I'd wanted to tear Graveman limb from limb when he'd refused to take me seriously. Of all people, I'd expected him to be more receptive. Then listening to Charlie degrade himself on the way back to his house was like throwing gasoline on an already blazing inferno.
 I followed Charlie to the front door. On cue, we both paused a few feet from the stoop and scanned, both of us anticipating another gift. Nothing was there. I reversed course and checked inside the mailbox as Charlie unlocked the front door.
 It was empty.
 I'd been to Charlie's a few times. I'd seen his bedroom, his office, and some of the main level. I knew Charlie was eccentric—*nervous*—

and had a touch of paranoia which had resulted in OCD tendencies, but this was the first time I'd witnessed the extent of some of his coping mechanisms.

When I closed the heavy front door behind me, Charlie locked it. Several times. He checked the crack between the door and jam, and I assumed he was making sure he could see the deadbolt in place.

As I kicked off my runners, he moved to the front room, where he checked the locks on each window, clicking them open, then back into place before moving to another room and another window.

I silently followed, observing the ritual and not interrupting.

Down a short hallway, he entered a room filled with several display cabinets anchored to one wall and floor-to-ceiling shelving lining another. A workbench sat in the middle of the room, littered with tools and paints and all the necessary instruments used for building models. There was a chemical scent in the air. Dozens of completed projects were balanced on tiny stands behind the glass doors of the cabinets. I crossed the room, mouth gaping as I admired them. As a kid, I'd been obsessed with shit like this. Not models in particular, but every historical machine that existed. Tanks, airplanes, helicopters, cars, everything. Especially war models like the ones filling the shelves.

"Holy shit. It's a P51 Mustang. That is so fucking cool." I crouched to get a better look, admiring the detail. When I noticed the one beside it, my grin widened. "Is that a Flying Fortress? No way. It is. Did you make these?"

"My father does. He's done modeling for as long as I can remember. It's a hobby."

"It's incredible. Look at the detail."

I scanned the others in the cabinet, recognizing a few more.

I pointed. "A B25 Mitchell, right?" I glanced at Charlie, who stood by the window, looking out from behind the blinds.

He shrugged without sparing it a glance. "I don't know. You'd have to ask my dad. I don't speak airplanes. It's his thing. I'm sure he's told me, but I don't retain it."

I continued to explore all the others on display, amazed and intrigued. Charlie moved to the door and waited. The heat of his gaze followed me around the room as I wandered and explored all the different models.

When I met his eyes again, he ducked his chin shyly. Straightening, taking one last look around, I asked, "Should we keep checking the windows?"

He didn't lift his head, worry and embarrassment radiating off him. In the next breath, he tangled his fingers together. "You think I'm ridiculous, don't you?"

"Why? Because you need to check all the locks?"

"Yes."

"I don't. I get it."

Or I thought I did. Charlie had been kidnapped and held for two weeks when he was twelve. Two weeks locked in a small room if the reports told me anything. His obsession with locked doors and security made sense. Was it obsessive? Yes. But I dared anyone to live through what Charlie had lived through and not feel those same urges. So I wasn't about to tell him his actions were unhealthy. Or ridiculous.

I nudged his arm. "Come on. Finish up so I can teach you a few things."

By the time Charlie had gone through the entire house, we were upstairs in his bedroom. Again, I was struck by how otherworldly it was. I had many questions but no words to ask them.

"Where should we do this?" he asked.

We'd been through every part of the house, so I had a general idea of each room's size and the space available. We hadn't gone into the basement nor was there a home gym anywhere. His room was busy and too full to accommodate the drills I wanted to cover.

Analyzing my options, I asked, "How about the media room? It's large. Can we push the furniture aside?"

"Sure. That works."

The media room was on the main level and consisted of a few large couches angled to face an enormous wall-mounted flatscreen. The room was carpeted, and once we shoved the couches and tables out of the way, it gave us ample room to work.

I informed Charlie we weren't using a switchblade to practice. We could pretend, and I hoped he picked up a thing or two. I wasn't sure a blade was a good self-defense weapon for Charlie to begin with. He would probably be better off learning a few hand-to-hand skills. Like I'd told him in the car, a knife wasn't ideal for self-defense unless a person understood how to use it. Most people didn't.

Immediately, Charlie showed signs of anxiety and discomfort. I was picking up on them more and more lately. The finger-twisting was a big one, and he was working his poor digits so aggressively, I wanted to reach out and stop him.

"Let's start with the knife." I waited until I knew he was paying attention before continuing.

He stood rigid and nodded.

"First of all, if your attacker has a gun, the knife won't help. Your best bet is to try and get the fuck out of there because he's carrying something far more deadly. I'm sure you've heard the saying never take a knife to a gun fight? If that happens, you fucking run. But let's say whoever attacks you has a bat or a crowbar, and he comes swinging at your head. What's instinct tell you to do?"

Charlie wet his rosy lips as he thought. "Um." His forehead scrunched.

I pretended to wield an imaginary bat, gripping it like a batter and taking practice swings before winding up and aiming for Charlie's head. "Okay. You have a knife, and I'm taking a swing at your head." I brought up my fake bat, telegraphing my moves. "It's coming at your head, Charlie. What do you do?"

Charlie did exactly what I expected. He thrust his arm out and stabbed me in the belly with his pretend knife.

I brought my arms around in a full swing, connecting with his temple, nudging his head to the side. "Crack! That gut wound isn't going to paralyze my system enough to stop me. It might hurt, but chances are adrenaline will mask the pain. I'm going to swing at your head again."

Charlie started stabbing my gut frantically while I took another crack at his skull.

"Still too pumped up to feel it, Charlie. Plus, if I'm three hundred pounds, your three-inch blade is barely getting through my padding. Who's taking more damage?"

Charlie dropped his arm, a deep furrow in his brow. "Me. I'm probably out cold now if you haven't cracked my skull wide open and left me with hemorrhaging on the brain. I'm dead, and maybe I've poked your kidney if my aim was lucky enough."

"I'm sure you've damaged me too, but did you stop me, and could you get away?"

"No." He peered at his hand where I thought he saw a knife even though he didn't hold one. "So, a knife is useless."

"Not necessarily, but it takes some training to learn how to use it to get the upper hand."

I held out my imaginary bat, a smirk on my face. I knew Charlie was frustrated, and I wanted to lighten the mood. "Here. Trade me. You take the bat and hit me this time."

Charlie's frown cracked, and he did all he could to fight a smirk. "You're an idiot." But he grabbed the bat from my hand as though it were really there.

We both laughed.

I waved him forward. "Do your worst."

Charlie grinned the whole time he wound up. When he took the swing, he went slow. As he came at me, I sliced across his forearm with a finger, mimicking a knife slash.

"What just happened to the bat and your swing?" I asked.

Charlie stared at where I'd pretended to cut him. "I dropped it?"

"I bet you did. You see, when you swing at me, you are giving me the best possible target to disable you. You presented me your forearm." I took Charlie's arm and extended it. He wore a short-sleeved polo, and his inner wrist was shot through with faint blue veins under his translucent skin. "Make a fist."

Charlie did. His tendons popped.

"See this? All the muscles and tendons here along your arm control your fingers and your grip. If I cut them, they'll no longer work, and you'll be disabled. You can't hold a bat. You can't crack my skull. This will most likely stop your attacker cold or at least shock him long enough for you to get away."

As Charlie processed this, he paled. In the car, he'd said he could use the knife if the situation presented itself, but in actuality, I wasn't sure he had it in him.

"Want to try again?"

Finding some bravado, he lifted his chin and nodded.

We ran through that scenario a few times. I let Charlie be the defender, and we sped up the pace so he got an idea of what action to take if someone came at him wielding a heavy object intending to strike.

"Okay. Now, there are two other hot spots for you to know about when disabling an attacker with a knife. The muscles and tendons in the forearm cut off all the mechanical workings of the hand, but if we cut higher"—I indicated above my elbow—"into the biceps or triceps, we can cut off the workings of the entire arm and disable what gives the arm its swinging power. But the best defense with a knife is cutting into the quadriceps." I sliced a finger over the muscle just above my knee. "If you cut right here, you will render the leg useless. The person can't chase you, and you can get away and get help."

Charlie was overwhelmed. I read it on his face plain as day. He absorbed everything I said, but there was a little voice inside him saying he couldn't do this. Fear was taking control, and the more I explained, the more I could tell he was envisioning himself in each scenario as he calculated his odds of getting away.

"Let's forget the knife for now. Chances are, it will be out of reach and useless if someone comes at you suddenly. How about I show you a few quick moves that will get you free of an attacker if they try to grab you?"

"Okay."

I studied his face. Pale skin with a dusting of freckles across his nose. Winter-sky eyes and long lashes. Thin, shapely lips. For a moment, I was caught in a trance, admiring the gentle beauty of the man in front of me. The idea of anyone going after him lit a fuse inside me. It had happened once, and I knew he feared it would happen again.

Charlie's gaze caught mine, and his cheeks colored before his focus slipped to the ground at his feet. He scanned the media room. "What's first?" he asked.

"Turn around." My voice cracked, and I cleared my throat.

Our eyes clashed again, but it was brief. Charlie couldn't seem to look at me for more than a few fleeting seconds.

He turned and immediately worried his hands.

While he wasn't looking, I took a second to process what I was feeling. It kept sneaking up on me, and I wasn't sure what was happening. Guys didn't normally have this effect on me. I hit Cage all the time, brought randoms home, or found an empty stall in the bathrooms if I didn't want to go to the trouble of shooing a stranger out of my house in the morning.

Fucking was fucking. Feelings not included.

I wasn't a fan of people in general. We clashed when they realized I was abrasive and judgmental. I carried a profound hatred for people who came from wealth, had privilege, or wielded power.

But Charlie was different despite ticking all those boxes.

I couldn't turn off the raging desire to protect him.

I couldn't ignore the pull that tugged at me whenever we were in the same room.

It didn't make sense.

We weren't alike in any way.

Ying and yang.

Charlie glanced over his shoulder. Winter blue. Mesmerizing. "What's happening?"

I cleared my throat and ignored the steady thrum of my heart and the slick coating of sweat on my hands.

"I was thinking. Turn around again."

When he turned, I went up behind him. I wrapped an arm around his neck and gently tugged him back until our bodies were flush.

Charlie gasped. His hands flew to my arm, and his delicate fingers wrapped around it, gripping hard, nails digging grooves into my flesh. I wasn't cutting off his oxygen supply, simply making a point.

Since the action seemed to kick up Charlie's anxiety, I pulled back a fraction on my hold, leaving it loose.

I brought my mouth to his ear, catching a whiff of his aftershave or cologne, and whispered. "I've got you. Now, what do you do?"

"Um." Charlie's breathing was ragged, and a tremor radiated through him. His soft hands clung to my arm.

I secured my other hand on his hip, keeping him in place.

When too much time passed and Charlie didn't speak, when his tremors intensified, I whispered, "It's just a scenario. You aren't in danger. I will never hurt you. Are you okay?"

His throat bobbed under the crook of my arm. "Yes. I'm… Um… I don't know what to do."

I peeled his fingers loose and moved his hands to the right spot. "Grip me here. At the wrists. Hard as you can. You won't hurt me."

He followed my instructions.

I kept my mouth against his ear as I spoke each new directive. My nose brushed the soft hair at his temple and made it hard to think. "Next, you're going to hang on tight and drop your body weight which is going to pull at my arm. At the same time, turn your head to the side so you don't choke yourself further."

Charlie turned his head first and stilled. The motion brought us even closer. His cheek brushed mine, and his lips were right there, a heartbeat away. His fluttering breaths feathered against me, warm and moist.

"Drop down. Make yourself heavy."

He wet his lips. His gaze flicked to mine. There was a long pause. Then he took action.

I let his weight loosen my grip a bit, showing him how the move would work on an unsuspecting attacker. "Good, now you have me off-balance, and you're low to the ground. Loop your leg behind mine and shove at the back of my knees. If you do that hard enough, I'm going down."

Charlie did exactly what I said with surprising efficiency. I lost my balance, and he laid me out flat on my back. Ideally, Charlie should have let go of my wrists when he felt me fall, but he didn't and wound up tumbling on top of me.

The weight of his body landing on mine knocked the wind out of me, and I grabbed hold of him out of instinct.

A look of surprise filled Charlie's face when he registered what had happened, and I burst out laughing. It didn't take long for the shock to drift away, then Charlie was laughing along with me.

He hadn't moved away, and I couldn't convince myself to unloop my arms from around his waist. Charlie buried his face in the crook of my neck and lost it. I'd never seen him so undone before, so happy. I hadn't known him long, but I would have bet anything he hadn't laughed like that in a long time.

And I'd done that for him. Me.

As the moment stretched, we remained on the floor, our legs entwined. Charlie lifted his face from my shoulder and peered down with a combination of interest and worry. It was a look I'd seen on him several times today. When his attention moved to my mouth, my blood pooled south. Charlie's Adam's apple bobbed.

What was it about him? He made me feel sixteen again, like I was experiencing attraction for the first time. Like the years I'd spent entertaining a different man in my bed every week no longer existed.

I slid my hands to the small of his back, adding a bit of pressure, letting him know it was okay to advance if that was what he wanted.

Charlie came an inch closer, hovering above me, gaze slipping from my mouth to my eyes and back. I was about to lift my head and help him take that last step when heavy footfalls moved down the hall.

"What the hell is going on in here?" Archie appeared in the doorway, and his words fell away the instant he took in the scene. "Oh."

Charlie rolled off me and scrambled to his feet. "Um. Dad. I didn't hear you come home. Takoda is teaching me self-defense."

Archie's gaze shifted between us. "Uh-huh."

I got to my feet, my shirt twisting funny around my body. I took a second to adjust it while trying to ignore how that might look to an outsider. "Good afternoon, Mr. Falkingham."

"Dyani." My last name came out curt and with a bitter edge. Again, his attention shifted from me to Charlie and back. "I guess I'll leave you to it." He reached for the door we'd left open and made a point of slamming it behind him as he marched off down the hall.

I glanced at Charlie, unsure how he'd feel about a closed door, but he didn't seem concerned. His cheeks were an inferno, and his fingers were taking abuse once again.

Before he could overanalyze what had happened, I jumped in. "How about we try that move again?"

Charlie watched while I replayed what I'd said and heard how it could be misconstrued.

"The defense move," I corrected. "Not the… Unless… You were supposed to let go when I fell."

A long pause followed my stumbling response.

Charlie fidgeted and looked everywhere but at me. "Okay. That… makes sense. We can try it again."

Neither of us moved. The tension in the room was at a boiling point. I didn't think Charlie had registered what that moment had done to me or how my jeans were suddenly a bit too tight in the front, and the last thing I wanted to do was draw attention to it in case it freaked him out.

Charlie cleared his throat and looked around. "How did I do? I mean… apart from…" He sighed.

"Good. Um… Next time"—I smiled, lightening the mood—"when you feel me fall, let go, and you won't land on top of me." I winked. Charlie found something interesting on the floor to stare at.

We practiced that particular move four more times, and Charlie got better each time we went through the motions. He didn't land on top of me again, and that was okay. He had enough to process. Maybe the almost kiss was one step too far.

Essentially, I was taking him through basic self-defense moves they taught in all sorts of classes. Arm grabs, chokeholds, invasion of space. It was the type of stuff Odina taught.

"Okay. Let's say your attacker is a lot bigger and stronger than you and somehow manages to get you on the ground. Now what happens?"

Charlie shifted his weight from one foot to the other, listening intently. He shrugged.

"Lie down on your back. We'll start there."

Charlie watched me cautiously as he maneuvered to the ground.

"Okay. So I've got you on the ground, and I'm coming at you. I'm going to choke you, except now I have mass and position on my side. You are pretty vulnerable like this."

I knelt and knocked Charlie's knees apart before wedging between his legs. His eyes widened. I bent over his body, placing my hands loosely around his neck, hovering over him and grinning. His pulse raced under my palms. We were close. Close enough I could smell his cologne again mixed with clean sweat.

"First thing you'll do is lock me in place. Take the control away from me, and don't let me get away."

Charlie frowned. "Don't I want you to get off me?"

"I'm bigger and stronger. At this point, you want to cripple your attacker, and I'm going to show you how. Wrap your legs around my middle and lock your ankles."

He did, and we both seemed to pause there for a few long seconds. The position could be flipped around and made into something much more intimate. My imagination raced along with my heart, and it took me a second to focus because my mind was fast sliding into the gutter. My body was reacting to the position without my consent, and if I didn't get my head in the game, I would be sporting wood again.

"Good. Nice and tight." I groaned internally at my own words. "What do you think you should do next? I've got my hands around your throat. I'm cutting off your air supply."

Charlie's gaze flicked to our tangled position, and I saw the cogs spinning in his head as he tried to figure out what to do. He placed his hands over my forearms, his touch light and tentative, but then he seemed stuck for options and frowned.

Without applying pressure, I leaned closer, inches from his face. "Come on, Charlie. What do you do? How do you stop me?"

His breath ghosted my chin as he peered up at me with his winter-storm eyes. My concentration turned to shit as he skated his soft hands up my arms and over my triceps.

"I don't want to stop you." Holding my shoulders, he lifted himself easily, ignoring my lax hold on his neck, and joined our mouths.

It was the most tentative and nervous kiss I'd experienced since my first kiss with a guy when I was a teenager. Charlie didn't do more than brush his lips against mine before pulling away. When he laid his head back down, I followed, releasing his throat and sliding one hand around to cradle the back of his neck.

I kept the kiss simple. Light. Gentle pecks a few times before glancing my tongue along the seam of his mouth, asking permission for more. Charlie fumbled, but he didn't push me away. Before long, he found the rhythm of our connection.

The kiss lasted less than a minute before I registered the vibrations running through his whole body, and I pulled back. "Whoa. You're shaking pretty bad there. Are you okay?"

"Yes. I just..." He ducked his chin, trying to hide his face.

I cupped his cheek and kept him in place. "Don't freak out. If you need to stop, we stop. No ifs, ands, or buts. You got that?"

"You must think I'm pretty pathetic, freaking out over a kiss."

"I don't think that at all, but I will kick your ass if you don't stop badmouthing yourself."

That earned me a hint of a smile.

I brushed my thumb along his lower lip, moved in, and kissed him once more, teasing again with my tongue. It didn't take much before Charlie's tongue came out to play too. We tested this new thing for another few minutes before I backed off yet again, sensing I could easily overwhelm him if I wasn't careful. What was worse was the aching swell in my jeans that made me want to tear his clothes off and fuck him into the ground. My body wasn't used to slow and steady, but I ignored its demands.

I didn't think Charlie noticed my erection, and maybe that was a good thing.

Tasting him on my lips, I offered him a coy smile. "Okay, so here's the thing. A-plus for distracting your attacker. I admit, I completely forgot to choke the fuck out of you, but I think your methods are flawed, and they may not work on everyone."

Charlie covered his face and laughed.

When he calmed, he put my hands back on his throat. "Okay. Do it again and tell me the right way this time."

It seemed like Charlie didn't want to focus on what had happened. Maybe he needed time to process. That was okay. For now. I needed time to ponder it as well, considering Charlie wasn't exactly like the guys I picked up at the bar. If what Archie had told me was true, I was possibly Charlie's first kiss.

I wasn't sure I was a deserving enough person to be worthy of any more of Charlie's firsts.

Twelve

CHARLIE

Dad had that look about him all evening, like he had a whole lot to say but wasn't sure how to say it. Takoda had left in the late afternoon after we'd exhausted ourselves practicing moves in the media room.

All I could think about was the kiss we'd shared. It hadn't happened again, but it had consumed my every thought since. I was still reeling at my bravery and the fact that he hadn't shoved me away.

Dad had an opinion. I saw it in his eyes. He studied me while we cooked dinner together. He kept glaring through our entire meal. It wasn't until I was loading the dishwasher after we finished eating that he finally spoke up.

"Charlie? What's going on with the young officer?"

I paused with a dirty plate in my hand then continued to rinse it before adding it to the rack. "He's teaching me self-defense."

"You know that's not what I'm asking you."

"I know." I glanced at Dad. He leaned against the counter, watching me with his arms crossed. It was a defensive posture, and I didn't like it. "I'm... I'm not sure. Why?"

"I think we should have a little chat because from what I saw, it looked like it was going somewhere that wasn't self-defense training."

"Dad, I'm an adult. It's a little late for *the talk*, don't you think?"

"To be fair, I've held off for seventeen years because you haven't shown any interest in stuff like this. I don't say this to hurt you, son, but I thought maybe..." He paused, then sighed. "I thought... I don't know how to say this."

I found the dishwasher soap under the sink and added a tab to the machine before setting it to wash. "You thought I was too messed up to be interested in sex, is that it? You thought that part of me had been ripped away because of.. of everything that happened?" I finished lamely, unable to say the precise words out loud.

"Yes."

"Well, you're wrong. It's always been there. I just... buried it. I wasn't ready to face it before." I wrung my hands, scanning the kitchen for something to do since having this discussion with my dad was making me agitated.

"And you are now?"

"I don't know. But if I am, it's no business of yours." I scratched at my arm, my insides vibrating. "And for the record, I don't appreciate you talking to Takoda behind my back. Especially when it comes to this. You don't know what goes on inside my head, and I'm capable of voicing things on my own if necessary."

"I won't apologize for what I said to him. You can stand there and act tough all you want, but that boy needed to understand some things. I've spoken with his sergeant, and I learned Officer Dyani is a bit reckless and out of control. Not exactly a rule follower. Sergeant Nikola has asked me to report any concerns immediately. You are my son, and I will not let some arrogant, sex-crazed—"

"Dad! Enough. I'm an adult. You don't have to coddle me." My tone was sharper than I intended, and Dad's eyes widened. I'd never spoken to him like that before. "I'm sorry. I shouldn't have raised my voice, but I'm tired of being treated like a child. I know I have anxiety. I know I have an extreme paranoia disorder—believe me, Sofia uses that label all the time, and I hate it. I know I have a form of OCD along with a slew of other issues, but I know my body, and I trust Takoda."

Dad's frown deepened, and I could see him wanting to have an opinion. I kept talking so he wouldn't interrupt. "I don't know if it's going anywhere. Probably not. I'm not stupid. I don't know if it can or how I'd react if it did. He's a lot more experienced than me. I know that. I know I'm tragically and possibly irreparably stunted in this area. Takoda probably won't want to deal with the obstacles I deal with daily. If I can't do more than kiss him, he'll likely get tired of me and move on. I know that. I'll deal with it if that's the case. And you're right. I have no clue if I can... have a normal relationship. I've been too afraid to try. But it doesn't mean I haven't thought about it a hundred times over the years. For the first time in my life, the desire for more is almost outweighing the fear. Maybe we won't get that far. Maybe it will all crash and burn the second he wants to... to have sex." My cheeks burned, and I ducked my chin, unable to meet my father's eyes. "You don't have any idea how embarrassing that is. Can you just be happy for me and recognize what it means for me to take this first step? To try? Don't ruin it, Dad. Please."

Dad scrubbed a hand over his head and frowned at a spot in middle space. "You're right. I'm sorry. I sometimes forget you're not a teenager anymore."

I knew my father was only being protective. My life had been challenging. The incident from my youth had changed everything. I couldn't blame him for being cautious and skeptical of Takoda's intentions.

"If I'm not okay, I will come to you. I always have, even when I couldn't express myself in the beginning, remember? You're my safety net. That hasn't changed."

Dad's eyes turned glassy as he nodded. This man had given up everything for me. His job, his wife, his life. I'd come home broken, and he'd never left my side. Piece by piece, he'd put me back together the best he was able. He'd hired the best doctors in the province and followed their advice. He had my best interest at heart.

I pulled him into my arms and hugged him. His grip was tight and comforting. He smelled like aftershave, old leather, and tranquility. We parted with mutual slaps on the back, and Dad held me by the shoulders.

"So, that boy kissed you, did he?"

I smirked and lifted my chin. "Actually, I kissed him."

Dad's brows winged up.

"But that's the end of this conversation. I have some work to do. Takoda is taking me to the station to look at a few pictures tomorrow, so I won't get anything done."

"Pictures?"

"Yes." I moved to the far window, commencing my routine of checking the locks before heading upstairs. "He wants to see if I recognize some faces. Just something he's working on."

I didn't want to elaborate. Dad wouldn't like it, and I was still unsure how I felt about the whole thing. The thought of seeing the faces of anyone connected to my past haunted me and made anxiety buzz under my skin, but Takoda would be there. I'd be safe with him beside me.

"Care to explain?"

"No. We can talk about it if it amounts to anything."

I headed upstairs, moving through each room on my way, thinking about the following day, what I'd promised to do, and about the kiss I'd shared with Takoda.

* * *

I woke up filled with dread and a sense of impending doom hanging over my head. It was Monday. There was no telling if the person stalking me was using a pattern. Not enough evidence existed to suggest I would receive another gift today, but I felt it in my bones.

A tiny part of my brain told me it was nothing more than paranoia. This was the kind of thing Sofia talked about. It was the reason I'd been given a diagnosis and why I took so many drugs.

I went through my morning routine, making a failed effort to ignore the uncomfortable sensations crawling under my skin. I got up, showered, dressed, and was downstairs for coffee and breakfast by eight.

No matter what, I couldn't stop my teeth from chattering.

"It's cold in here," I said when Dad noticed.

"It's the same temperature as always."

"Feels cold."

I didn't hang around, certain he'd call me out and connect my nervousness with whatever I was doing at the station later that day.

On my way upstairs again, I stopped on the landing and studied the street. The Beekmans and their herd of children were gone. The dogs no longer peered out the window, having retreated inside to sleep the day away.

Westly Huntington was talking to Ms. LaPointe on her front lawn. Both of them were widowed, and I always thought it would make a perfect romance if they found something with each other. The morning sun shone bright, and Francine wore big sunglasses that took up half her face, but her smile was equally radiant.

Westly was a good guy and lonely. He talked with his hands, and I guessed from the actions he was telling her about his moped.

I didn't want to spy, so I scanned the street in both directions, unable to shake the haunting sense of someone watching me. Was the person waiting around the next corner? What would it be this time? What did they want from me?

I clicked the lock a final time and continued upstairs. In my bedroom, I checked the backyard, scanning all the hiding places and shadowed corners. The hairs on the back of my neck stood on end. This was the kind of sensation that usually made me panic and call Stanley.

A *feeling*, but nothing more. No evidence.

I touched the phone inside my pocket and debated calling Takoda. Would he think I was crazy? I could see it for what it was. Intense paranoia. I hated that word. I hated my doctor for slapping a label on it, but I couldn't shut it off or make it go away. This was the kind of thing that made everyone lie to me so I'd calm down. How had I been so blind to the truth?

For years.

I closed the curtain and looked around my bedroom. For the first time, I saw it as everyone else did. My sanctuary was a joke to the outside world. A room of fantasy and pretend. A room more suited to a child. It had grown from the mind of a twelve-year-old boy, and in some ways, my life had stopped then and there.

I couldn't work. Not like this.

Crossing to the fountain, I sat on the floor and followed the flow of the water falling into the pond below. The soothing trickle usually helped calm me down. It was meditative in a way. But it wasn't helping. My insides were in a knot. I couldn't slow my breathing or stop twisting my fingers. They ached with the abuse. My lip stung, and

I ran my tongue along it, finding a small cut where my teeth had broken the skin.

I considered the bottle of Xanax in the bathroom. It would calm the storm, take the edge off, settle me down. But the pills made me foggy, and I didn't want to be a mess when Takoda came for me later. For once in my life, I wanted people to see me and not the layers and layers of problems I carried with me each day.

Closing my eyes, I listened to the water falling, pulling back all my senses like I'd learned to do as a child so I wasn't as overwhelmed. All that remained was the musical tinkling of the waterfall. I let darkness blanket me, soothe me, and comfort me.

My abandoned coffee grew cold where I left it on the ground at my side. I no longer smelled the rich brew that had filled the air a moment ago. I was neither hot nor cold. The taste of blood from the cut on my lip vanished. One sense remained, and only because I allowed it.

Retreating was easy. As a child, I could pass days in this coma-like state. Sometimes when that had happened, I would come back and find myself admitted to the hospital because Dad couldn't get me to eat or drink. As an adult, I was more in control. I was gone, but I remained at the edge of awareness. It was a choice, and it was how I knew the moment Dad entered the bedroom and called my name.

"Charlie?"

I didn't want to come back into the panicked state I'd left behind, but I knew if I didn't respond, he would worry. I fluttered my eyes open and glanced at the doorway.

"Is everything all right?"

"Just working through some plot points," I lied.

Although this level of detachment was similar to the times I ventured to Vrydindel, it wasn't the same. Vrydindel was a world of imaginary sensations, ones created in my mind. I'd learned to replace my real world with another. Sofia called it dissociating, but we agreed to disagree on that point. To me, I was merely letting my stories unfold in a virtual way without the assistance of computer technology. It was like dreaming, only better because I was in control. I didn't have to be Charlie anymore. I could be Calipnia, a powerful and magical hero with a vicious and protective dragon by my side.

"Have you been sitting there since you came down for breakfast?"

I touched the mug beside me. It was cold. "I... Yes. What time is it?"

"Almost lunchtime. I was in my workroom, so I wasn't sure if you came down at ten for more coffee or not." He glanced at my still full mug with a lifted brow. "I think you've been sitting there long enough, don't you?"

What he meant was, *Am I calling the doctor?*

"I'll come down for lunch."

"Good. I'm running to the store. I won't be too long. What time is Takoda coming for you?"

I had no idea. Pulling the phone from my pocket, I saw a missed text from him that he'd sent hours ago.

Sarge has me busy this morning. I'll b there around 3 or sooner if I can.

"This afternoon sometime."

"All right. If you leave before I'm home, text me. I'm just grabbing a few groceries. Do you need anything while I'm out?"

"No thank you."

I listened as Dad descended the stairs. A few minutes later, the front door closed, and the telltale click of the lock being engaged hit my ears. The car rumbled to life a few minutes after that, then he was gone.

For a while, I stayed present, analyzing how I felt and deciding if my anxiety had waned. I was better. My heart no longer knocked a frantic rhythm, and the uncontrollable shivers were gone.

I was being silly. Paranoia had gotten the better of me. Again.

But at least I'd managed it without drugs. That was a plus.

I headed downstairs and made a sandwich before returning to my office to work. Picking at the crust and popping little bites into my mouth, I reread the parts of my outline I'd written the other day. My ideas were solid. I'd set up the major conflicting events and worked from there. Calipnia and Rotkiv's next journey would intrigue the audience. When I considered how to expand certain plot points, my thoughts drifted and refused to stay focused.

In the end, once my food was gone, I resorted to sketching on my art pad, bringing a three-headed Chimera to life. He would be introduced in the ice realm as Calipnia's newest challenge. He was fearsome and legendary. Before this journey, he'd been nothing more than a myth, a story told by the people of Vrydindel for hundreds of years.

It was while hunched over, detailing the scales along his back, that I heard the car pull into the driveway. A few minutes later, the lock disengaged on the front door.

I was about to call out when a loud thunk made me jump. The walls vibrated. It sounded like Dad had thrown the heavy door open with enough force it had smashed into the wall.

I shot out of my chair when a second thump made me freeze. This one was accompanied by a grunt and the crinkling of plastic bags. There was a sound of shuffling, another grunt, and another soft thump I couldn't place.

My mind went on high alert, and the first thing I thought was that Dad had fallen and was trying to get up. I imagined a heart attack, a stroke, or something as simple as his knee giving out.

I raced from my office and was in the hallway, almost at the stairs, when I heard the voice. A muffled, low tone. Words too unclear to understand.

But it wasn't my dad's.

Like a breaking dam, adrenaline flooded my system. Fear was a noose around my neck. It locked up my joints and paralyzed my muscles.

Then three clear words floated up the stairs, shouted at full volume, thick with venom.

"Where is he?"

They were followed by my Dad's strangled tone. "He's not here."

"We'll just have to see if that's true, won't we? I think you're lying, old man."

A crash.

A deadening *whomp* like a foot connecting with a body.

A long groan.

I ran.

As silently as I could, I raced to my bedroom, my skin on fire, my heart in my throat. I was twelve again. At the bus stop. The cold February winds ruffled my hair. My backpack weighed heavily on my shoulders. I attended a private Catholic school and was the only kid from my neighborhood who caught that particular bus, so I was alone on the corner. It was snowing.

The panic was almost crippling. As quickly and quietly as possible, I wrenched open the closet door, scanning the interior before changing my mind. The closet was too obvious. Plus, it locked, and no matter how terrified I was, I couldn't make my feet move into a small space where I could get trapped inside.

My heart knocked so violently against my ribs I was sure it would leave bruises on the inside. Under my bed? Behind the curtains?

There was nowhere to hide.

The man downstairs called my name in a singsong tone. "Charlie. I have something for you. Come out, come out wherever you are." He chuckled. "We never did play hide-and-seek. What fun."

When I heard the steady thump of his feet on the stairs, I knew I was almost out of time. A heavy cedar chest sat at the end of my bed. It didn't lock, and it was probably large enough to fit an adult. It was filled with extra bedding.

I heaved the lid open and scooped the pile of blankets and sheets into my arms and tossed them into the open closet before sliding the door closed again. Then I climbed inside the chest and folded my body as small as I could make it. Before I closed the lid, I tugged my phone from my pocket so I had it in hand.

My heart pounded as I closed myself inside. It took all my concentration not to slip into a panic attack.

In the dark, squished so tightly I could barely move, with a man wandering my house, and my dad hurt somewhere downstairs, I typed a message to Takoda. My trembling fingers made it difficult.

Help me. He's in my house.

I hit Send and clutched the device in my hand until the plastic creaked. The man was on the second floor. He hummed a familiar tune. The cadence and flow made the hairs on my neck rise. I knew the song well. It lived in that dark hole in my mind. It was one of those haunting memories I couldn't quite grasp but knew was real. My throat constricted, and I wanted to throw the lid back on the chest and crawl out because I couldn't breathe.

Every now and again, the intruder sang a few words, asking if I was sad because I was on my own and then assuring me he'd get by with a little help from his friends. I wanted to throw up.

My phone rang, the volume piercing the silent bubble I'd tried to create. A new wash of cold fear enveloped me. It was Takoda. I smashed the decline button several times then turned the volume off, but it was too late.

The singing had stopped.

I held my breath and clenched my jaw so my teeth wouldn't chatter.

"I knew you were home." His footsteps moved toward my bedroom, then stopped. I could envision him standing at the threshold.

My ears rang.

My phone vibrated. Takoda. Calling. Texting. Calling again.

I couldn't answer.

"Well, well, well, look at this place. Amazing. We used to talk about dragons, Charlie. Do you remember that? Of course you do."

He was in my room, slowly making his way around.

I was sure he could hear my pounding heart. There was no way he couldn't. It drowned out all sounds.

"Why are you hiding? I thought we were friends. You said we could be friends."

I listened as he opened the closet and rustled around inside.

With trembling fingers, I pulled up the keypad for my phone and dialed 911 before hitting enter. Then I closed my eyes and prayed.

"I brought you chocolate, Charlie. You told me peanut butter was your favorite, so that's what I brought for you. How can you not remember me? All the games we played. The stories. The adventures we took."

He was closer now. He'd abandoned the closet and was nearing the bed.

"You were special. More special than the rest. Why are you hiding from me? Are you afraid? You know I'd never hurt you. We made a pact."

His footsteps stopped right in front of the chest. When he spoke again, he was about as close as he could be. In my mind, I saw him crouching, face at the opening.

Then he knocked on the lid. *Bang, bang, bang.*

I jumped as the sound and vibrations echoed through my bones. I almost cried out but bit my tongue to stop myself. A straitjacket of fear held me so tight I didn't think it would ever let me go.

"I know you're in there. I can hear you breathing and whimpering. Why are you scared? I thought I'd lost you. Everything fell apart that day. I thought you were gone for good. Imagine my surprise when I saw you on TV last month. There you were, calling out to me. You memorialized us, Charlie. You have no idea what that means to me. God, I've missed you. I brought you a present. This one's special. I've kept it with me every day since I lost you. I know you're having trouble remembering me. It's in there. I've been with you every day since we parted, haven't I? That's okay. It will all come back to you in time. Once you remember, then we can pick up where we left off. Friends forever, remember? Brothers. We made a pact. Here. For you. I've gotta run. I'll see you soon."

He cracked the lid on the chest and slid something inside. It fluttered over my head then fell down the edge of the box. I didn't move.

As the footsteps retreated back down the hall, I couldn't hold onto control anymore. The comforting darkness beyond my senses and reason enveloped me, and I let go, retreating as far away from reality as possible.

Thirteen

TAKODA

"I don't think you understand the severity of this situation." The vein on Sergeant Nikola's temple pulsed, a sure sign he was pissed off. Again.

"No, sir, *you* don't understand the—"

"You will speak when I tell you to speak, Dyani." He slapped a hand on the desk then wagged his finger. "I've had enough of your goddamn attitude. Not only are you disregarding a direct order, but you're aggravating a situation and making it worse."

The minute someone had caught wind that I was pulling photos for Charlie to view later, I'd been called into Nikola's office.

"You assigned Charlie to me. I'm telling you there is—"

"No. Stop. I explained how this works with him. I told you this was nothing more than paranoia, which is a common behavior with Charlie. A *diagnosed* condition. Are you a doctor?" Nikola didn't expect an answer, so I clamped my mouth shut. "We've been fielding his complaints for over a decade. I spoke with Stanley on the phone this morning, and I'm not pleased you went over my head. What part of 'let this go' did you not understand?"

I ground my molars, nostrils flaring.

"You're getting Charlie worked up, and the last goddamn thing I need is the crown attorney on my ass. Your job is to placate him, not stir this shit up and make it worse. Do you hear me?"

"Loud and clear."

"Is that attitude?"

"No, sir."

"Good. Now, you drop this nonsense today. I don't want to hear another word about it. Not one."

"You're making a mistake. Charlie is in potential danger."

If smoke could have come out Nikola's ears, I'd have been choking on it. "Do you want to rephrase that? Because it sounded an awful lot like another word."

I had a whole lot of other words to say, but I didn't trust myself at the moment, and my boss looked ready to strangle me.

Sergeant Nikola held my gaze for a long beat, waiting for my mouth to flap so he could put the final nail in my coffin. He injected as much authority into that venomous stare as he could.

Message received.

"You will return that file to the basement, and god help you if it is missing a single photograph or form. I forbid you to access it again. Then you will return to that desk and your assigned work. I don't want to hear another goddamn word about this. Understand?"

"Yes, sir."

"Get out of my face."

As I made my way to the door, my phone buzzed in my pocket. Uncaring that Nikola had eyes on the back of my head, I tugged it out, checked the message, and froze.

Help me. He's in my house.

The air caught in my lungs as I read it twice, absorbing what it meant, certain I was misunderstanding. Torn between racing out of the precinct and confronting Nikola, I pivoted in place, my boots squeaking on the linoleum flooring.

"Dyani, what the hell are you doing?"

My skin was alive with static. I thrust my phone at my sergeant, showing him the text.

"Care to tell me it's nothing again?" I snapped.

Nikola read the screen and frowned before lifting his narrowed gaze.

"I'm going—"

"You're not. You call Charlie, and you calm him down. This is your mess. You're the one who got him worked up—"

"This isn't his imagination," I roared. "He's in trouble, and I'm leaving."

"Dyani—"

But I was out of his office before he could find the words to scold me. I tapped Charlie's number as I grabbed a set of keys and darted toward the back exit, which led to the parking lot.

No answer.

I texted. *What's going on?*

Then I called again. And texted. And called.

The whole time, Sergeant Nikola yelled after me. I ignored him, registering in the back of my mind that he was telling people to detain me.

I picked up my pace, but before I hit the back hallway, someone grabbed my arm and yanked me off my feet.

I tried to shove whoever it was off, but then a second person grabbed my other arm, and together they dragged me back into the bullpen. Two detectives forced me into a chair as Nikola crossed the room, rage marking every inch of his face.

"You're finished, Dyani. You'll hand in your badge and your gun, and you'll pack up your things today. Do you hear me? This is over. I'm done." He slashed a hand through the air, emphasizing his point.

Every man and woman in the bullpen had eyes on me as they silently witnessed the situation. It was so quiet that when a phone rang, it echoed off the walls.

Everyone knew who this was regarding because I hadn't given two shits about keeping quiet when I'd suspected things weren't right and that Charlie had a stalker. The Falkinghams were a big name at the station, but no one was about to dispute the long-standing claim that Charlie was ill and his concerns were unimportant.

Nikola could fire my ass if he wanted, but I needed to get out of there. Charlie was in trouble.

"Sir," called a female officer from a desk on the other side of the room. She held a phone receiver to her chest. Her name was Dara

Juno. I didn't know her well, but something in her face told me I didn't want to hear what she had to say.

Sergeant Nikola turned, and Juno stood taller, tipping her chin up.

"What is it?" Nikola barked.

"There was a 911 call. Emergency vehicles are being dispatched to the Falkingham residence. Trampoline and Adina were the closest, and they called in, reporting they've just arrived on the scene." Juno's eyes danced to me before returning to Nikola's. "Dyani is right, sir. Someone was at the residence. Archie Falkingham is hurt pretty badly, and there's no sign of Charlie."

I was gone. An army couldn't hold me back at that point. Nikola shouted after me, but his words and threats meant nothing. The hallway was a blur as I ran.

In the patrol car, I hit the lights and sirens and burned rubber out of the parking lot. Even when cars pulled over for me, it felt like it took ages to get across town to Charlie's neighborhood. In reality, I made the trip in under ten minutes.

Sweat had gathered along my spine, and my fingers ached from the death grip I held on the steering wheel.

When I arrived, I parked at the curb and raced toward the house. An ambulance was on the scene, and two paramedics were assessing Archie, who lay on the floor in the front hallway. He was conscious but seemed to be incoherent and confused.

Kevin was talking with Corey, and they both looked up when I stormed inside.

"Did you find him?"

Kevin shook his head, but it was Corey who spoke. She gestured at Archie. "He says he saw his attacker leave alone, but we can't find Charlie anywhere. The back door is locked, and there's no sign he exited any other way. He's just not here."

"We searched," Kevin added.

"Koda?" Archie's strained voice drew my attention. I nudged a young paramedic, who couldn't have been more than twenty or twenty-one, aside and crouched down.

"Buddy, you need to move. We need to get this guy to the hospital."

I ignored the pimple-faced paramedic and took Archie's hand. It was cold and trembling.

Charlie's dad seemed to struggle to focus. Pain pinched his face, but he squeezed my hand when I said his name.

"Where's Charlie?" he asked.

"I'm going to find him. Don't you worry."

"He didn't take him." The words were slurred together, and I wondered if the medics had given him something for pain. Archie's eyes closed for a long time before opening again. "He's... scared."

"I know. I'm going to find him, Archie. Right now. You just get better."

He tried to nod, but the action failed when his body went limp.

"Move," the young paramedic said, shoving me aside.

I joined Kevin and Corey while the medical professionals moved Archie to a stretcher.

"We've gone through the entire house. There's no sign of him. No indication he was ever here. He might not have been in the house."

"You looked everywhere?"

Kevin shrugged. "I didn't look under the bed if that's what you mean, but I'm telling you, he's not here."

"He was here. He texted me."

If Charlie was afraid, and I'd have bet anything he was terrified, he'd probably hidden somewhere.

"We called for him. He didn't respond," Corey said as I raced up the stairs.

Charlie hadn't answered my texts, but that didn't mean he wasn't there somewhere, paralyzed with fear.

"Charlie? Charlie, it's Takoda."

At the top of the stairs, I glanced in both directions, unsure which way to go. One way led to his office, a large bathroom, and his father's bedroom. The other way led to the one place where Charlie went if he needed to detach from the world. His safety net.

I headed toward his bedroom, flying on instinct. It was dark within. The curtains were drawn over the window, blocking the midday sun. The fountain lights provided the only illumination. Remembering the one time I'd come over and witnessed Charlie's fragile mental health and how Archie had advised me to keep the lights off, I entered the dark room, letting my eyes adjust.

"Charlie? Are you in here?"

The closet doors sat open. Everything else seemed in order. There was no sign of a struggle. Nothing seemed to be out of place.

"It's safe now, bud. You can come out."

No response.

I crossed to the closet, finding Charlie's neurotic order inside. Perfectly hung shirts all in a row. Pants folded with perfect creases and organized by color. Underneath, his shoes were lined up one beside the other. But on top of them was a pile of blankets and sheets. Someone had tossed them there without a care. That wasn't like Charlie, and it set off alarm bells in my head.

I turned, scanning the bedroom. At the foot of the bed was a decent-sized cedar chest, big enough to fit an adult. One that I guessed had been filled with bedding before a frantic Charlie had needed a place to hide.

My heart lodged in my throat, fearing what I might find inside. If the intruder hadn't taken Charlie, was it because he hadn't found him? Or had he found him and done something far worse?

What was I going to find if I lifted that lid?

"I told you he wasn't up here."

I glanced at Kevin, who was framed in the doorway. Corey stood a few feet behind, glancing over his shoulder. Kevin was nothing more than a silhouette, backlit by the hallway light, his face shadowed.

He felt along the wall and flicked on the bedroom light.

"No. Leave it off."

Kevin frowned but did as I asked.

My vision was compromised for a second, and I had to blink a few times to readjust to the darker room. When I could see better, I indicated the chest at the foot of the bed, then, without words, told Kevin to stay back.

I approached the chest, my insides turning to liquid. I thought of the day Odina had been found beaten in the street, her skirt torn, bruises along her arms, thighs, and on her face. A trick that had gone wrong. She was my baby sister, and I'd felt so helpless and powerless. I'd always felt it was my job to protect her and keep her safe from the assholes of the world, and I'd failed.

I thought of Calian, my baby brother who was behind bars, barely eighteen when he'd been arrested. I thought of how I hadn't been there when he'd conned an older guy outside the liquor store into buying him and his buddies alcohol. How I'd been too busy to answer the phone when he'd called for a ride home hours later when he was drunk and stoned off his ass. Two counts of involuntary manslaughter. That was not a way to start a life. I'd failed him too.

As I knelt beside the chest, resting my hands on the cold surface of the wood, all I could think about was how I'd told Charlie I would protect him and how I wouldn't let anything happen to him.

I'd failed. Once again, I'd let someone who relied on me down.

If he was dead… I'd never forgive myself.

I didn't know what I was feeling for Charlie. It was something I couldn't quite explain. It was bigger than me. More powerful. When I thought about it for too long, it left me feeling out of control, and I hated not being in control.

A hand landed on my shoulder. Kevin. Was I sending out signals? Could he see the terror in my heart?

I lifted the lid.

"Oh shit," Kevin breathed. In the next moment, his heavy footfalls sounded as he ran down the hall, yelling, "We've got him. Get me a medic. Now."

For a moment, I couldn't breathe. All I could do was process what I was seeing.

Charlie was hunched over in a tight ball, his thin and delicate fingers laced around the back of his neck, his head tucked between his drawn-up knees. Apart from the steady rise and fall of his back, telling me he was alive, he didn't move. There was no blood or indication he was hurt, but he didn't respond when I called his name.

"Charlie? Hey, it's Takoda. Charlie?"

I touched his back, rubbing along the bumpy ridges of his spine. He didn't respond.

A storm of noise came barreling up the stairs, and I tensed, knowing it wasn't what Charlie needed. When more officers and another paramedic got to the door, I held up a hand, warding them off.

Once I was sure they weren't going to interfere, I tugged Charlie's shoulder, encouraging him to sit back.

"Come on. Can you sit up? It can't be comfortable all crunched up."

To my surprise, he followed my instructions. His face was blank and unreadable, his gaze far away, unseeing.

With his movement, something slid free and fell to the bottom of the chest. I reached for it. It was an old Polaroid. There was a young boy in the picture. He wasn't all that different from the man I'd gotten to know over the past few weeks if you shaved off about seventeen years. The young boy was sitting against a pitted and cracked concrete wall on a poured concrete floor. The room around him was unremarkable and empty, so far as I could tell. His blond hair, lighter than it was now, was ruffled and had a slight curl. His knees were dirty. His face was drawn and sad. His gaze was wary. He was in a dirty T-shirt, several sizes too big, and underwear. In one hand, he held a single Reese's Peanut Butter Cup. In the other, a stick of white chalk. The wrapper for the chocolate bar sat on the floor beside him.

It took me a few seconds to process what I was seeing. To understand the implications. My heart hammered like a war drum as I waved Kevin forward. Nausea climbed my throat.

"Gloves," I said, my voice thick.

The paramedic handed Kevin a pair of gloves, which he pulled on before I handed him the photograph. "Process this. There are two more things in my desk. They need to be processed too. Nikola won't be able to argue against it anymore."

Then I turned back to Charlie as Kevin backed off.

Charlie was hugging his knees. I hated the vacant look in his eyes. It stirred so much anger inside me. If the man responsible for putting that look there had been in the room, I'd have gutted him without a second thought.

Cautiously, I tipped Charlie's face toward me, brushing a thumb against his cheek. His winter-sky eyes looked through me without blinking. His lips remained slightly parted.

"Come back, Charlie. Come back. It's safe now. He's gone."

Although it didn't feel like he could hear me, his breathing changed, deepened. I kept talking, encouraging him. I scooped up one of his hands, holding it loosely but connecting us so he knew I was there.

"Come back. Please. You're scaring me. Come on, Charlie. Please. I want to help you, but I need you here with me."

He blinked, and his eyes shifted a fraction. Down. To our joined hands. I gave a light squeeze and continued to reassure him. His lips moved like he was trying to speak, so I held my tongue. Waited. Listened.

"My... my legs are cramped."

I smiled as tears burned my eyes. If I didn't think it would startle him, I'd have tugged Charlie right out of the chest and wrapped him in a bear hug.

Instead, I took a chance and leaned in, kissing his temple and whispering in his ear. "Let me help you get out of there. You were so brave. You did good hiding in here."

"He's gone?"

"Yeah. He's gone. But we're going to catch him. I promise you."

But Charlie didn't move.

When I tried to stand, he held my hand tighter. "Takoda?"

"Yeah." I stayed crouched.

"I don't want to take Xanax. They're going to give me Xanax. Please don't let them. I'll try to stay present. I promise."

A fire burned in my core, and I had to temper my rage before I said, "No one is going to drug you. You hear me? No one."

By the time I managed to get Charlie on his feet, there were more officers on the second floor along with a pair of detectives—Wan and Myers.

Charlie took a seat on the edge of the bed, his fingers working themselves into a knot. I put a halt to any questioning, but Wan pulled me aside and whispered, "Nikola wants you back at the station immediately. If you don't comply, we're to bring you in cuffs."

"That's fine. I'll go, but Charlie is coming with me. I'm not leaving his side."

Wan consulted his partner. They had a silent conversation, and Wan shrugged. "We need him at the station for questioning anyhow."

I didn't like the idea of anyone getting in Charlie's face, but I kept my mouth shut. We needed answers, and the only person with any information was Charlie.

The officers gave us space as we went downstairs. I kept a solid grip on Charlie's elbow, and he stuck close to my side. Outside, neighbors had gathered on their lawns. An elderly woman ran toward us the minute we were on the front stoop.

"Charlie! Oh, Charlie. Are you okay, sweetie?"

I was prepared to answer for him, but Charlie lifted his chin and spoke, his voice stronger than it had been a few minutes ago. "I'm okay, Ms. LaPointe."

"I saw they took your dad away in an ambulance."

Charlie's breath caught, and his cheeks paled as he glanced in my direction.

"He was awake and talking." Not a lie, but I didn't think Charlie needed to know his father had been fading in and out of consciousness. "We'll get a hold of the hospital once we get to the station. When we're done, I'll take you to see him."

Charlie considered that a moment, then nodded.

Francine held her hands over her mouth, eyes glassy as she looked between Charlie and me. She didn't say anything more as I guided Charlie to the cruiser and helped him into the front seat.

Before I started the engine, I shifted and took his hands in mine. He was going to break bones with his anxious fidgeting. "How are you doing?"

"Not good."

"People are going to have questions."

His throat bobbed. "I know."

"How do you want me to handle this? Nikola has basically fired my ass, so I can't guarantee he won't toss me out of the building the second we arrive. I'll go to war if I have to. I'll do what I can."

Charlie's brow creased. "He fired you?"

I shrugged. "He might change his mind since I have every intention of walking back in there and saying *I told you so* to that fucking prick. It wouldn't be in his best interest to fire me now. I'm sure the crown attorney would have something to say about that."

"Oh god. He's going to call my mother."

"I don't know what's going to happen. He isn't going to want to tell her, that's for sure. She'll find out eventually, and he's going to have to do some major ass kissing."

Charlie shrank in his seat. He didn't talk about his mother much, but I got the sense they didn't have a solid relationship.

"One step at a time. Are you ready?"

Charlie nodded even though he didn't look ready.

I kept hold of one of his hands as I set off toward the precinct. Our fingers stayed tangled together, and Charlie seemed to calm even more with the connection.

We arrived at the station at the same time as Wan and Myers. Wan carried an evidence bag with the photograph I'd pulled from the chest. It hadn't been an hour since the 911 call, and Nikola had already assigned this pair to Charlie's case.

The bullpen was utter chaos.

Crown Attorney Elizabeth Falkingham had arrived along with a guy I recognized as one of her assistant crown attorneys. He was in his midthirties and held a stack of brown folders like a shield. Like all the attorneys I'd met in the past, he was impeccably dressed in a designer suit, his tie pinched tight at his neck, his shoes buffed to a glossy sheen.

Elizabeth was a formidable woman and not someone to be trifled with. Dressed professionally in a black pencil skirt that landed just above her knees, a white blouse, and a dark blazer, she carried herself with the air of someone worthy of her position. She looked like her son. They shared a similar hair color, pale skin, and a trim physique, but that was where the likenesses ended. Elizabeth's gaze was deadly. It could slice through a diamond like it was warm butter. And that laser stare was directed at my sergeant.

They were in a heated conversation just outside his office, like they'd intended to seek privacy but had become too lost in their discussion before reaching their destination. A tense hush had fallen over the room.

From what I could gather, someone had tipped off Elizabeth about how Nikola had ignored a direct threat to her son. By the sound of it, he was scrambling to save his ass and failing miserably. She was railroading him every time he opened his mouth. It was rare to witness Nikola so rattled, but the CA was doing a fine job of knocking him down a few pegs—and in front of everyone. This was not going to go over well.

We walked into the middle of their conversation, Charlie moving ahead of me but stalling when the argument didn't cease. His mother's back was turned, and she was too angry to notice our arrival. Sergeant Nikola's face was beet red, his jaw like iron. He didn't notice us either.

"You're offering me assurances *now*? After the fact. Is that what you're telling me? Now that my husband is in the hospital and there's an active threat against my son, you *assure me* that you're putting every available officer on this case?"

"Liz, you know we—"

"No. You listen to me, Darren." She stepped forward, a finger raised, hovering an inch from Nikola's face. "This is my son we are talking about. Do not play games with me. I know he has problems, but your job is to assess each and every complaint he brings you. I know nine times out of ten they're bogus. But you *assess them*." She was practically yelling. "We had a deal. Rumors are spreading like wildfire that you ignored physical evidence. I don't care if—"

"Mother." Charlie's fingers were taking a beating again, but his voice was steady.

Elizabeth Falkingham's words cut off as she turned and found her son. There was no sudden wash of relief. She didn't haul him into her arms for a crushing hug like my mother would have done under the circumstances. Instead, the moment was just this side of awkward. Charlie held her gaze for less than a few seconds before staring at the ground while Elizabeth evaluated him head to toe.

Once during her scan, her gaze slipped to me, but she dismissed me just as quickly. I was nothing more than another officer to her. One of about a dozen in the room.

"Charlie. I heard what happened. Are you well?"

What kind of a question was that? Was she an idiot? Of course he wasn't well. Someone had broken into his house, attacked his father, and… and I didn't know what had happened after that, but it was enough to send Charlie into hiding—physically and mentally.

I stepped forward, intent on saying my piece, but Charlie touched my hand, stilling me.

"I'm fine, Mother. Shaken, but… I'm okay."

It was a lie. I could hear the quiver in his voice.

His mother was just as apt at reading Charlie as I was—probably better—and he was emitting all his normal signs of anxiety. She zeroed in on the finger-twisting, the subtle lip-gnawing, and the tension making his shoulders ride high. His face was ashen, and he seemed to be struggling to stay present, his gaze moving in and out of focus.

"I'm calling Sofia. These men need to interview you, and you're in no state to—"

"I said I'm fine." Charlie's chin rose, and he met his mother's eyes with determination. He was wretchedly pale, and his statement contradicted his physical appearance. Elizabeth saw it too. I was afraid she would go over his head.

A buzz from the other end of the bullpen caught Nikola's attention. More officers had returned from the scene. "Liz, the detectives are back. How about we take this into an interview room.

Charlie can give a statement, and we can go from there. We're going to sort this out. I promise you."

Charlie's eyes widened at the mention of an interview room, and we both said, "No," at the same time.

Nikola ignored Charlie's protest and pointed a finger at me as though just registering my presence. "You go sit your ass at a desk for a minute. I'm not happy with you. I'll deal with you when I'm finished here."

"We aren't using an interview room," I said, ignoring Nikola's order. "We can find somewhere else to conduct an interview. Somewhere Charlie feels comfortable, and I want to be the one *aksing* the questions. I was the one handling his concerns before this happened, so it's my case. My responsibility."

"Absolutely not. You're done, Dyani. Wan and Myers are taking it from here. At this point, I'm not sure if you deserve to wear that uniform."

The CA watched our exchange with calculated interest.

It was Charlie who spoke.

"I'm not sitting in an interview room, Sergeant, and I want Takoda with me. He's the only one who believed me until today. It's only fair."

"Listen, son." Nikola got out his gentler, placating tone. "I appreciate you've had an upsetting day. We're going to do all we can to find this person. I'm placing Officer Dyani under suspension until his actions can be reviewed by our board of directors."

Charlie went to respond, but Elizabeth held up a hand, stopping him. Eyes like ice sized me up. "My son came to you with complaints?"

"Yes, ma'am."

"And what did you do about them?"

I eyed Nikola, reading the fury all over his face. "At first, I followed the direction of my sergeant and told Charlie I'd taken care of it when I hadn't. I was instructed to brush it aside. A short time later, I was *aksed* to make a house call. Your husband requested I come by because Charlie was upset about something that had been left for him at the front door. I grew skeptical, but no one else seemed concerned. When another gift arrived, I knew something wasn't right. It couldn't be Charlie's imagination, not with the way he reacted. It didn't make sense. I took my suspicions to Sergeant Nikola, requesting further assistance, and he told me to let it go."

"Liz, we've been doing this for years. On your instruction. I realize we got lax and stopped assessing each complaint as they came in, but we're talking dozens and dozens. You know what Charlie's like."

"I'm right here, Sergeant. I don't appreciate being spoken about like I'm not in the room or I'm too stupid to understand."

"Son—"

"Enough." Elizabeth held up a hand. Her eyelids fluttered with annoyance before she fixed her attention on Charlie. "Are you well enough to talk with a few detectives?"

"Yes. Somewhere open."

Elizabeth eyed Nikola, who nodded and waved at Wan and Myers before turning and heading to the hallway that led to the interview room and breakroom. The CA and the ACA followed. Charlie grabbed my arm and dragged me along after them. I still hadn't been given permission to be present, but I left that obstacle up to Charlie. I wanted to know what had happened in that house.

Nikola cleared the same room I'd used when taking Charlie's complaint about the vehicle. The door was left open. Everyone swiveled the chairs around, forming a loose circle. This wasn't a typical interview. Ordinarily, it would have been an officer or two and the witness. But with the crown attorney present, Nikola wasn't going anywhere. She might not have direct control over his job, but she was in a position to have extreme influence, and he didn't want to piss her off further.

I encouraged Charlie to enter first and take a seat beside his mother. When I grabbed my own chair and moved it to his other side, Nikola spoke up, a sharp edge in his tone that dared me to argue. "Nope. Out, Dyani. We will discuss your position later. At the moment, you aren't part of this."

I wasn't doing Charlie any favors by going head to head with Nikola every time I turned around. Against my better judgment, I admitted defeat and was prepared to leave when Charlie spoke up.

"No. He stays." Panic filled his winter-sky eyes, and he lost another shade of color as he slid to the edge of his seat, looking ready to bolt.

"It's fine." I gave him the most reassuring smile I could muster, holding his gaze. "I'll be right down the hall. I'm not going anywhere. How about I call the hospital and see how your dad's doing?"

Charlie's forehead wrinkled, and his fingers twisted and tangled furiously.

"Find a seat, Officer. If my son feels more comfortable with you present, Darren will make an exception. Won't you?" Elizabeth skewered Sergeant Nikola with a look that dared him to object.

It took a long minute and plenty of teeth grinding before he nodded.

When I sat beside Charlie, Nikola refused to look at me.

Fourteen

CHARLIE

Too many emotions were hitting me at once. It was hard enough dealing with what had happened at home, but any time I was in my mother's presence, animosity and annoyance poured off her in waves. It was almost physical the way it touched me—*crippled* me. I hated it.

She had never been able to handle the repercussions of my kidnapping. The broken boy who'd come home had turned her perfect life into a tragedy. Everywhere she went, she was the mother of *that* boy. When it became obvious there was no easy fix and that I would be forever changed as a result of what I'd endured, she'd given up. I was an embarrassment. The damaged child she refused to take out in public because of the whispers and comments. Because of how it made people look at her. Elizabeth had wanted model children. She'd wanted Adelaide and me to shine and grow into powerful positions in the community.

But I'd become a burden.

When my father had taken early retirement so he could be home with me twenty-four seven, homeschool me, and coax me out of the darkness, my mother had decided it was too much, and she'd walked away. It wasn't the family she'd wanted.

She dealt with me from ten degrees of separation. I would forever be a stain on her life.

Adelaide and I rarely spoke. She'd been brainwashed by our mother to despise me.

As everyone crowded into the officers' workroom, the weight of my mother's judgment surrounded me. She could act angry at the sergeant all she wanted, but I saw the truth. It was my mother who'd instructed all those people at the station to coddle me and keep me happy.

It was her way of keeping me quiet and ensuring I remained in the background of her life. If I'd not had my concerns listened to, she knew the possibility of me winding up on her doorstep and *causing a scene* was high.

A man in a tailored navy blazer and designer jeans leaned forward, balancing his elbows on his knees. He was Asian with kind eyes and dark, neatly styled hair. "Charlie, my name is Detective Kim Wan. I want to go over everything that's happened since you first suspected something was wrong. Is that all right?"

"Of course." I was still jittery from earlier and couldn't seem to shake it off. My heart was beating too fast, and my palms were slick.

"How about you go ahead and talk. Tell me everything, and I'll interrupt if I have questions."

It didn't take long to recap the times I'd seen a white Pontiac, the chocolate bar wrapper I'd found at the front door under a rock, and the box of chalk that had been left in the mailbox. More than once as I spoke, I homed in on Takoda's presence beside me. Knowing he was there was the only thing holding me together. I wanted to reach for his hand, but I wasn't sure it was appropriate nor was I sure he would be okay with such a gesture. Everything that had happened in the media room the previous day felt like a different reality. Had we really kissed?

Inner tremors made me shiver, and I couldn't keep my hands still no matter how hard I tried.

"When did you know someone was in your house today?"

"Dad had gone to the store. A while later, I heard the car return. My office window overlooks the front of the house, so the driveway is right below me. I heard the sound of the lock disengaging, and I assumed Dad was coming inside. Then there was a loud bang like he'd thrown the door open with all his might and it had hit the wall."

I shook my head, frowning. "I've never seen my dad so violently angry. I couldn't fathom why he was so upset. It startled me. Almost right away, I heard another thump, but this time it was different. Like he'd fallen. I bolted for the stairs, thinking he was having a heart attack or stroke or something. Maybe that was why he'd shoved the door so hard. Then I heard him groan and another muffled thump. I couldn't make sense of it."

My forehead beaded with sweat as the fear I'd felt when I'd realized the truth returned. For those brief few seconds, I'd thought my dad was sick. What I'd been listening to was another person hurting him.

"I was just about to race downstairs when another voice yelled, 'Where is he?' I froze on the upstairs landing. It wasn't my dad's voice, and I knew then someone was in the house... looking for me."

"Man or woman?" Wan asked. His partner, a heavier set guy with a square face and buzzed hair, was taking notes, as was my mother's assistant.

"Man."

"Did you recognize the voice?"

I shook my head. "No."

"Go on."

"He came looking for me. Calling my name. I ran to my bedroom and hid in the cedar chest at the end of my bed. I texted Takoda."

"You texted Officer Dyani first before you called 911?"

"Yes. I was afraid. He was the first person that came to mind because I knew he would help me." I shrugged helplessly.

"Okay. So this intruder came upstairs."

"Yes." I wrung my hands until my fingers ached. "He wasn't in a hurry. He was humming a song, and he kept asking me why I was hiding from him. He said we were friends. He... he said he had something for me."

Myers handed an item to Wan. It was in a clear baggie. Wan examined it a moment, then glanced back up.

"Then what happened?"

I continued to stare at the item in Wan's hand. He kept whatever it was hidden from me, but a sinking dread told me it was important. *"I brought you a present. This one's special."*

I touched the back of my head when a memory flashed across my mind. Inside the chest. The man lifting the lid. Something falling on top of me and slipping down the side of the chest. I'd been so strangled by terror I'd forgotten about that.

The gift. Something special.

What was in the bag?

"Charlie?"

I blinked the room back into focus when Takoda touched my thigh. I shifted my attention to his face. Warm, hickory eyes stared back at me. Sage and sweetgrass all around. He squeezed my leg and nodded at Detective Wan.

I turned back to the detective. "The man kept talking to me. There was something familiar about the things he was saying. He said he brought me chocolate because he knew peanut butter was my favorite."

I tried to dig deeper, to find the missing pieces from so long ago, but when I came up against the solid door in my mind, I was too afraid to open it. Whoever the stranger was, he lived behind that door.

"He said we talked about dragons and that we'd made a pact to always be friends."

"Could this be another child who was kidnapped?" Myers asked, glancing around the room.

"Impossible," Mother said, frowning as she processed my story. "No other children survived. Only Charlie."

"What did he leave for me?" I asked Wan, staring at the baggie.

Wan glanced from my mother to Sergeant Nikola like he was looking for permission to proceed. Nikola gave him a nod.

Takoda bounced his knee, the motion jiggling my chair as Wan stood and brought me the baggie. "What can you tell me about this?"

My fingers shook as I reached for it.

Inside was a photograph. An old Polaroid. I hadn't seen one of those in a long time. I wasn't sure they existed anymore.

My breath caught as I stared at the young boy in the picture. Me. My vision darkened around the edges as a tidal wave of old fear threatened to take me out. My past was in front of me. The chocolate bar was clutched in one of my hands. A piece of white chalk was in the other. The cold, locked room I hadn't seen in seventeen years. I knew every inch of that room. Every crack in the wall, every slope and angle of the uneven floor.

The chill in my bones and the musty scent in my nose was as fresh as the day I'd sat in that corner on that thin, bare mattress.

Goose bumps crawled over my skin.

A noise climbed out of my throat as the picture fell to the ground. It was too much. I needed to lock that door. Get away from that room.

I squeezed my eyes shut as tight as I could, shoving back from reality, clicking off each sense as I retreated to safety inside my mind.

Before I could achieve full sensory deprivation, I heard frantic voices calling my name. My mother's rose above them all when she announced she was calling my doctor.

And there were hands on mine. Warm hands. Comforting hands.

Sage and sweetgrass.

Then there was nothing.

* * *

I didn't know how long I stayed gone, but slowly, one by one, I tuned back into the world around me, testing my senses as I returned to the present. Was it a conscious decision? It felt like I was being dragged back by a force I couldn't fight. But there was no more fear, so I allowed for it.

Maybe I'd been drugged. It wouldn't be the first time.

Familiar hands cradled my face, stroking my cheeks. The gentle timbre of a low voice wrapped all around me, its soothing tone whispering my name over and over, telling me I was safe, asking me to come back.

"You're safe. You're safe. I've got you. You're safe."

I believed it.

I blinked, refocusing my eyes.

The room was empty. The door stood open, which helped me breathe easier.

Takoda had moved his chair in front of mine. Our legs were pressed together.

We were alone.

"Hey, you. There you are. Welcome back. Those fuckers are pretty good at overwhelming you, aren't they? Fucking asshole dicks." A tiny smile touched the left side of Takoda's mouth.

"Where is everyone?"

"Getting a fucking clue. Don't worry about them. How are you doing?"

I considered. "I'm mortified."

"Why is that?" His thumbs continued to brush my cheeks.

"You must think I'm a real headcase."

"I think you've walked through hell and back."

It didn't change how I felt. No matter how hard I tried, I would never live a normal life. I would always be prone to these random moments of dissociation, thanks to my past. Even with Sofia's help, I wasn't sure I'd ever find a better coping method.

"Wan's not bringing that picture back in here, but he does have more questions. We need you to remember as best you can every single word that man said to you. Even if you think it's insignificant. Whoever this is, they were there when you were a kid. We need to figure out who he is and locate him so we can arrest him."

"What about the pictures you were going to show me? The ones of the guys who aren't in prison anymore."

Takoda paused and pursed his lips. He took my hands in his, brushing his fingers softly over my skin. "I'm not sure it's a good idea."

"But I might connect the voice to a face, right? I might recognize one of them because I've seen them around town recently."

"We're keeping it as an option. I know Wan and Myers want to show you, but maybe now isn't a great time."

I closed my eyes and stared into the darkness. If I could tap into that time period, I could probably figure out who the man was. There was something terrifyingly familiar about him, but I couldn't put my finger on it.

"Give me a minute. Are you okay for a second?" Takoda asked.

I nodded and stared at the floor as Takoda ducked out of the room.

When he returned, Wan was with him, but no one else.

Takoda sat again, leaving his chair in front of me. Wan pulled a chair closer, but he kept a respectable distance from Takoda and me. He carried a notepad and pen.

"Wan's going to take notes. I'm going to go through this afternoon with you one moment at a time. Is that okay?"

"Okay."

Takoda had me start from the beginning. This time, though, he stopped me repeatedly to ask questions.

"Was he frantically looking for you? Like, was he in a hurry?"

"No. It was… a lazy stroll. Like he had all the time in the world, and this was some sick game of hide-and-seek to him."

"You said the song he was humming was familiar. What song was it? Can you identify it?"

"'With a Little Help from My Friends.'"

"The Beatles?"

I nodded. "It made me uncomfortable."

"How so?"

"It's connected to… when I was there. He sang it before. Sofia would call it a trigger. Like the wrapper or certain smells, it called up memories of that time. I know… I remember him singing it."

"Him who?"

I shook my head. "I don't know." I couldn't look Takoda in the eyes.

He moved on and didn't push. I was glad.

"He knew you were in the chest. How do you think he knew?"

I twisted my fingers, sparing a glance at Takoda then Wan. "My phone rang. I hadn't silenced it."

Takoda blanched, and his lips parted. "Me?"

I nodded.

He closed his eyes and tipped his head back. "Fuck."

"There's nothing to be done for it now," Wan said, placing a hand on Takoda's shoulder. "Keep going."

It took him a minute to shed his guilt and fix his expression, but Takoda felt responsible. I saw it on his face.

He walked me through the incident at the house, up until the man was in the room with me. I remembered more this time and told Takoda and Detective Wan about the man's comments about thinking he'd lost me, then seeing me on TV. How he'd been pleasantly surprised.

"The timing almost fits," Wan said to Takoda. "This guy sees Charlie on TV and recognizes him. It ignites something inside him. Whoever this is, he seems to consider Charlie to be special. He's probably been living his life, figuring the past was behind him. They were caught. He served his time. It's over. But then Charlie is right there in front of him on the TV. He felt some fucked-up bond with Charlie as a kid, and seeing him again ignites those old impulses. Then it kickstarts his search for Charlie. How long does it take him to peg a location? With the internet, I bet it isn't too hard. A week? Two? Three if he isn't too bright. That's about the time Charlie claims he started seeing the white Pontiac following him."

I watched Takoda's face as he absorbed Wan's words. Takoda glanced at me, then Wan, then back to me. "I want to *aks* you something, Charlie. You don't have to answer me, but if you can, it might help."

"I'll try." For once, I had no inclination to correct his grammar.

"I know you don't have memories of the time when you were held. Are they gone completely, or do you know some things?"

I was about to start twisting my fingers, but Takoda must have sensed it and reached out, folding my hands in his.

My heart stuttered and found a steadier rhythm.

"I get flashes. I remember little things. Like that room. The smell. I remember being cold and scared. I remember how the T-shirt was so big I could tuck my legs inside to stay warm."

"The people? Do you ever get flashes of them?"

Those thoughts were dangerous. I shook my head.

"Do you remember anyone treating you differently? Anyone who called you special or brought you things the other children didn't get? Gave you privileges the others didn't have."

"I never saw the other kids. I wouldn't know what they got."

"So you remember being kept apart from the others?"

"I didn't know there were others until long after I was rescued. In the few memories I have, I was always alone."

"Do you remember the day that picture was taken?" Wan asked.

Takoda shot him a dirty look, warning him the topic of the picture was off-limits.

"I do."

Takoda's and Wan's eyes widened as they stared at me, waiting.

"Don't get too excited. The memory isn't as clear as you'd like."

"What can you tell us?" Wan asked.

My heart bruised my ribs, but I gathered all the self-control I could muster. "C-could you get the photograph again?"

Wan didn't move. He glanced at Takoda as though seeking permission. Takoda's gaze was locked with mine.

"Charlie, you don't—"

"I do. There's something in that picture that stirred a memory."

Takoda didn't look happy, but he tipped his chin at Wan, who got up and left. A few minutes later, he came back with the photograph in the evidence bag. For a second, I didn't think he was going to give it to me. He clutched it to his chest.

I glanced at Takoda. "I'll stay present. I'm in control."

"You can't make those promises."

"I can. I'm prepared for what I'll be seeing this time."

Sighing, Takoda washed a hand over his face and gestured at Wan, who gave him the baggie. Takoda studied it a minute before turning it around to face me.

The reaction I had on the second viewing was physical. My whole body went tight and on alert, but I clung to the present, looking once again at what I'd seen before. "My thumb. The one holding the chalk. It's tucked inside my palm." I pointed with a trembling finger. "If you look closely, you can see the white of a napkin that's wrapped around it. It's camouflaged by the chalk a bit."

Takoda turned the photo back around, and Wan leaned against his side. Together they looked at the picture and what I'd pointed out.

"Okay. I see it," Takoda said. "What does it mean?"

I held up my thumb, the same one that was wrapped in the picture. The scar was nearly invisible now. It had been seventeen years, but if a person looked close enough, they could see it.

"The day the person took the picture was the same day he made me take a blood oath. A pact. Brothers. Best friends. Always."

Fifteen

TAKODA

"I want him in protective custody. There is no chance in hell he's…"

"… can leave an officer camped at his house. We don't…"

"If the next words out of your mouth are…"

"I'm telling you. Look at the file. The only kid who was rescued was Charlie. That means…"

"This isn't the act of an adult. I'm just saying…"

"Erratic heart rhythm… three cracked ribs… keeping him for observation."

"… am not sending him back to that house alone…"

"I'm not saying we should…"

"If he'd look at these pictures, maybe we could…"

My head buzzed with the overlapping conversations and heated arguments taking place in Nikola's cramped office. I was grateful Corey had offered to get Charlie some water and sit with him while we sorted this shit out.

I hovered by the door, observing the scene, listening. Myers had the old case file spread out on Nikola's desk, and he was in a heated argument with Wan, pointing at the files and hissing his opinions. Elizabeth was making demands for Charlie's safety, and Nikola was stumbling, trying to please her while not blowing the department's budget for the year all in one go.

It was nothing but a mess of background noise. All I could think about was the absent look in Charlie's eyes that had remained for a solid fifteen minutes after he'd viewed that photograph the first time. It was haunting and scored me right to the bone.

The uproar that had followed had been intense, and I knew it hadn't helped Charlie's state of mind. When I'd shouted for everyone to leave the room, Nikola had lost his shit because I'd dared to order everyone around. We'd ended up in a yelling match I knew had done me no favors. Elizabeth had been ready to call Charlie's doctor. Wan and Myers had been confused about what was happening. It had taken Kevin's sharp whistle at the door to bring everyone down. He'd informed Nikola that I'd been able to bring Charlie around when this had happened at the house earlier. Elizabeth had seemed surprised. More arguing had taken place before Nikola had submitted and allowed me to sit with Charlie while everyone else cleared out.

Now we had more questions than answers.

Someone had a renewed interest in Charlie. Whoever the person was, they'd had a special bond with him in the past. The thought disgusted me. I agreed with Wan. It sounded like the person in question was another child. The way he'd spoken to Charlie, referring to their blood pact as making them brothers, talking about playing games, and telling stories didn't fit with the idea that it was an adult.

But it was impossible.

However, the thing that bothered me most at the moment was what would happen with Charlie. We'd received a report from the hospital. His dad was in rough shape, and they were keeping him for a few days. There was no way I was letting Charlie go back to his house alone.

"I'll watch the house," I said, cutting into the argument between my boss and Charlie's mom.

"No. Absolutely not. He's not going back there," Elizabeth said, her tone brooking no argument. "I want him in a safe house. I want twenty-four-hour protection. There is an active threat against my son."

Nikola ground his teeth loud enough I shivered. "Liz…"

She held up a hand, stopping him. "Find a way, Darren, or I'm reporting your incompetence."

My mouth got ahead of my thoughts—like it tended to do—and I spoke before Nikola could snap. "I'll take him back to my house. There's your twenty-four-hour protection. I won't let him leave my side."

"You're on suspension, Dyani. We're getting to that point, but as you can see, we have more pressing things to take care of first."

But my comment had snagged Elizabeth's attention. Her icy blue eyes, lighter than her son's, pinned me to the spot. "You would take full responsibility for my son's safety?"

I didn't have to think about it. "Yes, ma'am, and it doesn't matter if I'm suspended or not. I'll do it anyway."

Elizabeth pursed her lips to the side, her eyes narrowing. I could only imagine what it must feel like going up against her in a courtroom. Her look was predatory. She might not have much to do with her son, but god help anyone who hurt him.

A voice behind me spoke. "I'll hire you and pay you for personal protection."

Charlie.

I shifted around. Charlie's gaze, a thousand times softer than his mother's, skipped among the people in the room until they landed on Nikola. "I think you're making a mistake suspending him, Sergeant. Officer Dyani has been on top of this problem since day one. You didn't listen to him until my father was attacked and someone came after me, but he was right, and so was I."

"Officer Dyani and I have issues to discuss that go beyond this present case. I appreciate you sticking up for him, but it's a police matter, son."

Charlie held Nikola's gaze a long time before glancing at his mother then me. "Then I'll pay you."

An old burning rage sizzled in my core. "I don't need your fucking money. I'll bring you back to my place and keep you safe because it's the right thing to do, and I want to."

I turned to my sergeant. "Am I dismissed?"

"Not yet. We're having a chat."

* * *

Twenty minutes later, Charlie and I were in my beat-up Escort, traveling through the city to the general hospital. Nikola had given me an unpaid vacation pending a board review due to my behavior. I was not allowed anywhere near the case. He'd made that abundantly clear, but he'd told Wan and Myers I could be used as a consultant or go-between since Charlie seemed more comfortable talking with me than anyone else.

There was a lot to do, but they could only push Charlie so far. We couldn't force him to remember things he'd locked away, and too much pressure risked him retreating.

Charlie had spent some private time with his mother before we'd left. His doctor had shown up, and after Nikola had finished lecturing me, I'd eavesdropped enough to hear Charlie stand his ground when they'd suggested he take something to keep his anxiety in check.

"I want to pay you," Charlie said for the third time.

"No. It's not up for discussion."

"But you aren't working now because of me."

"No, I'm not working because I have a big fucking mouth and no self-control. *Aks* Nikola. He'll tell you."

"Please?"

"No. Drop it," I snapped.

Charlie startled at my harsh tone, so I dialed it back, taking a breath.

"I don't want your money. Please stop throwing it in my face, or I'm going to get angry."

Charlie didn't speak for the following two blocks. He went back to worrying his fingers.

"We'll stop at your house after we visit your dad so you can gather some things."

Charlie nodded but stared out the window. I didn't like the distant look in his eyes.

"I'm sorry I yelled."

"It's fine."

"Are you okay?"

"Not particularly. I feel useless in about every way possible. All the answers are locked inside my head, and I'm too afraid to tap into them. Even with the knowledge that it could help eliminate the threat, I can't do it."

"No one thinks you're purposefully holding back."

He sighed and rested his head on the window. I hated how tormented he seemed, and I wanted to reach out and touch his leg or take his hand, but I feared that would only put undue pressure on him he didn't need.

And now I'd gone and added more shit to the mix and upset him. I knew our vastly different financial positions would become a problem eventually. The last thing I needed was Charlie waving money in my face. He might not see it that way, but that was how I felt. I'd offered to keep him with me because the thought of him being alone terrified me. I didn't trust anyone else to care for him.

But of course I was too chicken shit to tell him that.

My phone rang, and my sister's name flashed across the screen. I'd called her earlier, before everything had happened, and had left her a message to get back to me. The clock on the dash said it was after four. She must have been done with school for the day. I was proud of her. She'd taken to college well and was eagerly studying to be a social worker. She wanted to help other teen girls so they didn't end up taking the wrong road in life like she had.

The old shit box I drove didn't have Bluetooth, so I connected the call manually and tucked the cell between my shoulder and ear. "Hey, Dina bean."

"You called me? Are you still at work?"

"Nah, I'm on the road. Special assignment." I winked at Charlie, who'd glanced over when I'd answered the phone. My comment earned me the first weak smile I'd seen on him all day, which I considered a win. "I gotta *aks* you a question. You got a minute?"

"Ask," Charlie whispered, winking back at me.

I flinched. "Hang on, Dina. I gotta smack the shit out of my smart-mouthed passenger right now." I grabbed my phone from the crook of my neck and feigned punching Charlie in the gut as I rolled to a stop at a red light.

He laughed out loud and shooed me away. I hoped it meant the hiccup we'd encountered was in the past.

I put the phone back to my ear, gracing Charlie with a smile before driving on when the light turned green. "I'm back. He's been properly disciplined."

"I don't know what's going on, but I get the feeling I don't want to know."

"I wanted to *ask* you," I emphasized the word for Charlie that time, "if you allow walk-ins for your classes or if people have to be signed up?"

"What classes?"

"Self-defense tomorrow night."

"Oh. You have to register. Why?"

Charlie's humor was gone, and he was attentively listening.

"Any chance you would make an exception for your adorable brother?"

It was Odina's turn to laugh. "I would if I had an adorable brother. Turns out the two I got are bottom of the barrel. Ugliest slugs I've ever seen."

"You're a brat."

"You know I'd make an exception for you. Why?"

"I have a friend who could use some practice. It would be two spots. Me and him."

"Him and me," Charlie hissed.

I sneered, and Charlie shrugged with a beaming smile.

"I'll be coming too," I continued. "I have to check with him first to make sure it's something he'd like to try, but if he says yes, then you're cool with us popping in tomorrow?"

"Sure. Text me as soon as you know. I'll even wave the fee, but not because you're cute."

"You're the best."

"Remember that."

I chuckled. The hospital intersection was coming up, and traffic was heavy. "Dina, I gotta run. I'll keep you posted."

I disconnected and dropped the phone into the cupholder. I caught the light as it turned yellow, spinning around the corner at the last second and pulling into the emergency parking lot on the other side of the street. I knew Archie had been admitted, but this lot saw the most turnover, and it was easier to grab a parking space without having to walk a mile.

The old car's brakes squealed as I turned into a spot. The engine coughed and died with a rattling sigh, and Charlie patted the dash like he was thanking it for getting us this far. It was cute, and I smothered a smile.

"So, self-defense classes?" he asked, hands tucked into his pockets as we waited for the elevator to take us to the care ward where his father was warming a hospital bed. It hadn't taken long to find out where he was.

"You can say no. I thought you might like it."

"I liked my private session yesterday. Why can't I have more of those instead?"

Was Charlie flirting?

I grinned and bumped our shoulders together as the elevator doors slid open. He bumped me back almost playfully. I liked this side of him.

"I don't mind showing you all the moves." I waggled my brows. "But Odina has more skill. She could teach you better than me. We can always practice afterward."

Charlie watched the numbers above the door light up one by one, a look of contemplation on his face. "I don't know. It feels like a waste of your and your sister's time. Someone came into my house today, and instead of confronting him, I ran and hid."

The elevator dinged as we arrived on the fourth floor. I tugged Charlie out and off to the side so we weren't in the way of the people waiting to get on. I backed him against the wall and stood close, getting in his face without touching as he stared at the floor.

"Look at me."

His eyes came up first, then he lifted his chin.

"What you did today was *exactly* what you should have done. What I taught you was how to disengage from an attacker if they manage to get their hands on you. It's not about being macho. It's not about confronting a bad guy. Hiding and calling the police is what I want you to do. Understand?"

"I was scared."

"When I got your text, so was I."

The stormy blue quality of Charlie's eyes held me in place. He searched my face and cut his eyes to the reception desk down the hall and back. His throat moved up and down. "I want to see my dad now."

He was overwhelmed. Too much had happened, and he didn't need me in his face. I nodded, backing up. "Come on."

Archie Falkingham had aged ten years since I'd last seen him. The attack had left him looking frail. His skin seemed to hang off his bones, and his eyes were glassy when they turned from the small TV hanging on the wall to the door when Charlie and I walked in. Pat Sajak was asking Vanna White to show him if there were any *R*s.

Charlie rushed to his dad's bedside as the TV audience gave a collective *aww,* telling me the player had lost his or her turn.

It was a private room—*of course,* the jaded side of me observed—and the heavy curtains over the window had been closed, leaving long shadows and a dull yellow glow from the bedside light. It smelled heavily of antiseptic.

Archie grunted as he tried to drag himself more upright, reaching for his son with the desperation of a parent who'd been losing their mind.

"Don't move. Hang on. Dad, lie back." Charlie felt along the side of the bed. "Where's the stupid control to raise the head of the bed?"

Archie didn't listen and tried to tug Charlie into his arms, all while making sharp noises of discomfort.

"Dad, lie back a minute. Hang on. Where the heck is it?"

"It's hanging on the rail," I said, moving in behind Charlie and resting a hand on the small of his back as I unhooked the device and handed it to him.

Charlie was vibrating with anxiety as he took the control.

He helped his dad sit more upright while I examined the man in the bed. Archie had bruising along his jaw and a small cut near his right eye held together with a butterfly bandage. His arm was splinted and wrapped, and when the sheet slid off his upper body as Charlie raised the head of his bed, I noted the bulk of more bandages under his hospital gown.

Archie was hooked to an IV and another monitor that beeped along with the steady pulse of his heart.

The old man caught me examining it and grunted. "The old ticker didn't like what happened, and it's giving me trouble. It's nothing. They're just keeping an eye on me. I'll be right as rain in a day or two. Nothing to fuss over."

Archie grabbed his son's hand. "It's you I'm worried about. Jesus, get over here." He pulled Charlie into a crushing hug that shouldn't have been possible from a man with cracked ribs. He breathed Charlie in as his eyes squeezed closed. It lasted a full minute before Archie released him. "I talked to your mother."

"She's making a scene at the station."

"As she should. It's about bloody time she stands up for you." Archie groaned and readjusted, taking the weight off his hip as his gaze moved to me. "I hear you're taking Charlie back to your place. Is that true?"

"Yes, sir. Your wife wanted a twenty-four-hour protective detail. I offered."

"We'll pay you."

I gritted my teeth. "No, thank you."

"I already tried, Dad. Let it go."

"Mmhmm." Archie's attention shifted to Charlie, then back to me, his mouth set in a firm line. "She twisted your arm, didn't she?"

"No, Dad. It was Takoda's idea," Charlie said with pure innocence.

I bit back a smile when Archie huffed a laugh and shook his head at his son. "Oh, I bet it was. Such a hardship taking you home with him."

In a flash, Archie's good humor fell away and was replaced with deep fret lines, the weight of a mountain's worth of worry weighing down his shoulders. Archie clung to his son's hand, dragging him in for another hug like he couldn't stand the idea of letting him go. "I'm so sorry this is happening. I'm sorry I was skeptical when you told me there was a problem."

"It's okay, Dad." Charlie's voice was muffled where his face was buried in his dad's shoulder. "They're going to figure it out. I'm going to be safe with Takoda."

The old man cracked an eye and peered at me from over Charlie's shoulder. "I want to believe that too, son."

In that look was a silent reminder of the things he'd shared with me the other day.

Charlie released his dad and dragged a chair beside the bed. He was obviously worried, but he didn't seem to know what to say. In an instant, he was working his poor fingers into a knot.

Archie noticed too and patted Charlie's hands until they stilled.

"Have they sent anyone to question you?" I asked, stepping to the foot of the bed.

"I talked to a young woman with her hair buzzed on the sides. Can't remember her name. She was at the house. Her partner was a redheaded fella. She followed the ambulance to the hospital."

"Officer Corey Adina."

"That's her. Told her the same thing I told her partner at the house. I didn't see the guy's face. He attacked me from behind as I was coming through the door. Must have been waiting for me to get home. Took me flat out, and every time I tried to roll over, he kicked me. Shoved my face into the ground and kept asking me where Charlie was." Archie looked at his son. "I'd have let him kill me before I told him anything."

A single tear rolled down Charlie's face, and he batted it away before cutting his gaze to me, likely hoping I hadn't seen it. I gave him a comforting smile and turned back to Archie.

"So you didn't see anything at all? Clothing? Height? Hair color? Ethnicity? Anything identifiable?"

"Not really. He was white. Wore dark jeans, and I think he wore a leather coat. I smelled leather when he was leaning over me."

"What'd he have on his feet?"

"Workboots. Black steel-toed suckers. That I remember. Hurt like a bitch." He massaged his wrapped ribs.

"Did you tell Adina all this?"

"Yup. Everything I could." Archie's eyes developed a glassy sheen. "I was so scared he was going to take my son again. I tried to delay him so Charlie had a chance to hide."

"I'm okay, Dad."

Archie swallowed a sob before he managed to pull himself together. He patted Charlie's hands. "I wouldn't survive if someone hurt you again."

The words weren't directed at me that time, but I felt them in my core.

I wandered the halls outside the room for awhile so Charlie and Archie could have some privacy. I was in uniform, so I caught a lot of attention from both patients and nurses. I was dying for a Mountain Dew or an energy drink, some kind of caffeine boost, but I didn't want to wander to the cafeteria or find a vending machine. Even in a hospital, I didn't want Charlie out of my sight.

The perp who'd attacked Archie and taunted Charlie was getting bolder, and I couldn't trust what his next move might be.

I sat in a chair outside Archie's room as I picked apart the things I'd learned about stalkers from when I was in college. We'd had a lengthy unit on it during one of my criminal psychology classes.

Stalkers fell into a few different categories. This guy wasn't a stranger. As much as Charlie didn't remember the men involved during his kidnapping, the perp knew who Charlie was. Based on Charlie's statement, it seemed the man had developed some unrealistic fantasy surrounding Charlie and their past. He considered Charlie a blood brother or a solid friend. He thought he'd done Charlie a service back then by bringing him chocolate or treating him special.

The problem with those types of freaks was that they lived in fantasy worlds and tended to push limits. Over time, those types of stalkers got braver. If the object of their fantasy refused to take on their role, the stalker upped their game and their demands of the person. The more unfulfilled the stalker felt, the more violent he might become and the higher the risk to the victim.

It seemed like the man was patiently waiting for Charlie to remember who he was, like he was doing Charlie a service by giving him time. He expected Charlie would figure it out with the gifts, then fall into his role. If that didn't happen, things would escalate.

Since this man was connected to Charlie's kidnapping somehow, it was a safe bet to assume he had some type of delusional belief or romantic ideation surrounding Charlie. The thought made me shudder.

Fuck what Nikola had said. I needed to talk to Wan and Myers to see what direction they were taking. I hated being curbed. I wanted to go through that old file again and examine every single person from Charlie's past.

It was over an hour before we left the hospital. I took Charlie to his house, weaving through the streets of his neighborhood while staying alert for suspicious cars or people. I wasn't in a cruiser, so if someone was lingering around, waiting for Charlie to get home, I had a chance of seeing them.

When I drove past the house once without turning into the driveway, Charlie sat forward with his mouth open, ready to speak.

"I'm surveying your street first. Being cautious."

He sat back, slumping lower in the seat and peering warily out the window. "You think he's around?"

"He could be. He left you a gift. He'll want to know what you thought of that."

"Well, I didn't like it," Charlie mumbled.

I chuckled, and it earned me a shy smirk. "What? I didn't. It was disturbing."

"Agreed."

After circling the neighborhood a few times without seeing anything suspicious, I pulled into Charlie's driveway and killed the engine. The response team was long gone. I had no idea how thoroughly they'd gone through the house or how long they'd been there, but it was quiet now.

"Keys," I said, holding out my hand. "I'm going in first. I want to do a sweep before you follow me. If the response team left a while ago, he could have found a way inside."

Charlie scanned the house. "I don't want to stay in the car."

"No, you'll stay in the front hall. I'm probably being overly cautious, but I don't care. Whoever this is, I don't trust him."

Charlie handed me his keys.

On the way up the front stoop, I unlocked the door and reached for my gun, only to find the holster empty.

"Shit."

Protective detail with no weapon. Lovely. I guess I was going in without. After the commotion from earlier, I didn't really expect trouble, but I wasn't taking chances. Stalkers didn't always think rationally.

I cleared each room on the lower level and returned to Charlie before moving to the second floor. By the time I deemed the house secure, Charlie had wedged himself into a corner of the front hallway and was gnawing his lip until it was nearly bloody and going to town on his fingers.

"No one's in the house. Pack a bag. Grab whatever you need for work too. You'll be with me for a couple of days at least. I'd rather not come back. I don't want to risk anyone tailing us and knowing where you are."

"Okay."

Charlie didn't move. He remained wedged in the corner, his gaze skipping from one place to the next, never landing anywhere for more than fleeting seconds. He was acting like a cornered animal. Terrified. Except Charlie wasn't about to lash out. He was ten seconds from curling into a ball and retreating inside his head.

I held out my hand. An offer. "I'm not going to let anything happen to you. Come on."

His gaze settled on my hand, then moved to my face. Winter blue like heavy clouds full of snow. So much trust burned behind his eyes, I almost flinched. Charlie took my hand, and he settled a few degrees.

Our fingers naturally linked together. His cold. Mine much warmer. The wild look in his eyes vanished. He'd stepped away from the ledge in his mind. His panic receded.

Without a word, we headed upstairs. In his otherworldly bedroom, with his fountain tinkling in the background, Charlie filled a suitcase. His gaze skipped more than once to the chest at the end of the bed. It had been dusted for fingerprints, and black powder remained all over its surface.

It was comforting to know the scene had been properly processed. Provided the perp hadn't worn gloves, there was a strong possibility they'd get a hit, and since all the men they'd arrested before would be in our system, it could be as easy as finding the match. I would have told Charlie if he wasn't doing all he could to hold himself together.

I hovered in the doorway while he carefully folded clothes and added them to a bag. He collected several items from the bathroom—including a slew of orange prescription bottles—and tucked them inside too. For a long time, he stared at the bed as though undecided on something.

He was still for too long. I was about to step forward when he came back to life and continued putting items in his suitcase. I could only imagine what thoughts were stirring around inside his head.

We stopped at his office where he collected a laptop, a sketchbook, notepads, and various other supplies. By the time he was finished, Charlie scanned the room and sighed. "I'm ready, I guess." He chuckled, and his cheeks turned pink. He ducked his chin, hiding an unexpected smile.

"What are you laughing at?"

Charlie shook his head, but his cheeks burned brighter. "Nothing... Everything." He blew out a breath and laughed as he strained his neck and stared at the ceiling. "God, you're going to think I'm crazy."

I waited him out, a curious smile tugging at my cheeks.

Charlie glanced at the packed bags sitting at his feet, shaking his head. "My life's in danger. My dad was attacked, and all I can think about is how I'm going to camp out at your house for a few days and what *that* might mean."

Heat pooled in my belly. Cautiously, carefully, I asked, "What do you want it to mean, Charlie?"

He met my eyes for the first time. "I don't know, but... Do you even have a spare room?" he blurted.

"Nope."

His breathing hitched, and when I thought his face couldn't get any redder, it did.

"But I'm happy to take the couch," I said.

He was a ball of nerves again. I crossed the room and took his hand before he could bust a finger. I needed to find this guy one of those squeezy balls or something. "Look. What happened yesterday—"

"I liked it."

"Me too. A lot."

"You did? I mean... really?"

"Don't act so surprised. You're kind of cute as hell in a straitlaced, nerdy sort of way."

"I'm not sure that's a compliment."

I chuckled. "It is."

He glanced at our joined hands. "I should be worried about this guy stalking me, but my brain is on overload right now. If I'm being honest, all I can think about is what will happen later and if I'll be able to handle it. Or... if you'll decide I'm too messed up to bother."

With my other hand, I tipped his chin so he'd look me in the eyes. "I'm going to put this right on the table. I'm a straight shooter. I don't have time for bullshit. I'm pretty sure your dad's pegged me as a player, and he's right. I've got a bit of a reputation. *Aks* Kevin." I chuckled. "But there's something different about you, Charlie. I like you in a way I didn't really expect. I'd be very interested in doing a whole lot more exploring with you. But," I said, shoving a finger over his lips when he went to open his mouth, "nothing, *absolutely nothing*, will happen unless you're okay with it. You've got a lot going on right now. There's no pressure from me. I'm not like that. Do you trust me?"

"Yes."

"Are you spinning all kinds of scenarios around in your head right now where you think I'm going to get *flustered* and run away because there's easier ass out there? Okay, forget I said that. That was crude, and I can almost feel my mother smacking me across the head for that."

"The word is frustrated."

"Really? Right now? You're a grammar Nazi, and you're *frustrating* me."

He smiled. It was shy and uncertain. "Just trying to help."

I brushed a thumb along his cheek, the intoxicating scent of Charlie all around me. "I will never rush you."

"Okay."

"Can I kiss you?"

"Yes," he breathed.

I kept it light and chaste, no tongue, as much as I wanted to taste every part of Charlie. He sighed against my mouth and brought his hands to my waist…

Then he jerked back with wide eyes, his hands in the air. "Oh my god. I touched your gun."

I almost choked on my spit, an undignified snort bursting out of me as I laughed. What made it funnier was how the double meaning went right over Charlie's head.

Charlie stared, perplexed, as I folded at the waist and laughed. "For starters, I don't have a gun. Nikola took it. You touched my holster."

And then I kept right on laughing because Charlie just had no idea.

Once I calmed, I didn't bother with an explanation, no matter how puzzled Charlie seemed. I grabbed one of his bags off the floor and hauled it over my shoulder. "Come on. I have cats to feed, and if I keep kissing you, my other gun's going to go off on its own because you are too fucking cute for words."

"Other gun?" he asked with all the innocence that was Charlie.

I winked and left him to puzzle it out.

I was halfway down the stairs when it sank in, and Charlie exclaimed, "Oh my god!"

Sixteen

CHARLIE

Takoda lived on the south end of town in an area that offered lower-income housing to people on assistance. Although he wasn't in one of the government-regulated apartments or townhouses, his neighborhood was rough. The houses along each side of the road were in disrepair.

His one-and-a-half-story bungalow was set back off the road, shadowed by a giant weeping beech and wild bushes that looked like they hadn't been groomed in decades. The grass was overgrown and filled with weeds and dead leaves that had been left to rot in the fall. A gravel driveway ran along the side of the house and was filled with more persistent weeds that had grown through the stony ground, some as high as midcalf. A dangerous-looking rosebush at the corner of the house, one that had long ago died, reached thorny arms into the path of the car, threatening to entangle us.

A rough, paver stone path led to the crumbling front stoop. The yellow siding was weathered and faded, lifting off the face of the house. The roof sagged, and several shingles were peeled up or missing.

It was a world different than where I lived.

Takoda caught my perusal and killed the engine on his beat-up Escort. The old car shivered and rattled as it died in the driveway. The heavy smell of burning oil and exhaust fumes filled the interior now that we were no longer moving.

"Go on. Say it. Get it out of your system. The place is a fucking shithole. It's not good enough for you. You can't stay here because it's a hazard to your precious health."

There was a defensive edge to Takoda's tone, one I'd heard earlier when we'd argued about whether or not I should pay him for his services. It didn't take a genius to guess he was sensitive about our vastly different financial positions.

"I'm a twenty-nine-year-old man who lives with his father because sometimes, when I'm having a bad day, I forget to feed myself. I'm too busy fighting dragons inside my head and deciding what spell might best subdue them. I'm so far gone sometimes, I drool on myself." I turned to Takoda, shrugging. "So stop. You said you have cats?"

Takoda took me all in, eyes narrowing before he turned and pointed at the big front window. It was cloudy with years of dirt that had never been washed away. Low hanging branches from the tree blocked the view, but he tugged me across the middle console so I could see better. "See them? Their beady little eyes glow in the dark. They think they're sneaky. They wait at the window for me to get home. Every fucking day."

Two sets of glowing eyes peered back at us, reflecting in the fading sunlight. With the glare on the dirty glass, it was hard to tell their coloring, but I thought they looked like gray tabbies. One was a bit larger than the other.

"What are their names?" I asked, my cheek so close to Takoda's I could hear each of his faint exhales and smell the hints of sage and sweetgrass wafting off his skin.

"Clover and Dandelion." He turned his face. He was less than two inches away, and my heart seized. "Want to meet them?"

My body buzzed at our proximity. I liked it, but it was overwhelming. I sat back, smiling. "I do. Dad would never allow me to have a pet."

"Come on."

Takoda helped me collect my bags and took me around the back of the house. We dodged the gnarly rose bush and passed through a rusty chain-link fence onto a cement pad. He had a small yard. It was as overgrown and neglected as the front. A weeping willow sagged in the back corner. Its long branches were full of new leaves that brushed the ground. The neighbor behind him must have been cooking. Their window was open, and the scent of garlic and herbs drifted on the breeze.

Takoda fumbled as he searched for the right key on his keychain to unlock the door. "Let me take the brunt of Clover's greeting. Hang back on the landing and only come up when I tell you it's safe."

I didn't know what that meant, but Takoda was grinning ear to ear, so I didn't think it was anything bad.

The front landing was tiny, no more than three square feet, barely enough room for two people to stand. Stairs directly in front of me went down to a dark basement, and to the right, a second flight went up to what appeared to be a kitchen. Takoda kicked his boots off, letting them sail into the basement where they landed with a clatter in the darkness below. I toed mine off and left them on the first stair leading down.

The second Takoda reached the kitchen, a blur of gray fur flew through the air and landed on his shoulder. The suddenness startled me, but Takoda burst out laughing and snagged the furry intruder, nuzzling and cooing a warm greeting.

"That's my girl. Always gotta be dramatic." Takoda dropped my bag on the ground and shoved it aside with a sock-covered foot as he turned around to display his prize. I climbed the stairs to his level.

Still using a higher-pitched, lovey tone, he said, "This is my little princess, Clover. She loves her daddy, don't you, baby girl? Yes, you do. Yes, you do." The cat head-butted Takoda and mewled, nuzzling him back. "I know. I love you too. Say hi to Charlie. Charlie's staying with us for a few days. Is that okay?"

I offered my hand for her to sniff. After a cursory examination, she rubbed her face against me and purred. As I greeted Clover, a second cat weaved between our legs, meowing loudly, seemingly not impressed at getting less attention.

"Hey, Dandy boy." Takoda squatted and gave the second cat love too. "This here is Dandelion. He's not half as snuggly, but he hates being left out. Ain't that right, buddy? They're siblings, and they're both fixed, so they can't do the nasty and make incest babies."

I snorted then pinched my lips together, trying to cover my reaction. It earned me a beaming grin from Takoda as he placed Clover on the ground and stood. "What? It's true. That would be bad and kind of gross."

"It would."

"Do you want a tour? There's not much to see, but I can show you around. I want you to be comfortable here. Or as comfortable as you can be without maids and butlers."

"I don't have maids or butlers."

"I'm teasing."

He was but only barely.

"Um… sure. A tour would be good."

However, when Takoda walked away, I couldn't convince my feet to follow. My OCD was a powerful thing. In a different and unfamiliar environment, it roared to life and clawed unpleasantly under my skin.

I glanced down the handful of stairs to the door we'd come through, then I glanced at the basement and all the unknown that lived beyond the darkness. The kitchen windows overlooked the yard. There were two of them. Deeper into the house was a front door, a giant front window, and who knew how many more?

The runaway rhythm of my heart made my palms sweat. A fast-growing flood of anxiety poured into my veins.

"Charlie?"

I jumped and spun around. Takoda had returned, and he was asking questions with nothing more than a hitched brow.

How did I explain my needs without sounding like I was out of my mind? I was sick of coming across as impotent and needy.

Takoda's gaze slipped behind me to the door and back, and I got the sense he was putting the pieces together without my having to say a word. I fumbled for a way to explain that didn't cast me in such a negative light, but Takoda's hand landed on my shoulder before I came up with anything.

"You know what I forgot? This is technically protective custody, right? I mean, even though I'm suspended, I told you I'd make sure you were safe. I'm such an idiot. First things first. We need to secure the house. Entrances. Exits. I have to check it all. Want to help me?"

My chin quivered once before I tightened my jaw. Relief made tears threaten to flood my eyes, but I held them back. I wanted to crumble to my knees. He knew. Takoda saw it in my eyes, but he'd given me an out.

Takoda winked, issuing me a soft smile, then moved around me to go back down the stairs to the door. He held my gaze as he clicked the deadbolt into place—not once but twice—before giving the door a good hard tug.

I swallowed a lump and nodded.

He tipped his chin to the basement. "It's unfinished. One big room. Steel supports. Clutter mostly. Shit I have no use for. There are two windows at street level at the front of the house. Tiny things. Hardly big enough for a person to crawl through. Do you want to check them with me, or do you trust me to check them alone?"

I considered. I hated unfinished basements. They were too reminiscent of my past. The cold concrete walls felt the same as the small room where I'd been held. The scent. The chill.

"Do the windows open, or are they sealed? What kind of latches are on them? Are they stiff locks, or do they move easily?" I sighed. "You know what? I'll come with you. I have to or else…"

Takoda held out his hand.

Maybe it was a tick against me, but Takoda didn't say a thing. He sensed I was uncomfortable in the basement but let me go through my lock ritual, never releasing his grip. On the way back upstairs, I tested the deadbolt on the back door myself. He let go of my hand once we were upstairs again, then we went from room to room, and Takoda let me check the rest of the doors and windows until I was satisfied.

Under my skin lived shame and embarrassment, but this was what I'd become. This was what those people had done to me, and I couldn't change it.

I needed to know I was secure while inside, but I also had to know the locks were under my control, and I could get out if I needed to. It was a fine balance that I'd fought with for years. One that caused me a lot of grief, but I lived with it.

The last place we checked was Takoda's bedroom. With the final latch moving under my fingers, the itch of my obsession faded. With its presence gone, it dawned on me where we were. A new spike of adrenaline crashed into me, but this one was entirely different and was accompanied by warmth and jitters.

Takoda's room was simple, if not disorganized. Clothes were falling out of a hamper by the door. His bed was unmade, navy blue sheets spilling onto the floor, and a comforter with a faded checkered pattern was in a ball in the center of the mattress. A basket of clean laundry sat on top of a plywood dresser by the window. There was a worn chair in the corner with random pieces of a uniform draped over the top. It was stuffy, but a familiar scent hung in the air. Sage and sweetgrass.

"You can have the bedroom. My couch is not in great shape, so I'll suffer there." Takoda crossed the room and stripped the sheets off the bed, dropping them in a pile on the floor. "God, I'm sorry for the mess. I have no clue when I washed these last. I'll find clean ones."

After tugging the pillowcase off the second pillow, Takoda gathered the bedding in his arms and pivoted, glancing around. "Make yourself at home. Take a few drawers in the dresser. Just shove my clothes in that basket, and I'll get it out of here. I'll make us dinner in a bit too. I might have something in the freezer I can *unthaw*. I'd order takeout, but I'm broke, and I don't get paid until next week. I have to throw my last twenty at gas for the car. Had I known this was going to be a thing, I'd have cut down my bar nights with Kevin this month." He shrugged. "Sorry." He glanced at me, looking sheepish, but when he caught my attempt at covering a smile, he scowled. "What?"

"You can't *unthaw* something."

"Yes, I can. What the fuck are you talking about?"

I pinched my lips and shook my head. "Never mind."

Takoda still looked confused, but I decided to let it go.

"I'll order us food," I said.

"No. No way. I wasn't saying all that so I could be your charity case. I'm just... This isn't a five-star hotel. I live in a shitty house on a shitty street in a shitty neighborhood, but it's mine, and I like it here. I'm proud of what I have, even if it doesn't look like much. I make decent enough money, but I just don't like saving it for a rainy day. I go out and have fun, and when it's gone, it's gone. On payday, I get more. I didn't expect to have company."

"And I don't want to burden you. I don't expect you to feed me. What you're doing is above and beyond, and you won't let me pay you, so let me get dinner. As a thank you. Not because you're a charity case."

Takoda's jaw ticked, and I thought he was going to object. In the end, he sighed and nodded. "Fine. Thank you." He headed down the hall with the pile of dirty sheets. "Oh," he called, "are you a TV person? Because all we watch in this house is *Animal Planet,* and good luck putting anything else on."

I smiled to myself. Somehow, I didn't think he was joking.

While I unpacked a few belongings, fighting with the discomfort of being somewhere that wasn't home, I heard Takoda talking softly to someone on the phone in the kitchen. His noisy washing machine clunked and rattled in the basement as it went through its wash cycle on uneven legs. Every now and again, I caught random words from his conversation that told me he was discussing my case with someone at the station. I strained to hear better, but with the noise from the basement, it was impossible.

Both of his cats lay on the freshly made bed, watching me as I paced the room, getting a sense of my surroundings and shaking the constant urge to test the lock on the window or peer out the curtains I'd closed. The sheer unfamiliarity of my surroundings was wreaking havoc on my state of mind. I didn't know how I was going to sleep.

Already on edge, it was harder and harder to keep the day's events from overwhelming me. I sat on the bed and offered my hand to the nearest cat. I thought it was Clover. She sniffed my fingers then laid her head down. I stroked her fur as she closed her eyes.

"Are you settling in okay?"

I glanced at the doorway and found Takoda leaning against the frame, cell phone in hand. He'd showered and changed into cargo shorts and a plain white T-shirt. It contrasted with his olive skin tone beautifully and drew my eye to the art decorating his arms.

"What are they doing at the station?"

He stared at me for a long moment, and I didn't think he was going to answer. "All right. I'm only going to tell you because you *brung* it up. I'll tell you what I got out of Wan, then we drop it for the night. Deal?"

"Brought."

Takoda's expression turned flat. "We need to talk about this little thing you have for correcting my words all the time."

I couldn't hide my grin. "I don't think you hate it as much as you let on."

His attempt at a serious expression cracked, and he laughed. "I still say *misunderestimate* is a word. I will die on that hill. Even Kevin agrees with me, and Kevin is stupid smart."

I pinched my lips together before saying, "Well, perhaps it is I who *misunderestimated* then. Forgive me."

"I'll think about it."

Takoda crossed the room and sat beside Dandelion, who turned indignant with the interruption to his sleep, stood, arched his back, then jumped off the bed and strutted from the room.

"Excuse me for disturbing you, Mister Snooty McSnoot Face."

Takoda rolled his eyes and stretched out on his side, watching as I continued to pet a sleeping Clover, waiting for an update.

"All right. Here's what I know. No fingerprints were found on the cedar chest or the photograph. The wrapper and box of chalk gave them nothing useable either. He must have worn gloves at the house. They're pulling files for all the men who've been released from prison who were involved in the original case. They'll be paying them a visit and bringing them in for questioning if necessary. That's all I know at the moment."

It wasn't much.

"How old are they?"

Takoda frowned and shook his head. "Who? Those guys? Now? I'm not sure. I only read the file once. I can't remember the ages of the men they arrested." He shrugged. "I don't think I looked, to be honest. Why?"

"I just feel like the person was younger."

"Younger then or younger this morning when he came after you?"

I tried to conjure memories of both earlier in the day and the day from my past when I remembered making a blood pact with someone in that drafty concrete room. Someone who'd brought me chocolate and sang The Beatles.

"Both. I don't know. I have no proof or evidence to support it. It's just a feeling. How old were the other children?"

"Nope. No way. We aren't doing this. Not tonight. If you want to head to the station tomorrow and go over some things, we can do that, but I'm not going down memory lane with you after the day you've had. We're packing it away before you end up with nightmares or go inside your head where I can't reach you."

I felt called out. The risk was real, and Takoda knew it.

He must have taken my silence for agreement. "Now, let's figure out what we're going to eat and choose an episode of *Animal Planet* that won't result in us getting our eyeballs scratched out of our faces while we sleep."

Clover was in a tight ball against my hip, purring and looking far more innocent than the picture of violence Takoda painted. "You make them sound vicious. I don't believe you."

Takoda chuckled. "Wait until you see them go at the screen. They fight over who can be closest. It's digital anarchy."

* * *

I ordered delivery from a little Indian place I enjoyed that was in the heart of downtown. Takoda didn't object, but I could see he wanted to. It was a pricey joint, and he must have known as much. I ignored his glares and placed the order anyhow.

He crouched by a cabinet near the TV, sifting through over a dozen DVDs of his cats' favorite program as he chose a disc.

"Did you *aks* them to make it super spicy? Wait. *Ask*. I meant *ask*. Oh god, don't say it. I swear to god, I will kick your cute little bubble ass if you correct my words again." He mock-sneered and pointed a finger at me. "Don't do it. I'm warning you."

"I *asked* for medium spice. Is that okay? I can't do really hot. It gives me heartburn."

"Fine. That works."

"Bubble ass?"

Takoda grinned facetiously as he waved a DVD case in the air at his cats. "*Frozen Planet* tonight, guys? Dandelion goes ape shit over the flying penguins," he told me.

"I don't have a bubble ass."

"I said a cute little bubble ass. You do so, and it was a compliment."

I glared—unconvincingly—and Takoda smirked as he loaded the DVD into the player. His comment had brought those butterflies to life in my belly again, and I couldn't help taking him in while his back was turned. It was hard to believe he looked at me the same way. Especially considering how different we were.

Once the program was playing, his cats bounded up onto the TV stand and sat directly in front of the screen, blocking the view. Takoda laughed and waved a hand at them as he flopped on the couch as if to say, *You see?*

"They're kind of rude like that. Hope it's okay. I've told them a dozen times to sit on the floor, but cats don't listen."

"It's fine. I might have seen this episode anyhow. You love animals. I saw the way you were with Stanley's dog."

"Yeah. People annoy me. Animals, not so much."

"Why is that?"

"Why is what?" Takoda tucked one knee under his butt, turning to face me as he draped an arm over the back of the couch. There was a good foot of space between us.

He was right. The couch wasn't a comfortable piece of furniture. The middle support seemed to be compromised. I had to prop myself in a certain way so I wouldn't fall into the center. I felt awful knowing I'd taken his bed and this was where Takoda planned to sleep.

"People. Why don't you like people?"

"I like some people. I like you. I like my sister. My mom. I like Kevin, even though he's a douche sometimes and makes me wait until he's hammered before we can scope out Cage, but that's a whole other story he's not prepared to talk about yet. Corey's okay. And Wan. I don't know. What I hate is fake or pretentious people. People who think they're better than me or more deserving just because they have money or a better job. All of a sudden, they get this superiority complex. It's bullshit. We're all the same deep down. Or we should be." Takoda shook his head and watched his cats go wild, batting at the TV screen. "I don't know. I'm talking out of my ass. According to most people, I'm a real dick. That's fine. At least I'm honest about it. I don't care what they think of me. No, I'm not perfect. I have my own problems, just like everyone else, but I can admit it. Sarge would tell you I don't play well with others. I've gone through two partners in four years." Takoda laughed, but it didn't feel like a joke. "You know, he assigned me to you, hoping I'd fuck up so he could fire me."

"Really?"

"Yup. I don't think he assumed we'd get along. Didn't matter. Still got suspended."

"What's Cage?"

Takoda's brows shot up. "Really?" His hickory eyes sparkled with his smile.

"I've never heard of it."

"It's a local gay bar."

"Oh." Blood swarmed to my cheeks. "I didn't know that. Do... you go there often?"

Takoda chuckled. "I don't know. What's often? I probably go once a week if I can talk Kevin into it, which, I'll be honest, isn't hard."

It was one of the distinctive differences between Takoda and me. He might have been younger by a few years—or at least I assumed he was—but he was a world more experienced. When it came to sex or relationships, I was seriously repressed. Most sixteen-year-olds had more knowledge about sex than I did.

I didn't think I wanted to hear about Cage or what went on there, so I changed the subject.

Our food arrived a short time later, and we curbed the conversation to eat and laugh at the cats who were so engaged in the program their tails were poufy, and the fur along their backs stood on end.

"Every time," Takoda said, shaking his head.

They were the real entertainment that night, and commenting on their obsessive behavior helped things flow when I didn't know what to say.

Night fell, and the sun that had bled around the heavy curtain in the front room vanished. With night came trepidation. This wasn't my home. Takoda might have been acting as a sort of bodyguard, but he was so far outside of my league, it took everything not to squirm

The cats grew tired of chasing penguins. Clover curled up on the back of the couch and slept near Takoda's head where she could have her fur stroked by her cat-daddy while Dandelion vanished into the house somewhere.

Takoda yawned as the narrator's voice on the video droned on, talking about the dangerous enemies who threatened and hunted the flying penguins. I knew I should excuse myself and let him go to bed, but the strange house and all its stranger noises were keeping me wound tighter than a spring. I figured I could retire and pull out my laptop to work for a bit. Maybe I could slip into Vrydindel, shut off the building anxiety, and uncover plot points or confront the unexpected.

It sounded lame and childish when I considered the good-looking guy beside me who had a world and a life far more normal for someone in their twenties. Why couldn't I be like him?

I knew sleep would be impossible. I didn't feel safe here, no matter how much Takoda tried to make me feel welcome. It was too unknown. My day was catching up with me.

"Are you drifting away?"

I blinked and refocused on Takoda. "What? No."

He looked tired. His eyes were red rimmed and his lids heavy, but they examined me. "Are you sure? You've got that whole, I'm-almost-freaking-out-again look to ya, and when your eyes start glazing, I know you're tucking away into that space inside your head where you feel safer."

"I'm fine, and I'm not. You look tired. I'm going to head to bed. Let you sleep."

"All right. Promise you'll come find me if you have any problems."

"I'm not going to do that."

"Don't make me get out my mean voice."

I couldn't hide my smile. "Your mean voice?"

"I'll do it. It's really scary."

"I'm sure it is."

"Oh my god, you think I'm joking. I'll do it, then you'll think I'm an asshole like everyone else." He nudged me with a sock-covered toe, smiling the whole time he talked.

Laughing, I ducked my head. "Yeah, yeah. I don't believe you."

"I'm serious. Come find me if you have a problem."

"Okay, but you don't have to worry about me. I'm a big boy. I'll probably try to work for a bit. It will calm me down."

"All right."

I stood and hesitated as I looked around the room. My fingers itched to check the locks on all the windows and doors again, to scan the house, to do something reassuring and familiar. I resisted, but it took all my effort.

Before I walked away, Takoda caught my wrist and dragged me back down on the couch where I landed nearly on top of him. Surprised, I tried to right myself, but he took my face between his hands and kissed me.

It was sudden but not unwelcome. I stopped trying to get away and let my body sag against Takoda's. I didn't know where to put my hands and spent far too long analyzing that issue. The kiss was gentle but much deeper than the first two times, and fire exploded in my bloodstream, burning me from the inside out. Every nerve ending tingled and came to life when his tongue sought mine.

It was exhilarating and terrifying at the same time.

The kiss didn't last long, and when Takoda pulled back, I was dazed, half on top of him, and breathing heavily. And my cock was hard—something that rarely happened. Did he know? Could he feel it? My heart tried to evict itself from my chest cavity.

Takoda smiled. "Goodnight, Charlie. I'll be here if you need me."

Was there a double meaning behind those words?

All I could do was nod as I peeled myself off the couch and Takoda's lap and retreated down the hall, all too aware of the ache in my pants.

Sleep was a joke. If I wasn't losing my mind over the strange environment, I was reliving the kiss I'd shared with Takoda, analyzing the overwhelming surge of heat that wouldn't leave me alone.

Dandelion was asleep on one of the pillows and didn't look like he intended to leave. For a while, I sat beside him, leaning against the headboard, the bedside light casting a soft glow across his fur. I'd put on a pair of sleep pants and a clean T-shirt. Goose bumps climbed along my arms, but they had nothing to do with the temperature in the room. I felt like a live wire, sparking and snapping with a current of electricity that had nowhere to go.

And I was *still* half-hard.

The bedroom door was open—because I couldn't convince myself to close it—and I hoped Takoda wasn't bothered by the light spilling down the hall. More than once, I considered my laptop and working on my outline, but I knew I'd be too tempted to retreat into my mind, and I was sick of escaping every time things got hard. Detaching. Dissociating from reality. Sofia said it was caused by the trauma from when I was little, but I wasn't little anymore. Shouldn't I grow out of it? Shouldn't I have better coping mechanisms?

So I sat, doing all I could to remain present, fighting the draw toward calmness. Fighting the ache in my sleep pants and desperately wanting to do something about it.

But I couldn't. Not with Takoda down the hall. Not with a wide-open door I couldn't shut.

In time, my mind slipped on its own. I didn't go as far into the darkness as I did some days, but I was far enough gone I didn't hear Takoda until he sat on the bed beside me, jostling the mattress.

I blinked and found his hickory-brown eyes studying me. In the next breath, I registered he was dressed in nothing more than tight boxer briefs.

And the inferno roared back to life in my blood.

"Can I sit with you?"

I glanced around the room, clearing my head, refocusing. The clock told me it was after two in the morning. How long had I been drifting?

"Did I wake you?"

"No. I got up to pee, and I saw the light. I thought we had a deal."

"I'm sorry. I didn't… I'm sorry." I resisted twisting my fingers together and picked at the blankets instead.

"Move over."

Dandelion was no longer on the pillow, and I had no clue when he'd left. I slid over, and Takoda dropped down beside me, leaning against the headboard as he yawned. He didn't leave any extra space, and our shoulders connected. The heat of his bare skin bled through my thin shirt. I was all too aware of his state of undress and our close proximity. More tattoos covered his chest, snaking down his ribs and over a firm, flat abdomen. Some slipped under the band of his underwear. There were thorny branches, a diseased-looking heart, a murder of ravens, a crown, a cross. There were symbols whose meanings were lost on me and script I couldn't read. Over his ribs was a detailed and realistic eye filled with tears that pooled into a pond underneath. There was a reflection in the pond, but I couldn't make it out.

I could have spent hours examining them.

"Talk to me, Charlie."

"What?" I blinked and darted my gaze across the room, realizing I'd been gawking at his half-naked body. "I… don't understand."

"You're not sleeping. You're not even under the covers, so I don't think you're trying either. I know you're buzzing right now. You didn't even know I was standing at the door because you were gone inside your head. There's a lot of shit happening. Scary shit. This isn't your home. Fuck, someone attacked your dad today and taunted you while you hid in a box. I know your anxiety is probably maxed out. I just want you to talk. That's all. About anything. *Aks* me whatever you want. Just don't think about that stuff anymore, okay?"

I smirked, and when Takoda caught me, he scrubbed his face. "Oh, fuck me. *Ask*. Fucking *ask*. Jesus Christ, I fucking hate you." But his face split into a devastating grin that defied his words. When he pinched my side, I squawked and shoved his hand away.

Takoda laughed and did it again.

"I didn't say anything that time. God, don't pinch me. It tickles."

"You didn't have to say anything. You get this adorable little smirk, and I know I fucked up my words. Now quit messing with me and pick a direction. We're going to chat until you're really tired, then you're going to sleep."

Taking the life preserver he was tossing, I asked what I'd been curious about since meeting him. "How old are you?"

"Twenty-six. Just a baby to you. I know."

"In a lot of ways, you're older than me."

"I'm also ten times douchier." He paused. "And I know that's not a word, so don't say it."

I grinned. "I'll add it to my Takoda dictionary."

"I ought to pinch you again for that. You're turning into a smartass, Charlie."

"You're a wonderful influence."

"Your dad's going to kill me. I'm just going to pinch you until you're all sweet and innocent again."

I tensed when he feigned an attack. "Okay. Whoa, stop. Another question."

He laughed and sat back. "Shoot."

"You have two siblings, right?"

"No. Three." He tipped his head to the side and watched me as he answered, his eyes catching the low light and shimmering. "There's Odina, who I've told you about. She's twenty-two. She got a late start with college. Took her a while to pull her shit together. Calian is twenty now."

Takoda paused and ran his tongue along his teeth as though considering his words. The humor he'd had faded. "He's locked up. Two years into a four-year sentence for involuntary manslaughter. Killed two people driving home one night, drunk and stoned off his ass. At the time, he was underage to drink but a legal adult. They threw the book at him. Istas is twenty-four. She's somewhere up north, married, popping out babies, doing her thing. I don't know. She doesn't care about us anymore. Got out the first chance she could. What about you? You've got a sister, right?"

"Adelaide. She's three years younger than me. She went to live with my mother when my parents split up. We don't really talk much. She resents me for all the problems I caused."

"Resents you? Are you for fucking real?"

I shrugged. "Yup."

"That's bullshit."

"It is what it is. Dad tells me not to worry over it."

"I'm going to try really hard not to have an opinion."

I laughed when Takoda growled under his breath and fisted his hands until his knuckles turned white.

"If you breathe any harder, you'll blow fire out your nose, and I'll have to write stories about you."

"Don't antagonize me, Charlie."

I bumped his shoulder. "She's not worth it. She and my mother chose their path a long time ago, and it didn't include me or my issues. I don't let it bother me anymore, so you shouldn't either. I have my dad, and he's been my pillar of strength through everything."

"I can tell. He loves you something fierce."

"I know. He gave up everything for me."

Takoda grew quiet. His fists were no longer balled, but he'd taken up my habit of picking at the blankets.

"I know what it's like not having the support of two parents. My dad abandoned us when I was eight. Calian was just a baby. Two years old. Dad up and left one day and never looked back. Left my mom with four kids to raise all by herself. He barely sent a dime to help her, which would make your blood boil if you had any idea how much money my father has."

"He wasn't ordered to pay child support?"

"Sure he was, but he weaseled out of it for years. He'd send the odd check, then stop. Mom didn't have the money to keep hiring lawyers to fight him every time he failed to pay her. He has his own company, so it was easy for him to shift funds and work things in his favor. He's a fucking tool is what he is. He's remarried somewhere with a new family now. I have three half-siblings I've never met who are living the easy life because that fucking sperm-donor asshole liked them better. Fuck him. I'm the only one of my siblings who really remembers him, so I guess I have the biggest problem with it. Mom used one of the few checks he ever sent to have all our last names changed to hers. Her little fuck you to him. I'm glad. I don't want any ties to that man."

"You never had visits?"

"Nope. He walked and never looked back."

"I'm sorry."

The root cause of Takoda's inner hatred toward wealthy people was shining loud and clear. I thought it best I didn't comment further. I got the feeling he didn't often share this side of himself.

He was tense now and agitated.

The muscles in his thighs twitched. I stared at their smooth, firm surface for a long minute before resting my hand on his leg. I tried to convince myself I was offering comfort or support, but the truth was, I wanted to touch him. His skin was warm—*hot*—and my pulse spiked at the connection.

I had plans to say something reassuring, but my thoughts scattered, and it took everything in me not to rip my hand away and apologize.

Takoda stopped seething. I felt the heat of his gaze on the side of my face, but I refused to look up. I couldn't look away from where I'd placed my hand. I didn't know if it was okay to touch him or if he thought I was nothing more than a joke. Takoda probably picked up guys at his weekly visits to the gay bar all the time. A simple touch on his leg meant nothing to him. To me, it was the first step down a pathway to the unknown.

His voice broke through the cluttering noise in my brain. "What are you thinking, Charlie?"

"I don't know." My voice was raspy.

Takoda placed his hand over mine. For a moment, I thought he was going to remove it, but he didn't.

"Charlie, I need you to be very clear with me about what you want right now. I don't want to fuck this up and cross lines I shouldn't. Your dad will kill me, and it won't be a quick death. I'm convinced he would tear my balls off and peel the skin from my bones."

A nervous chuckle surfaced with his vivid description. "No, he wouldn't. He's not a violent man."

"Oh, he would. Trust me."

"I won't let him."

Takoda's gaze was searing. "How about you tell me what you want so we're safe."

"I don't know," I whispered. "I've never…" I swallowed a thick lump. "I just want to touch you."

Takoda caught my chin, and there was no more avoiding his deep, hickory eyes. He was so close, his breath gusted over my lips. "If for one second you want to stop, you tell me."

I nodded.

"No. With words. Promise me, Charlie."

"I promise."

Seventeen

TAKODA

I was going straight to hell. Archie was going to spend a millennium torturing me until I begged for death.

Every cell in my body screamed for me to back down. Charlie had had a horrible, stressful day. The last thing he needed was someone pushing his limits or taking him places he wasn't ready to go.

I feared he wouldn't stop me if it got to be too much. I feared he'd force himself too far over the line, and I'd have a mess on my hands. A bigger mess than I already had.

When I studied him, when I searched his innocent, winter-sky eyes for the truth, all I saw was determination. A tiny fire burned inside him, and he was looking to me for guidance.

His fingers on my leg twitched, but I didn't know if he wanted to explore more or retract his hand.

"Please, Takoda." The pleading behind those two simple words was enough to drive me forward.

I caught his mouth, kissed him, drew him closer with a hand wrapped around his nape. When he parted his lips, I swished my tongue into his mouth, seeking his and taking our connection in a vastly different direction than before. If Charlie couldn't kiss dirty, there was no way we could go further.

He surprised me.

Letting go of my thigh, he caught my waist and encouraged me to move closer. I heaved myself up and straddled him, holding his face and drawing sweet little noises from his throat as I nipped his lower lip and rasped my tongue against his. He tasted minty like toothpaste with an underlying flavor that was all Charlie. It was that flavor I chased. It unearthed a hunger that growled in my core.

"Touch me anywhere you want," I said against his mouth. "Anywhere."

He didn't respond, just angled his head so we could kiss deeper. Tentatively, his hands moved from my waist to my abdomen. His touch was feather light as Charlie glided his fingers over my skin, exploring with all the confidence he could muster. It tickled, but I didn't pull away.

For all that Charlie had been sheltered from the world, he was incredibly brave when he wanted to be, and I admired that inner strength.

He broke free from my mouth, and his gaze fell to my chest. His lips were ripe and abused. He watched as his hands moved over my pecs, tracing the lines of several of my tattoos, brushing cautiously over one nipple then the other. Then he let his hands wander down toward my navel. He didn't go lower, but the attention was enough to stir my blood, and my cock swelled in my underwear. There was no way he didn't see what he was doing to me. It was right there in front of him, less than a foot away. Hard. Aching.

For him.

I remained alert for signs of anxiety, but I didn't see any.

"Can I touch you?" I asked when his hands stalled around my navel. "Just like you're doing."

His gaze flicked to my face. His rosy lips remained parted, and his chest rose and fell in quick little bursts. "Yes."

I sat back on his lap, teasing my hands under the hem of his shirt. "Can I take this off?"

He lifted his arms instead of answering, and I helped him shed the cotton T-shirt and threw it onto the ground. Charlie was thin and didn't have visible muscles. His stomach was flat, and his hip bones protruded above his sleep pants. Fine blond hair dusted his chest. His pale, almost milky white complexion made his nipples stand out, perky and hard. What would he do if I took one into my mouth? I salivated at the thought.

Something else I noticed but refused to draw attention to was the obvious tenting in his sleep pants. He was just as hard as me.

I checked in with Charlie again, looking for clues he wasn't doing well, but I didn't find any. What I saw was a man who was desperately seeking guidance in something he'd never explored before. Something he wanted to explore.

I flattened a palm on his chest, feeling the steady thrum of his heart like a battering ram as it raced underneath his ribs. Charlie's gaze took in every angle of my face. I watched him as I trailed my hand over his warm skin. My touch raised more goose bumps along his arms. I grazed a knuckle over one nipple then the other. It earned me a tiny intake of air. A silent gasp.

Then I moved my feathering touch lower. When I brushed my fingers through the trail of hair leading to the waistband of his pants, Charlie held his breath.

I paused there, teasing with a light touch just under the elastic as I leaned in and whispered in his ear. "Before we go any further, I just want to say something. I'm not going to fuck you, so take that thought out of the equation right now. And it's not that I don't want to. So don't think that either. One step at a time. I want to make you feel good, Charlie. I want to make you feel so good. Can I touch you lower?"

"Yes." The word stuttered out of him.

"Can I use my mouth to do that?"

A long space of time followed my question. When I was about to take back the offer, Charlie squeaked, "Oh, god. Um…"

"Never mind."

"Yes, you can."

"Nope." I pulled back and looked him in the eyes. "If you had to think about it, then no."

"That's not why I hesitated." His cheeks were crimson.

"Why did you hesitate? And if you can't answer me, then it remains a no."

"I just… I'll probably embarrass myself before you get that far." I didn't think Charlie could turn redder. He tried to duck his chin, but I caught it, unable to fight my smile.

"If that happens, I'll just take it as a compliment."

I kissed him for another minute, tangling our tongues together until Charlie's fingers dug painfully into my sides.

When I released him, I took my time, exploring every inch of his neck, sucking and marking his tender skin, nipping and brushing my lips over his shoulders, then kissing down his chest.

His taste was exhilarating.

When I flicked my tongue over a pebbled nipple, Charlie cried out and pushed me back.

"When I said I was going to embarrass myself, I meant it. You… you can't do that. I'm… Oh god…"

I chuckled and glanced between our bodies. There was a distinct wet spot on the front of his sleep pants.

"Am I too late?"

"No," he squeaked. "But if you keep that up, you will be."

My face hurt from smiling as I bumped his nose with mine. "You're too fucking cute, Charlie Falkingham. I can hardly stand it."

"I don't know how to take that."

"It's a compliment. How about you take your pants off?"

That way he was in control. I still wasn't convinced he was a hundred percent okay with me moving lower.

Charlie took a second to compose himself, nodded, then shimmied out of his sleep pants, kicking them off the end of the bed.

I didn't look. Not right away. I kept my eyes on Charlie, noting every emotion that crossed his face. He was nervous, but he wasn't panicking.

"Do you want to take mine off too?"

Charlie glanced between us. He ran his tongue along his upper lip once before nodding. The action was less sure.

"You have to do it. If you want them off, you take them off. But, Charlie?" He returned his focus to my face. "You don't have to."

"I know."

"Do you? I'm serious. You won't offend me."

"I want to," he said with more conviction.

He didn't spend as much time thinking about it that time. He caught the band of my underwear, and I lifted so he could push them as far down my legs as possible. I removed them the rest of the way using my feet, kicking them into the pile we'd made on the floor.

We were naked, and I still hadn't shifted my gaze from Charlie's face. His was riveted on what he'd exposed, and I let him look. There were still no signs of distress in his eyes, so I gave myself permission to keep going.

First, I tipped his chin and kissed him, slower and more gently than before, savoring his flavor and the tiny noises he tried hard to suppress. Our cocks bumped as I settled on his lap again, and Charlie whimpered.

I took my time before I moved my mouth along his collarbone and down his chest. I left his nipples alone as I followed the path of fine hair to his navel. I circled it once with my tongue, dipping inside, then moved lower.

Charlie fisted the sheets and was statue still.

"Are you with me?" I asked as I came closer to my destination. His cock was stunning, uncut, and so hard the head poked out the hooded top. It glistened in the low light of the room, wet and leaking.

He hadn't responded, so I glanced up.

Charlie's eyes were wide and wild. He was panting, lips parted.

"Charlie, I need an answer."

"I'm good." The words burst out of him like they'd been shot from a cannon.

I had a feeling I could blow a soft stream of air across his dick and he'd explode.

"P-please don't stop," he said, the words pinched. "I… want you to keep going."

I pushed his legs apart so I could nestle between them. His muscles jumped and spasmed under the surface of his skin. When I looked at his cock and wet my lips, it twitched in response, and I knew Charlie was watching my every move. Waiting.

Knowing it would be over quickly, knowing he was already riding the edge, I put Charlie out of his misery. I took his cock in my hand, drew back the foreskin from his tip and licked one circle around his head before sucking him into my mouth.

That was it. It was over.

Charlie's body jerked and stiffened, then he gasped, a silent cry filling the room as he came. One hand reached out and grabbed my head, his fingers scraping my shorn hair like he was searching for somewhere to hold on. He didn't seem to know if he wanted to pull me off or shove me deeper. I worked him through every pulse, dragging his orgasm out as long as I could.

When he squirmed, I immediately crawled up the bed, noting every inch of his face. Tiny tears wet his lashes, and his skin was flushed all down his neck and across his chest. His lips were bright and pink. I kissed him, taking my cock in hand and working myself hard and fast.

I didn't know if coming all over him was a good idea, but I was too far gone to ask permission. It was small potatoes compared to what I'd just done, so I rode the tidal wave.

I was trembling, cusping the edge of delirium, when Charlie's fragile fingers wrapped around my hand, interrupting my pace. I groaned and removed my hand, letting him take charge. His touch was tentative and far too light. I placed my hand over his and guided the pace, showing him how I liked it. It didn't take much before my orgasm slammed into me, and hot cum coated us both. I growled, dropping my forehead to his shoulder as each wave rocked through me.

My heart raced for a solid two minutes before my senses came back online. I was too far gone to register if Charlie was okay, but I knew I needed to check in. Lifting from his shoulder, I rested my forehead to his. "Are you okay?"

"Yes."

"Too much?"

"No."

"You're not freaking out?"

He touched my cheek with his clean hand, and I opened my eyes, blinking him back into focus. "Takoda, I'm fine. Trust me."

"Okay, because I'm wrecked."

"I'm kind of a mess though."

I chuckled, glancing down at the trails of cum coating his stomach and chest. "You definitely are. Go clean up. Maybe you'll sleep better now. A good orgasm always helps me."

"Will you stay here with me?"

"Are you sure?" I didn't normally let men share my bed, but Charlie was different. He'd been different since day one, and the idea of sleeping beside him made my heart skip a beat.

"Stop asking me if I'm sure. If I wasn't, I wouldn't have asked."

"Fair enough. Go clean up. I'll fix the bedding."

Charlie returned a few minutes later, dressed in sleep pants and a T-shirt once again. While he was gone, I'd found my underwear. He crawled under the covers, and I encouraged him to lie up against me. He tucked his head on my shoulder and curled around me.

He was asleep within minutes.

* * *

Charlie disconnected the call, and the glow he'd woken up with that morning vanished. He slumped in the kitchen chair and rubbed his eyes. His hair was a mess and his pajamas bed rumpled. He yawned. We'd been up twenty minutes, dancing awkwardly around the previous night's activities while sorting out our morning.

"What's up?"

"They want to ask me more questions. Detective Myers thinks I should look at the pictures of the men they arrested back when I was a kid in case I recognize anyone, or a picture rings any bells. They're heading out this afternoon to pay the men a visit, but he's not convinced it's going to give them anything. He said a few of these guys are repeat offenders on parole and aren't exactly known for being truthful. Unless they suspect something, they can't get warrants to check phones or houses. The best they can do is see if they have alibis for yesterday afternoon."

"Okay. So, what do you want to do?"

"I told him to look for a scar. That's all I've got." Charlie turned his thumb, staring at the faint silver line that ran across its surface. "Whoever the person is, they might have a scar just like me. I told him I would take a look at the pictures, but I didn't promise anything. I guess my mother is kicking up a fuss about it. Again. She doesn't want them to let me see the pictures. She said it could bring back too many memories and damage me more. But…"

Charlie didn't finish his thought, and his forehead creased as he stared into space.

"But what?"

"But if I could remember, they would probably be able to catch this guy, right? It's right there. The memory. I feel like I should know who it is. I just… need to break down the door. Sofia has always told me it's a barrier of my own making. It will only come down if I allow it. At this point, seventeen years in, she doesn't figure it will ever happen, but what if I can force it open? What if looking at those pictures unlocks that space in my mind where it's all hiding?"

And what else was beyond that locked door? What else might Charlie remember?

It sounded risky, and I understood his mother's concerns. At the same time, part of me wondered if Charlie wouldn't be better able to move past the trauma if he could face those demons head-on. I wasn't a doctor. For all I knew, remembering could make him a thousand times worse. But he was an adult, and to me, it should be his decision.

"Don't hate me for double-checking, but you're sure this is what you want to do?"

His body sagged, wary and heavy as he buried his face in his palms and scrubbed. "Yes. I just want the past to go away so I can be a normal person for once. I'm stressed. My routine is out of whack. I feel stupid checking your doors and locks every five seconds, but it's a burning itch under my skin I can't ignore. I need coffee, but you don't own a coffee pot, and my eight o'clock mug is at home, which sounds ridiculous, and you must be second-guessing having anything to do with me at all."

I pulled a chair up beside him and sat. The rickety wood creaked under my ass. We hadn't talked about the previous night or how we'd woken up wrapped around each other. Not once had Charlie admitted he was feeling anxious at not being able to do things he normally did that helped him stay calm—even though I saw how much it pulled at him. His routine was upside down. He was trying so hard to pretend it didn't matter, and I couldn't understand why.

When I placed a comforting hand on his back and rubbed up and down his spine, Charlie sighed, his muscles relaxing.

"I want to see the pictures. I want to remember all of it, even if it hurts, even if I'm afraid."

"Okay." I was about to tell him to go find some clothes, shower, and dress, but I stalled and added, "You know, Charlie, I don't see you as broken or damaged or whatever it is you think I see. For all the shit you've been through, I think you're brave and strong. If at any point today you need a break or you have to go to where it's safe for a while, it's okay. I'll be there. You know, when you come back."

"God, when you say it, it makes me sound like a loon. They should just lock me in a ward and throw away the key."

"Yup. That's it. I'm going to poke your fucking ribs now." And when I jabbed him once, he howled and dodged me, slapping my hand away. I poked again and again, aiming for the soft spot under his arm and the ticklish spot at his side. Charlie laughed as he launched off the chair and shielded himself against more attacks.

"You're evil. Stop it."

"No. Not until you stop badmouthing my friend."

He dropped his arms, his face flushed. "You're mean."

"You're cute."

"I'm trying to insult you."

"Mean is the lamest insult ever, and I'm trying to make you smile."

"It's not going to work."

"It already has."

Charlie caught himself grinning and worked hard to turn it into a frown. His effort made me laugh.

I backed him against the counter and head-butted him playfully. "You done shit-talking?"

"No."

I put my hands on his sides, fingers digging in enough to warn him, and I raised a brow. "You sure?"

He tensed, and his winter-sky eyes shimmered with his smile. "Okay. Yes. I'm done. Don't tickle me."

I kissed him instead. He sighed and brought his hands to my hips. I kept it tame. Before it could escalate, I pulled back. "Shower. We'll go to the station and hopefully figure out who this fucker is."

"You have a really nasty potty mouth."

"Then why do you keep sticking your tongue in it?"

"Because I like to."

"I like it too, but right now, you need to shower before I get other dirty ideas."

"Okay, but for the record, I'm still really upset about the fact that you don't own a coffee pot. I may have to reconsider your offer of protective custody."

"We'll stop somewhere on the way to the station. I'll even pay for your *expresso*, okay?"

Charlie snorted then pinched his lips together.

I groaned. "God, what now?"

"Espresso."

"That's what I said."

"No, you said—" Charlie squealed when I dug my fingers into his side. "I'm going to shower. Let me go."

* * *

The bullpen was buzzing with activity when we arrived. The door to Nikola's office was closed, but the blinds were open on the glass wall and showed he wasn't alone. Charlie's mother and the same ACA who had been with her the previous day sat on the other side of my sergeant's desk.

The heavy scent of stale coffee hung in the air with the murmuring of several different conversations. Charlie hugged his paper cup of takeout coffee between his palms, sipping it and humming like it was the best thing on earth. I'd chugged an energy drink on the drive over, and that was enough caffeine for me. Plus, it tasted way better.

Detective Myers caught sight of us the moment we arrived and called out across the room, waving us over. His and Wan's desks faced each other, but both men were going through a file together, their chairs side by side.

As we approached, Wan shut the file and stood, hand extended. "Charlie, my man. How are you doing? Did this guy take good care of you last night? I've seen his shit hole house. I hope he at least changed the sheets on his bed. God knows how many layers of old cum they've gathered."

"How about fuck off, Wan." I slugged his shoulder—hard—as a crimson blush climbed Charlie's neck and settled in his cheeks.

The last thing I needed was Wan planting doubt in Charlie's mind or painting descriptive pictures of my extracurricular activities.

"I'm teasing. He knows I'm teasing."

Charlie smiled, but it was tight. He sipped his coffee, avoiding my eyes.

"We came so Charlie could review those pictures. When are you talking to these guys?"

"Once we're done here, we're driving into TO. You sure about this?" Myers asked Charlie. Myers had a fresh coffee stain on his shirt that looked like he'd tried unsuccessfully to wash it out. His shirt was damp, and the brown smear was wide, drawing attention to his round gut.

"I'm sure."

"The CA wants to be in the room. I'll go let her know that we're—"

"No. I don't want my mother present. Takoda can sit in with me."

Myers and Wan exchanged a look. It was Wan who spoke. "It wasn't a request. She made that clear."

"Well, she can suck my fucking dick," I said. "I don't care if she's the crown attorney. I don't care if she's the Queen of fucking England, Charlie is an adult, and if he says no, the answer's no."

Charlie cringed and elbowed me in the side. "Thanks for standing up for me, but the visual was absolutely appalling."

It took a second for me to reassess all I'd just said and find the problem. When I did, I gagged. "Oh… oh god, it was. I withdraw that, but he's still not doing it." I glared at Wan and Myers.

Myers pointed toward Nikola's office. "Don't tell me. Tell her, and maybe leave out the part where you want her to suck your dick."

Charlie's face pinched with disgust, and he shuddered. "Everyone stop saying that. Please. I beg you. I'm an author. I'm cursed with an extremely vivid imagination."

Heels on linoleum flooring told me Nikola's meeting was over, and the crown attorney was approaching. I caught a whiff of her expensive perfume before I even turned around.

Elizabeth wore a navy, knee-length skirt with sheer nylons and two-inch pumps, bringing her close to my height. Her blazer was open, revealing a white silk blouse underneath. Her blonde hair was tied back in a professional bun, and her makeup made her already menacing glare all the more dangerous. She was a viper, and it was hard to believe she was related to the quiet, soft-spoken man beside me.

"Charlie, I strongly advise you to reconsider."

"Mother, it's fine. I need to do this."

"You don't. These men can sort this out without your help. Think of the hours of therapy you might incur if this goes poorly."

"I already spend hours in therapy each week, Mother. I have for seventeen years. You'd know that if you called on occasion."

Elizabeth's lips pinched. "What do you hope to gain from this?"

"I hope to find out who's stalking me. I hope to find out who came into my house. Who attacked my dad and put him in the hospital."

"But at what cost, Charlie?"

"I don't care about the cost. I want answers. I want to feel safe again, and if that means unlocking some of the stuff I haven't been able to access in seventeen years, so be it. I don't need you sitting beside me and holding my hand. You didn't want to do it when I was twelve, so you don't get to do it now." Charlie turned to Myers and Wan. "Detectives, if we could please get this over with. My mother will not be joining us."

My eyes blew wide, and Myers, Wan, and I exchanged glances. Charlie was as fierce as I'd ever seen him. Perhaps he had a touch of his mother's venom in him after all.

Elizabeth glared as we marched off down the hall to the interview rooms. I couldn't help thinking this would turn into another tick against me.

Wan seemed to remember Charlie's aversion to closed-off spaces and continued down the hall to the officers' workroom. Three patrol officers were writing up reports. One of them was Sullivan, my old partner.

"Everyone out," Wan shouted. "We need this space for a bit. Give us thirty minutes, and you can have it back."

He earned a few glares and muttered objections, but in less than three minutes, the room was empty. Sullivan gave me a look on her way out. We hadn't spoken since she'd ratted me out to Nikola. Even though it had been a few weeks, she didn't look any more pleased with me.

In the workroom, with the door propped open, we pulled a few chairs into a semicircle, and Wan bounced the brown folder on his knee as he studied Charlie. "Are you sure about this? Last time I showed you a picture, you shut down and put everyone in a panic. If that happens again, I'm going to have the crown attorney so far up my ass I'll be tasting her perfume for a month."

Charlie squeezed his hands into fists over and over. He checked in with me, then glanced between Myers and Wan. "Yes. I'm sure. I'll stay present... Rather, I'll try."

I debated taking his hand, but I didn't want the detectives to suspect there might be more between Charlie and me, at least not yet. Nikola would find out, and I was already in enough shit.

Wan shuffled forward and tapped the folder. "Okay. Anything you can tell us might help. Even if you don't think it makes sense, just talk it through."

I shuffled closer, resting my thigh against Charlie's, hoping he might draw strength from me, hoping it was enough.

Charlie took a shaky breath as Wan opened the folder.

Eighteen

CHARLIE

I didn't know what to expect. My entire system was on alert. The tenuous control I had over my emotions was on the cusp of breaking. If Takoda hadn't been right beside me, thigh pressed to mine, I knew I wouldn't have agreed to this. His presence gave me a sense of safety and security even when the enemy was my memories and what they could reveal.

Wan opened the folder. Inside was a stack of photographs. He removed two, closed the folder, then placed them side by side on top. One looked dated, and the second looked fairly new.

"We've collected recent photos to go with the ones taken seventeen years ago when these men were arrested. Have a good look. Let me know when you're ready for the next set. We have five to get through."

I held my breath as I examined the two pictures he'd pulled from the folder, waiting for the dam inside my head to crack, waiting for the collapse of my sanity. It didn't come. The first picture, the dated one, showed a man close to my own age, possibly a few years older. His dark brown hair was fashionably styled but with a noticeably receding hairline. He was thin with an angular jaw and cheekbones. His nose had been broken at one time and hadn't been set right, making it jut out at an odd angle from his face. The second picture showed the unkind passing of time. It was the same man, but in the newer photograph, he was nearly bald with only a ring of silver-brown hair circling his melon-shaped head. His skin hung loose on his bones, and he had several scars on his face he hadn't had in the first picture. One scar intersected his upper lip and gave it a crooked little jag.

I frowned, glancing from one image to the other.

"Charlie?" Takoda's voice was gentle, and I didn't know how long I'd been staring and processing.

I shook my head. "He's not familiar. He's not even stirring memories at all. I... I don't know. There's nothing there."

"Okay. Another." Wan passed the first pair of photographs to his partner and pulled two more from within the folder.

The second man was stockier, especially in the more recent picture. Rotund. He had a bulbous nose and big ears that didn't fit his face. Unlike the first man, I was immediately affected when I stared into the dark pits of this guy's eyes. They were too small for his face, and the slash of a bushy unibrow overtop tickled something to life in the back of my brain.

I thought of the concrete room with the thin mattress on the floor. I thought of the voice. The singing. I thought of the gifts left behind; the chalk and the chocolate bar wrapper. Blood brothers. Best friends forever.

"He's familiar, in a way, but it's not him."

"How can you be sure?" Wan asked. "You recognize him?"

"Kind of. On a subconscious level, if that makes sense. It's the eyes. I... I'm not comfortable looking at him. It's... I can't describe it." My skin crawled, and I knotted my fingers together until they ached as I stared at the face in the older picture. "But it's not him who's been stalking me. I know that much."

"Explain."

"He's too old. I remember the cut." I rubbed my scarred thumb along my pants, felt the memory of pain as the knife sliced the pad of my thumb. It was almost as real as it had been years ago. "The person was younger than him. A lot younger."

Myers sighed, and there was a hint of annoyance behind it. "None of the other children survived, Charlie. I know that's hard to accept, but it's the truth. Maybe the guy just looked young, but he wasn't."

Wan held up a hand to his partner. "Hold up." He passed the pair of photos to Myers and opened the folder again. He picked through a couple until he found what he wanted. When he closed the folder and placed another pair on top, he said, "This man was younger than the others. He was twenty-five when we arrested him. He could probably pass for a lot younger. How about him?"

My knee bounced as I took in the new man's features. Takoda's hand came to rest on my thigh, arresting the movement. He squeezed and left his hand in place, rooting me to the present. The heat from his palm and the sure grip of his fingers settled something that was fast unspooling on the inside.

The man in the photo had unruly reddish-blond curls, a round face, pouty lips, and angry hazel eyes. No one smiled for their mug shot, but this guy looked downright hostile. His image stirred no memories.

I shook my head. "Can I see the picture he left for me again? The one where I was in that room."

The three men surrounding me exchanged glances. Without a word, Myers rose and left the room. He returned a minute later with the evidence bag, the Polaroid tucked inside. He passed it to Wan, who laid it on top of the folder.

Unlike the pictures they'd been showing me, my reaction to this particular image was vastly different. Even knowing what I was about to see, the impression on the old print paper upended the scant amount of self-control I'd mustered so far.

It would have been easy to back away from it all. Shut down. Close my eyes and retreat. But I'd been doing that for years, and I was tired of being afraid. I was tired of how people looked at me, how they treated me like I was irreparably broken.

Takoda's grip on my leg tightened as though he somehow knew how hard I was fighting. In his own quiet way, he was reassuring me he was there.

I took his hand and laced our fingers together. He didn't object, and when Wan exchanged glances with Takoda, all Takoda said was, "I've got you, Charlie. You're doing great."

I picked up the Polaroid and tried to open my mind. I studied what I could see of the room, avoiding the young boy with distress in his eyes as he stared at the camera. It was there, like a word that got stuck on the tip of my tongue when I was writing, and I couldn't for the life of me remember what it was.

Amber eyes.

A crooked-toothed smile. A sparkling smile? It was friendly somehow, but there was something else.

Beads of sweat formed along my brow as I closed my eyes, staring into the abyss. Where I normally ran from my senses, this time, I tried to pull them toward me. I wanted to see it all. Smell it. Taste it. Touch it. It was always out of reach.

Blue jeans with pen-drawn pictures of devil horns and curse words, doodles that made no sense. Dirty nails chewed to the quick. A red Swiss army knife with all sorts of tools tucked inside. White powder on my hands.

"Give me your thumb."

"Why?"

"Just do it. Don't be a chicken shit."

Pressure. Pain. Blood. Laughter.

"Can't undo it now. Brothers for life."

"For life," I heard myself say out loud.

"Wanna keep playing? It's my turn."

"Here, I brought you something special."

"They're coming. Don't say anything. I'll distract them."

I gasped, snapping my eyes open as the room spun around me, the past melding with the present. Takoda was on his knees between my legs, holding my face. His voice was calm in the chaos.

"It's okay. You're okay. Deep breaths. You're safe. You're safe, Charlie."

My heart was making every effort to expel itself from my chest. It hurt, and I folded in half, pressing my hands to my sternum, wanting to alleviate the pain. Takoda guided my head to his shoulder and rubbed my back, reminding me to breathe.

In my ear, he whispered, "If you have to go away, it's okay. I won't leave your side, and I'll be here when you're ready to come back."

I did want to leave. Desperately. I wanted to escape the horror. It would have been easy. But I was done with easy. I was done being a coward.

Instead, I clung to Takoda's shirt, sucked in enough oxygen to stop the spinning, then rasped, "He was another child. He was *not* an adult. Amber eyes. He... I don't... I don't know more."

"It's okay," Takoda said, his hand tracing a path up and down my spine.

It wasn't. There was more information just out of reach. Little things I couldn't voice yet. Feelings. Certainties. They were there.

"He can't have been another of the kids," I heard Myers say.

Wan hushed him, and I listened to shuffling and harsh whispers as the two detectives left the room. I'd failed. They didn't believe me. We hadn't finished reviewing the photographs, and I'd fallen apart.

The minute we were alone, Takoda lifted my head from his shoulder and took my face between his hands. Concern marred his features.

"I want to remember. It's right there. I feel like I need a push. I can almost see it. There are things... that don't make sense."

"Don't be so hard on yourself. Maybe it's best you don't remember."

I took a few minutes to calm down before Takoda and I wandered back toward the bullpen. Wan and Myers were huddled around a desk with Nikola and two other detectives. Their raised voices traveled as they argued about the possibility of a child who'd been unaccounted for and had somehow gotten away. There was no evidence to support it, so my theory was causing a problem.

Takoda encouraged me to have a seat at an empty desk while he approached the group. Another heated conversation followed, but since my presence had been noted, it was nothing more than harsh whispers and jerky hand motions.

My mother was gone, which was probably for the best since she'd have likely bullied her way into the middle of it all with more threats and more fake concern for my wellbeing. In all likelihood, she would have insisted my mental health was too fragile, and she would have called Sofia.

When I'd been left alone long enough and the jitteriness from earlier had eased a fraction, I rose and approached the group.

At first, no one noticed me.

"Can I see the file?"

No one heard my request.

"Can I see the case file?" I asked again, louder.

Heads turned in my direction, and the buzz of energy waned. Sergeant Nikola was the one who stepped forward, pushing Takoda back when he went to move past him. "Son, maybe it would be best if—"

"It would help. I know it would. If I could see it, then—"

"Wan and Myers are heading out right now to touch base with these five men. They're going to have a chat with them and see what they can determine. If need be, we will get warrants and dig deeper. If my detectives suspect—"

"It wasn't any of those men."

"You didn't look at all the photographs," Myers said.

"I don't have to. I'm telling you, it wasn't them. If I could see the case file, read it, maybe it would—"

"I can't allow that."

Takoda took a step forward, looking ready to object, and Nikola pressed a hand to his chest, then continued. "Dyani is going to take you home, Charlie. If we need to consult with you again, we'll give him a call, and he can bring you back to the station. Right now, it would be best for you to relax and let us do our job."

"But I don't want to go home."

"He means my place," Takoda said, removing his sergeant's hand from his chest and shifting around him.

I peered from Nikola to Wan to Myers, sparing a quick glance at the other people I didn't know. "You don't believe me."

"It's not that we don't believe you," Wan said, his voice bordering on patronizing. He was acting like I was fragile and might crumble apart. "We'll talk to these other men and see where we're at. Especially this younger one since you think—"

"It's not him. I'm telling you. Why aren't you listening to me? He was a kid. I know he was a kid."

Wan held out his hands, shrugging. "I'm not going to fight with you, Charlie, but it's not possible."

"Come on," Takoda said, taking my arm.

I didn't want to leave. I wanted to view the case file. I wanted to tear off the Band-Aid and see what was underneath. If I came face-to-face with a nightmare, so be it. Someone was out there, stalking me.

They'd hurt my dad and put him in the hospital, and the answers were right there inside my head, hiding behind a murky shadow.

Takoda guided me toward the back door that led to the parking lot. I didn't fight or pull away, but I wasn't happy.

I didn't speak the entire drive as the dismissal of every single detective and Sergeant Nikola stewed and burned inside me. The unhealthy rattle of Takoda's car made my teeth ache, and he insisted on weaving through backroads and doubling back to ensure we didn't have a tail. When he braked at a red light, the sharp squeal resonated through my bones, and I cringed.

"Your car isn't exactly helping us go unnoticed. It's like a beacon." My comment had come out far snarkier than I'd intended, and Takoda shot me a dirty look.

"Not everyone has extra cash growing out their ass."

I bit back a reply, knowing I'd deserved that, knowing we would fight if I pushed.

When he pulled into the gravel driveway and killed the engine, neither of us moved or spoke.

"I know you're upset," he started.

"If everyone would stop coddling me, maybe I could figure this out."

"It's not about coddling you."

"It is, and you know it. Thanks to my mother, that's all anyone at the station has ever done with me. If I could see that old case file, maybe—"

"Charlie, I've read the file. There were no other kids who survived. There was an explosion. They all died. You're it. You're the sole survivor. I know you think you remember it being—"

"He was a kid," I yelled. "I'm telling you. They're wrong. You're wrong. Don't tell me I don't know what I'm talking about or that I'm crazy. I'm not inventing this. It was real. I remember it."

"Except you don't."

I fisted my hands, vibrating as I stared at the dusty dash of the Escort.

"I'm on your side, Charlie."

"It doesn't feel like it anymore."

"Look, I've put my neck on the line. I'm on thin ice right now. Hell, I'm fucking suspended. If I go to war over this, there will be no board evaluation. I have to back down. I don't want to. I want to help you remember, but my hands are tied."

"Fine." I got out of the car and headed for the back gate behind the house, dodging the dead rose bush and tripping once on a tangle of weeds.

Takoda cursed under his breath as he followed.

Inside, I stood on the small landing after Takoda had kicked his boots into the dark basement and retreated into the house. I could hear him talking to Clover and Dandelion in that high-pitched tone he used, but I couldn't move. Immobile, fingers twitching, tears filled my eyes. The fight was real, and I didn't know how to suppress it or make it stop. I couldn't simply enter a house and not perform my checks. It was like trying to ignore an insatiable itch.

No matter how many times I told myself to walk up the stairs to the kitchen and follow the hallway to the bedroom where I could be alone, I couldn't convince my feet to move. The whirlwind of noise in my head grew louder and louder.

I fell back against the door, slid to the floor, buried my face, and cried.

My safety net had been compromised. This new environment and all the troubles that had preceded it were too much. My routine was upside down, my life was inside out, and my dad wasn't by my side to reassure me. I was drowning.

I wasn't on the ground long when I sensed Takoda's presence beside me. He crouched, brushed my hair back, and encouraged me to my feet. Without a single word, he took my hand and placed it on the lock.

I clicked it. Twice.

Takoda kissed my temple and guided me through the basement before we went back upstairs. He stopped at every window and door while I performed my ritual. We ended in his bedroom once again, and he wrapped me in his arms and let me come undone. Through it all, he didn't say a thing.

* * *

The sky was a rich indigo speckled with a few pinpricks of stars that emerged as night descended. Light pollution ruined the effect. As

I stared at the sky, I wondered how devastating the view would be if we were in the middle of nowhere instead of in the heart of the city.

Takoda parked the Escort under a streetlamp in the strip mall's parking lot. A café occupied the corner space with neon signs advertising *Hot Brew* and *Fresh Baked Goodies*. An old print shop was in the store space next door. There was a sign in the window that read, *Closed*. A children's clothing store rented the spot beside it, then there was an empty store window with a sign that claimed it was available for rent. At the opposite corner of the strip mall was a Taekwondo club that took up the final two spaces, and that was where Takoda's sister taught self-defense classes.

It was almost eight o'clock. As much as I'd have rather stayed at the house, Takoda had insisted we go out since he'd already told his sister we were coming.

I'd spent most of the day alone in his bedroom, sitting on the bed, staring at a blinking cursor, unable to work. Takoda had checked in on me several times, but I hadn't been in the mood to chat. By dinner time, he'd shut my laptop and taken me by the hand to the table where he'd set out a small feast of spaghetti and meatballs.

We'd eaten in silence, and there had been hurt in his eyes when I'd retreated to the bedroom once again. In the end, he'd encouraged me to go out by asking if I wanted to visit my dad again. I'd spent an hour at the hospital while Takoda had warmed a chair in the waiting room. He'd refused to leave me on my own.

Takoda checked down the street in both directions when we got out of the car. We were in the heart of the city. Traffic was still heavy even though it was long past rush hour and we were on a side street and not the main thoroughfare.

Instinctively, I followed his gaze, looking for a familiar white Pontiac.

"Maybe we shouldn't be out," I said, scanning the lot and glancing at the buildings across the street.

"I'm staying vigilant. If anyone is following us, I'll know."

He held out his hand, and despite being upset, I took it. His nice meal and constant concern had smoothed the sharp edge off my anger.

With a gentle tug, he drew me closer, tucking me in his arms. "I know you're pissed at me because I didn't push harder at the station to get you that case file, but I won't let anything happen to you. I swear."

I stared at the small divot at the base of his throat, unable to meet his eyes. "I'm not mad at you. I'm frustrated."

"Don't you mean *flustrated*?"

I pinched my lips. "You're not funny. Stop it. I don't want to smile right now."

He chuckled and nudged me with his nose. "Can't help it, though, can you? I'm too cute, and you know it."

When I refused to meet his eyes and still wouldn't give in, he sighed. "Charlie. Look at me. Please." When I did, he asked, "What can I do?"

"Help me remember."

"How? You tell me how, and I'm all over it." He held up a finger. "Provided it doesn't mean getting my ass in more trouble. I can't afford to lose my job."

Except I didn't know how.

When I couldn't find an answer, Takoda pecked my lips. "Think about it. In the meantime, let's go learn how to kick some ass."

"I thought this was self-defense? Wasn't it you who told me it was about disengaging and getting away from an attacker? Not kicking ass?"

"You have a smart mouth, mister."

I laughed for the first time since we'd left the station that morning.

"Now I'm funny? Really?" Takoda reached around, grabbed a handful of my ass, and squeezed. "Get that cute butt moving, and we'll see who's laughing when they're flat on their back."

It was Takoda who ended up flat on his back. Multiple times. His sister was an excellent teacher and had encouraged everyone in the class to pair up and work through each move several times as she taught them. As we practiced, she walked around the room, giving tips, offering demonstrations, and delivering praise.

We all had a red mat designated as our practice space, and Takoda landed with a thud and a groan as I knocked his feet out from under him for the fourth time. Each time I performed the move, it was with more confidence.

Odina clapped. "Yes! That's exactly it, Charlie. Nicely done." She offered me a fist to bump as Takoda slowly peeled himself off the mat, glaring daggers at his sister.

"Don't encourage him. Jesus Christ, I think you put my back out."

Odina looked like her brother with the same warm skin tone, dark hair, and hickory eyes. However, she was half his size, slender and without an ounce of fat. She had a button nose and an oval face. She wore black spandex biker shorts and a tight pink tank top. Her smile showed the same mischief.

"This guy's being a whiny ass. Ignore him," Odina said. "Try it one more time. We're going to move on in a minute."

Odina wandered to the pair on the next mat over. We were the only men present in a class full of college-aged women, but it didn't bother me.

Every time I was able to take Takoda down or disengage from his grasp, I felt bigger, stronger, and more confident. Somehow less afraid. Each time, the moves were easier. I thought less about where to put my hands and instead moved on instinct.

Takoda watched his sister for a minute before shaking his head and facing me again. "She's a menace. She likes to see me in pain."

"I like her."

"You would."

He groaned and arched his back. His T-shirt pulled across his chest and rode up an inch, exposing his abdomen. I couldn't help admiring the long line of his body and remembering all we'd shared the previous night.

"Again?" he asked, snapping me from those dangerous thoughts.

"Um. Yes."

He grinned and wiggled his brows like he knew where my thoughts had spiraled. I averted my gaze as my cheeks warmed.

We'd been practicing a move that could be used when an attacker moved in behind their victim. It was similar to the one Takoda had shown me at the house the first time he encouraged me to learn self-defense. Odina's way was smoother and less complicated. Takoda had informed me she was a show-off and claimed his way was just as effective.

I turned, giving Takoda my back, waiting for his pretend attack. I cleared my head and closed my eyes, forcing the flow of each move into my brain.

It was strange how my head worked. When I wrote stories or came up with amazing plot twists, they often happened at random moments when I least expected it. The sudden surges of brilliance were often jarring, and I had to stop whatever I was doing to capture the moment before it slipped away.

That was what happened when Takoda moved in on me. I reacted; grabbing, turning, pushing, moving. I did everything robotically and instinctively as Odina had taught us. Only that time, when Takoda's back hit the mat, I didn't disengage like I was supposed to. His explosive *oof* sent a flashbang through my mind, and I landed on top of him like I had that day in the media room.

My head raced with a possibility I hadn't considered.

Takoda made the noise of a buzzer. "And that's a fail, ladies and gentlemen." He wrapped his arms around my waist and rolled us so he was on top. "The attacker has won the game."

The whole time, I was only half-aware of what was happening, his voice a distant hum.

The answers. I knew where I could find them.

"Hello? Charlie?" Takoda's humor had vanished by the time I refocused on his face.

I was underneath him, his weight pinning me down.

The room was hot, and the stink of sweaty bodies surrounded us, but I still picked out the calming essence of sage and sweetgrass in the mix.

"What just happened?" he asked, his voice laced with worry.

"I need you to take me somewhere."

"Um. Okay. That was random. What are you talking about?"

"You said you'd help me remember."

"I did. And?"

"And I want to go back there."

"I'm not following."

"The warehouse where I was held. To that room. Take me back there, and I know I'll find the answers."

Nineteen

TAKODA

Charlie's words echoed inside my head as the class came to an end. People filed out, the low hum of voices nothing but background noise. I'd been unable to focus on the lessons that had followed his declaration, and it had fueled my sister's teasing when Charlie had managed to toss me around like a ragdoll.

Charlie and Odina were chatting and laughing a few feet away while I dragged the mats off to the side of the room and organized them into a pile. It was good to see Charlie smile after he'd been so upset all day. I was torn. He was so adamant about the stalker having been one of the children from years ago, but how could I argue with facts?

Once the mats were cleaned up, I joined Charlie and Odina. Odina was being her usual sweet self, and Charlie was soaking it up. He couldn't see the menace I'd grown up with because she'd learned to skillfully hide that part of herself as an adult. It was still there, under the surface. She tormented me all the time, but I loved her.

Odina smacked my arm as I came up beside her, her smile coy. "You didn't tell me Charlie was staying with you at the house."

I glanced at Charlie and raised a brow. "That's because it was under wraps. Secretive protective detail."

"You're a twenty-four-hour bodyguard. Don't flatter yourself. Besides, she's your sister."

My jaw dropped. "You're getting cheeky, mister." I pointed at Odina. "And I have no doubt you're corrupting him. Stop it."

"Please." Odina rolled her eyes. "If anyone's corrupting anyone, it's you corrupting Charlie. So what's going on? Why the promotion to glorified bodyguard?"

"I hate you. I'm a cop. You should respect my authority?"

Odina snorted, and Charlie covered his mouth, hiding his own smile.

"I hate you both." Pointing at Odina, I said, "And I can't discuss the details of my assignment."

"God, now he thinks he's FBI or something," Odina said to Charlie, who was still doing all he could to fight a smile.

I growled at my sister and glanced at Charlie. "Are you ready?"

Charlie's good humor fell away, and he gnawed his lip, shuffling once before asking, "We're going, right?"

"We'll talk about it in the car."

Odina glanced between us.

"Thanks for letting us participate tonight. I think I'll be icing some solid bruises before bedtime."

Charlie's smile returned, wider than before. Seeing it made all my sore muscles worth it.

Odina pulled me into a hug, dragging me to her level and patting my back. While squeezing me tight, she whispered, "I like him. A lot. And I know there's more between you. Don't fuck this up."

I pushed her back and gave her my best what-the-fuck expression. How had she pieced it together in the span of one hour?

Odina rolled her eyes. "You think I'm blind. You're an idiot. I'm serious. Behave for once in your life."

I glared at my sister as I encouraged Charlie to head for the exit.

Odina called after us. "And call Mom. She wants to organize a dinner or something."

The parking lot had cleared out by the time Charlie and I walked to the Escort. He stuck close, our shoulders brushing. My head was busy rolling around his suggestion from earlier, so we were over two dozen feet from the building before I registered I hadn't scoped the area, and we were walking blind into a dark parking lot.

I grabbed Charlie's arm and tugged him toward me, spinning and scanning the street and endless shadows surrounding us. "For fuck's sake. You've got my head upside down and inside out, and I'm not on alert."

"We're okay. No one's around." Charlie scanned as well.

"Not the point. You've got someone following you. I need to keep my eyes open." We got to the car, and once we were safely inside, I started it up and turned to Charlie. "I don't know about this whole warehouse thing. This would be under the umbrella of 'Things I shouldn't do because it might cost me my job.'"

"I'm not saying we go inside, but—"

"No, that's exactly what you're saying, and you know it."

He pressed his lips together and glanced out the window. "The picture of me in that room brought a flood of memories to the surface, but they still weren't clear. I could just about grasp the moment. It's right there." He looked back, tapping his forehead. Determination sang in his eyes. "And it was nothing more than a photograph. If I could be back in that room, in that place where…" His Adam's apple rose and fell. "Well, it might bring it all back."

The desperation in his eyes cut me to the quick. I didn't want to discourage his surge of courage, but I didn't think he was looking at the bigger picture.

"Have you considered what that might mean?"

"Yes." His voice was small. "I have to do this. Please help me."

I blew out a long breath and scrubbed the back of my neck as I watched cars drive by on the road beyond the parking lot. This was as good as signing my own execution papers. "All right. All right, fine."

According to the time on the dash, it was after nine.

"We'll go in the morning. I'm not sure where this place is located, so I'll have to figure out a way to get that information from the file."

"No. We go tonight. Now. I know where it is. If we wait until morning, there will possibly be traffic and people around. The warehouse is near the shipping yard. It's been abandoned for decades. The whole area is a warehouse and factory graveyard. The building used to be used as a storage facility for shipping containers prior to transport. The company that owned it went under, and the building was left to rot. At this time of night, the area will be quiet and... Maybe we can get inside and explore."

Mouth agape, I stared at Charlie. "How the hell do you know all that?"

His fingers twisted together, and he shrugged. "That place has haunted me for seventeen years. You don't think I've driven by there a million times, wondering? My dad doesn't know. Neither does Sofia. It would be better if they didn't find out."

"And you want to break in and explore it so you can take a trip down memory lane?"

"Yes."

"And when you lose your shit, what do I tell your doctor and your dad?"

"Nothing because I won't."

I craned my neck, staring at the torn upholstery above my head. "I'm so getting my ass fired. It's a good thing you're cute, Charlie. When the unemployment office asks me why I don't have a job anymore, I'm going to show them your picture and ask them if they could say no to you."

Through all his nerves, Charlie smiled, and fuck if I could do anything but follow him on his journey for answers.

I threw the car into gear and pulled onto the road.

I jumped on the highway to get through the more congested parts of town faster and exited closer to the harbor. Charlie guided me in the direction of the shipping yard and the place where the big bust had taken place seventeen years ago in an abandoned warehouse. It was a more industrial part of town and home to two of the city's major steel manufacturing plants. Several other plants in the area had gone under years ago

He was right. It was quieter at this time of night than it would have been during daylight hours.

As we cut down an empty side road, Charlie told me to pull over. Huge empty structures surrounded us on both sides of the road. Rows of warehouses and factories that had long ago been shut down and abandoned. The city had left them to deteriorate. They were shells of what they'd once been.

Twenty-foot high, razor-wire fences surrounded each of them individually with signs bolted at intervals, warning that it was private property and trespassers would be prosecuted. Again, I asked myself what the hell I was doing.

I pulled to the side of the road beside a strip of brown grass that ran between two empty buildings thirty yards off the road. Four large steel shipping doors dotted the side of one. The other was nothing more than a pitted stone wall with small windows three stories above street level, peering down on us like dark vacant eyes. Graffiti covered both buildings. I scanned but didn't see a way inside. There was no gate or entrance in view. The trucks that would have used the shipping doors once upon a time had accessed a long drive that ran beside the building. The entrance and exit must have been around the back. "Which one?"

Charlie stared off down the road. I couldn't be sure he hadn't vanished inside his head already. He seemed distant. Withdrawn. If that was the case, I was turning the car around and taking him home right fucking now.

"It's farther down. I just… need a minute."

I killed the engine and popped my seat belt. "Let's walk it."

Charlie opened the glove compartment and frowned as he leafed through the junk I kept inside. "You don't have a gun?"

"Jesus, yes, I have a fucking gun." I scrubbed my face. "God, this is a mess. I'm in so much trouble."

Unless I was on duty, I wasn't in the habit of carrying a gun. I had permits, but unlike some officers, I didn't feel the need to be armed twenty-four-seven. I'd grown up on the south end of town where there were gangs and thugs and increased crime. Hell, I still lived in that area of the city. But I'd seen too much violence growing up, and I'd had guns shoved in my face too many times to not feel the effect deep in my core. One of my best friends had been killed with a gun in a back alley while buying a single ounce of pot. One fucking ounce.

I wouldn't voice it out loud, not even on my death bed, but I hated guns. I'd passed all my tests in the academy. I knew I'd use one if the situation called for it, but I hoped that never happened.

Sure, I was a cop. Yes, I was armed, but unless I was on duty, I couldn't justify carrying one around.

With Charlie under my care, I'd packed my personal piece under my seat before we'd left the house, thinking I should have it close just in case.

I unearthed a small locked box and selected a key from my keychain to unlock it. Inside was my Ruger SR9. I checked the chamber then slid the cartridge into place. There was a belt holster inside the box as well. After I'd pushed the lockbox back under the seat, I worked the gun snug inside and clipped it to my belt.

"All right. You ready?"

"Ready."

We got out of the car, and I scanned the empty street. There was no life in this abandoned area of town. No wonder this location had been chosen for nefarious purposes all those years ago. There weren't any streetlights or floodlights anywhere. It was dark and eerie with only the moon and stars to guide us.

Charlie stayed close to my side, and as we walked, I felt the weight of the gun at my hip and hoped I never had to use it while protecting Charlie.

"This one."

Charlie came to a halt in front of the tall fence outside a three-story warehouse building that was a clone of the rest of the ones lining the street. Same disrepair. Same skeletal remains. The corrugated metal siding was dripping rust. There was nothing extraordinary about this building that made it stand out more than the rest, and I wanted to ask Charlie if he was sure, but the stillness in his body and his shallow breaths gave me my answer.

A large cement pad ran for thirty yards beyond the fencing, all the way to a row of steel bay doors and loading docks. More graffiti dotted the building in places, which told me there had to be a way inside the fencing. If kids could get in to mark it up, so could we.

High above the bay doors ran a block of dark windows. Offices, I guessed. Some of the panes were cracked. Others were missing and had been replaced with plywood. All of them were dingy and murky under the moonlight. Years of dirt smeared their surfaces. There was a lone steel door off to the right of the bay doors, but I could see the heavy padlock from where we stood and knew we'd never get inside that way.

"Come on." I took Charlie's hand and guided him along the fence where it cut around the corner and ran along the east side of the warehouse. This building was close to the one next to it, and the path between them was only wide enough for us to walk single file. Charlie clung to the back of my shirt as I went first. There were large air vent ducts set fifteen feet off the ground. Their grills were rusted out or pulling up in places. Metal piping ran in vertical lines in one section, turning and vanishing at the roofline.

When we came out on the other side, we were in a loading area. Ramps led up to a half dozen more rolling doors. There was a service entrance in the gate where trucks had been admitted at one time. It had been electronically activated and looked solid even today. A wide parking lot sat beyond the security fence, unused dumpsters in a line, then an overgrown field with a second gated area, housing huge transformers that no longer hummed with power. An employee access gate sat on the far side near a single-story section of the building that jutted out from the rest. That section had a different type of aluminum siding and large, street-level windows. Based on the look of the outside, I guessed it had been the administrative part of the building back when it was in use.

Charlie had gone quiet. His grip on my hand was tight, but when I checked in, his eyes were alert as he scanned the back of the building. I took him around to the parking lot and the smaller access gate in the fence.

A rusty padlock hung open. Someone had cut it long ago and left it behind. A length of heavy wire wound around the two poles instead, keeping the gate closed and inaccessible. I tried to pry them apart, but they were stiff, and their sharp edges cut into my fingers. Getting them unwound was doable, but not with my bare hands. Whoever had put it there had probably used plyers.

"Here," Charlie said, removing his switchblade from his jacket pocket.

"You brought this with you?" I took it from him and stared in disbelief.

"I take it everywhere. Just in case."

The light of the low moon reflected off Charlie's face. It might have been the shadows playing against his features, but he looked pale. Sickly.

"It will help, but I need something else. A rock, maybe?"

We looked around the edge of the fence. Charlie retreated to the parking lot where the old asphalt was crumbling and there were large potholes. He grabbed a decent size rock and brought it over.

I used the knife's handle and the hard edge of the rock to help unwind the wire. It was still a challenge and required a lot of grunting and strength. The rock slipped at one point, and the wire scraped along the pad of my palm, cutting into the soft flesh.

"Fucker." I sucked the wound and shook my hand. "Now I'm going to get tetanus and die."

"Don't you have your shot?"

"Of course I've had my shot. I'm being dramatic. It hurt."

Charlie took my hand and examined it, angling it so the moonlight caught the scored flesh. "It's a scratch. It's not even bleeding. You'll live."

I sneered, but there was no heat behind it, and Charlie just smiled. I worked on the wire again and managed to get it unwound. It clattered to the ground, and I kicked it, cursing the stupid piece of metal and checking my palm again.

The gate squealed as I shoved it open, singing in my teeth. The shrill noise bounced back at us from the building. If anyone was nearby, they'd have easily heard it.

Charlie pocketed his blade again as I scanned the shadows. We crossed into the yard beyond the fence.

Nudging Charlie toward the administrative section, I said, "If we're going to get in, I have a feeling it will be over here."

The large windows set in the aluminum siding on this part of the building were in decent shape, dirty but intact. When I pressed my face to the glass and shielded my eyes to see inside, I confirmed my suspicion. Abandoned desks, filing cabinets, empty shelving, even an old switchboard.

A hallway led into the main section of the warehouse, and I debated what to do.

Charlie had moved to the main doors and tugged them, confirming they were locked. He glanced at me and shrugged. "What now?"

"You're sure this is the place? I don't see any leftover police tape or signs there was ever anything that went down here."

"It's been seventeen years." He studied the ramps leading to the rolling bay doors a couple dozen feet away. Something passed over his face before he looked back at me. "I'm sure. Look. There are scorch marks, and the high windows are all blown out and boarded up. There was an explosion."

He was right. Sighing, I paced back to the gate where we'd entered, grabbing the chunk of asphalt I'd abandoned on the ground.

I checked the area as I approached Charlie. He watched my every move. When he registered what I was about to do, he held up a hand.

"Wait. Let me."

"At this point, it doesn't matter. We're breaking in one way or another. If we're found out, it won't matter who broke the window. Hell, we can claim it was busted when we got here. They'd still have us on trespassing."

Worry lines marked Charlie's forehead. I could see him second-guessing asking me to do this.

"Do you want answers?" I asked.

"Yes."

"Will this give you answers?"

"I…" He glanced back at the rolling doors and the high windows. "I think so."

I threw the rock.

The pane shattered, and glass tinkled and fell to the concrete pad below. It was loud in the quiet night. The silence that followed was deafening. The crickets that had been chirping in the thick, grassy field beyond the parking lot fell quiet. In the distance, I could almost hear the crash of waves hitting the rocky shore at the harbor.

Charlie's face was priceless. His eyes blew wide, and his lips parted as he shifted his attention from me to the window and back to me like he couldn't quite believe what I'd done.

"Yeah, you saw it. I did that. You're a bad influence on me, Charlie Falkingham. I was this sweet innocent cop before I met you. Now I'm a rebel. Breaking and entering. Destruction of property. What's next? What have you done to me?"

Charlie snorted and covered his mouth.

I laughed and gestured. "Take off your coat. I need it."

I'd left the house without one. The spring evening was chilly, but I had thick skin and didn't get cold easily.

Charlie removed his jacket and handed it over. I wrapped it around my hand and used it to clear the remaining glass from the bottom of the frame. Once I'd gotten rid of most of it, I draped it over the sill and heaved myself up, climbing inside.

Charlie followed, shaking his jacket out once we were in and putting it back on.

I knew before I even tried that the power was shut off to the building, but flicking the light switch on the wall confirmed it. It was dark, so I dug out my phone and turned on the flashlight, sweeping it around the room.

Charlie stuffed his hands into his pockets and rocked on his feet as he followed the beam.

"Shall we?" I gestured to the hallway, which led to the main body of the warehouse.

Charlie's shoulders rose with a deep inhale. He set his jaw and nodded.

We passed through a short corridor before exiting into the main storage area and the location of the event from seventeen years ago. The ceiling was a good thirty-five or more feet above us. Charlie had taken out his phone as well but hung back, sweeping his light around the room.

There was no mistake we'd found the right building. Evidence of the explosion and subsequent fire surrounded us. There was a rickety worktable, charred and missing a leg so it sat at a sharp angle on the ground. Burnt and broken chairs were scattered around the space, and a dozen rusty old tools sat on the floor and hung from old hooks on the wall. Black scorch marks climbed as high as the ceiling.

On one wall, a line of huge shipping containers had survived. They were black with old soot and curling paint, standing like massive tombstones in a row.

Nerves and anticipation made me pull my gun. I knew we were alone, but this place had an ominous atmosphere I couldn't shake. Maybe it was knowing what had taken place within the walls.

Now that we were inside, my beam of light caught on old crime scene tape near one of the rolling doors. It was half-buried under debris and dust that had settled over the years. Another strip still hung on the frame, waving with the air current that flowed between the crack in the bay doors. A leftover cardboard box marked with a faded forensic logo was chewed and disintegrating. Rats, maybe? I didn't know.

Charlie hadn't moved. He hung in the entrance to the hallway from where we'd come. I wasn't sure how to help. I waited, keeping half an eye on him while getting familiar with the dark space around us.

Without a word, he started toward the back of the room. The light cast by his flashlight trembled as it swept the ground at his feet.

I didn't know what he was thinking or if he recalled anything. Was this burnt-out shell of a room familiar? Where had the children been kept?

A thought struck, and I spun, casting my light against the far wall. My blood turned to ice as I remembered what I'd read in the reports about cages. Ones intended for dogs or larger animals. They were gone now, but I'd seen pictures in the file. It was where they'd kept the children.

Most of them.

Not Charlie.

He'd been found elsewhere.

Alive.

Alone.

When I turned back, Charlie's light was far away and vanishing fast down a long corridor leading deeper into the warehouse.

"Charlie," I shouted, running to catch up.

He didn't stop.

"Charlie, wait. You can't go off on your own."

My foot caught on something, and I staggered and nearly fell, catching myself at the last minute on the leg of an upturned chair. The weak wood cracked and broke under my weight, and I landed on my knee. My phone tumbled and fell face up, blocking my flashlight and throwing me into darkness. I grabbed it, cursing, and checked the screen for cracks before glancing up.

Charlie was gone.

"Fuck me. Charlie!"

I ran, keeping my beam of light on the ground so I wouldn't trip again. I raced down the corridor where he'd disappeared. It ended at a juncture. On my left was darkness. On my right, a short way down, faint light bounced on the walls.

"Charlie?"

When I got to the room, I stalled. Charlie stood just inside the doorway, one hand on an old padlock that had been cut. It hung rusty in a hook on the steel door. Charlie twisted the lock absentmindedly in his hand, his gaze far away, his flashlight aimed at the far wall.

"Charlie," I said, much softer.

He didn't respond.

This was the room. I didn't recognize it from the picture, but I knew it was the case. I felt the impact as it rolled through Charlie and into me.

On the wall on the far side of the room was a faded chalk drawing of an old children's game.

Hangman.

Twenty

CHARLIE

The gentle hand on my arm made me jump. "Charlie?"

I sucked in a much-needed breath and blinked. My eyes were dry, and my skin felt like it had been shrink-wrapped to my bones. The cold padlock under my fingers was rough and flaking. I couldn't let go of it. Muscles seizing, I couldn't step any farther into the room.

The drawing on the wall had stopped my heart. If a steady whomp of blood hadn't been pulsing in my ears, drowning out all other sounds, I would have believed shock had done me in.

Tearing my attention away from the wall, I swept the light around the small room. It was no more than six by six. Poured concrete all around me. Pitted. Aged. Cracked. Cold and suffocating. The dampness amplified the thick scent of mold, and I wanted to cover my nose or hold my breath.

The mattress was gone, but I held the beam of light over the place it had once been. There were tuffs of its innards in the corner like they'd been blown there on a gentle breeze, but there was no breeze. The air was still.

The corner. Flashes of memories assaulted my brain. Cold nights curled up in a ball wearing nothing but an oversized T-shirt and underwear. Shivering. Hiding in that corner like I could disappear into the wall.

I squeezed the padlock under my fingers, tried to take a step into the room, and failed. In my mind's eye, I heard the heavy slam of the steel door and the soft click of this exact lock being fit into place, securing me inside.

If I moved, if I entered this place from my past, who was to say I wouldn't be back there again? Alone. Stuck. Terrified.

"Charlie?"

I jolted.

Takoda.

"I'm okay." My voice was weak, strained, and I knew he didn't believe me.

"I'm right here. Nothing is going to happen to you. Do you want to go inside?"

I nodded.

But when I tried again, I couldn't release the lock.

Takoda must have registered or understood my predicament. It wasn't the first time he'd read me like a book, and I wondered how it was he could be so in tune with me when everyone else in my life treated me like a mutant.

He peeled my fingers from the lock, unhooked it, and placed it in my palm. It was heavier than I expected.

"I'll stay by the door. No one is going to close it. I promise."

I fisted the lock until my skin pulled tight over my knuckles and my fingers ached. I took a step. Then another.

In my mind, I was walking down a dark tunnel from one reality into another. A flood of memories returned, but they were broken pieces of a whole. A stale piece of bread on a cold metal tray. Plain oatmeal in a cracked plastic bowl, cold and hardened like a brick. A cup of water with a sour, metallic taste that made it hard to drink.

Hunger pains.

Fear.

Tears.

Loud voices outside the door.

Shouting.

The firm grip of a hand around my bony wrist, yanking me off my feet.

Pulling me to safety?

I pinched my eyes closed, fighting against the barrier in my mind.

The rasp of my own labored breathing was loud in my ears. My teeth hurt. My palm ached.

When I opened my eyes, I narrowed my focus to the wall and the chalk drawing. That was where the answer lay.

Hangman.

"Want to play a game?"

White powder on my fingers. Chalk dust.

The slice of a knife.

Pain.

"Blood brothers."

Blue jeans with crudely drawn images done in pen. Devil horns. Curse words. Squiggly lines. A dragon.

Amber eyes.

A shining smile and crooked teeth.

A shining smile.

A shining smile.

No.

Twinkling?

Sparkling?

The hangman wasn't complete. At the end of the rope was a rough circle for a head, a long line for a body, two short stick legs, and one short line for an arm. The arm reached up like the stick man was falling. I could almost hear him scream.

Underneath were horizontal lines marking two unfinished words.

One more mistake and the stick man was doomed.

"We didn't finish playing."

I frowned at the game, squatting beside the wall. The answer seemed obvious. *Tomb Raider.*

"I'll give you a hint. It's my favorite movie. Angelina Jolie is in it. She's so hot. Come on. Guess. I've seen it, like, ten times."

A twinkling smile.

A sparkling smile.

Crooked teeth.

It dawned on me. "He had braces."

"What?"

"He had braces. On his teeth. He was older than me, but not by much. A teenager. I remember… floundering to keep up with things he talked about. The shows he liked." I waved a hand at the wall. "The movies. Angelina Jolie. *Tomb Raider*. I didn't know the answer back then because I was a bit too young for that."

The more I talked, the more the memory cleared.

Noises beyond the steel door.

Men's voices.

A piece of chalk in my hand.

White powder.

"Just play the game. They aren't coming this way. I promise. I won't let them. It's just us."

"He was in here a lot. We played hangman. He brought me chocolate. He… kept them away from me."

"How old was he, Charlie?"

Takoda's voice cut into my thoughts, and I fished for an answer. The boy's image still wasn't clear.

"A teenager. I don't know. Fifteen? Sixteen?"

"The age range of the children taken was nine to twelve. You were the oldest. There wasn't anyone older."

"He was part of it. Somehow. I don't know how, but he came and went. He had keys."

"The youngest arrest was the one you saw today in the picture. You said it wasn't him."

"It wasn't."

A noise made me turn and look at Takoda. He'd pushed away from the door and was intently staring at me.

"So what are you saying? Was this kid like you, or did he slip through our fingers? That seems kind of young to be part of this. Are you sure?"

"I… don't know. I mean… He… I remember hearing them. Down the hall. Voices. Men."

In the large room we'd passed through.

"I remember being afraid. He told me they would leave me alone. They weren't coming for me. He told me to relax. He was going to hang out for a while. He had yellowy-brown eyes. Like amber. Braces. Teenagers wear braces, right? Not adults. Not usually. He… drew on his jeans with a pen. I remember he had acne. His voice wasn't deep.

I'm telling you. He wasn't an adult, and he wasn't one of us. He was one of them."

Takoda didn't seem to know how to process what I was telling him. To be fair, I didn't understand it either.

"What else do you remember?"

I pressed a hand to my temple and spun, taking in the room. There was more. A lot more, but I was too afraid to push beyond the barrier. I shook my head, backing away from that place in my mind. "I don't want to go there."

"Okay." A hand landed on my arm, and I opened my eyes, unsure when I'd closed them. I'd backed myself into the corner, and Takoda was in front of me. "Let's get out of here. Let me think about this some more."

My stomach churned, and my skin was slick with sweat. I glared at the open door over Takoda's shoulder, my heart jackhammering out of control.

He took my hand, peeled the lock from my fingers, and guided me out of the room. He left the lock hanging on the hook again and took me down the hall to the main body of the warehouse.

I stalled before he could drag me back to the administrative offices and swept my flashlight around the room once more.

"Come on."

Takoda didn't let me linger. We were back outside in less than two minutes. I crouched, sucking in the fresh spring air, letting it wash over my heated skin as I worked myself down from the cusp of a panic attack.

We hadn't learned much, but it was enough to know whoever was after me was not anyone the police were looking for.

Who was this guy?

What had he been doing in that room with me all those years ago when he'd been no more than a child himself?

Why had I been the sole survivor?

While we'd been inside, the urge to retreat hadn't been present. I had been too on edge, knowing that if I didn't stay alert, I wouldn't be able to escape if the need arose. Now that I'd distanced myself from some of that danger, all I wanted to do was hide from the anxiety. It had raced to the forefront too fast and too suddenly.

I buried my face in my palms, the hard grit of the concrete slab biting into my knees through my pants.

Takoda kneeled beside me. I felt his presence and knew he would understand if I had to go away for a bit. But I didn't want to be a coward. I'd told him I could handle this.

He rubbed up and down my back, his soft murmurs by my ear not penetrating through the fog but soothing nonetheless.

When I lifted my head, he pulled me against his chest and let me find my center again.

"I'm okay. I just… It was a lot."

"I know. We need to get out of here. I don't like being in the open, even though this place is abandoned. Let me take you to my house."

Holding tight to his hand, I got to my feet and let him guide me back to the car. I tried to be proud of myself for not taking the easy way out, for not turning everything off and going away.

Takoda didn't talk all the way back to his neighborhood. I stayed quiet. He spent less time weaving through the streets and checking for a tail. It was late. After eleven. There was no one on the backroads of his neighborhood except us.

When we pulled into the driveway and he killed the engine, neither of us moved. Takoda tugged his phone from his pocket and stared at it for a long time.

I didn't know what he was thinking, so I waited.

Coming to a decision, he searched through his contacts and connected a call, tucking his phone by his ear. It rang a long time, and when Takoda sighed, I assumed he got the person's voicemail.

"Hey, Stanley, this is Takoda. Officer Dyani. I have some questions regarding the case from seventeen years ago. Charlie's case. I was wondering if we could chat. Give me a call when you can."

He left his number and disconnected. "He's probably in bed."

"What do you want to ask him?"

"He was one of the arresting officers. If anyone is going to remember details that aren't in the file, it will be him. I want a clearer picture. We seem to have an unknown variable, and I don't like it."

"Do you believe me?"

Takoda took my hand. It was dark, and his face was in shadow, but I caught the soft smile he returned. "I do. We just need more answers." He gave my hand a squeeze. "Let's go inside and not worry about this anymore tonight."

Easier said than done. In seventeen years, this was as close as I'd ever come to that incident from my past. I feared the nightmares it might cause and how I would handle them being in a strange environment.

We went inside, and without any cues from me, Takoda took me around the house and let me check the locks. I felt stupid, but after the night I'd had, I was also grateful he'd accepted my quirks without question.

In the kitchen, Takoda dug through the fridge and pulled out two beers. "You drink?" he asked, handing me one and leaning against the counter.

I turned the bottle in my hands, thumbing the label. "No. Not really. Sofia has always warned me against alcohol." I laughed humorlessly. "Add it to the list. It can mess with my meds, but it could also mess with my head. Like I need more things to mess with my head."

I set the unopened beer on the counter, yearning for something I couldn't describe. It was something I'd craved for many years. Something I might never achieve.

Takoda drank from his bottle, assessing me. I could only imagine what he saw.

"Do you need to talk about it? What you saw tonight?"

"No." I fought the urge to wring my hands, stuffing them into my pockets instead. I stared at the dingy tile that covered the kitchen floor. It was yellow, and I wondered if it was stained from age or originally that color. "Maybe I should try to get some work done. My publisher is expecting an outline, and I've barely worked in what feels like weeks."

"Okay." Takoda drank from his bottle then placed it on the counter. "I'll be lounging with the cats, watching *Animal Planet* or something until I crash."

A sad smile filled my face as I shook my head. "They have you wrapped around their little paws."

"Believe it. I wouldn't want it any other way."

Neither of us moved. There was something unspoken in the air, and it made my chest tight.

I thought it was time to retreat, but my feet wouldn't listen. It was late. Claiming I needed to work was nothing more than an excuse to avoid confronting Takoda about the previous night. It wasn't fair. We hadn't talked about it all day, but it had lingered in the back of my mind.

Maybe I had a mess of problems, but I liked to think I was adult enough to face them and admit them—even when there were risks. Even when I knew that confrontation could lead to disappointment and regret.

There were a hundred things I wanted to say. Takoda needed to know his efforts and attention, however much appreciated, were wasted on a guy like me. If the statements from his friends and colleagues were true, I didn't know why he was showing interest in me at all. He could find a willing and far less complicated man any time he wanted at the gay bar he so frequently visited.

"I feel like you're thinking yourself into a knot right now, and somehow it involves me, and I'm not getting to have a say because you're doing all my talking for me."

"How am I so transparent to you?"

Takoda swiped a hand over his hair and stepped forward so he was in my space. He'd grown serious, and my nerves ratcheted up. "I have three siblings I helped raise. Mom had her hands full, and I was the oldest. It was my responsibility to help out as best I could. Odina and Calian were little fucking rebels, but what they didn't realize was everything they did as teens, I'd done a thousand times worse. No, I'm no angel. I've been down the wrong road too many times to count. But it gave me an edge with them. Nothing they tried to pull fooled me. I saw through their lies and deceptions, and I knew the truth just looking at them. Odina was the queen of trying to think her way out of complicated situations. You get that same look sometimes when you're thinking really hard. Like you're trying to outsmart me."

"That's not what I'm doing."

Takoda hooked two fingers under my chin and angled my head up. "Then what has your head all in a knot right now because it looks to me like you're in the middle of a battlefield, waving the white flag."

"Okay." I blew out a breath. "The thing is, I really like you. Dad would say I'm infatuated because I see you as my protector, but that's not it... or rather, not all of it." I sighed. "Maybe it's part of it. You make me feel safe, and I don't feel safe very often. You've got a harsh edge to you. I've seen it. You push most people away. You act tough and mean, but you've been nothing but kind and understanding with me. You don't treat me like I'm broken. You don't get annoyed by my quirks. And... you have a soft heart under your brash exterior."

"You better not tell anyone. That has to be our secret. It will ruin my reputation." Takoda smiled and nudged his nose against mine. "I don't see the problem. Why the internal battle?"

"You're so far out of my league, I feel like I'm from another planet. Last night—"

"Was incredible."

"Was a joke." With a gentle hand to his chest, I encouraged Takoda to step back and give me space. "I'm a joke. What happens when you discover that I may not be able to go further than that? I've been thinking about it all day, and to be honest, I don't know if I can. You gave me an out last night. You told me it wasn't going to be... full sex." My cheeks warmed. "And you have no idea how grateful I was for that. The idea of crossing that line scares me. Not because I don't want to. I do—almost desperately—but I've spent seventeen years dealing with random triggers that throw me so far over the edge I go away inside my head for days. Then I get pumped full of drugs just so I can feel safe enough to come back."

The more I talked, the more the words flowed, and the more the truth surfaced. "I'm dying on the inside right now. All I've ever wanted was a taste of a normal life. I didn't get to go to high school like the other kids because I was a wreck. I didn't get to go on dates. I didn't get to explore my sexuality when I was a teenager. This is the first time I've ever felt attracted to someone without a mountain of fear holding me back. I feel safe around you, but I can't be a normal guy. I'm not like those men you find at the bar who you can just throw in bed and fuck however you want. And yes, I said fuck. Sue me. They can give you what you want. I don't know that I can, and it's not fair to you. I'm... damaged goods. I'm—"

"Hey." Takoda's sharp tone stopped my momentum. "What did I say the last time you talked shit about yourself?"

I didn't respond and ducked my chin. "You have no idea how badly I want this, but—"

He was there, in front of me, forcing my face up again. Two warm hands cupped my cheeks. There was fire in his hickory eyes. A blaze of heat that burned me inside and out. "You don't get to tell me what I can and cannot handle. You don't get to choose my limits and boundaries, just like I don't get to choose yours. And you absolutely do not get to talk bad about yourself. Not in my house. Not when I'm around to hear it. Let's get one thing straight right now. I will never, *ever* ask you to give me more than you can handle. I will *never* push you to cross lines you don't want to cross. I told you this last night, and I meant it. And what's this shit about guys at the bar giving me what I want? You don't know what I want, Charlie. If you did, you wouldn't be making this speech, trying to push me away."

"I'm not trying—"

"You are. Yeah, I've had a lot of guys in my bed. So what? They never meant anything to me. Sex was something to do because it can get really fucking lonely when you isolate yourself from everyone. I like you too, Charlie. A lot. It's a rare thing for someone to chisel through the stone-cold barrier around my heart. Odina knows. My mother will tell you too."

"I'm going to frustrate you."

"You mean *flustrate*?"

I laughed, and Takoda tugged me against his chest. I buried my face in the soft cotton of his T-shirt.

"You know what *frustrates* me?" he asked.

"Me correcting your words?"

"That too. But it's the way you've already decided that you aren't worth it and that I should walk away. I don't want to walk away. I want to see what this is. I want to help you discover all your strengths because I think you focus too much on your weaknesses. I want to keep making you feel safe."

"You know what I want?"

"It better be positive, or I'm going to pinch your sides until you beg for mercy."

I tensed at the thought and lifted my head, unable to hide my smile. "I want to share your bed again."

Takoda's smile grew. "Yeah?"

"Yes, and I want to explore more of what we did last night… If that's okay."

"Are you sure?"

I sobered and stood taller. "I am, and I need you to trust me when I say that I'll let you know if I'm not. You don't have to ask me every five seconds."

He studied my face and nodded. "Okay. You better."

"I will."

Takoda descended and joined our mouths. His lips were soft and tasted of ale. We kissed for a long time in the kitchen, tasting one another, learning how we fit together. It was new and fresh and exhilarating. In time, Takoda took it deeper, and when our tongues brushed together, my skin came alive.

He was careful and respectful, stopping and checking in without saying a word, then we'd join up again and start the dance anew.

Takoda held my face, cradled the back of my head, and took me places I'd only ever dreamed.

He pulled me away from the counter, crushing me against his body as he wrapped his arms around my middle. The steel length of his erection pressed against my leg. He moved his hips, grinding against me. I was equally hard, and the movement sent a thrill through my blood as the soft brush of fabric rubbed against my sensitive skin.

I whimpered, and he smiled against my mouth. "Bedroom," he whispered.

Takoda guided me backward down the hall, his hands roving under my shirt, soft caresses that made me shiver with need.

In the bedroom, he pulled my shirt over my head and tossed it on the ground. Then he peered deep into my eyes as he moved my hands to the hem of his, wordlessly telling me to do the same. I pulled his shirt off and left it on the floor with mine.

In his arms again, bare chest to bare chest, Takoda kissed me deeply, nipping my lips, sucking my tongue, and drawing out sounds that embarrassed me.

We didn't stop.

His warm skin, his explorative touch, his mouth, taste, and scent engulfed me. I was floating on a cloud of bliss, and I never wanted to come down.

The back of my knees connected with the bed, and Takoda guided me to the mattress, our mouths never parting. The friction below continued. Takoda dragged his erection against mine, and wild sensations pulsed through my system. I groaned, deep and throaty, and he chuckled.

"You like that?"

"Yes."

"You know, sex doesn't have to be penetrative. Some guys don't like it at all. There are all kinds of things we can do. I just want to make you feel good, Charlie. That's what's important to me. Can I do that? Will you let me take care of you?"

I nodded, unable to voice a single word, the sting in my eyes catching me off guard. Here was a man who went to great lengths to hide behind a tough exterior when deep inside he was caring and thoughtful and more patient than I ever imagined.

He helped me out of my pants, and his followed. Takoda dug through the bedside table and came back with a bottle of lube. He filled his palm and brought it between us. I hissed when he took me in hand, the wet glide shooting pleasure through my whole body.

I closed my eyes, arching into his touch as he stroked me with agonizingly slow tugs.

He didn't kiss me, but he watched my face. I could hardly catch my breath, caught in the shimmer of his eyes. Then he coated himself and took us together, pumping a few times, moving up and down our lengths. I writhed and gasped, wanting more and needing him to stop before I lost it too soon.

When he released us, he resumed rocking his hips, grinding us together. The friction was made all the more perfect with the addition of lube. We kissed, rocked, groaned, and found a rhythm that wasn't too slow or too fast. It was a gradual build that took over every cell in my body. I felt alive.

We coasted on those blissful sensations for a long time, limbs and bodies entwined, mouths joined. It was just the two of us. Rocking. Exploring. Moving as one.

Takoda touched me everywhere, buried his face in my neck, inhaled, whispered in my ear. He pulled me into his arms, and we were as close as two people could be. My toes curled as my body tingled and sang with growing pleasure.

Every movement, every touch took me closer and closer to the finish line, but I didn't want it to end. I never wanted it to end.

Takoda held himself up on his arms, rutting and peering deep into my eyes. A sheen of sweat covered his forehead and chest. His lips were parted, and he panted and trembled.

"I'm close. Can't hold off much longer."

I traced his tattoos, memorizing every inch of the beautiful man above me. I soared higher and higher, unable to voice the sheer intensity of my pleasure. My stomach muscles tightened. Heat swelled and burned low in my belly.

Takoda reached down, taking us together in his hand again.

Then I was there.

Lightning shot across my vision. I cried out as I peaked and came. Takoda wasn't far behind me, his voice cracking as he shouted his pleasure, his hand jerking us through every wave.

Twitching, lightheaded, and dazed from the experience, I caught Takoda when he collapsed in my arms.

We lay still for a long time, hearts racing in a synchronized rhythm, skin damp and flushed. We were a mess, but I didn't care. I never wanted to leave this moment. It felt fragile. Although Takoda had claimed he understood, I still didn't think it would last.

I was exhausting. Someday, he would grow tired of me.

"Stop doing that?" he mumbled against my throat. "I can hear you again."

I chuckled. "I can't even think in private now?"

"Nope. I'd poke you if I could, but I'm too tired."

"We need a washcloth."

"Yeah. I'll get it."

It took another few minutes of cuddling to come down from the high of our orgasms before Takoda could roll off the bed and find his feet.

Once we were clean, he encouraged me to curl up beside him, and in no time, I drifted off to sleep.

No nightmares.

Just peace in my lover's arms.

Twenty-one

TAKODA

I woke the following morning to blaring music. "Seek & Destroy" by Metallica. At the time, it had seemed like a good idea to make it my ringtone. I regretted everything. It was early. Too early. Groaning, I stuffed my head under a pillow, seeking silence. It was then I registered the warm body pressed to my side and stilled.

I was suddenly far more awake and ten seconds from panicking when I remembered.

Charlie.

It was a rare thing for me to wake up next to a guy. I wasn't used to it. I always sent hookups packing the minute the fun stuff was over. Charlie wasn't a hookup. At least, I hoped he'd understood that the previous night. I wasn't good at expressing myself, and this was new territory for me.

Poking my head out, I was met with a bed-rumpled Charlie who was wearing a far too sexy smirk as he lay next to me, hands folded under his head. There was a hint of blond scruff marking his jaw.

The sun was up, and it hit his face in such a way that the winter-sky blue of his eyes glimmered. He seemed content. Happy.

I liked it.

"Are you ignoring your phone on purpose?"

"Yes."

"What if it's about the case?"

"They can call back at a reasonable hour. You're safe here with me. It's too early." I hooked an arm around Charlie's waist and drew him against me, nuzzling his throat and weaving our legs together. I was already hard, and by the feel of it, Charlie was interested in where this could go too. I inhaled his sweet essence, letting it hum through my veins as I kissed his collarbone and hitched my hips forward, seeking that same delicious friction we'd enjoyed the previous night.

I kissed up his neck and captured his mouth, rolling us so I was on top.

My phone rang again, and I growled.

"Maybe you should answer it."

"Whoever it is, they're gonna die. I will fucking kill them with my bare hands. They will never find the body."

Charlie laughed and nudged me over.

It took effort, but I crawled to the edge of the bed, abandoning Charlie's warm body and my aching cock. My phone was in my discarded pants. I hung off the edge of the bed, reaching and dragging them toward me so I could retrieve it.

Stanley.

I flopped onto my back and angled the screen to show Charlie before I tapped to accept the call.

"Dyani."

"Good morning. I got your message. I know it's early, but I thought I'd give you a call before you headed to work. What's up?"

I yawned and scratched my bare chest, shoving the blankets down so Charlie could have a nice view. We'd fallen asleep naked in each other's arms, and I wasn't complaining.

"Well, first of all, I'm not working. I'm on an unexpected vacation for a while, pending a board review. Could be permanent. I hope not."

"Got your ass suspended, huh?"

"Little bit."

"If that's the case, I don't think I can talk to you. If you're already up shit creek, I'm not getting involved."

"How about you clear your morning and listen to what I've got to say first? Me and Charlie will be there in an hour."

"Charlie and I," Charlie whispered as his gaze skipped down my chest and lingered lower.

I jabbed him in the ribs, catching him off guard, and he squealed, slapping a hand over his mouth as his eyes blew wide. His cheeks flamed crimson.

"Charlie? He's with you right now? Was that him I just heard?"

Charlie had gone still. Stanley's voice carried. I was sure he could hear both sides of the conversation.

I shrugged. "Yeah, we're both here. I'm playing bodyguard. Keeping him safe while the big boys figure out who's after him because we were right and someone's stalking him for real. You know his dad's in the hospital, right?"

Stanley remained quiet for a long time. "I didn't know."

"Well, he is. Someone attacked him, trying to get to Charlie. We have some questions about the old case. Charlie's memory isn't good, but it's coming back in bits and pieces. He's hoping you can help fill in some blanks."

"Put Charlie on the line."

"No. I'll put you on speaker." I clicked a button and placed the phone on the bed between us.

"Hey, Stan," Charlie said, his cheeks still announcing his embarrassment.

"How are you doing, Charlie?"

"I'm all right. Takoda is taking care of me."

Stanley made a noise in his throat, and I would have bet there was a whole lot more he wanted to say, but he held his tongue.

"Your dad okay?"

"He will be." Charlie toyed with the sheet. "Can we come by this morning?"

"Who's taking care of this?"

"Myers and Wan," I said, reaching for Charlie's hand and stilling his fidgeting.

"Good detectives."

"I agree, but the pieces aren't slotting together, and Charlie has some memories that don't add up to what's in the file, so we were hoping you could clarify some stuff."

"I'm going to have to call Nikola."

I was about to speak when Charlie held up a hand. "It's my past, Stan. My life. Why can't I seek answers? Why can't I ask questions?"

"I don't want to upset you, Charlie, but you have no idea what you're asking."

"I do." Charlie turned his hand over and laced our fingers together. "I know what happened to me. I'm not stupid. Maybe I can't remember it all, but there are certain things I do remember, and I need more context. I'm not asking for all the grit. I'm asking you to listen to what I know and see if it rings any bells. See if it makes sense to you. That's it. Please."

There was cursing in the background, and I knew we'd won. "Fine. I'll put the coffee on."

"We'll be there in an hour," I said before disconnecting the call.

It was just shy of seven in the morning. We needed to shower and dress and drive across town to Stanley's, but there was enough time to be lazy for five minutes, so I tossed my phone back on the ground and rolled Charlie until I had him crushed to the bed again.

"Now, where were we?"

* * *

I parked on the curb outside Stanley's craftsman-style house and killed the engine. The whole car rattled and sputtered, making an awful racket as it died.

Charlie cringed. "You really need to get this thing looked at."

"Why? It works fine. It's just a little noisy."

Charlie shook his head with a smile and reached for his seatbelt. I caught the back of his neck and dragged him in for a kiss before he got out. I was having trouble keeping my hands off him. He smelled like my body wash, and his hair was still a little damp from our shower. He hadn't shaved, and I loved the rasp of his scruff under my thumb.

He'd been reluctant at first, but I'd convinced him to join me in a shower after our early morning activities. Everything sexual was pretty new for him, and I took great pride in watching his confidence bloom.

For as inexperienced as he was, he was eager to explore and learn. He'd curbed his fear—to a point—and pushed his own boundaries. So long as he didn't push himself too hard, I let him be the guide for how far we took things.

A couple of handjobs in the shower after a mind-blowing frotting session was nothing short of perfect.

"He's probably watching us make out in your car from his window," Charlie said against my mouth when I wouldn't let him pull away.

"I don't see him."

"He's a retired detective. You wouldn't, but he's watching. I guarantee it."

I chuckled. "The guy isn't too fond of me already. I'm sure this isn't helping." I kissed Charlie once more, cursing my interested dick. "Come on. Let's hope Mr. Smarty Pants detective has a good memory and senility hasn't set in yet."

"Be nice. I like Stanley."

"I'm always nice."

Charlie snorted as he got out of the car.

The neighborhood was quiet, but I took a minute to looked down the street in both directions, noting the vehicles in the driveways and parked along the curbs. There was a man in a suit getting into his Mustang three houses down and a mother pushing a baby stroller across the street, heading in the opposite direction.

Nothing suspicious.

I'd thrown on my holster before leaving the house, even though I didn't like it. If Stanley had anything useful to tell us, we might need to make a stop at the station, and I'd also promised Charlie we'd head to the hospital to visit his dad later. Plus, I was in serious need of groceries and couldn't put shopping off any longer since I was feeding two people and hated the idea of Charlie constantly ordering out.

If I couldn't keep Charlie tucked away indoors, then I needed to respect my role as his bodyguard and make sure nothing happened. Which meant carrying a gun even while off-duty.

Stanley's front door opened before we made it up the paver stone path. I was surprised to see Angel on her feet, hovering behind him, poking her nose out the door from behind Stanley's leg. Stanley's hand rested on the old girl's head, scratching between her ears. She woofed as we approached, and I thought maybe she recognized me.

My heart swelled. I dropped to my knees and patted my thighs. "Come here, pretty girl. Do you remember me? Come here."

Angel slinked past Stanley's leg and hobbled across the front porch toward me. She sat, pressing her face into my palm as I loved on her and kissed her furry head.

"You're up and moving today. Feeling okay?"

"She's stronger in the mornings," Stanley said, eyeing us with a sad smile. "She was having a bit of breakfast. Her appetite is going."

Angel jammed her nose against my shirt, sniffing and pawing like she wanted to shake. I obliged and laughed as I tried to hold her nose back. "You smell my cats, don't you? Bet you'd love to get your paws on them."

"Come on, girl. Let them get inside. You go back and finish your food. Angel! Let's go." Stanley had to raise his voice before she registered him talking. I guessed her hearing wasn't the same as it had been when she was younger.

Angel peered back at Stanley, then resolutely ignored him, snuffling my hand again and asking for more ear scratches. I stood and encouraged her into the house. "Come on, silly girl. You need to eat more."

Charlie stuck close to my side. I didn't miss the subtle glances from Stanley. He was trying to piece together a suspicion. Well, I supposed if he'd seen us kissing in the car, it wasn't a suspicion so much as a realization. The old detective was astute and had probably figured there was something more between Charlie and me the last time we'd visited.

Based on the hard look in his eyes, he didn't like what he'd seen one bit.

Stanley took Charlie and Angel into the kitchen—Charlie, so he could help himself to a coffee, and Angel, so she could finish her breakfast.

I settled on the couch in Stanley's overheated front room, layers of deep brown in every shade surrounding me. I guessed he kept it warm for Angel since her nest of blankets lived in front of the fireplace. He was a man who loved his dog and sacrificed his own comfort for hers.

Charlie returned with a mug between his palms, steam from his hot drink licking his pale cheeks. He'd groused about my lack of a coffee pot again that morning.

Charlie settled beside me. Angel hobbled into the room too, but instead of heading to her blankets, she came and plunked herself down at my feet, laying her head on my knee.

I chuckled and scratched her ears.

"She likes you," Stanley said, settling into his recliner with his own mug of coffee.

"I like her too. Come here, girl. Come lie down on your blankets, and I'll sit with you."

I encouraged her to nestle down by the fire. Once she was comfortable, I stroked her fur and glanced between Charlie and Stanley.

Stanley waited expectantly to be let in on whatever was going on.

Charlie's wary gaze landed on me like he didn't know how or where to start.

"Want me to catch him up?" I asked Charlie.

"Sure."

So I told Stanley everything that had happened so far, including the intruder at Charlie's place, the attack on his father, how Charlie had hidden in the chest in his bedroom and was taunted by the man stalking him, and about the third gift—the photograph.

Stanley's face had gone ashen by the time I was finished. He set his coffee aside like he no longer wanted it and folded his hands in his lap, leaning forward. Deep crevices marked his forehead.

Charlie cleared his throat and took over the story. "The picture, the third gift, it brought back some memories. Mostly it's a lot of bits and pieces, but the person who took the picture is the same person who's stalking me now. I know it is. He wants me to remember him. He thinks we've bonded. The problem is, there's a discrepancy with what's in the case file."

Stanley frowned. "Go on."

No detective wants to be told they'd missed something or made a mistake, and I could see it all over Stanley's face, the urge to jump in and deny there were any errors.

I watched Charlie for signs of distress. He held tight to the mug of coffee without drinking it. It was preventing him from worrying his fingers, but he still had tells. His muscles were tight, his knee jiggled, and he was ghostly pale, which brought out the freckles across his cheekbones and nose. All the calm energy he'd woken up with was gone.

"Do you want me to talk?" I asked.

He shook his head. "No. I can do this. I have to."

Before we'd arrived at Stanley's, we'd discussed our adventure at the warehouse the previous night and decided to keep it to ourselves. There was no sense admitting we'd broken into the building and risk getting both of us in trouble. Charlie was going to attribute all he remembered to having seen the photograph.

"This might sound disjointed, but I'll tell you the things that have come to me. I remember the room in the photograph. It's the same room where you found me. Where they kept me. I remember the mattress in the corner, the texture of the walls, the smell, the dampness. I remember wearing a big T-shirt and underwear and being constantly cold."

Stanley made a noise in his throat, a strangled sound that was a mixture of pain, anger, and anguish. Concerned, Angel lifted her head and glanced at her daddy, whimpering once before lying down again. Charlie also heard the emotion in Stanley's noise and paused.

"I'm sorry. Keep going," Stanley said. His jaw ticked, and his nostrils flared.

I could only imagine the shit he'd seen in that takedown. That kind of stuff stuck to you and never left, no matter how many years went by.

"I remember a person visiting me often in that room, and it wasn't... for that, you know?" Charlie glanced up, and Stanley nodded.

"The guy wore blue jeans with holes in the knees. He liked to draw on them with pen. Pictures. Curse words. Dragons. I remember it because I remember thinking my mother would have given me hell if I'd drawn on my jeans like that. He had amber eyes, like little golden suns. Acne. And braces. I can't remember his hair color or what he looked like beyond that, but he was young. Older than me, but young. He would bring me chocolate, and we'd play games. Hangman, using chalk on the walls. He liked talking about medieval video games and dragons and quests. We talked about dragons a lot. I remember that now, and I made up stories on the spot. He told me about his favorite movies and TV shows, but mostly I didn't know anything about them because they were things older kids watched. Things my mom would never allow."

Charlie put his coffee down and dug his fingers into his knees, picking at the seam of his pants. Tremors rocked his body, and the scant control he was trying desperately to hang on to was fleeting fast. I left Angel alone so I could sit on the couch.

Uncaring what Stanley might think, I wrapped an arm around Charlie and pulled him against me, rubbing his shoulder. "Keep going. You're doing great."

Charlie stared at a spot in the distance as he continued. "I remember hearing the voices of the men down the hall. I remember being afraid of them. The boy told me they wouldn't come for me. He pinky swore and promised I was safe. He said they were going to leave me alone because he was visiting. He visited a lot. On one of his visits, he pulled a Swiss army knife out of his pocket, and we made a blood pact to be best friends and brothers for always. He cut me." Charlie held out his thumb, showing Stanley the faint scar. "Then he cut himself, and we sealed the deal."

Stanley examined Charlie's thumb and stared between us with a look I could only describe as perplexed.

"The thing is, Stan," I continued when Charlie fell silent. "Charlie's convinced this guy was a kid. A teenager not much older than him."

Stanley was already shaking his head. "No other children survived. When we found Charlie, it was a miracle, and he was alone."

"We know that. We also know Charlie was the oldest in the age bracket of the boys taken. Charlie says this guy had keys and came and went as he pleased. Visited him often. He was one of them, not a captive."

Stanley scrubbed his face and fell back in his seat. "Impossible. Absolutely impossible. He kept shaking his head. "We didn't arrest any teenagers."

"We know. That's where you come in and tell us what we're missing. Charlie distinctly remembers a boy of about fifteen or sixteen in that room with him on multiple occasions. Think. Something is missing here."

"No. I'm telling you, we tore that place apart. Everyone involved tried to flee out a side access door after setting off the explosives in the main room. We were on them. Immediately. No one got away. We had all exits covered. Mateo Fabian, the ringleader of the whole thing, took a plea for a reduced sentence. He gave us the names of everyone involved who wasn't there at the time of the takedown. We made several arrests in the following days. The children..." Stanley buried his face in his palms. "We weren't fast enough. They tried to cover the evidence. Burn the place to the ground."

"I survived because I wasn't with them in the main room." Charlie's voice warbled as he stared at the floor without seeing it. He was far away. "Why wasn't I with them?"

"We don't know. No one knew."

"It was because of this kid. I don't know why, I don't know how, but I know it. I need to figure out who he is because he's after me."

"Give me a minute," Stanley said.

He stood and paced, chest heaving, brow furrowed. He made three laps of the room before coming to a stop at the window, where he went rigid. "Jesus fucking Christ."

"What?"

He shook his head like whatever thought he'd had couldn't be true.

"Stan. What? Even if it's nothing, you've got to tell us. Maybe Charlie will remember more."

"That's just it. I thought it was nothing. I forgot all about it until now. I thought he was just a kid in the wrong place at the wrong time. Fuck me. It's not possible." He slapped a flattened hand against the windowpane, making it shiver.

Angel barked. The poor girl didn't know what was happening, but she sensed her daddy's tension and didn't like it.

Stanley turned and faced Charlie. His face was drained of color, and I thought the poor man was going to be sick. "We had a full tactical team surrounding that building. Over twenty men ready for the takedown. We'd been hunting those motherfuckers for months. Those men were prepared to cover their tracks. They knew we were there before we were properly situated. The minute they caught wind of us, they detonated a few batches of small explosives and tried to escape during the chaos. In his interview, Fabian admitted everything. Two birds with one stone. Distract us with an explosion. Destroy evidence. Clear the building unseen. It didn't work out for them how they hoped because we got them. He threw every one of his accomplices under the bus. We were stunned he would so readily give them all up just to make his life easier. We knew a child molester wouldn't survive in prison, and we were right. Lesser sentence or not, he was dead within a year. They failed. We outnumbered them, and we were ready enough to take action. What we didn't plan for was a burning building with children stuck inside.

"The firetrucks had moved in at that point. We couldn't get near the place until they got the blaze under control. We had a team making the arrests, and my partner and I were desperate to get inside, knowing there were kids in there. I was sick to my stomach. Helpless. I couldn't sit still, so I paced around the building."

Stanley went quiet for a moment, staring into the past. It was obvious he'd carried this guilt and failure with him through his entire career.

"That's when I saw him. I ran into a kid. He was hiding around back, mesmerized by the fire. There was a line of dumpsters on the far end of the back parking lot. He didn't hear me approach, and I startled him. He tried to run, but I snagged his shirt. I was full of adrenaline, shouting in his face. I scared the shit out of him."

Charlie's breathing changed as he listened. I found his hand and laced our fingers together.

"The kid was panicked, which I assumed was because I'd snapped. When I asked him what he was doing there, he said he'd been hanging out with some buddies a few properties over. They'd heard the explosion and came to investigate. When they saw the cops, his buddies took off. The kid reeked of dope. He couldn't have been more than fifteen or sixteen like you said. I called him on the drugs and told him to empty his pockets. He had a few joints but nothing else. He begged me not to arrest him. Said he'd already been to juvie once, and he didn't want to go back. I was tempted to take him in and question him to see if he'd seen anything, but he was pretty freaked out. That whole area is hot for drug deals and illicit activities, so his story wasn't unusual."

"So you let him go?" I asked.

"I asked him if he knew anything about what was going on. He said he didn't. I asked for his name, gave him my card, and told him to call me if he remembered anything useful. Basically I gave him a slap on the wrist about the drugs, kept the joints, and told him to fuck off. I had bigger concerns that night than some teenager smoking pot with his friends."

"What was his name?" Charlie asked. His voice was small and tight.

"Jesus Christ, it's been seventeen years. You don't know that this is the same guy. In fact, it probably isn't."

"It is. It has to be. There's no other explanation. Why would he have been there?" The frantic note in Charlie's voice rose.

"Drugs, Charlie. Smoking up with his buddies."

"Or he was lying. You have to remember his name. I need to know."

"Were daily logs a thing back then?" I asked, knowing the practice of officers recording their daily activities might be newer than the case. It was brought into play when the people in charge wanted to ensure their money was being properly spent and not wasted. If they could prove officers had too much time on their hands, they would chop numbers.

Stanley's eyes lit up, and he stood straighter. "You know what? I think they were, and that is exactly the kind of thing I would have noted. Hang on."

He vanished into another part of the house on a mission. I turned to Charlie and wrapped both my hands around his. "You're doing great."

"This is him. He's our guy, right?"

"I don't know, but he fits, and if Stan can give us a name, we'll look into it."

Charlie was too pale. I brushed knuckles along his cheek. "Is this too much?"

"No. I just... need answers."

"We'll figure it out."

I encouraged Charlie to rest his forehead on my shoulder so I could rub his back. He relaxed several degrees and pressed his face into my neck, inhaling before sighing.

When Stanley returned, Charlie moved away, but not before Stanley registered our close connection. He wasn't a stupid man, and he narrowed his eyes, issuing me a warning without saying a thing.

He carried a banker's box and set it on the floor in front of the recliner. When he lifted the lid, I saw a long line of neatly ordered journals inside. The spines were marked with dates. The man was not only smart but far more organized than I expected.

He spent a minute shuffling through the journals before he found the one he wanted. He tugged it free and leafed through the old brittle pages, turning them one at a time, scanning his notes.

It took another few minutes before he found what he was looking for.

"Write this down," he said, finger poised over a spot on the page in front of him.

I removed my phone from my pocket and pulled up the notes app.

"Victor Istomin."

Charlie glanced over my shoulder and took my phone when I made a butchery of the spelling. Then he asked, "Victor as in V-I-C-T-O-R and Istomin, I-S-T-O-M-I-N?"

"Your guess is as good as mine. I didn't ask him to spell it out. That's what I've got. I'll be honest. I never bothered looking him up. Had no reason. We had bigger worries."

Charlie handed back my phone. I stared at the name. I wanted to run it through the system and see if I got a hit. The kid had claimed to have had a juvie record. People like that didn't always change as adults and sometimes had minor infractions on their rap sheets. Sometimes worse.

"I didn't add any more notes than what I told you. I swear, I talked to that kid for less than five minutes, then I sent him on his way. Like I said, I chalked it up to wrong place, wrong time. He had a bike with him, which to me corroborated his story. A red BMX. He jumped on and took off when I told him to get lost. Never saw him again."

I stood and thrust my hand out to Stanley. "Thank you. We aren't hanging out. I want to take this name to the station and look him up. Update Wan and Myers and see what they think."

Charlie was lost in his head again, frowning at a place on the floor. Stanley eyed him then glared at me.

"You be careful, Dyani." But what Stanley didn't say was, *if you hurt him, I'm coming after you.*

Message received.

"Yes, sir. Come on, Charlie."

I held out my hand, but it took a second for him to register and accept it. I pulled him to his feet, and he blinked away from whatever thought had taken him, focusing on the old detective.

"Thank you, Detective Graveman."

"Anytime." Stanley got to his feet.

Angel opened her eyes and whimpered.

I crouched and gave her a pat. "Take it easy, girl. Maybe I'll see you again."

Stanley saw us out and stayed in the doorway as we headed to my vehicle and got in.

Charlie was stuck in his head again. Not gone away like he sometimes did, but he looked deep in thought.

"Want to say it out loud?"

"What?"

I turned the key, but the engine choked and sputtered and wouldn't catch. Frowning, I tried again, then a third time, giving it a bit of gas and encouraging it to life. When the car finally started, it chugged and threatened to die before leveling out.

I glanced at Charlie. "You're thinking hard about something. Might help to say it out loud."

"Oh. It's… I don't know. Something about his name."

"You remember it?"

"It's familiar. I think. But it's… not what I called him."

"What do you mean?"

Charlie peered back at Stanley, who was still at the door. "Drive. Let me think more. I'm not sure, but I feel like the answer is right there."

Halfway back to the station, Charlie asked to see my phone. I dug it from my pocket and unlocked it before handing it over. He found the notes app and stared at the name he'd entered.

I didn't speak. His mind seemed to be spinning around something, and if I interrupted, I feared the thought might flee.

We hadn't confirmed this guy was who was stalking Charlie, but Charlie seemed convinced. Until we could track him down and get him into an interview room, I wasn't sure anyone would believe him.

I pulled into the lot behind the station and killed the engine. The car rattled, and something clunked, then it shivered to a standstill. Charlie didn't react.

"Ready?"

He sighed and shut off my phone, handing it back. "Yeah. This is him. I know it."

"Then let's try to find him and prove it."

Charlie followed me inside.

In the bullpen, we were immediately tagged by Nikola, who was having a word with a pair of officers just outside his office. His brows met in the middle, and he excused himself, stalking across the room in our direction.

"What are you doing here?" he snapped, eyeing Charlie but aiming his question at me. "Did Myers call you in for more questions?" he asked Charlie.

"No. We have possible information and need to look into it," I said.

I went to move around him, but he planted a hand on my chest. "What kind of information?"

"A name. Are you going to let me do my job?"

"Takoda." Charlie placed a calming hand on my arm.

I was a bit fired up and knew I was only making things worse. I took a steady breath and squared my shoulders. "We think it might be our guy."

Nikola considered me for a long moment before waving us toward Wan and Myers's area. The two detectives weren't in the bullpen, and I had no idea where they might be.

"Where'd you get a name?"

Charlie looked at me for answers. I figured there was no harm in telling Nikola the truth, so I explained how Charlie had wanted to talk to the old detective because of memories that didn't line up, then I told him all we'd learned about the kid outside the warehouse that night.

Nikola seemed skeptical, but he wasn't about to blow us off. Not after the last time and knowing the crown attorney was crawling up his ass. He might not be happy with me, but he knew where to draw the line.

He sat at Wan's desk and picked up the phone. "Find me Myers and Wan," he barked at whoever he'd called.

He hung up and jiggled the mouse, bringing the computer screen to life.

I wanted to tell him I could handle it, but Charlie's presence reminded me to keep my cool. I was technically suspended. Nikola could have easily taken details and promised to call if he found anything.

He keyed in his access code and pulled up one of our databases.

"Victor Istomin," Charlie said when Nikola glared at him expectantly.

He typed the name, clicked a few boxes, and waited as the search ran.

It came back with a whopping zero hits.

"No record."

"Graveman claims the kid owned up to having been in juvie," I said, one hand on the back of the chair as I leaned over Nikola's shoulder.

"If the record's sealed, it won't be in the system any longer."

At that moment, Wan came from the back door of the bullpen. Myers wasn't with him. He steered in our direction, glancing between Charlie, the sergeant, and me, looking for answers.

Nikola shoved back from the desk and stood, speaking to Wan. "We have a possible lead. I'm not convinced it's anything just yet, but we should look into it."

Nikola brought Wan up to speed. Wan informed us Myers was headed across town to talk with one of the old arrest's parole officers, double-checking an alibi.

Wan took his seat, and Nikola headed back to his office. "How sure are you?" he asked Charlie.

"Almost certain. It's too similar. It… feels right."

"How about a loose search? We could be dealing with an alternate spelling," I said.

Wan studied the screen and unchecked the little box marked *Exact Match*. He hesitated over the area parameters. Nikola had set it broad, covering all of Ontario. He left it then ran the search again. When the results came in, four entries were marked as close matches, and about fifteen or sixteen were marked as loose matches. Three of the first four were alternate spellings on the last name Istomin, while one was a variation on the name Victor.

Charlie made a noise, a tiny gasp that I might have missed had we not been standing shoulder to shoulder. His body tensed.

Wan heard it too because he glanced back at the same time I asked, "What is it?"

Charlie's gaze was riveted to the screen. "Rotkiv. Oh shit. Oh god. How did I not see it sooner?"

Wan looked confused and glanced between Charlie and the computer screen, a deep frown on his face.

I felt just as lost. Rotkiv? It took me a second to place where I'd heard the word before. It was the name of one of Charlie's dragons. He'd spoken it several times when telling me about his books. I hadn't been paying close attention because fantasy books and dragons weren't my thing.

"Charlie?"

"I forgot. I... How could I have forgotten? Oh my god."

He looked like he was about to collapse, so I shooed Wan out of his chair and encouraged Charlie to sit.

I crouched to be at his level, keeping one hand on his thigh. "You need to explain what's happening. What does this have to do with your books?"

"Not the books. Rotkiv. He was created in my mind long before I wrote his story. I-I invented him while in that room." Charlie glanced at the results on the computer screen. "He liked video games and fantasy comic books. He told me the ones with dragons were his favorite. It was the one thing we had in common. *I* drew the dragon on his jeans. I remember now. I invented him on the spot and told stories off the top of my head when this guy came to visit me. He was enthralled. He loved it. The dragon didn't have a name at first, and he asked if he could name him. Rotkiv, he said. I laughed because it was a weird name but somehow fitting for a dragon. He shrugged and told me it was his name spelled backward. We tried my name like that too, but it was too hard to pronounce, so we called the dragon Rotkiv. His name is Viktor, but with a *k,* not a *c.*" Charlie pointed at the screen and the one entry with the alternate spelling on the first name.

Wan beat me to it. He leaned over Charlie and took control of the mouse, clicking the name. It turned out Viktor had a few misdemeanors. Possession, petty theft, and a few reckless driving charges. He'd done four months a few years back, but there weren't any major charges.

"All right. Shuffle over, buddy," Wan said, patting Charlie's shoulder. "I have to look into this."

"You're gonna find him and bring him in for questioning, right?" I asked.

"Because of a possible connection to a fictional dragon name? That won't get me anywhere but laughed out of the station, but I am going to poke into this guy to see what I can find in relation to the case seventeen years ago. I need to know how a fifteen-year-old kid ties in with a massive kidnapping and sex-trafficking operation."

Charlie had gone pale. "You don't believe me."

"It's not about believing you, Charlie." Wan opened a new screen on his computer as he tugged his cell from a pocket in his shirt. "It's about finding proof. Otherwise, we can't hold him." A second later, whoever Wan had called—Myers likely—answered. "I need you back here. We have a possible lead."

I knew how this stuff worked, and I knew it would take some time. We could hang out at the station, but I feared it would make Charlie antsy.

He was already lost in his head, staring at Wan as he worked on the computer and spoke on the phone.

"Come on. We can get lunch and touch base later. Maybe you'll think of more things that will help. If this guy is connected, maybe we can figure out how."

It took another moment for Charlie to break his gaze from the computer. When he looked at me, there was a world of pain in his eyes.

"They don't believe me."

"They do, or they wouldn't be looking into it."

"I want to go to my house. I… Please. I need to see something."

I didn't like the idea of bringing Charlie to his neighborhood where this Viktor guy could be lurking and waiting for Charlie to return, but something told me he needed this, so I nodded at the back door. "Let's go."

Twenty-two

CHARLIE

Dragons.

Vrydindel.

The many adventures of Calipnia.

All of it had been born in this room.

A series of twelve books.

As a young boy, too afraid to face the real world, I'd learned to escape into another.

And it was Viktor who'd started the ball rolling. He'd encouraged the stories. He'd sat and listened to them all.

When I'd been rescued, the trauma had been so great that I'd abandoned my fantasy world for a time. Not long, but long enough for the walls to go up. Long enough for my mind to break. Long enough I hadn't remembered where the fantasy had truly begun. All I'd known for a long time was it was a place of safety and fun and peace.

Far from the dangers down the hall. Far from the fear that lived behind a barricade in my mind.

I stood in the middle of my bedroom, surrounded by the world I'd created as a twelve-year-old boy and let the memories return.

All of them.

Viktor's face morphed and cleared. Curls of reddish-brown hair. Braces over crooked teeth. Acne. The broken voice of a teenager going through puberty. And an odd sense of safety even when surrounded by danger.

I felt Takoda's presence in the doorway. He was worried. I wasn't retreating inside my head, but I was sure it looked that way from the outside.

On the wall, Rotkiv peered down from a huge frame, rows of sharp teeth on display. A fighting stance. Claws like needles, scales like rubies, and a tail that could level a building. He was fierce. The most dangerous dragon I'd ever created.

And he'd turned from enemy to friend.

"You need to make him vicious and strong. He should be smart and witty, always escaping capture. The evilest dragon that ever lived."

"But Calipnia will get him. No one can defeat Calipnia."

Viktor thought about that. "But Rotkiv is older and stronger."

"And Calipnia is younger and smarter."

"You're not smarter than me. How about this? Maybe they'll battle and realize they're equally matched. They end up as friends and work together to save the realm. Rotkiv can be Calipnia's protector. Just like I'm yours."

"A team?"

"Blood brothers. He's a blood dragon after all."

"What's a blood dragon? Is there such a thing?"

"There is now. We just invented it."

Noises. Shouting. Men.

"Don't worry. Rotkiv will protect you. He will always protect you. If you're my blood brother, Calipnia, then you can't be harmed. Family doesn't hurt their own."

It was right there. The answer.

"Family doesn't hurt their own."

"What was that?" Takoda moved in behind me and wrapped his arms around my middle. It was protective, and I exhaled a shuddering breath as I leaned back into the embrace.

"When I was hiding in the chest, he said I had been calling out to him all this time. He meant through my books. He thinks I wrote them for him. A calling to my brother. He thinks I've honored our bond and that I've been seeking him for years. He is Rotkiv, and I am Calipnia. He's not wrong. They were invented in that room. The dragon and the demi-elf bonded long before I wrote their books. He said, because we were blood brothers, he could protect me. From the men. Family doesn't hurt their own."

Takoda's phone rang, but instead of answering it, he spun me around to face him. All the pieces were falling into place, but it was taking a second.

There was doubt in his eyes. He was second-guessing the state of my mind and my memories. He didn't trust his instincts anymore.

As though just registering the shrill cries of Metallica, he dug his phone from his pocket. Wan's name flashed across the screen.

He hit accept and immediately put it on speaker.

"Dyani. You're on speaker, and Charlie's with me."

"We have a connection. You aren't going to believe this."

He was wrong. I'd already figured it out, and Takoda was only two steps behind. "Viktor is Mateo Fabian's son. His father was the mastermind behind the whole operation." A pause followed my statement, so I added, "I just fit it together. I wasn't leaving out details on purpose."

"But you're right," Wan said. "Viktor Istomin shares his mother's surname. She and Fabian never legally married, but they filed taxes as common-law partners for years. We're still unearthing things. Graveman wouldn't have connected it. Viktor was a minor at the time and therefore exempt when they interviewed the common-law wife and other family members."

Myers cut in. "We think it might be why Fabian was so quick to sell out. His son was part of it. They knew something was going down, and the kid managed to slip away in time. If Fabian gave up his crew, there was less chance of another guy being offered a plea as well. Anyone else might have revealed his son's involvement. The cops had all the answers because Fabian didn't hold back a damn thing."

"He would have known he was toast in prison either way," Wan said. "Guys like him don't survive behind bars for long. He wanted his son left out of the mess. Viktor would have landed in juvie at the very least. With a crime this serious, it's possible they'd have tried him as an adult, and he'd have gone away for a long time."

"So you have enough to bring him in? That's a solid connection," Takoda said.

"Yup. We're still working on a current address. At this point, nothing is coming up. I just wanted you to know we're on the right track. I'll keep you posted."

The line went dead, and my pounding heart was the only noise in the room. It thrummed loudly in my ears and made me lightheaded. I had to sit down.

I fumbled to my bed, and Takoda sat beside me, spinning his phone end over end in his hand. "We're going to get this guy. We're close because of you."

"I don't feel so great."

I looked around my room. The place where I'd taken refuge for years. The fantasy world I'd created that had become bigger and more popular than I could have ever imagined.

"How can I ever go back, knowing where it all came from?"

Takoda followed my gaze around the room and seemed to understand what I meant. "I don't read a whole lot of books. In fact, I don't read at all, but isn't that the beauty of the written word? Stories grow and change with an author. They're the essence and heart and soul of their creators, but they come to life in the readers' minds. The reader will never know the impact a story had on an author because they don't know their life. They haven't walked in their shoes. It's an individual journey for each person who picks up that book. Maybe Vrydinhoof, or whatever you call this place, has served its purpose. Maybe young Calipnia is done fighting the big bad dragons because he's realized they don't frighten him anymore. He doesn't need Rotkiv to protect him because, maybe, he's strong enough on his own."

Takoda weaved his fingers with mine and raised them to his lips, kissing my knuckles. "Maybe it's time to start a new journey and write a new bestselling series." He shrugged. "I'm just talking out of my ass."

"No. I think you're right. You're a pretty great guy, you know that? And you're smarter than you give yourself credit for."

"I have my own evil dragons, Charlie. Maybe it's time I stop fighting them too."

Something passed between us in the quiet minutes that followed. Takoda never stopped looking into my eyes. His were glassy. More than once, he looked like he wanted to say something else, but the words never surfaced.

The afternoon was getting away from us. "How about we hit the grocery store and go back to your place and eat," I suggested.

"Then we'll head to the hospital and visit your dad?"

"Okay."

Takoda leaned in and kissed me, a soft brush of lips. A whisper. A promise.

Butterflies roared to life in my belly, and I tugged him against me. I let Takoda press me down on the bed and invited him to take the kiss deeper.

Groceries would have to wait.

The moment was magical, and it had nothing to do with the fantasy realm surrounding us. This was goodbye and hello wrapped together in one neat package.

For too many years, I'd been nurturing a deep wound created from a torturous and unthinkable past. I'd convinced myself there was no way out of the horror and that I'd be forever stuck in a whirlwind of fear and uncertainty.

But I was wrong.

Like Takoda had said, my story didn't have to end here. I didn't have to keep walking this same path. I could step beyond the fear and the pain and forge a new one. Maybe it was scary, and maybe I'd run into new obstacles along the way, but unless I took a pen to paper, then I would never know how this new chapter would play out. My past didn't define me, and my future could be anything I wanted it to be.

It could be the best one yet.

I didn't need Vrydindel or Rotkiv to protect me anymore. I was strong enough on my own.

*　*　*

Blue-tinged smoke appeared from beneath the hood of Takoda's vehicle, along with an awful smell. I coughed and brought my shirt to my nose. The car had developed an ear-splitting whine, and I wasn't sure if the two were related or if the whole vehicle was just on the verge of collapse.

"Pull over. I think we're going to blow up."

"It's fine. It does this sometimes."

"That's not normal." I pointed at the swirls of smoke rising from under the hood.

Takoda sneered and kept going. "It's still driving. That's what matters. Point A to point B. We're good."

"Look. Take that spot there. We can walk. It's only a block. I'm going to die from toxic-fume inhalation at this rate."

Takoda couldn't argue. He was trying not to cough too as the car filled with the scent of burning oil.

We were close to the hospital, and the metered parking on the street was far cheaper than what they charged in their parking lot anyhow.

Engine screaming and whining, Takoda pulled to the curb. The breaks squealed, adding more noise to the mix. It was followed by a bone-jarring grind and more smoke. There was one last horrendous clang as he shut off the car. It coughed and died.

"I think it's getting worse," Takoda announced as he squinted out the windshield at the billowing cloud rising from under the hood. "I might need to take it in."

"Might I suggest the wreckers? I think it's beyond hope."

"I can't afford a new car."

I stayed quiet. Takoda was sensitive when it came to discussing finances, and I walked a thin line. It was easy to get myself in trouble if he thought I was waving my money in his face. Somehow I'd need to convince him to let me pay him for his bodyguard services, even if he was too proud to take the money. The least I could do was offer to get his car fixed since he'd been driving me around everywhere. That might make a good excuse. I filed it away to discuss later.

It was evening, and dusk had turned the city into a palette of monochrome. It was cool, and I was glad for my jacket. Takoda was in short sleeves, but he seemed impervious to the chill in the air.

We got out, and Takoda dug through his jeans pockets before feeding a few coins into the meter, ignoring my offer to help. Dimes and nickels clinked one after another in a steady rhythm. It took a while for him to empty his pockets. Then he stared at the display and frowned.

"Fuck me. Fifteen fucking minutes? How the hell much does parking cost? If you'd let me hit the emergency lot, I could have parked free with my police pass."

I dug coins from my pocket and shoved him aside. "Move. The old beater wasn't going to make it to the end of the block, never mind the parking lot at the other side of the hospital."

Takoda begrudgingly moved over, arms crossed as I added a pair of loonies and a couple of quarters into the machine. "There. We have two hours. We don't have to visit that long, but we don't have to worry now. Better?"

Takoda didn't respond. He stewed and seethed and glared daggers.

"Stop it. You're too sensitive. Now, aren't you supposed to be playing James Bond or something?"

Takoda's spine stiffened, and his gaze flicked around the street. He wasn't the most astute bodyguard and was far too easily distracted. I tried not to point it out since I'd already bruised his ego over the parking meter. It didn't matter. I felt safer just being near him. Alone, I was vulnerable. I didn't think this Viktor guy would come after me when I was with Takoda. That would take guts. Even when he wasn't on alert, Takoda was the definition of intimidating.

We headed toward the hospital at the end of the road, passing a line of shops on our right that were closing for the day. A family-owned hardware store, a candy store called Grandma's Treats, a pizza joint, and a pet store, which called Takoda's attention.

He stopped in front of the display window and cupped his hands to the glass to look inside. It was closed for the night, and the interior lights were off.

"I should come back here and grab something nice for Angel. A toy or a treat or something. It would give me an excuse to visit her again. She's a good dog."

"I'm sure Stan wouldn't care if you just showed up to visit without a reason."

Takoda shrugged, and we kept walking.

The hospital was brightly lit. We crossed the road and headed to the main entrance where we went through the automatic sliding doors. An information and preregistration desk sat on the left. A bank of elevators was on the right. They would take us to my dad's floor.

I wasn't sure what I'd do if they discharged him before the police tracked down Viktor. I didn't want to go home without Takoda at my side, but I didn't want Dad alone at the house either.

The fourth floor was quiet. The scent of antiseptic and cleaner was sharp and tickled my nose. The fluorescent lights hummed. Our shoes squeaked on the linoleum floor as we headed down the short hall to my dad's room. Takoda paused outside his door and gestured at a small cove with a group of chairs that sat under a window a few feet away.

"I'll hang out over there. No rush or anything. Take your time."

"You can come in. It's fine."

"I don't think your dad likes me too much."

"Well, then he'd better learn to like you." I hesitated, unsure if it was a good time to bring this up. "I mean. This..." I waved a finger between us. "It's something, isn't it? Because if it is, my dad's going to find out about it eventually, and he's going to have to get used to it."

Takoda smiled. "I'm pretty sure he already suspects. It's half the reason he's not too fond of me."

"Well, too bad for him. Come on."

I took Takoda's hand and tugged him into the room after me. It was a private room, and Dad had the head of his bed raised to watch the small TV on the far wall. He held a remote and was flicking through channels when we entered, a frown bringing out the deep wrinkles in his face.

When he saw us, he set the remote beside him and grinned. "Thought you were a nurse coming to bug me. Not sure how much damn blood those people need to take, but if they don't stop, I'll have none left."

His color was better than the previous day, even though he still looked tired. "Nope, not a nurse. How are you, Dad?"

"Bah, sick and tired of being here. Just ready to head home. Tomorrow maybe. We'll see what the doctor says." He eyed Takoda, and his eyes grew sterner. "Dyani."

"Sir."

"It's Takoda, Dad."

It was then Dad's gaze drifted to our joined hands. He stared at our connection for a long minute before lifting his gaze again. "Is it now?"

There was a moment of tension as Dad stared at Takoda, who, for the first time since I'd known him, looked uncomfortable and unsure. It was out of character.

"Well, come on in then. Been a boring day. I wouldn't mind some company. Grab a seat." He waved at a few abandoned plastic bucket chairs that had been shoved to the other end of the room.

I glanced at Takoda and gave him a smile. We grabbed the chairs and dragged them over, taking a seat.

"Your mother was here earlier with your sister."

"Adelaide came? I'm shocked."

Dad chuckled. "I think your mother dragged her by the scruff of the neck. Probably told her I was biting the big one or something. Beth told me they have a lead on this stalker. The sergeant called her up this afternoon. Is that right?"

"It is, but can we talk about something else? I've been dealing with it all day, and I'm exhausted and a bit overwhelmed."

Dad checked in with Takoda before nodding. "All right. Your choice, but you know, that only leaves one other topic of conversation that interests me at the moment." A grin spread across his face, taking the heat out of his next words. "I think the young man beside you, who hasn't let go of your hand, best tell me his intentions with you since he's chosen to ignore my warnings."

"Um." Takoda opened and closed his mouth, gaze shifting frantically between Dad and me.

"Dad. It's not your business."

"Oh, it sure is. If my son has his first boyfriend, his old man has a right to know about it. Is that what this is?" The question was for Takoda.

"Um."

"Dad, you can't—"

Metallica pierced the air, and Takoda slapped his pockets, looking for his phone. "Oh, thank god. I have to get this. It's probably important."

Dad laughed as Takoda scrambled upright and pulled his phone out. "It's Nikola. See? I was right. Super important. I'll take it in the hallway."

And I guessed by the expression on Takoda's face that when the call was done, he wasn't returning. He would plant himself in the chairs in the little nook down the hall and stay there, avoiding the inquisition that was my father.

The door closed behind him, and Dad chuckled.

"Way to go. Thanks. You scared him off."

"It was too easy." Then he sobered. "So am I right? Is he your boyfriend?"

My cheeks burned, and I resisted the urge to fidget. "Yeah. I think so. I mean… It's definitely something."

"Definitely something. Hmm. And you're doing okay with it?"

"Yes. He knows… He knows I might have limits. He understands."

Dad took a second to examine me, likely looking for signs I was lying or exaggerating the truth. I wasn't. "Good. I'm happy for you. I wasn't sure this would ever be a possibility. I'm so glad I was wrong."

"He's really great, Dad. He acts all tough, but he's been patient and kind."

I would have explained more, but there was only so much about my sex life I cared to share with my father.

Dad was about to say something more when the door opened and Takoda poked his head back into the room. "They've got a location. Wan and Myers went to knockity knock on his door to talk to him, but there was no fucking answer. They also have a white Pontiac Grand Prix registered to a Viktor Istomin. Surprise, surprise. With Viktor's connection to Fabian and the car, it was enough to get a warrant to search the premises. They have guys moving in as we speak. Nikola's tearing up my asshole right now because this Viktor guy is in the wind, and I don't have you somewhere safe, so we've got to get you back to my place before I get extra suspended."

"What does that mean?" I asked.

"I don't fucking know. He said something like, 'You think you're suspended now? Just you wait, Dyani.' So, there's that, and I'm not really prepared to find out what it means. And… Oh my fuck, I just realized I'm swearing like a sailor in front of your dad when I've been trying to show I'm a good boyfriend—or whatever I am. Sir, please withdraw all the F-bombs and remember I care very much for your son. Shit."

Dad just laughed and tugged me in for a kiss and hug. "Be safe," he whispered in my ear. "Don't tell him, but I think I like the guy."

Twenty-three

TAKODA

"Does your dad own a shotgun?" I asked as I hit the down button on the elevator.

Charlie chuckled and bumped my shoulder. "No."

"That's good. I don't make a very good first impression. Hell, I don't make a very good second, third, or fourth impression. I've never really dated, to be honest. I've mostly just been the type to screw around, and I don't take names when I do. Shit, don't tell him that. In fact, let's pretend I never said that because you didn't need to hear it either. God, he must hate me. He does, doesn't he?"

I hadn't been prepared to walk into Archie Falkingham's room as anything more than Charlie's bodyguard, but that had all changed when Charlie had grabbed my hand and dragged me into the room after him.

Charlie was smirking. "Dad likes you, and so do I. Stop fretting. Now tell me what's happening."

"I did. The guy owns a white Pontiac. The house is in his mother's name, and so are all the bills. Records say she died last year, and I guess he's never changed it. Wan and Myers couldn't get an answer at the door and said it looked like no one was inside. The garage is sealed, so they couldn't tell if the vehicle was there or not. Once they have some backup, they're moving in."

The elevator doors opened, and we entered. Charlie wrung his hands as he bounced on his toes, staring at the numbers as they counted down the floors.

I touched the small of his back. "They're going to get him. It's almost over. He doesn't know we're onto him."

"I know. It's just… scary."

The elevator doors slid open. "I've gotcha. I promise."

Visiting hours were coming to an end, and the main lobby on the first floor was quieter than when we'd arrived. We headed out the automatic sliding doors into the night. It was colder now that the sun had gone down, but I didn't feel it. I'd been rolling the latest update around in my head since getting off the phone with Nikola.

Part of me wanted to be there when they entered the house. I wanted to get my hands on this guy and fuck him up for taunting Charlie and hurting Archie. The piece of shit needed to rot in a cell.

I scanned both directions on the main road, looking for a familiar white car or anyone suspicious. The traffic wasn't heavy, but there was enough activity on the road to help me relax. A few people came out of the hospital behind us, and I noted each of them as I guided Charlie back toward the side street where we'd parked earlier.

We crossed the four-lane main road at the light and headed down the less populated street with the now-closed storefronts—the pet store, the hardware store, and even the candy shop. The only one still open was the pizza joint on the corner closest to the hospital. There were a few other cars parked in the metered spots along the road. A beige Camry was in front of my Escort, and a blue Neon was parked behind it. A guy in a Dodge van pulled into the road from a space farther down and drove off.

At the end of the block of storefronts, about three car lengths from the car, my phone rang.

I stopped walking to fish it from my pocket just as Charlie said, "What is that?" and pulled free from my hold.

He approached the car, and I checked my phone screen—Wan—before following his gaze to try to figure out what he was talking about. There was a folded paper under the windshield wiper of the Escort.

"Is that a fucking ticket? Jesus Christ, I will kick someone's ass if they fucking ticketed me. We fed the meter, for fuck's sake."

Growling deep in my throat, I hit *Accept* on the call, put the phone to my ear, and barked, "Yeah. What?" as Charlie plucked the paper from under the blade.

"Where the fuck are you?" Wan snapped.

"Just leaving the hospital. We were visiting Archie Falkingham. I'm taking Charlie back to my place now. Nikola called with an update. Why?"

"Because you're a fucking idiot, that's why." There was an edge to Wan's voice I didn't like, and him calling me an idiot instantly got my back up.

But I didn't respond because the look on Charlie's face when he opened the paper stole my voice. He looked like he'd seen a ghost.

My phone vibrated in my hand, and Wan said, "We're in the house. I just sent you pictures. Look at them. This guy has been following you and Charlie everywhere. You should not be on the street at all right now."

I pulled my phone from my ear even though Wan kept talking. I opened the message he'd sent and scanned. They were pictures he'd taken of a wall behind someone's bed. Supposedly at Viktor Istomin's house. There were dozens of pictures of Charlie. At his house. At the gas station as he filled his car. The supermarket. The library, post office, and a bookstore. There were pictures of us together. In the driveway at my house, at the Taekwondo club, in the precinct parking lot, and even at the abandoned warehouse. A few showed intimate moments we'd thought were private.

Ice slipped down my spine, unearthing goose bumps along my arms. I'd been careful, at least, I'd thought I had. This guy had been on our tail the whole time, and I hadn't seen him at all.

Wan was still talking, but everything in my brain was happening in slow motion. I glanced at Charlie, who was still immobile as he stared at the paper in his hand. It trembled in his grasp, and I knew, subconsciously, this was all going south.

"Dyani!"

Wan's shout jarred me back to the present, and I pressed my phone to my ear again, eyes glued to Charlie.

"Did you hear me? Get the fuck off the street and find somewhere safe. Now! This guy isn't at the house, but Myers just got intel that he could be in a blue 2007 Neon. It's registered to his mother's name, and it's not here. We've got the white Pontiac in the garage, but there's evidence another vehicle is usually parked beside it."

A blue Neon. I darted my gaze to the vehicle parked directly behind the Escort, Charlie less than five feet from its bumper.

And far too many shadows surrounding them.

As though sensing something was wrong—or hearing something I hadn't—Charlie diverted his attention from the paper just as I reached for my holstered weapon.

Charlie didn't look at me though. His gaze drifted over my shoulder, and his eyes blew wide at whatever he saw. I knew then I'd made a big mistake. Viktor wasn't by his car, hiding and waiting for Charlie.

He was behind me.

The impact hit my temple. My teeth cracked together, and a flash of searing white pain tore through my head and radiated down my spine. I registered a momentary explosion of fireworks across my vision, but that was all.

My world went dark before I hit the ground.

Twenty-four

CHARLIE

I reached for the paper as Takoda answered his phone. It wasn't a parking ticket. I knew that before I picked it up. I was close enough to see the tears from where it had been pulled from a coil-bound notebook.

Unfolding it, my breath caught. A crudely drawn hangman game stared back at me. The little stick man was nearly fully drawn. He was missing one arm, the same as the one drawn on the cement wall back in the warehouse. One mistake, and it was game over. The dashes underneath were partially filled in, enough I could easily guess the answer.

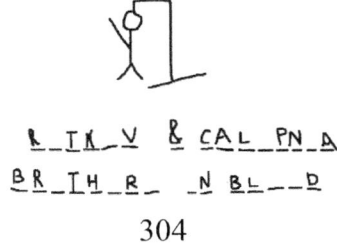

Rotkiv & Calipnia. Brothers in Blood.

My hand trembled. No air moved in or out of my lungs, and I was dizzy. My ears rang. Takoda's voice came from far away. Another voice, someone yelling on the other end of the phone, traveled across the space between us. Whoever it was sounded angry.

He was here. Viktor was here.

I glanced up to warn Takoda as a form emerged from the shadows at lightning speed. My eyes widened.

Takoda's hand moved to his holster, but he was too late. I didn't have time to warn him.

Viktor swung the metal bat he carried like a baseball player, aiming to knock the ball out of the park. It collided with Takoda's temple with a sickening thunk, the bat resonating and ringing with a twang of metal.

I flinched at the impact.

Takoda went down like a sack of potatoes, knocked out cold in an instant.

The paper fluttered from my hand as I came face-to-face with the boy from my past. Viktor Istomin. Rotkiv. My protector once upon a time. But what I hadn't known or understood as a twelve-year-old boy was how twisted and wrong it was that he'd been present among such dangerous men.

Fear clamped around my heart, and I couldn't take my eyes off Takoda's unmoving body.

"Calipnia." Viktor's voice was no longer that of a teenager. It was deeper. It was the voice of the man who had walked through my bedroom a few short days ago, taunting me, leaving me gifts while I'd hidden inside a cedar chest. "You remember me now?" There was a hopefulness to his tone that sounded out of place among such savagery and violence.

Paralyzed by terror, I stared back into amber eyes. "I remember."

He smiled. His braces were long gone. "I knew you would. When you went to the warehouse, I knew it would all come back. You've been calling out to me for years, haven't you? I didn't know, brother. You were always smarter than me. Why did you hide behind an alias? Kingston Fireborn. That's clever. Was it a test? A game to see if I could find you? I won, didn't I? You told our stories. Rotkiv and Calipnia forever. Adventuring through Vrydindel. Amazing. When I saw you on TV, I couldn't believe my eyes. I thought I'd lost you forever, but then you were right there."

He tossed the metal bat aside, and it clanged against the asphalt, bumping Takoda's leg before rolling under the beige Camry. Takoda still didn't move, and my gut twisted. The sound of the bat hitting his head resonated in my ears.

In the distance, traffic rolled along the main road by the hospital, but we were far enough down the side street that we might as well have been in another town, on another planet. It was desolate. Not a single car or soul around. The stores were all closed for the night, save for the pizza joint at the end of the block. It was just out of reach.

Viktor stepped closer again, closing our distance. He crouched and picked up something from the ground. Takoda's cell phone. The caller was still yelling on the other end of the line. Wan. Viktor disconnected it and tossed it under the Camry as well.

"We need to get out of here."

While he was distracted, I slipped my hand into my pocket and tucked my switchblade up inside the sleeve of my jacket. My palms were slick, and I almost dropped it when I removed my hand again. It took all my effort to calm my racing heart and act normal. Tremors rocked my body, and my teeth chattered, giving me away.

"You look terrified. Why? You don't have to be afraid of me. I won't hurt you. I didn't then, and I wouldn't now. You're my brother, Calipnia. Do you want me to call you Charlie? Is that it? Are we too old for nicknames?" He chuckled. "That's okay. Charlie it is."

I spared a glance at Takoda. A slick of blood covered the side of his face, and my stomach dropped. He needed a doctor. The hospital and help were a short block away, but it might as well have been miles for all the good it did when I was trapped by a delusional lunatic.

I wanted to run to Takoda to check if he was breathing, to scream and yell at the top of my lungs for someone to help, but Viktor was moving closer, and I didn't know what to do.

He noticed my diverted attention and glanced back at Takoda once before meeting my eyes again. "He's going to have a long nap. I didn't want to hurt him, but he never leaves your side."

Viktor was in front of me now. When he reached out and took hold of my left wrist, I flinched. He raised my hand and examined my thumb. I was grateful the switchblade was safely tucked away in my right sleeve. He angled my thumb so the streetlight reflected off my scar, then he grinned devilishly.

He held up his thumb, the same scar marking its surface. In the same fashion as he'd done seventeen years ago, he pressed our thumbs together. "Brothers in blood forever."

I couldn't move or breathe. I had the knife, but the blade was still tucked inside. If I tried to eject it, he'd know, and I didn't want to alert him I had a weapon.

"I'm sorry I abandoned you that night, Charlie." His words were soft and wistful. Sad. I could almost believe he meant it. "It tore me up. If I could have taken you with me, I would have. You believe me, right? I heard my dad yelling, and I knew something was wrong. I didn't have much time. He'd always told me in an emergency to use the venting system to escape. I barely made it. I'm so sorry. I'm here now. I'll never leave you like that again. Will you forgive me, brother?"

My throat was like flypaper, sticking to itself when I tried to swallow. I had to formulate a plan. Takoda needed help, but I didn't know what to do.

"I-I forgive you."

His face shifted into a brilliant smile. "Good. I was so afraid you wouldn't. Come on. We have to get out of here fast. I have a plan."

When he reached for my hand, I backed up a step. "I don't want to go with you. Takoda needs help. I have to help him. He's hurt."

It was the wrong answer, and I saw my mistake the moment the words left my mouth. Viktor's joy at finding me transformed into an ugly, twisted rage. His amber eyes darkened. His lips curled over his teeth, and his body went rigid.

"Who cares about him? We're brothers. We made a pact, remember? I kept you safe from all of them," he roared. "I protected you. I was your fierce dragon."

I backed up a step, my pulse throbbing in my ears. All I knew was, if I got in a car with him, it would be over. The police would never find me. Viktor was clearly unstable, and maybe he believed everything he said about protecting me and keeping me safe, but it was sick and twisted.

He'd created a fantasy world where we would be brothers and never leave each other. Maybe he wasn't all that different from me. Who knew what kind of trauma he'd suffered at the hands of his psychotic father. Except, I knew that Vrydindel wasn't real. I knew it was nothing more than a peaceful escape and a slice of fiction.

"You're scaring me."

"I'm not scaring you. I'm saving you."

He was yelling, and I wished there was someone in hearing distance who would take note of the situation and help, but no. I'd insisted we park down a side street, and now Takoda was unconscious and bleeding while some crazy freak tried to convince me he was my savior and that I should run away with him.

I backed up another step, grateful he'd abandoned his weapon on the ground. The problem with retreating was, I was heading in the wrong direction. The hospital and a greater chance at getting help was behind Viktor, and I was moving farther down a desolate street.

Viktor kept pace, advancing with my retreat.

"Don't you get it, Charlie? I thought we'd lost each other. I knew you survived that explosion. You know how I knew? Because I put you in that room," he spat. "He wanted you in a cage with the rest of them, but I gave you something better. I saved your life. You should be thanking me."

I sped up. The knife in my palm trembled as I tried to work the blade free one-handed without dropping it.

Viktor moved faster, closing our distance.

"My dad gave you to me. You were mine," he yelled, slapping his chest. "Mine. I got to do whatever I wanted to you, and I chose to take care of you, Charlie. I made you my brother because I didn't have a brother, and I'd always wanted one. We were a team. I taught you games. I brought you gifts. I swore I would never let them hurt you, and I kept my promise." Spittle flew from his lips, and his nostrils flared. "Stop. Running. Away!"

He broke out into a sprint.

There were ten or twelve feet between us, but I couldn't keep going backward or he'd catch up to me for sure.

I turned and ran, shot off down the road, tears blurring my eyes, my heart pumping. In the few seconds that Viktor had been advancing, I'd concocted a weak plan that would probably fail, but it was all I had.

I wasn't a runner. I sat behind a computer most days.

Viktor was gaining on me fast.

I brought the switchblade from my sleeve and ejected the knife. Perspiration coated my palms, and the small weapon almost slipped out of my hands. The wind sliced against my eyes, bringing more tears to the surface.

I'd gone less than half a block, and my lungs burned. It was now or never.

I slowed my pace, letting Viktor catch up, knowing what he would likely do. If I was wrong, I was fucked.

I thought of Takoda lying bloody and unconscious on the ground with a head wound that needed medical attention. I thought of my dad in a hospital bed and how it was Viktor who'd put him there.

I thought of gentle kisses and tattoos over warm olive skin, of tender touches and eyes the color of hickory. I thought of the future I'd been too afraid to reach for. Of the years I'd lost because I'd been a coward hiding in a world that didn't exist.

Strong arms grabbed me from behind, and for a moment, fear erased everything I'd learned. But I knew if I didn't find a way out of this, Takoda could die on the street behind me.

I'd only practiced the move a dozen times or so, but when I cleared my head, my reflexes took over. I grabbed his wrist, dropped my weight, which threw him off-balance, and tucked a leg behind his. Then I shoved. In seconds, Viktor was falling, a surprised cry on his lips.

He landed hard on his back, stunned and wide-eyed.

"What I taught you was how to disengage from an attacker if they manage to get their hands on you. It's not about being macho. It's not about confronting a bad guy. Hiding and calling the police is what I want you to do."

Not this time. I had the element of surprise, and I used it. With the blade exposed, I pressed it to Viktor's throat, right over his jugular.

He froze, eyes bulging, hands open and submissive at his side.

"Don't move," I screamed. Tears rolled down my face, and I couldn't stop them. "I will kill you. I will fucking kill you."

The past and present collided. My entire body quaked violently. I couldn't stop shaking. My teeth rattled, and I was at risk of cutting him even if he listened, but I didn't back down, and I didn't loosen my grip.

In my mind, I kept hearing the deadening thunk of the metal bat hitting Takoda's head. The sight of him landing on the ground in a heap was burned into my retinas. Blood. Tender kisses. Gentle hands.

A future I wanted desperately.

"Don't fucking move," I screamed again, over and over.

I could feel myself slipping into hysteria but couldn't find my way back. The blade was slick in my hand. Fear was rich and flowing through my veins.

"Could you stab a man if you were in trouble?"

I didn't know anymore, but the risk of inaction was too much to think about.

I was crying. Uncontrollably. My chest heaved. My vision was compromised.

"Hey. Hey now. See, baby brother? You don't want to hurt me. It's okay. I'll take care of you."

Viktor moved his hands toward me, and I jerked, spitting venom in his face. "I said don't move. Don't move, you fucking freak. I'll do it. I swear to god."

"I'm not going to hurt you. I promise. Please take the knife off my throat. I forgive you. You're just scared."

I wasn't scared. I was terrified.

I couldn't release the knife. Blinking heavily, I managed to clear my vision enough to see bright red beads of blood forming under the blade. Viktor's amber eyes were steady and focused on my face.

"Ease up, man. Charlie. Calipnia. Whatever you want me to call you. You're hurting me. You don't want to hurt me. We're brothers. We made a pact. Come on. We can make this right. Together, like before."

Sirens wailed in the distance. I gasped, jerking my head up at the sound and glancing down the street as hope bloomed in my chest. But they were far away. For a brief, gratifying moment, I thought they were heading toward us.

Help was coming.

Until I remembered we were near the hospital, and it was likely an ambulance on its way to the emergency room.

That flash of inattention was all Viktor needed. Before I registered what was happening, the knife was no longer in my hand, and he flipped me. I landed on my back and cracked my head against the road.

Our positions were reversed.
The cold steel of the blade touched my throat.

Twenty-five

TAKODA

When the darkness receded, there was nothing but pain. Like a thousand knives, it stabbed into the soft tissue of my brain. My face was sticky. Blood drained into my mouth. It combined with saliva before dribbling over my lips and creating a pool on the ground.

I groaned and tried to move, but a slash of red-hot lightning shot through my temple and down my neck. The peaceful darkness threatened to take me away again, and I wanted to go toward it to escape the agony. Instead, I stilled until it retreated.

I remained unmoving, focusing instead on opening my eyes. The world blurred and tilted, shattering into a prism of cut images I couldn't process.

My stomach roiled. I was seeing three of everything, and no amount of blinking made a clearer picture.

It took a long minute to put the pieces back together and remember where I was and why I was lying on the ground.

Charlie.

A surge of adrenaline made me jerk my head up too fast. The world spun and exploded into a kaleidoscope of broken pieces that refused to reform. My stomach heaved, and there was no stopping what was coming. I vomited, and each convulsion speared more needles of pain through my head.

When my stomach settled, I carefully looked around at the ground directly in front of me, doing all I could to bring it into focus. Under the car on my left, I saw my phone—or rather three phones. I reached out, grabbing for the device but coming up empty each time.

Army crawling forward, gritting my teeth against the lashing agony shredding my brain, I swiped my hand over the ground, hoping one of those phones was real and not an illusion created by a bad blow to the head.

My fingers scraped hard plastic just as a roaring shout pierced the air from down the road.

"Don't fucking move!"

Charlie. Oh god.

I dragged the phone across the asphalt as I worked at getting my legs underneath me. They wouldn't cooperate, and I went down hard on a hip. Again, my stomach lurched, but nothing came out. I tried again and succeeded at getting to my hands and knees.

The phone screen lit up at my touch, but it was too bright, and I squinted and turned my head. Peering through slits, I looked back. It was nothing more than a warped image. I couldn't bring it into focus no matter how hard I tried.

Going on memory, I punched my finger in the general vicinity of the call button.

The colors on the screen changed, and three and a half blurry keypads, overlapping and fuzzy, stared back at me. The numbers were indecipherable.

"Fuck, fuck, fuck, fuck."

More yelling from down the road. How far away? Where was he?

Charlie, I'm coming. I'm coming.

I jammed a finger over the buttons, hoping I was hitting the mark. For all I knew, I'd hit #-4-4 and not 9-1-1.

I listened to it ring, and a wash of relief hit me when the operator came on.

"911. Do you need police, fire, or ambulance?"

My tongue was thick, and each effort to bring words to my lips failed. I tried to say, "Police," but I thought it came out slurred, and I wasn't sure she understood, so I settled for "Help" instead.

Charlie was yelling—screaming—and the frantic tone in his voice sent a chill down my spine. Fear unlike any I'd ever felt made me abandon my phone and crawl toward the noise. I fumbled for my gun, dropped it, picked it up, and kept crawling.

But I wasn't moving fast enough.

And I couldn't see straight.

And where the fuck was he?

The commotion down the road was elevating. Another voice cut through the air. Male. Saying things I couldn't piece together. Whether it was my head not making sense of the words or that I was too far away to understand, I didn't know.

All I knew was, I needed to get to my feet and move faster.

At my car, I grabbed the driver's side door handle and cried out through the pain as I pulled myself upright. Again, I dry heaved. The world spun and tilted on its axis, and it would have been so much easier to collapse into a ball and wait for help to arrive.

But Charlie needed me.

If I waited, he could be taken.

Or worse, he could be killed.

Viktor was dangerous and had already proven he was violent.

Time was not on my side.

When my stomach calmed, I tried to aim for the ruckus down the road. It was like walking on a Tilt-A-Whirl. Every step threatened to topple me over. With my vision compromised, it was easier to move with my eyes closed. I told my feet to run, to ignore the blinding pain tearing me in half, but the best I could manage was a staggering shuffle.

I wasn't sure how fast I was going, but I was moving and listening.

The voices grew angrier, wilder, and closer.

My foot caught on something—or nothing—and I went down hard on my hands and knees. The gun skittered a few feet ahead of me, and I almost passed out. I fought through it, slapping the road in front of me until I got hold of the weapon again.

When I glanced up, I saw them. How many fucking people were here? In the middle of the road, there were about seven or eight blurry images. But only two voices. I squinted, blinked, and did everything to clear my vision, but nothing worked. Charlie. I saw Charlie on top. Was it Charlie? He was holding something to Viktor's throat, and my gut told me it was his knife.

I was about to call out when the image in front of me changed at nauseating speed. An army of people blurred and moved too fast for my broken mind to comprehend.

But when it slowed again, Charlie was no longer on top. A sickening crack and a cry of pain arrested my heart. I couldn't make out what was happening, not clearly, but I knew Charlie had lost the advantage, and Viktor had him pinned down. A lot of Viktors. Too many Viktors.

I raised the gun and found my voice. The slur hadn't left, but I added as much authority as I could muster behind the order. "Police. Get off him, or I'll fucking shoot a bullet right through your fucking head, asshole."

All six of your fucking heads, I thought.

He didn't have to know that the chances of that happening were slim since I didn't know which head was the real one. All he had to do was believe my threat.

The fighting stopped. Viktor went rigid.

He didn't turn to me nor did he move off Charlie.

Was Charlie okay?

"Charlie? Charlie, talk to me. Are you okay? I can't… Talk to me."

All I got was a whimper, and the fear that came from that tiny noise surged through me like a hurricane.

"Get off him," I screamed. "Get the fuck away from him, or I'll kill you right now."

I waved the gun at all the Viktors.

Darkness threatened to close in on me from all sides. Blood roared in my ears. I was too close to passing out. The pull of gravity worked against me. It tugged at my arm, compromising my aim. I wanted to cry. Charlie needed me. I'd promised to protect him.

Did this guy know I was in no shape to rescue anyone? Was that why he hadn't moved?

"Motherfucker," Viktor muttered. "Charlie, tell that asshole to back off. We can go now. You and me."

Charlie didn't respond.

Viktor roared and flew to his feet. I was right. He saw no threat in the gun. I was probably aiming miles off course. He marched toward me, gaining ground too fast. It was an army of Viktors, and I didn't know where to aim.

"Stop moving, or I'll shoot," I screamed.

He kept advancing. Laughing.

I aimed skyward and fired a shot. The crack of the gun echoed and resonated off the buildings, slicing hot knives through the soft tissue of my brain, but it did its job. When I lowered the muzzle at Viktor again, he stood still. I got the sense he was sizing me up, deciding if I'd really shoot. Deciding how good my aim would be.

"I fucking dare you," I said through gritted teeth.

I saw motion. A blur of movement from behind Viktor's legs. Viktor launched at me, and I tightened my finger over the trigger but hesitated. Charlie was out there but where?

It took a moment for me to realize Viktor wasn't coming at me. He was falling forward because Charlie had tackled him from behind. I stilled my finger on the trigger just in time to see the two of them land on the ground a few feet away in a rolling, messy ball of too many limbs.

My ears were screaming from the gunshot. A whining, pulsing wail filled my ears and ached in my teeth. Lights flashed across the ground and the world all around me. Blues and reds and whites. My head was breaking. I couldn't take the pain anymore. Not like this.

Shouting. Doors slamming.

"Police," someone yelled.

It was help. They'd arrived.

I lay on the ground, unable to do anything more. I felt like I'd been shattered into a thousand pieces.

Sounds drifted, growing more and more distant. An army of Charlies scrambled away from a pile of Viktors, throwing their hands in the air and saying something I couldn't process.

All the Viktors stayed down.

Good, motherfucker. Good.

I let go of my gun and reached for Charlie, but I couldn't move. I tried desperately to hold on to consciousness, but the world was falling away. Closing my eyes, I curled into a ball and welcomed the peaceful darkness.

Help was here. Charlie would be okay.

And I was tired.
So fucking tired.

Twenty-six

CHARLIE

I'd stabbed someone, and I couldn't stop shaking as I stared at the wet slick of blood that coated my hand and fingers. Wheezing, unable to catch my breath, I couldn't break away from the sight. Blood. Another man's blood. I'd plunged a knife into another human being.

Sirens sang through the night. Red and blue lights flashed and rolled across the buildings at the side of the road. A storm of boots raced onto the scene. People yelled things I couldn't decipher.

All I could see was the blood on my hand.

A woman with a blonde ponytail and mousy features knelt in front of me. She carried a bag and set it on the ground before tipping my chin and forcing eye contact. "Hey, hey, sweetie. Deep breaths. In and out. Are you hurt?"

I didn't know, and I couldn't answer since oxygen refused to enter my lungs. My windpipe had shrunk to the size of a straw, and no matter how deeply I sucked and gulped for air, there was none.

She continued to speak, talking me through each breath as she checked me head to toe. Only as the panic receded did I realize she was a paramedic.

Police cars and ambulances filled the street.

I wanted to scream for her to check Takoda. I was fine. She didn't need to worry about me, but Takoda was not okay.

"T-t-takoda. Takoda. W-w-where is he?" A vise clamped around my heart.

I looked around, frantic to find him when the young woman placed a calming hand on my arm. "They're loading him into an ambulance right now. Your name is Charlie, isn't that right?"

I nodded, seeking the ambulance, needing to see it with my own eyes.

"Charlie, are you injured? I need to know if you're hurt. There's blood on—"

"It's not m-mine." My voice was airy and weak. "I s-s-stabbed him."

"I know."

"Is he d-d-dead?"

She chuckled, which curdled my stomach. I didn't see what was so funny. "You stabbed him in the shoulder. He'll live, and for the record, in case you're concerned, he's been arrested. He's in police custody on the way to the hospital. Now, I think you're in shock, Charlie. Do you think you can get to your feet? We have an ambulance here for you too."

"I'm f-f-fine."

Why couldn't I talk? What was wrong with me?

"You were very brave tonight."

"Is Takoda okay? H-he was... Oh god, Viktor hit him s-s-so hard." The sound would be with me always.

"The doctors will take care of him. Come on. Let's get you to your feet."

"I'm c-cold."

"It's shock, hun. We're going to get you checked out at the hospital too."

As the kind paramedic helped me to my feet, Wan approached. I didn't know he'd arrived.

"Hey, Charlie. How are you?"

"I s-s-stabbed him." I showed him the blood on my hand, still mesmerized by its appearance.

"You did good, considering this whole thing turned into an epic clusterfuck. Viktor Istomin has been arrested. Once they take care of that small flesh wound you gave him, we'll be taking him in." He squeezed my shoulder. "And once you've been checked out and given the green light, we're going to have a little chat. I need a statement."

"What about T-takoda?"

Wan's mouth flattened, and he looked grim. "He's going to need some medical attention, but don't you worry. He's in good hands."

Another paramedic came over with a thick blanket and wrapped it around my shoulders. My teeth were chattering nonstop. The pair then guided me to a waiting ambulance.

From there, everything moved at lightning speed, or perhaps I was just too exhausted to comprehend what was happening.

In the emergency room, a doctor checked me out. A police officer who told me he was friends with Takoda stayed by my side, chatting casually like I hadn't endured a terrifying battle in the street that had resulted in me stabbing someone.

Hours later, after the doctors had cleared me and Wan had listened to and documented everything I could remember about the evening, my mother appeared from behind the small partition where the doctors had been treating me.

She wrapped her arms around me, drawing me into a crushing hug. Despite our poor relationship, she was still my mother, and the warmth and safety of her arms around me was everything I needed.

When she whispered how much she loved me, I broke down and cried.

Adelaide never came, but that didn't shock me. We'd grown up in two different worlds, and most days it was hard to acknowledge we were related at all.

Mom took me up to the fourth floor to visit Dad, who'd been frantic since hearing what had happened. I stayed with him overnight since the doctors weren't allowing Takoda to have visitors outside of family until the following day.

* * *

At eight o'clock the following morning, still dressed in the same clothes I'd worn the previous day with a kink in my neck from sleeping in a hard, plastic hospital chair, I stood outside Takoda's room in the ICU, my nerves in a knot.

Odina had stopped by my dad's room the previous night and had shared that Takoda had suffered a hairline fracture to the skull. The doctors were monitoring him for bleeding, seizures, or leaking of cerebrospinal fluid, but they were optimistic the injury wasn't as severe as it could have been.

He would have headaches and pain for a while, but both were treatable. They'd started a course of antibiotics as well since the impact had split the skin across his temple, which risked introducing an infection to the brain. Otherwise, he was sleeping, and Odina had shared I could see him the following day.

So there I was, outside his room, my stomach in a knot. Takoda had been hurt because of me.

A squat nurse in mint green scrubs waddled out of his room, pushing a blood pressure machine. When she saw me standing there, she smiled. "He's awake."

I nodded, unable to choke out a response. Once she lumbered off into another room, I braced myself and entered Takoda's room.

His eyes were closed, deep purple bruises surrounding them. Soft breaths passed through his slightly parted lips. An IV fed into his left arm, and a monitor beeped on the other side of his bed, a steady, calming pulse that matched the beating of his heart.

I shuffled to his side, and his lashes fluttered, eyes squinting open to slits.

"Charlie?" His voice was scratchy like sandpaper.

"Hey." My chin wobbled, and tears filled my eyes.

Takoda reached out, wiggling his fingers. "Come here."

I took his hand. His grip was loose and weak.

"I'm so glad there's only one of you," he said.

I chuckled and batted at my eyes. I didn't know what that meant.

"How are you?" I asked. It was a stupid question.

"Been better. Have a bitch of a headache."

"You have a skull fracture."

"Bah. It's nothing. I've got a hard head. It'll heal." He tugged my hand—or tried to.

I moved closer. With waning strength, he tugged me into his arms and hugged me. "I was so fucking scared," he mumbled against my neck.

The tears came again, and I couldn't stop crying.

"I heard you were one badass motherfucker," he said. "Stabbed him, did ya?"

I choked on a laugh. "In the shoulder. Barely. He was going after you. I had to stop him."

Sobbing, unable to speak more, I buried my face and let the tidal wave of emotions take me away. Takoda shushed me and held me close.

Takoda fell asleep not long after I arrived. I held his hand and sat beside his bed, watching each breath as it passed through his lips, thanking god he was alive.

A knock at the door an hour later jolted me from my thoughts and made Takoda stir. Odina was at the door with an older woman I knew immediately was Takoda's mother. She shared the same warm skin tone, dark hair—except hers was streaked with silver—and deep brown eyes the color of hickory. The genes were strong on that side of Takoda's family.

"Mom, this is Charlie, Takoda's... He's the man Takoda was protecting."

I stood and offered my hand. "Takoda's boyfriend," I added, unashamed and standing tall. "Nice to meet you."

Takoda's mother's eyes widened, and she held a hand to her mouth, dashing her gaze from the bed to me.

"Yeah, Mom, shocking, I know," Takoda's sleepy voice said from behind me. "Don't go making a big deal of it."

Odina just smiled. "I knew it was more."

Takoda's mother took both my hands, shaking them once before yanking me into her arms. "Oh, I'm so happy to meet you. So, so happy."

"Good grief. Save him," Takoda said to his sister.

"Mom, enough. The poor guy went through hell last night, and now you're suffocating him."

Takoda's mother released me and wiped stray tears from her eyes.

"Jesus," Takoda said. "You'd think I've never dated."

"You haven't," Odina said, a teasing note in her voice. "How are you, Charlie?" She dragged me into a hug, rocking us side to side.

I wanted to thank her for teaching me how to escape an attacker. If not for her, I might never have gotten away from Viktor. No, it hadn't gone as well as I'd hoped, but her lessons had helped nonetheless.

The words caught in my throat with the clog of emotions I couldn't swallow, so I just hugged her back.

We all sat and chatted quietly for a while. Takoda's mother wanted to know everything about me, and Takoda made a weak effort to get her to back down and let me breathe.

A half hour before lunch, Wan and Myers showed up at the door.

"Knock, knock. It looks like our patient is doing better."

He wasn't. If anything, Takoda looked gray and was growing quieter the longer he had visitors. I knew he probably wanted to close his eyes and sleep.

"Tell me you have that fucker locked up."

"We processed him last night. Feel up to a chat?" Wan asked.

"Not really, but let's do it."

Odina offered to take me home, and I agreed. They were releasing Dad later that day, and I wanted to shower and clean up so I could get back to the hospital to pick him up.

"Everybody out," Odina announced, clapping her hands. "Let the man say goodbye to his boyfriend."

Wan and Myers shared the same expression. Their brows shot up, and they glanced between Takoda and me.

"Yeah, yeah, go ahead and give me shit later. Now fuck off for five minutes," Takoda said, shooing them out with a weak wave in their direction.

Wan chuckled as he followed everyone else out of the room.

I took Takoda's hand when he held it out. "Well, that knock on the head didn't smooth out any of those harsh edges, did it?" I said with a grin.

"Nope. I feel as ripe as ever."

Gently, I leaned in and kissed him, lingering and absorbing the moment, knowing how close I'd come to losing him.

"I'll come back later. I want to get Dad home and settled. Mom said she'd come by and keep an eye on him over the next few days so I can be here with you."

Takoda lifted his hand and grazed his knuckles along my unshaven jaw. "I was so scared he was going to take you away from me."

I clasped his hand and held his palm to my cheek. "I'm right here, and I'm not going anywhere."

Takoda kissed me again, and a salty tear landed on our joined mouths. For once, it wasn't mine. When I pulled back, he tried to hide his tears but failed. "You've done something to me, Charlie." His voice quivered, and his eyes filled as his chin trembled. "I don't ever want to lose you. I'm going to do my best not to fuck this up. I promise. I want to be the best boyfriend you've ever had."

I smiled through my own watery eyes. "Well, you don't have much competition since you're the first."

He chuckled, but his tears continued to fall. There was more beyond that look in his eyes, but instead of words, he pressed our mouths together and told me with a kiss.

Twenty-seven

TAKODA

Desk duty was where it was at. At least I'd had my badge and gun returned without having to endure a meeting with the board. Three weeks after my discharge from the hospital, Sergeant Nikola had sat me down for a long talk. I was far more subdued than usual. My experience with Charlie and his stalker had jarred something loose inside me. I'd spent a lot of years being a dick to everyone, feeling jaded and hard done by, but I'd learned that money and privilege didn't always equate to an easier life. Charlie had taught me that. Money hadn't saved him from a lifetime of mental-health struggles. Deep down, we were all the same. Maybe our battles in life were different, but we all fought to some degree. We all had challenges and obstacles to overcome.

Nikola spent a long time discussing my behavior. When he explained that Solomon was willing to give me another chance, I was more grateful than I could express.

However, until the doctors cleared me for active duty, I was confined to paperwork. My headaches were fewer and farther between.

They ailed me on occasion, but the real risk was taking another hit to the head too soon.

So I typed up reports and offered to help where I could. And I did it all without complaining.

Charlie and I had been dating for a month. It might not have been a great mountain of time in most people's books, but we'd been through a lot together, and we'd grown close fast.

He spent his days with his dad, working on a new book series, and every night in my bed. We'd developed a system, and it worked for us. He still had to check the locks several times a day, he still had a rigid routine and an abundance of pills to help manage his anxiety, but overall, he was better.

I checked the clock for the hundredth time, counting the minutes until I could clock out and drive across town to see him. We had a date planned tonight. Bowling. Charlie's idea. Odina and her current boyfriend were meeting us at the bowling alley later that night.

I had one more hour of work to get through, then I could rush home, shower, and spend my evening with Charlie.

I studied the file in front of me as the sound of clicking nails on the tiled floor caught my attention. I spun in my chair, a wide grin on my face just as retired detective Stanley Graveman entered the bullpen with Angel beside him.

The old girl was getting by one day at a time, but with the way her tail was wagging and the full-blown doggie smile on her face, she looked years younger.

"Hey, girl."

Stanley undid her leash, and she hobbled over to my desk, burying her face in my side and chuffing. I stroked her fur and nuzzled against her, greeting her with the same enthusiasm. She licked my face, and I laughed.

"How are you? You're up and about. That's good." I ran my hands over the soft golden fur of Angel's head.

"She's having a good day. We thought we'd go for a car ride since walks just tire her out anymore."

Charlie and I had visited Stanley and Angel a couple of times since the incident with Viktor. Charlie and Stanley had become good friends, and Angel and I shared our own connection.

I gave up on paperwork and spent my last hour loving Angel while Stanley visited with his old coworkers. I'd moved up a few notches in Stanley's book, but I also knew he kept a watchful eye on me. Charlie was important to him, and he wouldn't see him hurt again.

* * *

It was six when I pulled into Charlie's driveway. The old Escort had bitten the big one, and I'd visited a few used car lots until I'd found a decent replacement that was affordable. I'd refused Charlie's offer to help and took a small loan instead, figuring it was the adult thing to do. If I could stop blowing through my paychecks at breakneck speed at the bar, then I'd have plenty extra to spend on a car loan. With Charlie in my life, I had no need for Cage.

So the new-to-me Nissan Rogue felt pretty spectacular when all was said and done. It was my new baby, and I planned to take good care of her.

At the door, I rang the bell and waited, bouncing on my toes. The older woman next door must have heard me pull up. She poked her head around the corner, smiled, and waved.

"Hello, Takoda."

"Hello, Ms. LaPointe. How are you today?"

"Just lovely, thank you. You here to see Charlie?"

"Yes, ma'am."

She beamed.

Across the street, an army of children spilled from a minivan, followed by two tired and weary-looking parents. A couple of dogs barked in the front window, greeting them as they headed inside.

The door to Charlie's house flew open, and Archie greeted me, peering over reading glasses that were balanced precariously on the end of his nose.

"Just who I've been waiting for. Get in here quick before Charlie decides he's ready to go. I think he's behind. He's been writing up a storm and barely taking breaks. Come on, come on."

I chuckled and followed Archie, unsure what the rush was all about. I kicked my shoes off at the door and followed him through the house to his workshop. The chemical scent of model cement hung in the air, and several desk lights illuminated his workspace.

He snagged a box off the corner and thrust it into my hands. "Check this out. Got it today at the hobby shop downtown."

"No shit. A P-16 Black Widow? This is badass."

"And..." Archie reached behind him and handed me a second box. "I got one for you. I thought we could build them together. I could teach you the ropes. Charlie never cared to learn. What do you think?"

"Are you serious? Hell yeah. Oh my god, this is the coolest thing ever. When can we start?"

Archie chuckled. "Not tonight, or Charlie will have my head for ruining his date. How about this weekend? I'll make room on the bench, and we can go through it step by step. I'll make a pro out of you yet."

I couldn't wipe the grin off my face. "This is amazing. Thank you."

Archie clapped a hand on my upper arm. "No, thank you. You gave me back my son. You brought him out of that dark place in his head. I've never seen him so alive and happy."

Before I could respond, Archie crushed me in a hug. It started as a tight squeeze and ended with a back slap before he pulled away. "You better go find him. He's been waiting all day for you to get here."

I thanked Archie again and made my way upstairs. Charlie wasn't in his bedroom. In fact, he didn't spend a lot of time there anymore. On a few occasions, he'd mentioned remodeling it but then dropped the subject when I'd inquired about his plans. What I wanted to suggest was that he move in with me. I didn't have a beautiful home or a whole lot to offer, and I knew he wanted to stick close to his dad. It was a topic for another time. It wasn't like we spent many nights apart, and Charlie relied a lot on his familiar routine.

Every day he was stronger. I thought with patience, there would come a day he would be ready to break free altogether. Like he was slowly doing with his bedroom and the fantasy series in Vrydindel he'd set aside—much to his publisher's dismay.

One day in the future, I knew we'd take those bigger steps together. Today, I treasured all we had.

I found Charlie in his office, typing frantically on his keyboard, oblivious to the world around him. His new series was still high fantasy but without dragons. An adult series he was keeping close to the chest. When I'd asked about it, he'd smiled and reminded me I didn't read books.

I was ready to change that once his new book was published. He had me curious, and I wanted to be part of Charlie's world.

The curtains over the window were open. The summer sun reflected against his blond hair and brought out the freckles across his nose.

His delicate fingers raced away, turning his thoughts into words.

"Should I cancel?" I asked after a time.

Charlie gasped and swiveled on his chair to face me, a brilliant smile taking over his face.

"Hey. You're here."

"I've been here a while. Do you still want to go bowling? If you changed your mind, you're the one who has to tell Odina."

"No, no. I'm..." He glanced at his computer. "I'm good. Let me save this, and I'm ready."

He clicked a few times, shut down his computer, and stood. I didn't move from the doorway. I couldn't stop staring at the amazing man in front of me. He'd been through hell, and he could still smile. He was stronger than anyone I knew.

"What? Why are you looking at me like that?"

"Because I love you."

Charlie's eyes widened, and his lips parted. "What?"

I crossed the room, unable to go another minute without touching him. I took him in my arms and kissed him deeply, cradling his face and savoring every ounce of him.

"I love you so much, Charlie. I can't even describe it. It overwhelms me in the best possible way."

Tears filled his eyes, and he wiped his thumbs over my cheeks. Apparently I'd shed a few tears of my own.

"I love you too. You saved me."

"No. You saved me."

THE END

Want more romantic suspense?

The Endless Road to Sunshine

My name is Jason Atkinson, and I married a serial killer.

My world shattered on a cold April morning when they took my husband away in cuffs.
The life I knew, the man I loved, and the world I believed in was nothing but a lie. He stole my trust, my happiness, and my faith in humanity, and I'm not sure how to move on.
With my mental health hanging by a thread and a media circus following me everywhere I go, escape seems like the only answer.
Shedding my old life and starting fresh.
A new city. A new job. A new name.
Maybe everyone will leave me alone and let me wallow in peace.
But Skylar Dawson, a student almost twenty years my junior, has a different plan.
Everything about him is endless—his eyes, his smile, even his babbling mouth.
He shines with a blinding inner light I can't ignore.
He's a ray of sunshine in my dark world.
Skylar Dawson will not be ignored.
But will his energy and patience run out when he realizes I'm too tormented and broken to love him back?

OTHER TITLES BY NICKY JAMES

Audio Books
Love Me Whole
Owl's Slumber
Shades of Darkness
No Regrets
New Beginnings
Clashing Hearts
Confused Hearts

Standalone Contemporary
Trusting Tanner
Twinkle Star
Love Me Whole (available in audio)
Rocky Mountain Refuge
The Christmas I Know
Long Way Home
The Devil Inside
The Endless Road to Sunshine

Hometown Jasper
Clashing Hearts (available in audio)
Confused Hearts (available in audio)
Forgetful Hearts
Concealed Hearts

Death Row Chronicles
Inside
Outside

Trials of Fear
Owl's Slumber (available in audio)
Shades of Darkness (available in audio)
Touch of Love
Fearless

Lost in a Moment
Cravings of the Heart
Heal With You
A Very Merry Krewmas (Trials of Fear Special)

Fear Niblets
Rigger's Decision
Slater's Silence

Healing Hearts Series
No Regrets (available in audio)
New Beginnings: Abel's Journey (available in audio)
The Escape: Soren's Saga
Lost Soul: AJ's Burden

Taboo
Sinfully Mine
Secrets & Lies
End Scene
Risk Takers
Rule Breakers

Historical
Until the End of Time
Steel My Heart

Tales from Edovia Series
Something from Nothing
Buried Truths
Secrets Best Untold

Printed in Great Britain
by Amazon